SILENT EVIDENCE

RACHEL GRANT

JANUS
PUBLISHING

Evidence: Under Fire

Into the Storm

Trust Me

Don't Look Back

False Flag

Absent Without Leave

Evidence

Concrete Evidence

Body of Evidence

Withholding Evidence

Night Owl

Incriminating Evidence

Covert Evidence

Cold Evidence

Poison Evidence

Silent Evidence

Winter Hawk

Tainted Evidence

Broken Falcon

False Evidence

Fiona Carver

Dangerous Ground

Crash Site

Flashpoint

Tinderbox

Catalyst

Firestorm

Inferno

Romantic Mystery

Grave Danger

Paranormal Romance

Midnight Sun

Writing as R.S. Grant

The Buried Hours

This one is for Toni Anderson.

Fabulous author and dear friend. I thank the universe every day for the gift of your friendship. Thank you for being the kind of person who makes the world a better place. Even my books will take a bullet for you.

<h1 style="text-align:center">Chapter One</h1>

Virginia
October

The lake, surrounded by the bright, vibrant colors of fall, would be beautiful if it were still a lake and not a boggy nightmare, a forest of long-dead tree stumps erupting from acres of mud. But Anderson Lake wasn't a real lake, and thanks to a twelve-foot drawdown, it was now not even a fake one. Once upon a time, this had been a river valley, then the hydroelectric fairy came along and transformed it into a reservoir. Now a crack in the dam required the deep drawdown for repairs.

The four-foot-tall tree stumps made it possible for Hazel MacLeod to envision the extent of the woods along the river thirty years ago, before the dam was built. A glimpse back in time to the valley this had been.

Hazel had visited this reservoir several times in the five years her cousin's company had owned property that abutted the water, but seeing it during drawdown was vastly different from the serene lake when the reservoir was full. She turned her gaze to the north end of the muddy lake bed with its tree-ghost forest and tried to guess where Raptor land started and stopped. She'd never been on this eastern edge of the reservoir; it wouldn't look familiar to her even if the lake were at normal capacity.

She knew she was in the right spot because she'd spotted Isabel's blue Prius and the sheriff's SUV in the line of cars, and she'd had no trouble finding the path through the woods Isabel had indicated. She'd been told it was important she enter from the utility company's access point because the adjacent property owner would not allow egress across their land. The landowner feared Isabel would find and record an archaeological site that could put restrictions on land use.

The objections had been so vehement, the owner had delayed the survey for days as lawyers sorted out what the property line and easement was between utility reservoir and landowner.

Now Isabel was up against the wall to get the survey done before the lake was refilled, and she'd called Hazel in a state of panic, needing her particular expertise at the lake immediately. Hazel had done the only thing she could and grabbed her backpack with field equipment and borrowed the Range Rover from Alec's fleet of vehicles to drive an hour from Gaithersburg to northwestern Virginia and the muddy shores of Anderson Lake.

According to Isabel, she needed to follow the lakeside path south for a half mile, where she would spot Isabel and her crew documenting the find that had her so alarmed. The path, being well above the usual level of the lake, was hard, dry, red Virginia clay and easy to follow as it cut through trees or skirted the high water shoreline. At last, Hazel rounded a bend and spotted her cousin's wife, Isabel Dawson, along with the county sheriff, a deputy, and five other men and women. Three were Isabel's field crew, while the remaining two wore coveralls that labeled them as utility workers.

Isabel shoved her phone in her pocket and smiled broadly when she spotted Hazel. She waved her over, yelling, "Thank you for getting here so quickly! You're a godsend." She turned to the others when Hazel reached the group. "This is Dr. Hazel MacLeod, forensic anthropologist."

Hazel passed her credentials to the sheriff to verify her expertise.

"You work for Talon & Drake, the engineering firm that was contracted to fix the dam, Miss MacLeod?" he asked.

"Dr. MacLeod," she corrected to establish that if he didn't like her initial assessment of the bones, his opinion didn't matter. She was the expert here. "I'm a consultant. I've worked with Talon & Drake in the past when human remains were found during construction and they needed an estimate of the age of the skeletons to determine if they were archaeological, historic, or recent."

"And that's what you're supposed to do here?" the sheriff asked, his tone skeptical.

"It's why Dr. Dawson called me, yes," she said, using Isabel's degree as well for the same reason. Isabel had warned Hazel when she called that the sheriff was eager to write off this find as a prehistoric burial ground and move on. He'd been irritated at Isabel's insistence on calling Hazel in to examine the bones.

Which was a pretty major red flag in her line of work.

Usually, sheriffs were more worried on the other side of the equation, fearing bones of crime victims might be released to tribes under the Native American Graves Protection and Repatriation Act, preventing further investigation into a homicide. In her experience, it was a rare law enforcement officer who was quick to write off a find that included human remains. Especially when there were no artifacts present, as Isabel had indicated on the phone. But then, there was a strong likelihood—given the number of skeletons involved—this could be a slave burial ground, which brought different issues all around, but that wouldn't be the sheriff's problem either.

Hazel had scheduled her second appointment with her psychotherapist for this afternoon, but the urgency in Isabel's tone as she expressed her concerns about the sheriff had convinced her to reschedule. She turned to Isabel. "Shall we get started?"

Isabel looked at her feet. "Do you have rubber boots?"

She shook her head. She hadn't purchased a new pair since returning from a five-month assignment in Croatia a week ago. She hadn't expected to go into the field so soon. She had enough money saved to take time off from work—a mental break she needed after spending months identifying victims of genocide in the Balkans—and had been lucky to find her old field kit stocked and ready to go after Isabel's frantic call. "I'll sacrifice these shoes to the cause," she said, referring to the worn running shoes that were about to get filled with red clay mud.

She followed Isabel into the muck and mud that defined the high water level of the reservoir. Isabel's employer, Talon & Drake, was the contractor hired to repair the dam. Knowing archaeological sites would be exposed when the artificial lake was lowered, Isabel, the Bethesda office's lead archaeologist, had been tasked with documenting changes to the old village sites that would be exposed. It was a pretty standard project. The bones had been an unexpected discovery.

Isabel and her crew had been in the field since last Wednesday—working through the weekend because the repairs were nearly complete and refilling the lake would begin on Friday. Their job was to photograph and measure prehistoric features and survey the stump forest to record new sites exposed after thirty years of inundation. During today's survey, the team came across a pile of bones in the water, just beyond the drawdown zone. Following the management plan agreed to by the utility company, Talon & Drake, and the State Historic Preservation Office, Isabel had notified all parties to the agreement along with the local sheriff's office, as these remains had never been documented as being part of a previously recorded archaeological site.

If the bones were prehistoric, they would be left in situ, remaining where they'd rested for hundreds or thousands of years without disturbance, as intended at the time of their burial. But if Isabel's crew had found an historic slave burial ground, it could be argued that they should be examined. Documented. Reburied in a place where their descendants could visit and honor them. They could be counted and acknowledged in death in a way they hadn't been in life.

The bones could give voice to a past that many tried to erase.

Hazel wasn't a fan of unnecessarily disturbing the remains of the deceased, but sometimes, as with her work for the International Commission on Missing Persons in the Balkans, disturbing remains was the only way to acknowledge victims of genocide. To be counted.

There was no way she'd give these bones the cursory once-over the sheriff wanted.

Her feet sank into the thick, saturated silt. The clay grabbed her submerged shoe and held on. Her foot popped free, leaving the sneaker behind. She grimaced and grabbed the shoe, tossing it along with her sock to the shore before removing her other shoe and sock, tossing them as well.

"Sorry," Isabel said. "You gonna be okay barefoot?"

She shrugged. "I'll have to be." She could do a preliminary examination today, then decide if she needed to come back tomorrow with better footwear. The water was cool, but not achingly so on the early October afternoon. She followed Isabel, stepping carefully to avoid cutting her feet on buried rocks or tree roots as they wound through the eerie dead forest in which all the stumps were chest-high.

The sheriff, deputy, and utility workers remained on shore. Isabel's field-workers, one young woman and two young men, accompanied them, the woman pointing to the pin flags protruding from the water, marking the first bones they'd spotted, several meters from the bulk of the remains.

At last they reached the bones that were the reason Hazel had dropped everything and made a mad dash to the reservoir. A fine layer of orange silt covered the bones, obscuring them at first, disguising them as sticks, branches of the stump forest. But Hazel knew those curves and lines. They weren't the irregular shape of tree limbs. They were human limbs. Condyles, sockets, curved ribs. The shapes were so familiar. And among them, she spotted a bony brow ridge, empty eye sockets, and a wide nasal aperture.

Like spotting fish underwater, once she spotted one cranium, her vision adjusted to take in the whole school. She scanned the water for meters in every direction. Skulls and long bones. Ribs and scapulae. Pelvic bones and vertebrae. Thousands of bones. Two dozen or more individuals, from the looks of it.

Just like Bosnia. Just like Croatia. Just like Rwanda and Darfur. A mass grave.

Sean Logan spotted Isabel's Prius in the line of cars that included a sheriff's SUV. He pulled out his cell phone and called his boss. Well, sort of his boss. Alec Ravissant owned Raptor, but since he'd been elected to the US

Senate, he'd handed over management of the company to Keith Hatcher, Sean's official boss.

But today, Rav had called the office and asked Sean to drive out to Isabel's project area, which was near Raptor's auxiliary wilderness training area, to pick up his wife and bring her home. An odd request considering he'd also asked Sean to bring Chase Johnston to the reservoir so he could drive Isabel's perfectly fine car back to Gaithersburg.

Even stranger, Rav had told Sean to look out for anything suspicious at the reservoir and be on guard, but not to share that detail with anyone, not even Chase or Isabel.

He'd offered no explanation as to why he was sending Sean on this errand, nor had he said anything about a sheriff being at Isabel's job site…which could qualify as suspicious. "Rav," Sean said into the phone. "We're here. Does Isabel know to expect us?"

"No," his boss said. "She said there was some sort of issue at the site and she'd call me back. She was in a hurry to get me off the phone, so I've been not very patiently waiting for her to call as promised."

"Issue?" Sean asked, looking at the bar of lights on the sheriff's SUV. "Did you know the county sheriff is here?"

"What?" Rav cursed. But it wasn't an angry sort of sound. Sean recognized the ring of fear. He climbed out of his Raptor-issued SUV, one of the many perks of his job. "I'll find Isabel and call you back," Sean said.

"Tell Isabel to call me. Now."

"Sure thing." He hung up and tucked the phone away. To Chase, he said, "Let's go."

"Rav's worried?" the kid asked. Chase wasn't really a kid…but he looked like he was about fifteen. Combine that with the eager, gung-ho enthusiasm of a boy who'd never served in the military, never seen combat, and Sean couldn't help but think of him as a kid, even though he knew the young man had been more than tested a few years ago.

"Yeah. Isabel said something about an issue at the site without explaining. The sheriff's vehicle is worrisome."

The kid frowned. "Should we draw our weapons?"

Sean shook his head. Chase, with his pale white skin, lived a life with fewer concerns than Sean ever could.

"As a Black man, it's unwise for me to approach a police officer with gun drawn, even if they know to expect me. This guy has no idea we're here."

Chase flushed bright red. "Right. Sorry."

Sean patted him on the back as they started down the path. "Just a fact of life. Frankly, it's not good for you to approach weapon drawn either, but you stand a better chance of surviving the encounter than I do."

They hurried down the path, not bothering to be silent. Sean had no wish to startle anyone at the other end. Relief settled in when he rounded a bend and the reservoir came into view. But there was no sign of Isabel or her crew. He glanced to the north and south, taking in the exposed lake bed with stunted trees seeing sunlight for the first time in at least thirty years. He'd run scuba trainings in this lake, he'd seen the stumps underwater, but still, this was nothing like the Anderson Lake he was used to.

He spotted the path to the south that cut through the living forest. Fresh footprints told him that was the route to Isabel. After a quick half-mile walk between forest and lake, he caught sight of Isabel with her bright orange curls, wading in the water amidst the stump forest with four other people.

The sheriff and a deputy stood on dry land with two men who appeared to be from the utility company. Whatever the emergency was, no one appeared to be agitated. He wanted to call Rav to give him the heads-up, but the boss was more interested in speaking to his wife, so he sent a quick text: *Eyes on Isabel. She's fine. Will have her call you after we speak. SL5X*

SL5X was Sean's Raptor signature, only used when the person on the receiving end might want confirmation that the sender was really the operative and not someone who might have gotten hold of his phone. Probably not warranted in this situation, but Rav was worried about his wife, so Sean would leave nothing open to misinterpretation. He liked Rav a lot, and he liked his big, steady paycheck and top seniority.

Sean was about to approach the sheriff and introduce himself, when Isabel turned and caught sight of him. She said something to a woman bent over looking at something underwater, then headed to the shore where Sean waited.

The second woman stood and turned, and something shifted in his chest as he recognized another redhead. Unlike Isabel, Hazel MacLeod's hair was on the auburn end of the color spectrum and bone straight. Today, her thick hair was tied in a casual high ponytail that effortlessly highlighted her perfect cheekbones and slender neck.

Shit. He hadn't expected to see Hazel today. Hell, he'd thought she was still in Bosnia. Or was it Croatia?

It didn't matter. She was the last person he wanted to see. He'd never get that night in Grand Cayman out of his mind. No matter how hard he tried.

And he'd tried.

Hazel MacLeod was the center of several fantasies that would never be fulfilled. And apparently, there would be no avoiding her today.

Isabel grinned broadly and made a beeline for him, splashing through the shallow water. "Sean, Chase, what are you two doing here?"

He held out his phone as she approached. "You need to call Rav."

Her features darkened. "Shit! I totally forgot. Oh, hell. I

hope he's not mad. He didn't send you because he was worried, did he? When I told him there was a problem with the site, I hope he didn't think it was an emergency." Her gaze landed on the law enforcement officer who waited on the shore. "The sheriff is here due to technical details, not because there's any sort of trouble." She frowned. "But how would Alec know Sheriff Taylor is here?"

Sean gave her a look and waved his phone, glad that the sheriff's presence wasn't a real problem. "Just call him."

She ignored his offer and pulled out her own phone. Sean scanned the lake, avoiding watching her as she called her husband, his apparent disinterest part of the bodyguard's role. Nothing was private when he was assigned to guard someone, but he knew how to refocus his gaze and stance to remain alert while not seeming to eavesdrop, even when he was listening to every word.

In addition to hyperawareness of Isabel's conversation with Rav, he could feel Hazel's thorough perusal before she turned back to whatever it was she found so interesting underwater, ignoring him as if eight months hadn't passed since she'd begged him for sex in a hotel room in the Caribbean and then they'd both spent an awkward three days pretending nothing happened.

He'd loved his job with Raptor right up until that moment, when his employer's sexy cousin threw herself at him at a time when there was no way to catch her without screwing up everything that mattered. The months between then and now had been easy, knowing she was on a different continent. But now she was back, and damn, she looked good in those skintight jeans that cupped her ass as she bent over in the water, examining something as if it held the answers to the universe.

Hazel MacLeod was back, and somehow, months had slipped by without him mentally preparing to face her again.

Next to him, Isabel Dawson apologized to her husband and gave a long-winded explanation about bones and more bones causing a problem with the environmental review for the Talon & Drake dam repair project. At last she hung up from her conversation with Rav and eyed Chase. "Alec says he wants you to drive my Prius home."

"Yes, ma'am."

She handed him the key, not even bothering to ask why. He took it and nodded, then walked away.

Isabel watched the young man with the same look she always did. Like a mother hen. Once Chase was out of earshot, she asked the same question she always did, the one Sean had come to expect like the sun rising in the east. "How's he doing? Any problems?"

"He's fine, Iz." In truth, Chase wasn't a quick thinker, and Sean fully believed it related to the ordeal he'd suffered at the hands of supreme mind fuckers a few years ago, but with each passing day, Chase's cognitive abilities increased. He could recover. He would recover. He was ninety percent there. It was the homestretch that was taking longer than anyone had anticipated.

"You'd tell me the truth, right?" Isabel asked, as always.

"You know it," Sean said, repeating his line. He appreciated that her lines were borne of genuine concern, not simple rote behavior. His responses weren't placating either. He did believe it. If he didn't think Chase was up to the job, he'd have insisted Keith let him go with a massive severance package a year ago.

But Chase needed Raptor, and Raptor, in its own way, needed him.

With the Chase ritual behind them, Sean could once again focus on the unsettling fact that he was about to talk to Hazel for the first time since Grand Cayman. He really should have used the gift of time he'd been given these last several months to figure out what to say to her. But Hazel had thrown him off-balance since their first meeting four and a half years ago.

The woman who haunted his fantasies gave up her study of the muddy waters and waded across the manufactured lake to greet him.

Her gaze slid up and down Sean's body like a caress, and much as she tried to hide it, Sean knew she liked what she saw. The feeling was mutual. And that, right there, was the problem. In an instant, a new fantasy of Hazel popped into his head. This one involved bending her over one of the ancient tree stumps and making her come so hard, her moans echoed across the fake lake.

Goddamn but he was in a mood today.

No one had warned him Hazel would be here. He should have had a Hazel clause written into his contract during the last renewal. Thirty days' notice before he'd have to face her, with a bonus for the hazard of turning down the owner's cousin. Again.

He wouldn't screw with his employment, especially not by getting involved with a flighty party girl.

Hazel's smile was stiff as she approached. "Sean, what brings you here?"

"Hello, Hazel. Good to see you again." His words were crisp and precise, not his usual speech pattern, but then, no one had warned him Hazel would be here. He was off his game.

Isabel's gaze flicked between the two of them, her expression both speculative and alarmed.

Good thing Keith was running Raptor, not Rav. Sean and Keith got along great, and Sean's status as top operative had been earned and established years ago. As long as Sean didn't make the mistake of fucking the owner's sexy cousin, he couldn't be fired. "How was

Bosnia?" he asked, trying to add more warmth to his tone.

"Croatia," she corrected, an edge to her voice. His fault, he knew, but it was too late now. "And the country was lovely, but the job sucked, as to be expected. How have you been?"

"No complaints." To Isabel, he said, "Rav wants me to drive you home. You going to be here much longer?"

Isabel looked to Hazel. "How much more time do you need?"

"I'll photograph and collect several bones to examine in the lab, but I need to come back tomorrow and take more pictures before collecting a broader sample. See if I can get an MNI count."

"MNI?" Sean couldn't help but ask.

"Minimum Number of Individuals," she answered.

He glanced at the reddish-brown water. "What's going on here?"

"Isabel and her crew found a lot of bones," Hazel said.

He frowned. He knew enough about Hazel's expertise to know she was talking about human remains; if Isabel had found animal bones, she'd have called someone else. "What do you mean by a lot?"

"A mass grave, upwards of twenty people."

"A prehistoric or historic burial ground? Or something more recent?"

"That's what I've been wondering," the sheriff said from behind him. "What's the word, Miss MacLeod?"

"Doctor," he and Hazel said at the same time.

She smiled at Sean, and warmth bloomed in his chest. To the sheriff, she said, "I won't know anything for certain until after I've taken a look in the lab. I'll take a few bones tonight to examine for a preliminary assessment, but I still need to come back and work up a ballpark estimate of the MNI based on the major elements readily visible."

"If those bones are Indian, the Menanichoch and other tribes in the area won't be pleased with you removing them," the sheriff said.

"The sample is being collected in accordance with the burial treatment plan they agreed to with the State Historic Preservation Officer. They might not like it, but they know it's the only way to ensure the remains are Native American and not something else entirely. I know my profession, Sheriff, but thank you for your concern."

The man's eyes narrowed, and Sean had to admit he liked the way Hazel didn't take any crap. But then, there was a lot he liked about Hazel MacLeod. Probably too much. That had always been the primary problem.

Hazel looked to Isabel. "The faster we get the bones bagged, the sooner we can go home." Together, the two women waded back to the deeper water about fifty yards from the bank. The grade was shallow, and they were only calf-deep when they stopped and joined the crew.

At last, Hazel and Isabel had their samples. They headed to the shore, zigzagging between the stumps. Hazel took a step, then let out a sharp screech. She jolted and lost her balance, then landed on her ass in the water, cursing all the way down.

Her face flushed a bright red as Isabel hovered over her. "Are you okay?"

Hazel sucked in a sharp breath between her teeth as she grasped her foot. "I stepped on something jagged. A rock, I think. Damn. I sliced my foot open."

Sliced her foot?

She raised her leg, revealing a bare foot. Of all the idiotic things to do. Why was she wading barefoot in murky water? He'd read an article about her some years ago—it popped up in a simple search, he wasn't internet-stalking her, nope, defi-nitely not—and read that she had a ridiculously high IQ. Not as smart as her supergenius sister, Ivy, but still well into the genius range. Sean was no genius, but even he knew you didn't wade barefoot in a submerged forest.

Blood oozed from the bottom of Hazel's foot and dripped onto her ankle and calf. That was a nasty cut.

With a curse, Sean waded into the water, soaking his good shoes and the bottom six inches of his slacks. He scooped Hazel from the water and held her with one arm behind her back and the other under her knees. Her wet, silt-covered clothing pressed to his chest, drenching him in the same rust-colored water.

She wriggled against him, threatening to upend them both. "I can walk!"

"But you weren't, and I haven't got all day. Where are your shoes?"

"I'll get them," Isabel said. "You carry her to your car. I'll get her shoes and the samples and meet you there."

"I can walk!" Hazel repeated.

"No, you can't," he and Isabel said in unison.

At last she settled against him, and he had to admit, it was sort of pleasant to have her there.

Dr. Hazel MacLeod. Witch Hazel. A sorceress who'd inhabited his dreams more often than he cared to admit, and not just since last winter in Grand Cayman, but in the years since they'd met at that dinner party at Rav's house, not long after the man had purchased Raptor. Sean had been fresh out of the Navy and plotting with his new boss on how to rescue Raptor from the crappy reputation created by its previous owner. Hazel, the boss's vivacious cousin, had been there, stealing all his attention, threatening to turn him into a complete idiot.

He'd followed her into the garden that night to look at the Milky Way and had been tempted to do things that would cost him his brand-new job.

Not his best moment.

"I can walk, Sean," she said softly.

"You're welcome," he said. "I know it was kind of me to ruin my best shoes and suit to help you. So glad you noticed."

She pursed her lips and let out a heavy sigh. Finally, she said, softly and with no hint of facetiousness, "Thank you, Sean. And it *is* good to see you." She looked down and murmured just loud enough for him to hear, "Although I could have done without you seeing me fall on my ass."

He wanted to make a comment about her fine ass, but she was still his employer's party-girl cousin and remained off-limits. "How've you been?" he asked. He'd worried about her while she was away but hadn't dared ask Rav or anyone else how she was doing.

She draped her arms around his shoulders, and he adjusted his hold, remembering that night on Grand Cayman when they'd danced and her chest had pressed to his and she'd smelled of flowers and sunblock, which was nothing like her current scent of iron-rich clay and lake water.

"Not great," she said, surprising him with an honest answer to his question. "I left Croatia early because…" Her voice trailed off, then she cleared her throat. "Because the nightmares got to be too much. I excavated a grave that was filled with children—eighteen of them, between the ages of six and ten. It was a school. I've excavated babies and children before, but…this one was my tipping point. I stopped sleeping. Eating. Sometimes it felt like breathing wasn't happening either. I decided to come home. Take a break."

"And you ended up here, in a lake full of bones."

She shrugged. "Isabel was frantic. The forensic anthropologist at the university is teaching today and couldn't get away. I'm living with Alec and Isabel until I find a place to live, and I have the expertise. I was the logical choice."

"You're living at the estate?" This shouldn't surprise him.

Rav's home was a mansion with over a dozen bedrooms, and he never shied away from opening his home to family. Hell, before Rav hooked up with Isabel, the mansion had been used as a safe house when they needed a secure place fast.

"For the next month or so, yes."

"You gonna be okay working on these bones?"

She frowned. "I think so." Her voice lowered. "I hope so. If I can't work…" The words trailed off, and he tightened his grip, an embrace under the guise of carrying her.

He reached the parking area and opened the rear door of his SUV with the remote. He set her in the back so she was seated facing out. "I've got a first aid kit. We'll clean up that cut." He took out the kit, then reached for her foot.

She resisted. "I can do it."

He merely gave her a look. She sighed and raised her foot so he could see the bottom. He rinsed her sole with water from his canteen, then studied the cut. "Shit. It's deep." Bright red blood flowed from the inch-long slit.

He hadn't been a medic in the Navy, but like all special forces, he'd had extensive training in treating wounds in the field, and his kit was stocked by Raptor, so he had everything he needed to clean the wound, glue it shut, and bandage it to prevent infection and reopening.

As he wrapped gauze around her foot, padding for the wounded arch, he admired her red toenail polish. His interactions with Hazel had always been when she'd been off work, in play mode. She'd always worn airy dresses and toenail polish and her hair down in a flowing auburn curtain. He'd never seen her wearing glasses before and realized from the thickness of the lenses, she must've been wearing contact lenses every other time they'd crossed paths.

Except for the toenail polish, this was a different Hazel. Her hair was pulled back, and her glasses had a heavy, dark plastic frame. Sturdy work glasses.

Sexy in a way that wasn't intended.

He really needed to stop finding everything about her sexy.

He'd just finished wrapping her foot when Isabel and the crew arrived with their field gear and Hazel's samples. They loaded their gear in their cars, and Sean told them to put the bones on the backseat of his SUV.

"No, they go in the Rover," Hazel said.

"You can't drive with this foot."

"Sure I can. It's just a cut."

"We can leave the Rover here tonight, Haze," Isabel said. "Alec won't mind, and you need to come back to photograph and do an MNI tomorrow anyway."

"I suppose," she said softly.

The sheriff and utility workers left. Hazel scooted forward and slid from the SUV's open hatch, placing all her weight on her left foot, which now was encased in her wet and muddy sneaker. Before Sean could step up to help her to the passenger side of the vehicle, Isabel moved forward and offered her shoulder. "Lean on me."

Hazel did, and Isabel guided her to the front passenger door. Hazel used the inside handhold to pull herself up into the seat. Before she turned, Isabel placed a hand on her knee. "You okay? You know I wouldn't have called you if it hadn't been urgent."

Sean watched the interaction between the two women, appreciating the display of genuine friendship. Isabel and Hazel were closer than he'd realized.

Hazel nodded. "I'm fine. It… I didn't see any children's bones. So far, none of the bones are small."

"I'll make calls tomorrow. Someone else can take over analysis. I just needed you today to get the sheriff off my back. Now that we've established the need to examine the remains, we can move slower."

"No. I can do it. I think it'll be good for me. Back in the saddle. Dr. Parks will probably approve." She gave Isabel a hopeful smile, and Sean felt a twinge in his chest. He was such a sucker for her smile.

Isabel's reaction wasn't what Sean expected. "Shit! Dr. Parks! You were supposed to see her again this afternoon."

"Don't worry. I called and rescheduled for Wednesday morning."

"Wow. I'm impressed she was able to squeeze you in that fast."

"Well, Alec is paying her big bucks to fix me."

"Good point. I think I financed her vacation home."

Sean guessed Isabel was referring to the therapy she'd gone through after what had happened to her in Alaska three years ago. He stepped forward and offered Hazel her purse, which he'd grabbed from the Range Rover before locking it. "Was there anything else you need?" he asked.

She shook her head as Isabel climbed in the backseat. He circled around to the driver's side, and a minute later, they were leaving the parking area. It would take an hour to get to Isabel and Rav's estate from here.

He hoped to hell when they got there, Rav would explain why he'd sent Sean on this errand.

Chapter Two

Hazel's head pounded as Sean drove the winding road through the forest. The headache could be a sign of dehydration, but she didn't think that was the cause. She didn't even think it was the cut on her foot, which throbbed after Sean's careful cleaning.

No, her headache came from one of two sources, or maybe both. She hadn't been mentally prepared to see a massive pile of bones today, nor had she expected to see Sean Logan so soon after her return from Croatia. But then, she would happily have put off seeing Sean for months, years even.

Piles of human bones she could handle. Sean Logan? Not so much. Not after the humiliation of Grand Cayman.

Seeing him again, out of the blue like that, had brought up every excruciating detail. It didn't help that he remained utterly, perfectly perfect. She'd taken a survey once and seven out of seven male-attracted people agreed that Sean Logan was objectively hot. In addition, one hetero man said Sean made him question his sexuality and one lesbian agreed that if she were into guys, he would do it for her.

The poll was statistically valid. Sean was certified hot.

His smooth mahogany skin, firm, square chin, full lips, broad nose, thick brows, and deep brown eyes were all beautiful on their own, but the moment he smiled? It was enough to make a single hetero woman weak. Or maybe it was just Hazel, but based on her nonscientific but still valid poll, she knew she wasn't alone.

But she was the fool who'd thrown herself at him in Grand Cayman. The idiot who'd then had to suffer through days of vacation after his gentle, but no less embarrassing, rejection. It had taken her years to build up the courage to go all in and tell him what she wanted, and then she'd crashed and burned on liftoff.

How great was it that the next time she saw him, she fell on her ass in three inches of water after thoroughly slicing up her foot like an idiot? She'd known better than to step with her full weight until she was certain it was safe. But she'd been distracted—by him—and wasn't thinking about bare feet and sharp objects.

He'd been kind, and she'd been bitchy, and he'd called her on it. Now she felt like an ass, but it was too late. She'd been frazzled by the sheer number of bones and seeing Sean. She couldn't draw upon the person she'd always tried to be around him, the flirty party girl who didn't give a damn. That persona had been her shield, and she was without it now.

It took work to get into that headspace. She couldn't pull it up on a dime. Especially not when she was at work, looking at human remains and wondering if these people had died natural deaths or if they were victims.

In the six years since she'd earned her PhD, she'd examined thousands of bones, many of which had been silent evidence of stolen lives. The crimes ranged from manslaughter to genocide, and she'd borne witness to every part of the spectrum.

She'd catalogued marks on victims' bones and provided testimony at trial. She'd mentally inhabited their missing skin and described entry and exit wounds made by knives, screwdrivers, hammers, saws, bullets, axes, rocks, glass, and random household objects.

She'd seen nothing in the lake to offer a clue to cause of death or even if there was a reason to examine these remains further. They could be prehistoric burials. Natural deaths, respectfully interred and disturbed in their eternal slumber by her intervention. The sheriff wasn't the only one hoping for that finding.

That was always Hazel's hope. She would speak for the dead, but she was grateful when it wasn't necessary.

They'd gone about fifteen miles when the oddity of Sean showing up struck her. She'd been so focused on her fluster, she'd forgotten to question why Chase Johnston had been assigned the task of driving Isabel's car home. "What's going on? Why did Alec send you to the lake?" she asked Sean.

"He didn't say," he said.

If she hadn't known Alec since before she'd taken her first steps, and if she didn't love him like a brother, she'd worry that he was some sort of controlling husband. But that wasn't Alec. He'd sent Sean for a reason.

"Has he ever done this before?" she asked, hoping past reasons would offer a hint.

"Nope. Never," Isabel said.

"Not entirely accurate," Sean said. "Remember when the Capitol was on lockdown a few months ago? You were home, so he had a team sent to the estate to make sure you were okay."

Hazel grabbed her phone from her purse and opened up the Twitter app. "Anything going on in DC we need to know about?"

There was a lot, as always, but nothing directly related to Alec or the Senate or anything that would explain Isabel's armed—because Sean was certainly carrying—escort home.

"Come to think of it, Alec received some threatening emails last week," Isabel said. "But honestly, he gets so many of those, I'm pretty much numb to them. They're always investigated. Half the time, they're bots or someone who was riled up by Voigt Forum or another extreme alt website."

"Maybe he received something he couldn't ignore," Sean said.

That was unsettling. Alec had been a magnet for threats from the moment he decided to run for office. Ironically, once upon a time, Isabel had been the FBI's top suspect.

They settled into silence for the long drive. Hazel couldn't help but lean toward her left so she could take in Sean's scent, which was much better than the smell of dried lake water that clung to her clothes. At last they reached the metal gate that was the only vehicle entrance to the property, which was surrounded by a six-foot-high stone wall. When Alec first bought the place, he'd considered tearing down the wall, but after Isabel had been abducted and held for ransom in Alaska, he'd opted to add electrical wiring to the top, bringing the height up to eight feet.

Sean entered his code, and they passed through, the bars closing shut behind them. Hazel understood the necessity, but she looked forward to finding an apartment and leaving the enclosure behind. She'd spent enough of her work life under guard. She didn't enjoy living it after hours.

Sean parked in front of the large garage. A glance inside the bay window showed Alec's car was there, but the bay next to it was empty. Not a surprise because that was the spot for the Range Rover Hazel had borrowed to drive to the site. A painful reminder that she was trapped here for the night.

Not that she had anywhere she wanted to go, it was just that with Sean here, this was the last place she wanted to be. She still ached with mortification. Beautiful, perfect Sean. He'd done nothing wrong. She was the one who'd drunk rum to give herself courage to strip and plant herself in his bed and offer him a no-strings vacation fling.

He was the one who was sober and shocked and more than a little horrified.

She'd give anything for a do-over. But there were no do-overs in this life. And really, if a time machine were ever invented, it would be silly to waste it on something so trivial when instead she could go back in time and assassinate Hitler years before he rose to power.

She needed to get her priorities straight.

She opened her door and started to exit, but both Sean and Isabel shouted no, and in a flash, he'd circled the vehicle and scooped her into his arms.

This sucked, to be swept into Sean's arms because she was an idiot who didn't know how to walk barefoot in a shallow lake. Being close to him while knowing he'd never want her in the way she'd wanted him for years triggered an ache.

He carried her into the house as Isabel led the way, opening doors that connected garage to mudroom to hallways to laundry room and eventually to the kitchen.

Isabel had drawn the line at live-in help, so only Alec, Isabel, and Hazel inhabited the house after six p.m., but during the day, there was sometimes cleaning staff, a gardener, and, twice a week, a personal chef who prepped meals.

The chef had been in today, and the kitchen smelled heavenly of some kind of pasta, garlic bread, and cheese. This was the best part about living with her cousin. Restaurant-quality meals without the need to put on pants.

Alec was in the kitchen when they arrived, and he pulled Isabel into his arms and gave her a kiss that made it clear he didn't give a damn they weren't alone. But then, it was his house. He could make out with his wife if he wanted. Hazel wouldn't care except she was very awkwardly in the arms of a man she'd wanted to kiss for upwards of four years.

Sean carefully set her down next to the breakfast nook table, and she dropped into a seat.

Alec released Isabel and held his wife's gaze. Ignoring Hazel and Sean, he said in a stage whisper, "Why was Sean carrying Hazel?"

"She cut her foot in the lake," Isabel whispered loudly back.

"What happened to her shoes?" Alec asked.

"She didn't have mud boots, and the clay sucked the sneakers right off her feet."

"Did the sheriff give you any more trouble?" he asked, still speaking in a stage whisper.

"I'm not telling you more until you tell us why you sent Sean to drive me home."

Alec eyed Sean and Hazel. Finally, he shrugged and said, "Dinner's hot. Let's serve up, and we can talk in the dining room."

Hazel wanted to change out of her damp clothes but knew Sean would insist on carrying her to her bedroom, and the last thing she wanted was to be carried up the grand staircase like some foolish damsel. She'd crawl if she had to, but dammit, Sean Logan wasn't going to carry her another inch.

Instead, he carried her plate of food as she hobbled, resting her weight on the side of her foot as she traversed the necessary distance to the formal dining room. She might lack grace, but she didn't lack pride.

Once they were all seated, Alec poured wine for Isabel and Hazel. It wasn't lost on her that he and Sean weren't drinking. She presumed that meant Sean was still on the clock. Still on duty even though Isabel was home inside a walled fortress with her former Army Ranger husband? Alec must be really worried about something. "What's going on, cuz?" she asked.

Alec sighed and pushed a file folder that he'd set next to his plate toward Isabel, but his hand remained on the top, holding it closed as if it were a jack-in-the-box ready to pop. "Isabel is aware of the threats I received via email last week."

"And they looked like the usual bots trying to cage you."

"Yes, but still. All threats must be taken seriously until proven otherwise. Today, I received another threat, and this one…I can't ignore. It didn't come via email and yet it had similar wording to the generic notes. It also contained information that's highly classified. Information few outside the Senate Select Committee on Intelligence have access to. Which means I can't share much from the note itself. Even the Capitol Police haven't read the whole thing. The FBI has assigned a deputy special agent in charge to head the investigation.

"Given my unique position of owning a private security company, she and I came to an agreement on how to handle this that keeps everything under wraps. With the exception of a few select FBI agents, no one outside this room knows all the details. And I'm sorry, but I can't share more than the unredacted portions of the note."

He opened the file folder and lifted a sheet of paper. "This is the note I received. It was found in the middle of a stack of papers related to the Intelligence Committee." He offered the paper to Isabel. "It's a copy, obviously. The FBI has the original."

Isabel held up the paper so Sean and Hazel could see the simple text—Times New Roman font, eighteen or twenty point—with thick black stripes covering the redacted text.

Isabel read aloud. "*Resign*, redacted. Redacted. Redacted. *Resign, or the redhead will pay the price. You are a traitor who doesn't deserve your seat.* Redacted. Redacted. Redacted. *The redhead will expose you.* Redacted. *Do the right thing, or your family will get smaller. Resign*, redacted." She looked at her husband, her jaw agape. "What the hell?"

"I am taking this threat very seriously," Alec said, his voice slow and measured. This was deliberative Alec, the methodical soldier, protective husband. Caged lion—or rather tiger, as Isabel sometimes referred to him. "It killed me that I couldn't drive to the reservoir and check on you myself, but I needed to talk to the FBI, so I sent Sean. When Sean said the sheriff was at the reservoir, I nearly lost it."

Isabel squeezed his hand. "I'm sorry. I didn't mean to blow you off. I had no idea. Finding such a massive pile of bones was sort of a big deal, and the sheriff was trying to shut down the work before Hazel could get there." She frowned, looking at the note again. "Redhead. Family." She met Hazel's gaze. "This threat could mean either of us."

Hazel stiffened. She'd assumed the author of the note was referring to Isabel.

"The minute you stepped into the kitchen with Hazel injured, I realized the same thing." Alec said. "There's an intentional vagueness to the wording."

"But who even knows I'm living here?" Hazel asked. "Ivy and Laurel and our parents know, but I haven't told anyone outside immediate family. The only person I've seen aside from Ivy, you guys, the cook, housekeeper, and gardener is Dr. Parks." She hadn't reached out to friends since returning stateside. She'd been content to play hermit as she tried to figure out what came next.

Isabel frowned. "Everyone at Talon & Drake knows. JT was in the office last Tuesday for a senior staff meeting. During a break, he and I were chatting and I mentioned you were back and staying with us. He asked if you'd be on call again if T&D needed forensic consulting and I said yes—I didn't think you'd want word to get out that you were refusing work."

"I appreciate that," Hazel said. The last thing she needed was a reputation that she could no longer do the job, and JT Talon was the CEO of Talon & Drake, a massive engineering firm that subcontracted out to firms all over the globe. A whisper coming from T&D could spread far and wide.

"Anyway, when the meeting resumed, JT told his assistant to put your name back on the on-call list. I never dreamed something would come up so quickly."

"So it was a matter of record at a company you've consulted for in the past," Alec said. "Plus," Alec grimaced, "I, um, paid the fee to have you added to the guest list for a black tie fundraiser for National Geographic that's coming up. Ivy is going to be there, and I thought you might enjoy it, plus it's a good cause. My aide handled all the details and when he asked your address, I said to use the estate. All my charitable donations are a matter of public record."

"So basically, anyone who is monitoring you could know Hazel is here," Sean said.

Alec nodded. "And on a personal end, I told the guys at JT's gym when we were sparring last week."

JT's gym was a private gym in the heart of DC where several of the guys from Raptor and a few other select friends of JT's sparred regularly. Former US Attorney General Curt Dominick was among the regulars, which was one of the reasons they all preferred to keep it private. Curt, JT, and JT's stepbrother, Lee Scott, had all studied karate together when they were in their early teens at that very gym, and JT purchased the property a dozen years before when the original dojo closed. Hazel knew there was an excellent gym at Raptor's Virginia compound, but that was an hour's drive from the Gaithersburg estate, while the gym was just minutes from Capitol Hill.

"So between work and friends, it's probably been well established I'm here. Not that any of your friends could be the source for *that*," Hazel nodded to the piece of paper.

"No, but it's possible whoever sent it is monitoring friends too." Alec's jaw was tight, and Hazel wondered what the hell was in the redacted parts of the letter.

"I hadn't heard Hazel was back," Sean said, "So the news isn't traveling in Raptor circles."

"That's right. You weren't at the gym Friday," Alec said. "How's your sister doing?"

"She's a trooper." To Hazel, Sean said, "Friday, my sister had chemo. I was on babysitting duty so her husband could be with her."

She'd had no idea his sister was ill. But then, she didn't even know he had a sister. "I'm so sorry. She's doing okay?"

"As well as can be expected. She's too tough to let breast cancer beat her. But the fight isn't pretty."

"Is she set for help while you're at Ian and Cressida's wedding?" Isabel asked.

"Yeah, our mom is in town. She arrived yesterday." Again, Sean addressed Hazel. "Katrina has had a really bad reaction to chemo. She doesn't want her daughters to see her at her worst, doesn't want to scare them. The last few months, I've stuck close to home, only taking assignments in the DC area so I can help her out. With the wedding being in West Virginia this weekend, my mom decided to take time off for an extended visit to be with Kat for the last rounds of chemo."

Hazel had known the wedding was soon, but hadn't realized it was this coming weekend. She didn't know the bride and groom well, but her sister, Ivy, was close to both and would be going.

Alec cleared his throat. "That brings us to the problem of what to do this week and weekend if Hazel is the redhead in the letter. I had a plan for Isabel, but this changes things. The problem is, because of the national security issues, we can't let anyone know. Not coworkers or friends." Alec met Hazel's gaze. "Or family, Haze. You can't tell Uncle Will or Aunt Diane—or even Ivy and Laurel."

"I can't think of why I'd want to tell my parents, but it's crazy to think they or my sisters aren't trustworthy," Hazel said.

"It's not about trust. You know I trust each and every one of them." Alec grimaced. "Please understand, there's a good reason that letter was so heavily redacted. If word leaks to anyone—including my colleagues in the Senate—about this threat, there will be serious repercussions. Honestly, I wouldn't even be telling *you* if you weren't living here and a potential target. I need your cooperation on this to keep you and Isabel safe. Promise me you'll cooperate."

All she could do was nod. Alec and Isabel had taken her in, were giving her a place to live and recover. Just as she didn't hesitate to drive to the reservoir to help Isabel, she couldn't refuse Alec's request, especially when he was trying to keep his wife safe.

"Okay, then." Alec smiled. "All I want is for you and Isabel to be protected."

"I know. I doubt I'm the target, but I'll do what you ask."

"Thank you." Her cousin put on his strategizing face. She'd seen the expression since they were kids and he planned midnight raids on the kitchen to steal desserts. Alec never wanted the sweets, but he'd loved developing intricate schemes to get past parents and housekeepers, and he'd reveled in the role of commanding his MacLeod cousins. "We need a plan for the fieldwork this week. We need a Raptor operative at the reservoir. Isn't one of Keith's recent hires from the Menanichoch tribe? You can tell your crew he's there as a tribal monitor. I'll figure out some excuse to tell Keith."

"Wait, not even *Keith* knows about this?" Isabel asked.

"Not even Keith."

Across the table from Hazel, Sean cocked his head. "What did you tell him today when you asked for Chase and me to drive out?"

"Nothing. I called before I had a game plan." He drummed his fingers on the table, then looked at Isabel. "We can tell Keith that you told me Sheriff Taylor made you uncomfortable and you wanted Sean there in case he challenged Hazel's authority to examine the bones. Now you want a security guard who can pose as a tribal monitor just in case the sheriff tries to shut you down again."

Isabel's brow furrowed in thought, then she nodded. "That could work. We could even tell the crew that story. Easier to keep track of the lies that way."

Alec nodded. "So that covers fieldwork and gets us through Thursday, which brings us to the wedding this weekend. Hazel, you'll be safe if you come with us. Half the guests are Raptor employees and former special forces of one type or another. Plus, I'm going to hire a couple of operatives from another company to embed with the hotel staff."

Hazel looked at him in confusion. "I can't go to the wedding. I'm not invited, nor should I be. I barely know Ian or Cressida."

Alec frowned, then he got that look he always did when he'd come up with the perfect scheme to get what he wanted. When she was seven and it meant extra dessert, she'd loved that look.

Right now? Not so much.

"You can go to the wedding if you're Sean's date," he said with a smug smile.

Hazel's stomach dropped. No. No. No. No. *No.* Fear for Isabel had addled his brain if he thought that was a solution.

He turned to Sean. "Do you already have a date?"

Hazel's heart wanted to collapse inward. Her cousin was *not* going to force an employee to bring Hazel to a wedding. It was wrong on so many levels.

"Actually, I do," Sean said quietly.

Something twisted in Hazel's belly at that. Of course Sean had a date. The guy was a fricking Adonis. He was a masterpiece. A work of art. He was what you'd get if Captain America and Black Panther had a love child. All muscle and beauty and eyes that drilled into your soul.

Yeah. She might've been thinking about Sean way too much during her months in Croatia. She wasn't surprised he had a girlfriend. He'd been single in Grand Cayman, but there was no reason to expect him to keep that status. It wasn't like he was sitting around thinking about *her*.

"Is it something you could break off?" Alec asked.

"Alec, no!" Hazel and Isabel said together.

"You're asking too much," Isabel added.

"Depends," Sean said. "What are you thinking?"

Alec shrugged. "If you bring Hazel as your date, you can share a room, keep an eye on her twenty-four seven with no one being the wiser. It will get us through the weekend, give us time to come up with a long-term plan." The scheming look returned to Alec's eyes, and Hazel knew he was falling in love with this idea. It was locking in place, and no amount of begging would sway him.

Isabel was Hazel's only hope. She was the only one who could make him see reason when he was being pigheaded.

"If you and Hazel pretend to be involved, that could work after the wedding too. If you take unpaid leave from Raptor —maybe claim you need a break after the intense schedule you've maintained the last few years—then you could guard

Hazel during the day, but it would appear you're hanging out with your new girlfriend. I'd pay you, and your break wouldn't burn any sick leave or vacation time."

Alec was going to need sick leave if he continued pushing this plan. He wanted to force Sean to pretend to be her boyfriend? *No.* This was a nightmare.

She could put a stop to this. Alec might know military tactics and politics, but he didn't know forensic anthropology. Today, a big project had landed in her lap, and she could use that to argue her way out of this. "But I need to do analysis of the Anderson Lake bones in a lab. Probably at a university, if they'll grant me the space. Sean can't hang out pretending to be my boyfriend while I'm working. It would be…weird."

"We can set up a lab here, in the office annex. The security here is solid—probably better than the university's because fewer people have access. What do you need besides a microscope?"

The truth was, not much beyond a good camera, tables, large rectangular trays to lay out the bones, and some big, heavy-based magnifying glass lamps. She could probably borrow most of what she needed from Talon & Drake.

Security was vital when it came to dealing with human remains. If her work was questioned in a court of law, she'd need to show an unbroken chain of evidence. But the bones had already been brought here tonight, not to Talon & Drake's offices in Bethesda. An argument could be made that the estate was even more secure because no one knew the bones were here and Alec and Isabel's home had a massive metal gate, an electrified stone wall enclosing the property, and an alarm system that went to local police, fire, and Raptor.

The office annex was just as secure. It had been Alec's home office for Raptor before he ran for the Senate. It was now mostly unused because he met with constituents at his office in Annapolis or in DC. One of the rooms in the annex would be perfect.

Dammit.

"Would the annex work?" Alec asked when she didn't respond.

"Yes. But you can't ask Sean to dump his date for the wedding. That's just cruel."

"Someone might've threatened your life, Hazel." This statement came from Sean.

She startled and faced him. "*Might.*" She studied his expression. Closed. Thoughtful. Intent. "You aren't seriously considering this? Dumping your date to pretend to be my boyfriend?"

"I'm not going to force this on you, Sean," Alec said. "You wouldn't be able to tell your date why, maybe not ever. If you say no, I'll ask someone else in Raptor, but you are my best, first choice. I trust you, and you've known Hazel for years. The idea that you two are involved wouldn't come out of the blue like it would if one of the other operatives took the job."

Sean gave a nod. He stood from the table and said, "Before I give you my answer, I need to make a call."

Alec nodded, and Sean left the room.

Hazel took a big gulp of her heretofore ignored glass of wine. She wanted to chase after Sean and tell him no, but two things stopped her: She'd promised Alec she'd cooperate, and the damn cut on her foot made running—even walking—impossible.

Sean braced himself as he dialed Tricia. He never should have asked her to be his date for the wedding. In truth, he'd regretted it the moment the words slipped from his mouth. Not because he didn't like her, but because he didn't like her in the same way she liked him. He might be pouncing on Rav's plan because it neatly extracted him from a potentially awkward situation, but he wasn't about to share that detail with Rav or Hazel.

He'd figured going to the wedding with Tricia would be convenient for them both. She'd dreaded being single at yet another couples-dominated event, and he'd wanted a companion for Friday's caravan to the inn in West Virginia, because Trina, matron of honor, had warned him she'd planned something that would be more fun with a partner.

Next thing he knew, he'd asked his coworker to ride with him to West Virginia, but his heart wasn't in it. Which didn't make sense. Smart, beautiful, and a tough-as-hell operative, Tricia was one of his favorite people. She was Raptor's private security branch's secret weapon, because no one expected the curvy, tall, dark-skinned woman with vivid blue kinky hair to be a former police officer and badass bodyguard.

The blue hair was key. Unlike male bodyguards, she didn't try to blend in, and she came across as sexy and wild and fun. Tricia didn't walk into a room; the moment her foot crossed the threshold, she owned it. No one expected her to be an expert in martial arts and firearms, and he'd personally witnessed her disarming men twice her size without breaking a sweat.

The last thing in the world he wanted was to hurt her feelings. But he was about to in a big way, and it sucked. He closed his eyes, took a deep breath, and hit the Call button.

She answered right away—a relief, because there was no way he could drop this in her voice mail like a coward—and her tone said she was happy to hear from him. "Sean! You sure took off like a shot today. What's going on with Rav?"

"Isabel was having trouble in the field. No big deal." He

rubbed the back of his neck as he paced the veranda. It was warm for early October and the crystal-blue water of the large swimming pool looked tempting even though darkness had settled in. "Listen, something has come up about this weekend."

"What do you mean?" Tricia's voice turned guarded. Less warm. With good reason. "You aren't going to the wedding? But you're best man."

He smiled at that, still a little surprised that Ian had asked him and not one of his former Delta Force buddies, but at the same time, he knew why. Sean was close to both Ian and Cressida, and his friendship with the former spy had begun with Sean telling the fool to get off his ass and tell Cressida how he felt.

"No. I'm going. It's just…" Hell. He would rip this bandage off in a way she'd understand. "There's this woman I've been into for a long time. I never thought it would work because of complications, but maybe it's not so complicated after all."

"Ohhh," she said, as if air was releasing in a slow seep.

"And…she's going to be at the wedding this weekend."

"And you can't hit on her if you're there with me." Her voice wasn't cold so much as guarded.

He wished he could use that excuse, but Hazel couldn't just show up at the wedding unless she was his date. "Not that exactly. Shit, Tricia, I'm so sorry, but I really like this woman. I have for a long time. And nothing's happened yet…but I think it will, and I wanted to call you and break our date before I do anything I'd have to explain to you or her later."

"What, are you on a date with her right *now*?" Tricia's voice was strained, and he couldn't blame her. This was an odd call between friends and coworkers. He never should have asked her, but part of him had wondered if the weekend might trigger something real. The problem was, he knew she'd thought the same thing. And then today he'd come face-to-face with Hazel and knew he wasn't attracted to Tricia in the same way he wanted Hazel.

"I'm sorry, Trish. I'm a total asshole."

"Oh my God! You *are* on a date with her!" She surprised him by laughing. "Listen, I'll be honest and admit I thought something might happen this weekend and I'm disappointed. But I appreciate that you respected me enough to call me before your magnificent hookup, even though you really didn't have to. It's not like we're in a relationship. Or even dating."

"Maybe there'll be some interesting single guys on Cressida's side of the aisle?"

"Have you ever met the historians at NHHC? No, thank you."

Sean couldn't help but laugh. "Thanks for understanding, Trish."

"You owe me. Big-time. Who is this mystery woman, by the way?"

It was weird to be having this conversation, which was composed of lies piled on lies, but his attraction to Hazel was the one truth he couldn't admit to Rav or Hazel, yet he could tell Tricia. "Hazel MacLeod. Rav's cousin."

Tricia squealed. "No shit! What's the big complication, then?"

"Uh…that she's Rav's cousin?"

"So?"

"If this goes south, it could screw with my job."

"Then why are you going for it now?"

Because Rav is paying me? Because she could be in danger? Because the idea of another man even pretending to be her boyfriend makes me wild with jealousy?

"I guess I decided life is too short to not go after what I want." He turned to face the windows, and there was Hazel, the warm yellow light of the dining room highlighting those high cheekbones and glinting off her dark auburn hair. He would be spending nearly every minute of the next week, maybe two with her.

He didn't know if he should be thrilled or terrified.

Chapter Three

As expected, Hazel didn't sleep much. It was hard to know if the cause of her insomnia was her abrupt return to work or the impossible situation with Sean. She'd been doing better on the sleep front since moving in with Alec and Isabel, but the previous night had been nearly as bad as her last weeks in Croatia. The appointment with the psychotherapist had been bumped to Wednesday, and she was eager to see the woman again.

Her session last week had been an introduction. They'd only had time for an overview of Hazel's issues, but even that had felt good. Like she was doing something.

One question Dr. Parks had asked Hazel had stuck with her. She wanted Hazel to look for links to the past, reasons why seeing the children's bones now could have triggered anxiety. She'd found herself up and pacing in the middle of the night, wanting to call Dr. Parks in hopes that talking to her would break the infinite loop her thoughts traveled.

But it probably wasn't cool to call the nice doctor at three in the morning when the situation wasn't life-threatening. She figured she'd wait until after the second appointment before she latched on to the psychotherapist like a burr.

Taking the doctor's question seriously, she considered whether or not the mass grave of children she'd excavated reminded her of Chelsea, the childhood friend who'd disappeared at nine and whose bones had been found—and her murderer arrested and convicted—when Hazel was in high school.

It was no secret that what happened to Chelsea had contributed to Hazel's passion for her work. So why would the anxiety happen now? Hazel had handled children's bones before, even children like Chelsea, abducted by a family member and discarded like refuse when they were done committing horrors on the young body.

Maybe it was the discarded part. The way the bones had been piled up in Croatia, offering zero respect for the destroyed young souls.

But she'd seen that far too often too.

Her mind circled the questions, and her heart raced and she paced. At last, the light of dawn came, but then a different kind of apprehension set in, something that a session with Dr. Parks wouldn't ease. Today, the great fake boyfriend charade would commence.

If she had to pretend to be involved with someone, did it have to be Sean Logan, a man she'd lusted after for years? The man she'd made an ass of herself with just eight months ago?

She'd been shocked when he returned to the dining room last night and announced he would be taking Hazel to the wedding. She'd also learned that Sean wasn't just a guest, he was in the wedding party—as in, best man. She'd glared at her cousin for the audacity of asking a man to work while he was supposed to be celebrating his best friend's marriage, but her death glares rolled off her thickheaded scheming cousin.

Alec didn't give a damn about what he was asking of Sean, and he refused to give any further explanation as to why secrecy was so damn important Sean would have to lie to his closest friends and Hazel would lie to their family.

US nuclear codes had better be at stake, or Alec was overreacting.

Last night, they'd hashed out a schedule to carry them through the weekend. Sean would call in to work today and say Alec had asked him to help injured Hazel retrieve her car from the reservoir and be on hand in case Sheriff Taylor showed up again. Sean and Hazel could leave once Alec arrived with the Raptor operative who could pass for a tribal monitor. That was the plan, anyway, if the Native American was available and willing to take the assignment.

Their whirlwind romance would also magically happen this afternoon. Sean would claim last night's dinner at Alec's ignited his interest in Hazel, and they'd ended up talking into the wee hours of the night. Then today, after they left the reservoir and Sean was "officially off duty," the chemistry from the night before would flare again and yadda yadda yadda…by tomorrow morning, he'd be calling the groom and asking if he could bring a different date to the wedding.

As Alec had said, given that Sean and Hazel had known each other for years—and had even spent a week together in Grand Cayman several months ago—this was a plausible scenario. But they would have to sell it to the group over the weekend, acting like they were in the first flush of a new relationship and serious enough to warrant Hazel's tagging along to the wedding.

For the next week, at least, Hazel would be with Sean nearly every waking hour. And starting on Friday when they checked in at the inn—an old Victorian mansion nestled in foothills on the edge of a national forest in West Virginia—they'd be sharing a bed.

As agreed, Sean arrived at seven a.m. sharp to drive Hazel and Isabel to work. Hazel answered the door and felt a rush of fluttery nervousness as she greeted her body-guard/fake boyfriend. She'd have to get over that damn quick if she was going to pull off the ruse.

Sean smiled. "Good morning. How's the foot?"

She glanced down at her bandaged appendage. "Tender, but your glue held, so a lot better. I can walk as long as I keep my weight on my toes."

He reached to the side of the door and produced a pair of mud boots and a cane with a sturdy base and four legs. "I figured you'd need something like this for wading in the lake."

"Thank you. That was very thoughtful." She looked at the boots. "And these are my size. How did you manage that?"

"I checked your muddy shoes before I left last night."

She'd left her sneakers by the back door before she'd gone up to shower while Alec and Sean worked out the details of her and Isabel's protection. She smiled and placed a hand on his arm to balance herself as she rose on her toes to kiss him on the cheek. "Thank you," she repeated. She got a whiff of soap and Sean and wanted to close her eyes and just breathe him in, but she restrained herself and pulled back.

"You're welcome." His face turned serious as he studied her. "Don't take this the wrong way, but you look like you didn't sleep well."

She grimaced. "I didn't."

He raised a hand as if he would stroke her cheek, but then dropped it. "I won't let anyone hurt you, Hazel."

She shook her head. "I'm not scared of the threat Alec received—well, except for being worried about Isabel. You *know* I'm not the target."

"We don't know that, and assuming such a thing is dangerous," Alec said, stepping into the foyer behind her. He shook Sean's hand and looked approvingly at the mud boots and cane. "Just got off the phone with Keith. Daniel Howe is lined up and will arrive at the site by one p.m."

Daniel must be the Menanichoch tribal member who worked for Raptor. Hazel was relieved to know Isabel would have protection in the field, because Isabel was the one they really needed to be worried about.

"Dan's solid," Sean said. "And he's done a lot of wilderness trainings at the Anderson Lake property. He's familiar with the area."

Alec nodded. "He's also had a run-in with Sheriff Taylor while working there and isn't a fan of the man. He's more than happy to act as tribal monitor if it will irk the sheriff."

Isabel stepped into the foyer, entering from the kitchen. She was dressed for the field and holding a cup of coffee, her corkscrew curls contained in a ponytail. Hazel envied her hair. Isabel always looked gorgeous without any effort at all. "We all set?" she asked.

Hazel was glad to see Isabel hadn't lost sleep over the threat. She'd taken the whole thing in stride, insisting that she go on with business as usual. She wasn't about to let anyone control her by manipulating her fears.

Alec slipped an arm around Isabel's waist and pulled her to him. He kissed her, then said, "I'll bring Daniel to the reservoir at one. Sean and Hazel can leave then and head to Baltimore to get the supplies she needs to analyze the bones here. Dan will drive you home at the end of the day in the Range Rover. He'll stay with you until Sean and Hazel return to the estate. If I'm still at the Capitol, you'll both be safe with Sean until I'm home. I've hired four security guards to monitor the grounds twenty-four seven, but Sean or me or someone with personal protection experience needs to be in the house whenever either of you are home. Preferably in the same room with you."

Hazel glanced from her cousin to her bodyguard. There was no way she would start bunking with Alec and Isabel, so surely the "same room" rule didn't apply to her. Unless he intended to ask Sean to move in?

Seeing her gaze flit back and forth, Alec must've read her mind. "I haven't decided yet, Hazel. This week it might be best to have you move to the room next to ours while we establish the relationship cover story."

"You can't be serious," she said.

"This is what I do, Hazel," Sean said softly. "Working twenty-four seven on a regular basis is why Raptor pays me the big bucks. The only reason I can't stay over before we take off for the weekend is my mom is staying in my condo. She'd ask questions about why I'm moving in with my new girlfriend on day two of our relationship, and she'd be more than a little upset that I'm not spending time with her."

Hazel turned to Alec. "You need to hire someone else to babysit me."

"I'm fine with it, Hazel. Unless there's a reason you don't want me?" Sean's voice was cool, and the look he gave her was spiked with anger.

Don't want him? No. That definitely wasn't the problem. Wanted him too much was far closer to the truth.

She gave a sharp shake of her head. "No. I just don't think this is fair to you. Your mother is visiting. Your sister is sick. Your best friend is getting married. You should be taking a vacation, not working while at the wedding and lying to all your friends about it."

"That's a fair argument," Isabel said.

"If I don't have a problem with it, and you don't have a problem with *me*," Sean said, "then this isn't up for debate."

Yeah, Sean was definitely pissed. Did he think she was trying to sabotage his job? She was trying to save him from an awkward situation so he could enjoy his mother's visit and his friend's wedding. But she wouldn't argue about it in front of Alec and Isabel. She firmed her jaw. "No. No problem."

"Good. Now, I've got a job to do and you and Isabel are going to be late for work." He picked up Hazel's field pack which she'd set next to the door, and shoved the handle of the cane toward her hand as he opened the front door.

She took the cane and hobbled outside, following him down the front walkway to his big company-issued SUV. She climbed into the backseat as Sean placed her pack in the rear compartment.

She'd had a bodyguard for less than ten minutes, and already she'd managed to piss him off. She should have stayed in Croatia. She'd be quite happy to have an ocean between herself and Sean Logan right now.

*H*e hadn't meant to snap at her in front of Rav, but damn, he'd broken off a date and rearranged his entire life so he could protect her and she was looking for ways to get him fired? And all because the party girl was embarrassed about Grand Cayman.

Thank goodness he hadn't slept with her. He could only imagine the drama she'd have created if that were added to the equation.

And why did she think he was so judgmental about her advances that night? He didn't care that she'd been drunk, and frankly, he'd been flattered by her advances. There was no reason for this drama now. They'd have to air this dirty laundry the next time they were alone, because there was no way they'd pull off the relationship lie with this much tension between them.

Isabel lingered inside the house saying good-bye to her husband before finally climbing into the front seat and closing the door. Rav stood beside her window, his focus entirely on his wife, and Sean recognized his worry over Isabel's safety overrode everything. The man probably hadn't even noticed Sean's anger or Hazel's stiff response.

Rav just wanted Isabel to be safe. Protecting those he loved was the only thing that mattered to Senator Alec Ravissant.

Sean glanced in the rearview mirror and caught a glimpse of Hazel's auburn hair, and he was flooded with a thousand and one fantasies. Some of his fantasies of Hazel were dirty and some were sweet, but in each and every one, he had his fingers in her hair.

Rav just wanted to protect the woman he loved. What did Sean want?

He watched Hazel in the mirror and didn't like the immediate answer that surfaced. *I want the same thing.*

But that could mean his sister, who was battling a disease. Or his mother, who struggled with watching her daughter fight something that was beyond her ability to soothe, after losing Sean's dad to cancer almost five years ago. And maybe, just maybe, it included Hazel too, but it wasn't necessarily a romantic love. He'd known Hazel a few months shy of five years. They were friends and had shared moments that hinted at something more. One way or another, she mattered to him. It could be as simple as that.

The only thing he knew for certain was he felt a fierce need to protect her, strong enough to lie to his closest friends if it meant he would be the one by her side. Taking a bullet for another human being was literally in his job description, and he was the only person he trusted to watch Hazel twenty-four seven. If someone came after her, he wouldn't hesitate to do what needed to be done.

He met his boss's gaze and recognized how hard it must be for the man to watch Sean drive his wife to the lake. But Isabel wasn't going to give up her work and freedom because of a threatening letter, and Rav had his own rather important job to do. These variables put Sean in the driver's seat, responsible for the safety of the women in Rav's family. "I won't let you down," he said to his boss.

Rav nodded. "I know. That's why I asked you. See you at one." He stepped back and rapped on the roof, sending them on their way.

*A*fter the tension at the house, examining the submerged bones was downright relaxing for Hazel. Isabel and her crew were busy recording an archaeological feature that had been exposed by the drawdown, while Hazel photographed bones in situ. She collected several more skulls for examination in the lab after recording their three-point provenience and photographing them. Other skulls she simply photographed. Craniums were the most obvious and simple way to estimate minimum number of individuals, but there were so many bone fragments in addition to the intact craniums that it was likely her MNI count would be lower than the actual number if she based it on skulls alone.

At the end of her first sweep of the bone garden, she'd counted a minimum of twenty-six individuals, all adults, and the majority of the bones weren't gracile, leading her to believe most, if not all, were male.

The remains were a little too uniform for a slave or

prehistoric burial ground, both of which would have women and children in the mix. The back of her neck twitched with her preliminary field assessment, but she was a scientist and expert witness who didn't rely on neck twitches for confirmation.

She glanced up to see the entire crew gathered on the shore. Sean and Isabel sat apart from the field techs. They must be on break. She vaguely recalled hearing a call announcing the break ten minutes before, but she'd ignored it, too engrossed in her work. Plus she was a contractor and would be leaving the site early. No need for her to break with the crew.

She leaned on the cane and studied the submerged, robust bones. Had these men been slaves? Was she staring at the remains of humans who had never known freedom? Men who had either been transported from Africa or born in the New World and spent their lives in labor for masters who considered them property?

As always, she would remove herself from the narrative and speak the truth the bones told her. When she spoke for these departed souls, would she be speaking for dead slaves?

The voices of dead children slaughtered in the Bosnian genocide surged forth. She'd been a coward and fled instead of speaking for them, and they were pissed. Images of the dirt-coated skull of a five-year-old child—gender unknown due to the prepubescent skeletal age—flooded her. She'd failed that child. She'd failed them all.

She stared into the occipital opening of a submerged skull, not seeing the adult male cranium before her. She smelled the dirt and heat of a dry site more than an ocean away. She wasn't in a lake; she was in a field in Croatia. Sweat trickled from her temples and down her neck in both worlds. She swiped at her brow as she gazed down on the high, straight frontal bone of a child the same age as her nephew, Julian.

She could hear Julian's laugh as she stared at the empty eye sockets. She remembered the mnemonic device someone in her undergrad human osteology class had come up with: *"No, Mom, Larry eats Spam."* Those words translated to: nasal, maxilla, lacrimal, ethmoid, and sphenoid, the names of the eye socket bones starting at the medial—or center of the body—and moving toward the lateral.

She was long past needing mnemonic devices to remember the names of bones, and the sudden reminder of that silly phrase triggered an uncontrollable laugh followed by a sharp pang of grief.

This skull before her wasn't Julian, it wasn't that child in Croatia, and it wasn't her childhood friend Chelsea. She was staring into the empty eye sockets of an adult male who had probably never eaten Spam nor was he named Larry. But he was a man. Who'd lived and died.

He was an adult, so it was safe to assume he'd experienced the full range of emotions that came with humanity. He'd laughed. He'd cried. He'd probably fucked. Hopefully he'd made love. And maybe he'd loved. But given his ignominious internment in this fake lake in Virginia, he'd been wronged in his life or in his death. And odds were, no one would ever know his name.

But she'd try.

Tomorrow in the lab, she'd assign this skull a number based on the location where he'd been found. He would henceforth be known as Specimen X101 or whatever naming convention she chose. The impersonal designation would probably be the only name he'd ever have in death.

She couldn't stop the garden of child skulls from flooding her vision. Even though she was thousands of miles away, working a wet site of questionable origins, not a dry mass grave, known to be part of a genocide. She couldn't fight the mental images.

She stared into the empty eyes of not-Larry-who-didn't-eat-Spam and grief—or panic—overtook her. Her weight shifted, and her hand slipped from the top of the cane. Her brain drained of blood and thought. Darkness closed in. She pitched forward into the shallow lake.

Chapter Four

Sean was on his feet in an instant, charging across the water, staring at Hazel's still body, shouting to Isabel to stay put. If Hazel had been hit with a tranq dart, he didn't want Isabel in the line of fire. As he ran, his gaze darted to the woods that surrounded the lake, looking for the source.

Before he reached Hazel, she jolted and pushed up from the water, coughing, but breathing.

Thank God.

Still crouching in the water, she shook her head and swiped her hand over her eyes. Finally at her side, Sean scooped her into his arms. She let out a squeal between coughs and pushed at his chest. He held her tight and headed toward the shore.

Her coughing subsided enough for her to speak. "Sean! Put me down. I'm fine."

"No, you're not. You passed out in the water. We need to check you out."

"I didn't pass out. I fell. I was standing with my head down, examining the bones too long, got a little dizzy when I raised my head, and tripped. That's all."

"You were still in the water for five to ten seconds." It had seemed like a minute, but she'd been less than thirty yards from shore. He'd sprinted the distance, only slightly hampered by water. Ten seconds was a high estimate. She'd probably only been still for seven or eight. But if she'd simply tripped while dizzy, she wouldn't have been still at all.

"I'm fine, Sean. Please put me down."

He ignored her and made a beeline for Isabel, who'd obeyed his command—something he was grateful for. It was vital that clients cooperate or he couldn't protect them. Rav must have underscored that point with Isabel last night, because her instinct to help Hazel must've been high.

The three people on her crew were on their feet, as anxious as Isabel. They were probably confused by the order to stay on shore, but they'd stayed with their supervisor. Now that it was clear Hazel was conscious and breathing, Isabel told the trio they should get back to mapping the site while she and Sean checked on Hazel.

"You okay, Dr. MacLeod?" one of the young men asked.

"I'm fine," she said as Sean set her on her feet. "Just clumsy and embarrassed."

The man nodded, then turned with the others to grab his tools and resume work. The site they were recording was fifty yards down shore, giving Sean, Hazel, and Isabel enough privacy to talk freely as long as they kept their voices low.

"What happened, Haze?" Isabel asked.

"I was bent over too long and the blood rushed to my head and I got dizzy. That's all."

"You landed face-first in the water and didn't move," Isabel said. "It looked like you passed out."

"I didn't pass out. I'm fine. I was just dizzy."

Hazel was lying. He'd bet anything she'd fainted. She'd said she'd had problems in Croatia. That was why she'd come home early. She hadn't been exaggerating. She would probably claim it didn't relate to his job of protecting her, and from her closed-off body language, she didn't want to discuss it.

"I should contact the university," Isabel said softly. "The professor was busy yesterday, but he can take over now that the sheriff isn't breathing down my neck."

"No!" Hazel said sharply. "I can do this, Iz. I was just dizzy."

Yeah, and maybe if you say it enough, it will become true. But Sean said nothing. This wasn't his fight, and the last thing he needed was to piss her off by voicing his concerns. He needed her cooperation if he was going to be able to do his job.

"Really, I'm fine," she insisted. "I need to do this. For Larry." She mumbled the last part.

"Larry?" Sean asked.

She shook her head. "Nothing. Just a lame osteology joke." She turned and walked over to her backpack, pulled out her water bottle, and took a long drink.

Isabel leaned toward Sean and said, "I need to get back to my crew. You got this?"

He nodded, and she left. He turned back to Hazel to see her tilt back her head and splash water over her face, rinsing off the lake water. Water dripped down her cheeks and neck, drawing Sean's gaze to where it disappeared into the V of her top. Not appropriate for him to be staring, given the situation, but he couldn't help it that a different memory surfaced.

She'd been naked in his bed with just a thin sheet pulled up over her hips. Her breasts had been on full display that night in Grand Cayman, and they'd featured in several fantasies ever since.

Hazel was tall like her sisters, at least five eight or nine, lithe with the muscles of an athlete. He imagined fieldwork and hiking kept her in shape. Over the years, she'd spoken a lot about camping and hiking, and there had been talk of them hiking together, but he'd never had the courage to take her up on the offer. He had a feeling if he ever got her alone in the woods, he'd give in to temptation.

He met her gaze, and she cocked her head as her eyes narrowed, letting him know without words that she'd caught the direction of his stare, but her expression didn't indicate if his ogling irritated or not.

On one hand, it was thoroughly unprofessional, but on the other, they both knew she'd deliberately shown him a lot more in the past.

"I should finish up in the next half hour," she said.

"Good. Rav called about ten minutes ago. He and Dan are on their way and will be early—arriving before noon. We can leave when they get here."

She nodded and headed back into the lake. He followed. From here on out, he wouldn't let her get more than an arm's reach away as long as she was in the water.

For the second time in two days, Sean had plucked Hazel from the lake and carried her to shore because she'd injured herself. This week was going just swimmingly. In that she kept swimming in a damn shallow lake that was determined to kill her.

She huffed out a deep breath. When freaked out over the fact that she'd fainted from anxiety, best to blame the lake.

She forced herself to finish photographing the bones and recording three-point provenience for the obvious skulls. It was important to get back on the horse—or back in the water —for both herself and to show Isabel she could do the work. She was fine.

Perfectly peachy.

Sean hovered way too close, but she understood his

concern, so she gritted her teeth and said nothing. She was doing her job; he was doing his.

"Rav's here," Sean said as she bagged a skull.

She glanced up and saw Alec on the lakeshore introducing a tall man who must be Dan to Isabel. "Can you do me a favor?" she asked.

"Depends on what it is."

"Can you not tell Alec I fai—fell in the water?" She caught herself just in time from admitting the truth.

"Sure, but you know Isabel will tell him. She might be telling him right now."

She cursed, knowing Sean might be correct. But she hoped Isabel would wait and tell him in private, when they had their nightly "How do you solve a problem like Hazel?" conversation she was certain they'd been having since she moved in with them.

"Put your hand on my chest," Sean said suddenly.

"What?"

"Put your hand on my chest. In a way that's casual, but could hint at interest because it's unnecessary. Dan's watching us, and he's one of the people we need to sell on the fake relationship. When he hears rumors about us—everyone in the office gossips worse than teenagers—he'll remember this."

While he spoke, she did as he asked, taking a step toward him and looking up at him, relaxing her shoulders so her body language toward him was open. Sean's handsome face split with a wide, sexy grin that brought out his dimples.

God. The man had dimples. It just wasn't fair.

"Yeah. Like that." He raised a hand to tuck a strand of hair behind her ear.

She knew this was all for show, but her belly fluttered. He was so damn appealing.

He slowly dropped his hand and stepped back, as if reluctant to end the moment, then his gaze flicked to the shore and his body stiffened slightly, as if he feared being caught being inappropriate with a client.

Sean was a good actor. He'd make this easy, as long as she didn't get carried away with the idea it was real.

"I should finish up so we can hit the road."

He nodded and stayed by her side.

"Talk to Alec. I'm just going to collect a few more bones."

"I'm not leaving you."

"I'm fine, Sean."

"I'm guarding your body, just like my contract says. You got an issue with that, complain to my boss, but I'm pretty sure he'll side with me on this one, especially after I tell him you fainted."

She didn't bother to correct him with a lie. Instead, she let out a heavy sigh and finished collecting samples. When she was done, she headed toward the shore, leaning on her cane and carrying what she could with one hand. Sean carried the rest of the sample bags.

"Don't forget to look at me like I make you all swoony in front of Dan. In fact, we can give that as the reason you fainted. I'm so hot, you lost your head."

She snorted. "Nah, we'll say I faked it so you'd carry me out of the water again."

He laughed.

Their debriefing with the others on the lakeshore was short, and ten minutes later, they were in Sean's SUV, ready to head back to Gaithersburg so Hazel could shower and change before they set out for Baltimore to meet with a precision microscope supplier. An extra shower hadn't been on the original schedule for the day, but her impromptu swim made it necessary.

As Sean pulled onto the dirt road, she realized this was the first time she'd been alone with him since Grand Cayman. The walk down the path yesterday didn't count.

Once again, she felt excruciating embarrassment, remembering vividly the feeling of being naked in his bed and being told—no matter how kindly—that it wasn't going to happen. Not to mention she was making him uncomfortable as well as putting his job at risk.

Her face flushed with mortification, remembering Sean's look of pity and disappointment, cloaked by a professional demeanor.

She hadn't had rum since that night and probably would never drink the deceptive stuff again. Rum could convince a woman she was beautiful, desirable. When really she was nothing special.

Better to focus on the other chores on their list for the day. She'd wanted a better microscope for years but the one she'd wanted was out of her range. But now, Alec had offered to pony up the price. Considering he was the one who wanted her working at the estate instead of making arrangements to use a university lab, she'd decided to let him. If she ended up hanging out a shingle and working as a forensic anthropology contractor, having the sweet microscope would be a boon for her business.

If she kept the microscope, she'd pay Alec back in installments. He'd refuse, but she'd insist. After all, she was living in his house, eating his food, and driving his cars, completely rent-free. She was willing and grateful to accept his charity, but it could go only so far.

When they finished in Baltimore, they'd head to Talon & Drake in Bethesda so she could borrow other items she needed to set up a lab on the estate.

They'd been on the road a few minutes when Sean cleared his throat. An ominous sort of sound.

Shit. He's going to say something about that night.

"I'm sorry for the way things went down in Grand

Cayman," he said, proving her mortification detector functioned perfectly.

"No need to apologize. I was out of line."

"You were on vacation. You were fine. I was the one who was working and should have handled it better."

"Can we please…never talk about this again?" Her face was hot. She imagined if she checked the visor mirror, she'd look like a tomato.

"It's okay, Hazel. You were adorable, and I was flattered."

"I was awful, and you were sexually harassed."

"You were not, and you also weren't my client or my boss. It wasn't sexual harassment. Not even close."

"Whatever. I thought we were going to stop talking about it." She said the last bit under her breath, but he heard her and laughed.

"Hazel, it killed me to turn you down that night."

"Right. You have a thing for drunken braniacs who lie in wait in your bed."

"Cut yourself some slack. You were on vacation. You drank too much. It happens."

"It doesn't happen to thirty-five-year-old grown-ass women. I'm old enough to know my limits. Can we please stop talking about this *now*?"

But that wasn't about to happen. Christ, now he was smiling. "Nope. We're going to keep talking about it until you get over it. Until you stop judging yourself so harshly. I don't give a damn that you were bombed. All I care about is that we're going to be spending a lot of time together over the next week or more and need to put that night behind us.

"When you look at me, people need to believe we're dating. Like we're lovers. Like we're eager to spend every damn minute together. Meaning this won't work if you turn bright red with embarrassment if someone asks about Grand Cayman. And they will ask, because it's part of our story, part of why us as a couple after spending just two days together is plausible. So I'll say it again. You were on vacation. You had too much to drink. It's no big deal. It happens to the best of us. Hell, I'd have joined you in the drinking if I'd been on vacation too, but for me, it was a job, and I take my work seriously. Because not taking it seriously can get someone killed. Now will you forgive yourself so we can move on and play our roles, and I can keep you safe?"

"You know I'm not the target."

"No. I don't know that."

"Why on earth would anyone threaten me? Going after Isabel would *destroy* Alec."

"You're like a sister to him. So are Ivy and Laurel. Lots of people saw how he reacted—and how much money he spent —when Ivy was in trouble in Palau. I'm not about to take the chance the threat is bogus or directed at Isabel when you fit the description. Rav hired me to protect you, and I'm going to do my job. But I need you to participate, or no one is going to believe we're a couple."

He reached across the console and took her hand in his. "Most of my closest friends are going to be at this wedding. You can bet they're going to be watching us closely. Hell, Trina's been trying to set me up since the week we met. She's going to flip when she finds out I'm taking you to the wedding." He leaned toward her without taking his eyes off the road. "Body language is really important in selling a cover story. You did good in the lake for Dan's benefit, but we're going to have to practice more. Leaning in to each other." He pulled her hand to his lips. "Little gestures like this. Relax your hand. Your body needs to be loose and inviting."

Her hand tingled from the feel of his mouth on her skin, which was why she'd stiffened—trying to hide her reaction. The last thing she wanted was for him to know how very much she still wanted him. Now she did as he asked and relaxed her arm. She leaned toward him, close enough to feel his body heat along her left arm, even though their arms weren't touching.

She closed her eyes. She could do this. All she had to do was resist the urge to hide her attraction, and everyone would see what they needed to. And she would just have to hope Sean would believe it was an act.

She pulled away, slipping her hand from his and scooting over in her seat so she could look at his profile as she asked the question that had been driving her nuts since last evening. "Why do you think secrecy is so important? Why not just tell everyone you're protecting me? The guests at the wedding are Alec and Isabel's closest friends too. Why can't he tell Curt? The guy was US attorney general for nearly four years. He was seventh in line for the presidency. I'm pretty sure he can keep a secret."

"*Was*. He's not AG anymore. Sure he's still got clearance, but he's not part of this administration, not part of government. Anything related to intelligence is the highest tier secrecy. Rav can't screw that up. You saw how much that letter was redacted. Even you and Isabel weren't allowed to see it, and it was a threat directed at *you*. I have no clue what was redacted from that note, but my guess is, it was big." He took his gaze off the road for just a moment to look at her, then focused on the narrow forest road again. "So, are you going to cut yourself some slack and work with me, or are you going to keep beating yourself up and make this difficult for us both?"

"Is it really necessary for you to be so logical about this? I mean, you could be a total dick and then I wouldn't care that you rejected me. When you're so understanding, it only makes it worse."

A dimple appeared in his right cheek, and she wished he

weren't driving and facing the road so she could take in the full beauty of his smile.

"I was on duty, Hazel. I couldn't have slept with you even if you weren't too drunk to consent."

"And what if things get out of hand this weekend?" she dared to ask.

"I'll be on duty. Twenty-four seven. Just like in Grand Cayman."

"It's your friend's wedding! You're best man. Surely you won't be on duty then?"

"I love Ian like a brother and am honored he asked me to stand up with him. I'll enjoy the wedding and reception, but won't forget the job I'm being paid to do."

Hazel couldn't help but stare at the man. He was crazy to take this on. "Do you have a life?"

He shrugged. "Not really."

"I'm sorry you had to break off your wedding date. I feel terrible about that."

"It's fine. It wasn't serious."

She wanted to believe that, but who knew with Sean? He prioritized work over life, so he could be lying. Maybe he'd ended an important relationship because he lacked work/life balance.

She didn't have balance either, so she really couldn't throw stones. But her issues were different. She worked too hard and played too hard, but the ratio was off and the extremes, instead of balancing each other out, were damaging. Her teeter-totter didn't maintain an even rhythm. It was stuck at the top or at the bottom, never in between. She was tossed up and slammed down, like booze in a cocktail shaker.

Grand Cayman was an example of the play-too-hard end of the spectrum; she'd overdone it on her break. Croatia had been months of being slammed down, and the mental bruises had triggered a fainting spell in a lake.

She'd arrived on Alec's doorstep looking for a break to give her that balance at last. No party-girl fun. No work. Just rest. But now she had dozens of skeletons to identify and a surprising invitation to a cozy wedding celebration.

"Are we cool now?" Sean asked.

She nodded. "We're cool." And she did feel better. It *was* good that he'd brought it up so she could put the mortification behind her. "But you have to promise to never bring up Grand Cayman again."

He laughed. "Deal, so long as you don't try to get me reassigned again. You tell Rav you want someone else, and I'll tell everyone how sexy you looked in my bed."

She couldn't help but smile. He'd found her sexy that night? He was probably just saying that, but for the moment, she'd try to believe it. "Resorting to blackmail?"

"Whatever it takes to keep my job."

She laughed. Sean was a good guy. She needed to remember that this couldn't be any easier for him than it was for her. Harder, in fact, because he would be lying to Ian while standing up with him at his wedding.

They reached the estate, and she was quick with her shower, and soon they were on the road again for Baltimore. They were lucky and traffic was light. It was just after two when they reached the supplier. The microscope was a beauty, and Hazel was practically giddy with the excitement of it, but damn, the price. She felt guilty buying it, even though Alec had insisted.

The amount Alec was expending for Hazel's protection—an expensive microscope, Sean's protection twenty-four seven, with bonus pay because he was supposed to be enjoying his best friend's wedding—it didn't make sense. Her being the target made no sense.

Unless there was something Alec wasn't telling her.

Chapter Five

Alec sat with his back to the headboard and watched Isabel comb the tangles from her curls. She wore a pale blue satin camisole and matching pair of shorts that he planned to remove as soon as she finished her nightly ritual. He never tired of this view. Never tired of these quiet moments.

Isabel's cat, Gandalf, jumped on the bed and stood on Alec's legs, staring him down as the cat always did before settling down to accept Alec's petting as his due. Alec stroked the animal, always amused that Gandalf had adopted him from practically the moment they met. As if the cat knew he'd be stuck with Alec for the rest of his days and so he might as well get the bonding over with.

The old tom had a certain bossy charm. He was especially clingy in the evenings, when he knew he was about to be banished from the master bedroom. The cat didn't share their room at night, because he inevitably wanted to sleep on Alec's chest, which was great for Gandalf, but not so great for Alec.

The furry beast never tried to disturb Isabel's sleep. What was up with that?

Isabel glanced over and smiled. "It's nice having you home every night."

"Yeah," Alec said. "I hate the reason behind it, but I shouldn't have let my schedule get so out of hand." He'd been working so late these last few months that he'd been spending at least three nights a week in their DC condo. He was lucky to live driving distance from the Capitol. He was one of very few senators who could sleep at home every night, but lately, he and his staff had been putting in extra long hours, and it had been easier to stay in the city. At the same time, Isabel was too busy with her job to join him in the condo.

With the threat to her safety, he'd made it a priority to be home every night. Sean would be here in the evenings, but that wasn't the same as Alec being able to watch over her himself.

"When all this is over, you think you'll keep this schedule?" she asked.

He pet the cat, who'd begun to purr. "I plan to. As much as possible."

"I'm going to hold you to that."

"Please do."

She smiled and set the wide-tooth comb on the dresser, then crawled up the bed and settled facing him. She stroked Gandalf's thick gray fur. "Hazel's got a thing for Sean. This weekend is going to be awkward."

Her words surprised him. "Really? No way. I'd have noticed."

She laughed. "Yeah, right." She stroked his cheek. "Honey, you've been so focused on work and whatever this threat is, you barely see *me*."

"Sweetheart, the day I don't see you when you're within a

thousand yards of me is the day you'll be tossing dirt on my casket."

She gave him a wry look, then leaned forward and pressed her mouth to his in a soft kiss. She started to pull back, but he cupped the back of her head with a palm and pulled her in to deepen the kiss, adding his tongue to the equation.

Claws bit into his leg—Gandalf didn't like the fact that Isabel was getting his petting—but Alec ignored the pain. He'd been looking forward to this moment all day. He slid a hand under her camisole and cupped a breast. Her nipples were hard peaks he wanted to taste. He released her mouth. "Let's get the cat out of here."

"But what about Hazel and Sean?"

"They can get their own cat."

She rolled her eyes. "I mean about how awkward this weekend is going to be. Sean is *best man*. He should get to enjoy this wedding. But he's going to be pretending to be involved with Hazel in front of his closest friends. Can't we save him that weirdness and just tell everyone what's going on?"

"I wish we could, Iz. It's not that simple. Plus, it would cast a different mood on the event. I'm freaked out enough about the threat. I don't want to scare the others."

"We've received death threats before. Why is it different this time?"

He wanted to tell her the truth, but the truth would only terrify her. "I'm sorry, love. I can't tell you." He stared into her eyes and remembered the worst day of his life. Hers too, but she didn't remember it. And never would, if he had any say in the matter.

"So, Hazel likes Sean?" he said, deliberately changing the subject. "Any chance it goes both ways?" He liked the idea of them as a couple.

Sean Logan had been one of Alec's first hires when he bought Raptor. The former SEAL had been his right-hand man throughout the transition from old management to new. Alec had considered Sean for the job of CEO when he left to run for the Senate, but Sean had nixed the offer, preferring the travel and flexibility of being an operative. He'd again turned Alec down when offered the job of Alaska Compound Director.

Isabel shrugged. "If it's reciprocal, Sean hides it well."

"Too bad."

"You're missing the point. You can't do this to Sean. Or Hazel. This weekend is going to be excruciating for them both."

"Sean agreed to do it, and honestly, there is no one I trust more with Hazel's life."

"But what if Hazel isn't the target? You might be ruining Cressida and Ian's wedding for Sean for no reason."

"I can't take that chance. And Sean didn't want to take that chance either." When Alec considered it in this light, he suspected Sean might have feelings for Hazel. "He could have said no."

Isabel shook her head. "For a brilliant man, you can be dense at times. Do you really think he'd have felt comfortable saying no to you? You're his *boss*."

"Keith's his boss. I just own the company."

She fixed him with a look. "Right. Like he's going to be splitting those hairs in the moment. You are his ultimate employer, and he knows it. *Of course* he said yes."

Alec sighed. Isabel was right. But dammit, Sean was the best choice. Plus he was single and knew Hazel, making the charade possible. "I'll talk to him tomorrow, give him the opportunity to change his mind before he talks to Ian about the wedding." At her look he added. "Without repercussions, of course."

"And what will you do if he wants out?"

"I don't know. All the DC operatives are either on assignment or going to the wedding. I guess I'll see if the FBI can stash her in a safe house."

"You know she's not a piece of jewelry, right?"

Now it was his turn to fix Isabel with a look. "Hazel, Ivy, and Laurel are the closest thing I have to siblings. It's my fault she might be in danger. I'll do whatever is necessary to protect her."

"Necessary in your mind, Alec. But to Hazel? She doesn't really believe she's in danger. And frankly, I'm inclined to agree." She cocked her head, her wild red curls flopped into her eyes rendering Alec's mind blank.

Isabel was always the ultimate distraction. She made him defenseless. And stupid. He was as infatuated as when they'd first met. Even more so, because now he knew her, heart and soul, and there wasn't a thing about her he didn't love. She challenged him, even pissed him off at times, but his love for her would never waver.

Not being able to tell her the reason behind his fears when she was at the heart of his worry? When he would die to keep her safe? It was a painful test, and a challenge no marriage should have to endure.

*H*azel paced her bedroom. She'd convinced Alec she could sleep in her room, which was at the opposite end of the house from the master suite, mostly because she knew Alec slept lightly—and assumed he'd be even more alert than usual tonight—and her pacing would wake him.

She'd managed to sleep for only an hour before the dreams started. This time, the skulls of children were interspersed with the bones in the lake, as they'd been in her mind when she fainted.

So that was a fun twist.

For the first time, she honestly asked herself if she could do the job. She'd assumed she could power through, as she always had, but today, she'd passed out in a frigging lake. Facedown. The sting of water in her sinuses had revived her, but still, that was scary as hell.

Who would she be without her job? How would she support herself? More important, her work was her life. Her frequent and lengthy trips overseas meant she was losing touch with many of her friends. Her sisters were married with children and careers of their own.

Laurel's child was neuroatypical and thriving thanks to Laurel and her husband's attention to their daughter's needs. Ivy and Matt were still practically on their honeymoon, and Julian was adjusting to life with new parents after losing his biological parents in a car accident when he was four years old. Neither of her siblings had time or emotional energy to give her, and she wouldn't ask that of them.

Alec and Isabel were probably about ten minutes away from starting a family, and the last thing they'd want was Hazel in their space as their family grew. Although they might enjoy the easy access to a babysitter.

But she hadn't gotten a PhD in forensic anthropology so she could be her cousin's live-in nanny. If she was going to take care of babies, they'd be her own.

But she didn't have children or a lover or anyone in her life outside her parents, siblings, and cousin, because she'd been too consumed with work to take the time to attempt a real relationship.

In some ways, her infatuation with Sean Logan was her longest adult relationship. She paced her large room, feeling rather pathetic about it all. As soon as she got her head together, she'd sign up for a dating app. For real this time.

The few times she'd attempted online dating in the past, she'd turned cold at the initial contacts. She'd examined the bones of too many women who'd been dumped in the woods. She knew the statistics, knew the man on the other end of the message was probably perfectly safe, but knife wounds leave marks on bones, and those had left marks on her psyche.

So maybe she'd been struggling with the job longer than she thought. At least she had an appointment with her psychotherapist tomorrow. She glanced at the clock, seeing it was just after midnight. Today.

There were a lot of hours between now and dawn. Maybe if she worked for a few of them, she'd be able to get some sleep.

It might be counterintuitive to think staring at the bones that were giving her nightmares would help her sleep, but she never had problems dealing with bones in the lab. It was when they were in the ground—or water—or garbage can or incinerator or trunk of the car that they got to her. Labs were where bones had a rightful place. It might not be their natural habitat, but at least they belonged there. Not like in a trunk or piled together in a mass grave.

She and Sean had put the equipment and bones in the annex, but she hadn't had time to set up the lab. Now was as good a time as any. She picked up her cell phone. Sean had spent the afternoon configuring the alarm system on the annex so she could access and monitor it through her phone. She'd never known he'd been involved in the technical end of the business, but it made sense, considering he traveled a lot for work and was often the only point of contact for the client —no technical support staff available.

Now she entered her pass code so she could monitor the alarm system for both the house and annex. She could turn alarms off and on as she left the mansion and entered the annex. Her thumbprint and pass code were required for both, which would speak well to the security of the analysis should the bones end up being evidence in a legal proceeding.

She pulled on a thick flannel shirt and buttoned it up, then slipped on a pair of boots for the short walk across the yard and headed down the stairs. At the front door, she flicked off the alarm using her code and stepped outside. As she secured the alarm behind her, her phone vibrated, causing her to jolt with surprise.

She had a text. From her fake boyfriend.

SEAN

What the hell do you think you're doing?

She paused on the porch, staring at the screen. The wind blew across the driveway, scattering dry leaves that had just started to fall. Another message quickly followed the first.

Where are you going?

HAZEL

Well, that's not creepy or anything.

If you are safe, use the password. And sign with your code so I know it's you.

Shit. He really was worried. She leaned against the column and tried to remember the password that meant she was safe. He wouldn't let her choose any word that people might guess she would use. Anything to do with bones or family was out.

What else did she have? And then she remembered what she'd tossed out in frustration.

HAZEL

Rum. HM3zj

SEAN

Okay then. Back to my original question.
What the hell are you doing?

Going to the annex. To work.

At midnight?

Couldn't sleep. Figured I'd set up the lab.

You can't leave the house. Not unless you
want to get me fired.

Alec wouldn't fire you because I left the
house when you weren't here to stop me.

He'll know I knew you left the house—my
phone is set to alert me anytime you or
Isabel turn the alarm system on or off. So
you need to get your ass back inside and
wait forty-five minutes so I can get there,
unless you want me to be fired.

Shit.

Without wasting time responding, she turned off the front door alarm, stepped inside, and turned the alarm back on again. A moment later, her phone buzzed.

Good. I'll be there in forty. Maybe sooner.
Traffic is light.

You don't need to come. I'll go back to bed.

Too late.

All at once, she saw the "is" part of the sentence, "Traffic is light."

SEAN

HAZEL

You can't already be on your way. Are you texting and driving?

SEAN

I am. There's a new invention called voice text. You should try it sometime. You type too slow. I think it took you a full minute to text the word rum.

Guilt filtered through her. She hadn't expected to need a code word so soon, and she'd been too excited setting up the new microscope to pay much attention to the list of words they'd settled on—all with different meanings should she end up in a situation. At least she'd remembered her code signature. But that had been easy: HM for her initials, 3 because she was the third child, Z for her niece Zoe, and J for Julian.

Turn the car around. Get some sleep.

No.

She climbed the stairs and paused at the top to type some more, thinking the voice thing might be a good idea, but not wanting to give him the satisfaction so soon. Plus talking might wake Alec—if he wasn't spying on this conversation, which was entirely possible.

I promise I'll be good and go back to bed. I'm on my way up the stairs now. But you probably know that since you're spying on me through my phone.

SEAN

Nah, I'm using the security cameras to spy
on you. You're on the upper landing.

Crap. She forgot the interior cameras were on at night
now. Alec had never used them before. She glanced up at the
camera and debated how to respond. She was tempted to flip
him off, but it wasn't his fault he was spying on her. In fact,
she was the one who'd dragged him out of bed. She owed
him. She smiled and set her phone on the bannister and
slowly began unbuttoning the flannel shirt, as if performing a
striptease.

Her phone immediately buzzed.

I'm trying to drive here.

HAZEL

Eyes on the road, Logan.

Keep your clothes on, MacLeod. Or at least
wait until I get there.

She stared at the screen. Was Sean flirting with her? She
moved away from the camera and headed toward her room.
There weren't cameras in this part of the house. She was safe
from spying eyes.

Back inside her room, she kicked off her boots and settled
on the bed.

You can't be serious about coming over. I
won't leave the house. I promise. I won't
even leave my room. Consider me grounded
until morning.

I'm coming.

HAZEL

Why?

The typing symbol swirled on the screen for a long moment, longer than she'd had to wait for a reply so far. It disappeared and appeared three times before a text delivered.

SEAN

You said you couldn't sleep.

Her body flushed. Was he concerned on a personal level? What were the messages he'd started then deleted?

I'm fine. Just…wound up.

I can't sleep either.

She touched his words on the screen, then jerked her hand away when the window popped up that would let her mark it with a heart. Yeah, she wasn't hearting any of Sean's messages, even if that was how she felt.

I have an idea about how we can use this for our cover story.

All at once, she deflated. She should have realized this was only about the job for him. She sucked in a deep breath and typed as if she hadn't felt all fluttery for a moment, only to be crushed with reality.

What's that?

SEAN

I told my mom about you tonight, just like we planned today. Tomorrow, I'll tell her that after she went to bed, I just had to see you. So I did.

HAZEL

You're going to tell your mother you drove to Gaithersburg for a booty call??!!

No! I mean, I'm sure she'll assume. But she also knows I wouldn't bolt like this when she's visiting—and wouldn't take you to the wedding—if there wasn't more to it. To us. So the fact that I took off tonight like I did will make it look like I really am crazy about you.

There wasn't a single thing he'd said wrong in the text. And he was right, this was a great way to sell the sudden-relationship story. Everyone had to believe that Sean fell in love with her hard and fast for this weekend to work. It was already Wednesday. They would drive to West Virginia in two days.

She stared at the last sentence. *So the fact that I took off tonight like I did will make it look like I really am crazy about you.*

Like he really was. This was just a job for him. He couldn't be more clear than if he'd straight out said he wasn't interested.

And that hurt, because in spite of months of telling herself to move on, she was just as infatuated with Sean Logan as she'd been when she'd thrown herself at him on Grand Cayman.

Chapter Six

Even though Sean could control the security system, he had Hazel meet him at the front door. He wanted the security team that was monitoring the grounds to see him entering the house with one of the residents so they wouldn't wonder if he was working another side on this job.

"Wave to the camera and smile, Haze," he said, nodding to the security camera mounted above the door.

She smiled wearily, her big eyes even larger behind glasses he was still getting used to seeing on her, and led him inside. He followed her up the stairs and across the landing to a casual family room nestled between two bedrooms, one of which was Hazel's.

He nodded to the interior camera in the foyer and the one on the upper landing as he passed by. At least there were no cameras in the living areas of the house, not that it would matter if there were. He wasn't here for a booty call, no matter how nice Hazel's booty looked in yoga pants.

She'd removed the flannel top she'd been wearing earlier, revealing an oversized T-shirt with the Rwandan flag on it. If he remembered correctly, she'd worked in Rwanda for seven or eight months a year or two ago. Then there'd been a stint in Ukraine, prior to returning home to be with her sister while Ivy's ex-husband was tried for treason and arms dealing.

It had been after Ivy's ex was convicted that the sisters had gone to Grand Cayman to celebrate. Sean had accompanied them to guard Ivy, who'd received death threats thanks to her marriage to Patrick Hill, and months before, she'd been abducted in Palau.

But neither Hazel nor Ivy had known that Rav planned to use the vacation to reunite Ivy with the Russian spy she'd fallen in love with in Palau. He had a new identity, giving him a chance to start over with Ivy and the boy she was trying to adopt—the former spy's biological nephew.

Hazel knew none of this. Her job had been to witness her sister and Matthew Clark meeting for what the world—and Hazel—needed to believe was the first time.

Sean's job had been to guard Ivy until Matt—who was more than capable of protecting her, as he had in Palau—could take over, but Sean still had to watch Matt's back and couldn't let himself be distracted by the boss's sexy cousin.

Now the boss's sexy cousin *was* the job. And the job was pretending to fall in love with her.

"Can I get you anything?" she asked. "Water? Beer? Cheese puffs?"

He was about to say no when her last offer surprised him. "Are they the nuclear-orange kind?"

"No way. All-natural white cheddar."

"There is nothing natural about cheese puffs."

"I suppose that's true. But they're so addictive."

She grabbed a bag from a cabinet and filled a bowl with them. He didn't really want cheese puffs, but it was something to focus on. She looked tired and worried. He assumed she hadn't been able to sleep because of her work in Croatia, but passing out in the lake was scary too.

"Do you want to talk about it?" he asked as she settled on the couch.

She sat with her back to the armrest, facing him, and pulled her knees to her chest, wrapping her arms around her legs. Her body was a tight ball and he didn't miss the sadness in her eyes. Was she upset with him? Or was it stress and fear? She certainly had plenty of reason for all the jumbled emotions.

"Not really."

She'd gone silent on their text conversation after he explained why he was still on his way, and it wasn't until he'd pulled up to the gate and stopped the car to punch in his code that he had a chance to reread their conversation and it hit him how his last line sounded.

It was the damn "really." It stressed a point that didn't need stressing. He could just as easily have said, *So the fact that I took off tonight like I did will show her how crazy I am about you.*

But he hadn't said it because it was too damn close to the truth. He didn't even remember the trip from his apartment to the car. One moment, he was sitting on the couch watching TV, then his phone buzzed, letting him know she'd logged in to the security system. He'd had his shoes on and keys in hand before she reached the front door.

He'd scribbled a note to his mother by the time Hazel stepped outside and turned the alarm back on. From there, it was a blur until he was on the GW Parkway and she'd sent the code word that meant everything.

Rum.

It wasn't lost on him why she'd selected rum, and it wasn't because it was only three letters and easy to type quickly. She'd cursed rum vehemently that night in his room.

He reached out and took a cheese puff from the bowl. It

made a satisfying crunch, and he had to admit, the white cheese was good. He'd had several more and caught Hazel's tired smile. "See," she said. "Addictive."

"Agreed." He licked the cheese powder from his fingers and wished she'd eat some so he could watch her do the same. Apparently, he was a masochist.

If he made love to her, she'd lose the shadows in her eyes. Maybe if she ate some puffs, he could lick the cheese from her fingers. From there, he would explore her body…and in the end, she'd be so exhausted and satisfied, there'd be no room for bad dreams. She'd fall asleep in his arms and would wake up fixed.

Except life didn't work that way. He couldn't fix Hazel with sex any more than he could fix his sister with thoughts and prayers. Hazel needed therapy and his sister needed chemo. And he was at a loss how he could help on both fronts.

"I'm sorry I got you out of bed," she said.

He shook his head. "I wasn't sleeping. I was watching TV."

"Yeah? What were you watching?"

"*Battlestar Galactica*. The reboot."

"Ooh. I've always wanted to watch it. Never had time."

"It's a great show."

"Is it streaming? We can watch it here."

"You really need to start with the first episode."

"I don't mind. We can watch whatever you were watching."

"Nah. The first episode is fine." He'd watched the whole series years ago. Tonight, he'd been flipping through the episodes, trying to find good ones without the cancer storyline.

Hazel grabbed a remote and hit a button. A panel on the

facing wall retracted, revealing an eighty-inch TV screen. "Sweet," Sean said.

"Living here has its perks."

He laughed. "I bet."

Not surprisingly, Rav subscribed to every streaming service and had broadband speed that would make Silicon Valley envious. It only took a minute for Hazel to find the show and hit Play. "You sure you don't want anything to drink? More cheese puffs?"

"Nah. I'm good."

Hazel dimmed the lights and settled back on the far end of the couch. The volume was low, but the sound system was set to quiet music and sound effects as needed to hear dialogue. They were twenty minutes into the story when he noticed she was just as tense as she'd been when he arrived. And he didn't think it was triggered by what was happening on the screen. Although a show depicting genocide was probably not the best choice for her at the moment.

Smooth move, dipshit.

The couch was deep and comfy, an L-shaped sectional that could easily accommodate two people lying side by side on his end of the L. He had an idea. Maybe not a good one, but it was better than his brilliant suggestion of watching millions of people get nuked by Cylons.

He paused the show, grabbed the thick fleece blanket draped over the back, and patted the cushion next to him. "Come'ere."

She cocked her head but didn't move.

"Come on. Let's get comfortable. Then if you get sleepy, you can drift off."

She looked skeptical, but she inched toward him.

"I promise I won't bite." *Unless you ask me to.*

Her lips twitched. "If I had a dime for every time I've heard that."

He chuckled.

She inched closer but stopped short, reminding him of a wary cat. He wanted to pull her in his arms, hold her, but not if it would make her uncomfortable. She hadn't exactly been thrilled both times he scooped her out of the water. "Will you let me hold you, just for comfort?"

Her brow furrowed. "I can't remember the last time someone just held me."

"Me neither." He'd dated plenty over the years but hadn't gotten serious with anyone since he'd been in the Navy. Sure, there'd been sex, but not much in the way of cuddling or emotional investment.

Her mouth twisted. "The last time might be when I was twenty and caught my boyfriend cheating. Ivy held me as I cried and promised she'd wreak cyber revenge."

He laughed. He didn't want to know what sort of revenge computer wizard Ivy was capable of. "Okay, then. Pretend I'm Ivy."

She smiled as she shook her head. "I don't think that will work."

He reached out and stroked her cheek. She looked so vulnerable and achingly beautiful in the dim light cast by the paused TV. "I want to help you, Hazel, but I'm not a psychotherapist. I don't know what to do." And frankly, the broken look in her eyes when she'd answered the door tonight scared the hell out of him. He was so out of his depth.

She crawled forward and settled next to him, stretching out lengthwise beside him but keeping air between their bodies. He put his arm around her and pulled her close. She let out a soft sound of surprise and pleasure and relaxed against him.

His heart shifted or opened or maybe it grew three sizes. He didn't know what the hell happened in his chest, but it was something. Maybe he could do this. Be the friend she needed and not screw up his job by sleeping with her.

Thirty minutes later, Hazel drifted to sleep. He could tell by the way her body relaxed into him as much as by the even cadence of her breathing. He hit the remote to power off the TV. The room descended into darkness. He wrapped his other arm around her, shifting position slightly to get more comfortable, then he buried his nose in her hair and breathed her in. She'd long since washed away the scent of lake water. Now she smelled of shampoo and something nutty that held notes of chocolate. He'd noticed the scent on her before. Whatever it was, he thought of it as sweet, pure Hazel.

He closed his eyes and relaxed with her curled up against his side and couldn't remember the last time anything felt so right.

Chapter Seven

$\mathcal{A}$lec leaned against the arched entry and stared at the sleeping couple. He smiled, already hearing Isabel's "I told you so" in his mind.

He doubted there was more to this scene than what was before him. They were both clothed, and if they'd wanted to fool around, Hazel's bedroom—which had a door for privacy, unlike this living room—was mere feet away. He'd been woken by the security system at midnight and had seen Hazel step outside on the security monitor. He'd been about to chase her down when she stopped and looked at her phone. Sean was on duty, even when home in his DC condo.

Alec had waited to see what she'd do and had been satisfied Sean had things under control when she stepped back inside. He'd been alerted again when Sean arrived, and at that point, he'd rolled over and gone back to sleep, secure in the knowledge there was another trained operative in the house. He didn't figure the man was here for a booty call, but even if he were, they were all safer with another operative on the premises.

He still wasn't sure why Sean had come over after Hazel

was safely back inside, but seeing them nestled together on the couch made him think it had more to do with Sean caring about Hazel than bodyguard duties. So, there was a good chance Hazel's feelings went both ways. He liked the idea, not that it was any of his business one way or the other. He liked Sean, and he loved Hazel. If this worked out, great. If it went south, well, he knew them both well enough that it wouldn't be the kind of drama that would force him to pick sides.

Hazel shifted in Sean's arms, and Alec retreated, glad they'd carpeted the upper floor so his steps were silent. Hazel had been having trouble sleeping, and this was the first time she'd slept past six in the morning since she'd arrived ten days ago. He'd let them both wake up naturally. They deserved that luxury this morning. Alec had planned to talk to Sean before he called Ian to tell him he wanted to bring a different date, but it looked like that might not be the issue Isabel feared it was. Alec would still talk to him, but it could wait until Sean had coffee.

Hazel and Sean. It might not be hard for them to pull off this fake-relationship thing after all. He'd tell Isabel this had been his plan all along. She'd know he was full of shit, but it would make her laugh. And there was nothing he liked more than that.

A heavy weight pressed on Sean's chest. He slowly opened his eyes. Morning light filled the room, and two dark eyes were staring down at him. Feline eyes, which came with feline breath that was being expelled just an inch from his nose. Gandalf didn't look pleased to find Sean sleeping on what he could only assume was the cat's favorite couch. Or maybe it was Hazel he'd claimed, and he didn't like the way Sean was holding his girl.

She's mine, cat.

Not hardly. But for the next few weeks…sort of.

He reached up to make peace by petting the cat, and Hazel stirred at his side. She jolted as if she would spring up and back away from their intimate position—her body tucked against him, her shoulder nestled between his side and his arm with her cheek on his chest—but he tightened the arm that cradled her, stopping her from fleeing. He didn't want her to bolt and make this awkward. Having her curled against his side was the most pleasant way he'd woken up in months.

Well, except for the perturbed cat staring down at him. "No sudden moves, or Gandalf might shred my chest." Okay, so the cat had given him the perfect excuse to keep Hazel close. *Thank you, Gandalf.*

She let out a soft giggle. "He can be pretty territorial when it comes to men." She reached up and pet him, and said in a singsong voice, "It's okay, Gandalf. Sean's not all bad."

He laughed, causing his chest to shake, and the cat's claws dug in. Thankfully, the blanket was thick and Gandalf didn't draw blood. "Not *all bad?*"

She smiled up at him, and his heart might've flipped if it weren't in jeopardy from a territorial cat. "Some parts of you are even good."

"Which ones?" His hand, which rested on her waist, itched to explore and caress. But he controlled the wayward appendage. He didn't want to ruin this by doing something they'd regret.

"The parts that held me so I could sleep without dreaming for the first time in weeks."

Gandalf settled on his chest, apparently accepting Hazel's

endorsement. Wasn't there a cartoon Hazel who was a witch? Maybe Gandalf was her familiar. "You slept well?"

She nodded, stroking the cat, then she rose on her elbow and kissed his cheek. "I slept great. Thank you."

He might be sore from sleeping all twisted up with her, but it was worth it, seeing her eyes clear of exhaustion and sorrow. "You're welcome. Anytime."

"Having a fake boyfriend isn't so bad."

"Whoa. Don't go crazy with the compliments this morning. I might develop a big ego."

"Hey, you moved up from not all bad to not so bad."

Oh, but sweetheart, you will like me when I'm bad. Thank goodness he had the control to not say those words aloud. Flirting with Hazel was just too damn easy.

She slid from his side and sat up. "I should jump in the shower. We need to hurry if you're going to have time to get home and change before my psychotherapy appointment this morning."

"I'll just shower here. I've got a bag in the trunk. When your job is twenty-four seven, you learn to be prepared."

"All right, then. I'll jump in the shower while you grab your bag. If Isabel's up, she'll have started coffee. If Alec is the only one up, you'll be on your own. He doesn't drink coffee and doesn't know how to use the coffeemaker. It's scary complex for something that's just hot water poured over ground beans. I only just finished the prerequisite course to learn how to operate it."

He shifted, and Gandalf jumped from his chest. "I was certified on that baby years ago. Before Isabel moved in, we'd sometimes hide people here in a pinch. Do you want cream or sugar?"

Her eyes widened with joy. "Cream, please." She stepped into her bedroom. "I could get used to this fake-boyfriend stuff if it means a solid night's sleep and fresh coffee."

He smiled as the door closed behind her. He could get used to this too if it meant she woke up happy and energetic, like the Hazel he'd met years ago.

He was still smiling as he entered the kitchen and found his boss sitting at the breakfast nook with a mug of hot chocolate and a tablet. Rav glanced up from his reading. A slow smile spread across his face as he leaned back in his chair.

"Mornin', boss," Sean said as casually as he could manage. Like it was an everyday thing that he waltz into his boss's kitchen at seven a.m. after holding his beautiful—and vulnerable—cousin in his arms all night. He cleared his throat. "For the record, nothing hap—"

Rav cut him off with a wave of his hand. "Don't worry, I pieced most of it together from the security log. *And* for the record, it would be none of my business if anything did happen."

"Disagree. You're my client. You hired me to guard her. That makes it your business. I want you to know I don't screw around on the job."

"I know you don't, Sean. And technically, you weren't on the job last night. Once Hazel was back inside the front door, she was safe to the level we agreed to. You didn't need to come here. That was your choice. So don't tell me you landed on my doorstep at one a.m. because you were concerned Hazel wasn't protected."

Sean could give the line about coming over to make the relationship lie more plausible for his mother, but Rav would see right through it. "She said she couldn't sleep. And after what happened in the lake yesterday, I was worried about her."

"Thank you. I've been worried too." His brows pulled in. "Can we step into my office? I need to talk to you about this weekend."

"Of course." He was curious why this couldn't be said in

the kitchen, considering the only people in the house were the four who knew the truth. Isabel must've been up already because there was a full pot of coffee. He poured himself a cup, then followed Rav down the hall to his ground-floor office.

Once they were in the room with the door closed, they each took seats on the opposite sides of Rav's large, modern desk. This wasn't a stately office for show. The furniture was made of fine wood, but it wasn't frilly or ornate. Each piece was sleek and functional. It suited Rav much more than his office in the Senate, which was antique in keeping with the architecture.

"Isabel reminded me last night that I didn't really give you a choice about this job and suggested you might've felt coerced into saying yes. I want to be clear. You can refuse. If you don't want to go through with the charade at the wedding, just say the word and we'll scrap the plan. I'll figure something out for Hazel's security."

Sean held Rav's gaze, trying to read him. Was this a cursory offer to placate Isabel, or did he mean it? But when did Rav ever say something he didn't mean?

In Sean's experience, never.

Did he want out? To be able to enjoy the wedding and celebrate with his friends? The idea held a certain appeal. He'd be solo at the wedding. No Tricia as his real date or Hazel as his fake one. But there was one problem with that idea. "Do you believe Hazel is in danger?"

Rav nodded. "Yes. I think they both are."

"I'm in, then." He wouldn't be able to enjoy the wedding if he was worried about Hazel's security. "Can you tell me anything more about the threat? It would help if I knew what to look out for."

Rav planted his forearms on the desk, leaning forward. He wore his calculating expression. The one that indicated he was weighing his options as well as his words. "I can say this. If what I suspect is true, we need to be on the lookout for white men between eighteen and…seventy?"

Sean snorted. "Way to narrow it down."

"Yeah. Sorry. Definitely white, though, if that helps."

"Does this have to do with that white supremacist conspiracy website? The one you've been pushing the Senate to investigate?"

Rav cleared his throat and gave an almost imperceptible nod.

If Sean remembered correctly, the modus operandi of the online "news" site—Voigt Forum—was to dox those who openly opposed them and to sic their racist followers on the exposed, asking them to stalk and harass and basically make the person's life a living hell. Rape threats and death threats were just the starting point. A month ago, a Black man who'd been profiled on the site had been lynched, and Rav had called for the site owners to be held accountable, to be tried and convicted for murder along with the white men who'd actually done the lynching.

A senator from West Virginia, Christopher Small, had been a regular contributor on Voigt Forum prior to his election. He'd taken exception when Rav had called for a Senate investigation into the lynching. It appeared Senator Small hadn't broken all ties with the website as promised.

"Do you think Senator Small is behind this, to get you to back off?"

"I'm not naïve enough to dismiss him as a suspect, but it seems improbable."

"I'm with Isabel. I don't understand the need for secrecy," Sean said. "I mean, I'm fine pretending to be with Hazel, but why is it necessary? It's just going to be us at the inn the first night. Can't we pretend for the other wedding guests but tell our friends the truth?"

"Too much room for error."

Sean studied Rav, and slowly, the truth dawned. The redacted part of the note hinted at—or outright stated—a connection to one of the wedding guests. And maybe that person was involved somehow.

It was easy to rule out ninety-five percent of the guests. He'd trust all but one with his life. And that one was a newcomer with a top secret past. "Motherfucker. Matthew? You don't think he—?"

But Rav's suspicions did make sense. Matthew Clark had, after all, been a Russian spy and assassin. But the CIA, FBI, DOJ, and probably a dozen other letters Sean didn't know about had vetted him. As far as Russia knew, Dimitri Veselov—also known as the Hammer—died in Palau along with his handler. The man had spent months in intensive debriefing with the CIA and FBI. How was it possible they'd missed something?

Rav was silent. Finally, he said, "We can't be too careful."

But dammit, Dimitri—*Matt*—was crazy about Ivy, crazy about the son they were in the process of adopting.

He frowned. "I've never picked up racist vibes from Matthew," Sean said. "And believe me, I notice."

"I'm glad to hear it," Rav said. Silence settled between them. There were a lot of words cloaked in that silence. Finally, Rav let out a deep sigh and said, "We're good for this weekend, then?"

Sean nodded. "I'll protect Hazel and make sure we're convincing."

"Thank you." He cleared his throat. "This situation is… delicate. Any action I take that triggers Hazel—or anyone— to get wind of Matt's past, and Ivy could lose Julian. That little boy can't be put through losing another mother. And Matt could very well be innocent, and his carefully constructed new life could be yanked away if I screw this up.

There's a lot at stake here. Probably even more than *I* realize. I want you to know I wouldn't have asked this of you if I didn't believe it was necessary. Having you guard Hazel is the only way I can think of to keep this under wraps while keeping everyone I love safe. This way, even Matt is protected."

Sean nodded. He was starting to get an idea of the stakes, and the secrecy at least made sense, even the fact that he couldn't explain it to Hazel.

If Hazel ever learned the truth about all the ways she'd been lied to—by Rav, by Ivy, and even by Sean, she'd be livid. It was a good thing she would never, ever find out.

Chapter Eight

"Aside from the death of your childhood friend, there's another area I want to explore that could be a trigger for your anxiety." Dr. Parks's smooth, even voice was comforting, even as she said things that made Hazel uncomfortable. "You mentioned last week your experience in Ukraine, which predated your work in Croatia. Being detained for thirty-six hours by Russian separatists must've been a huge ordeal, yet you downplay it. It's possible you suppressed that trauma, and in Croatia, other work stress piled on and it all became too much."

Hazel considered the doctor's words carefully. She hated thinking of what happened in Ukraine. Detained and accused of being a spy, she'd been terrified. Yet she'd known the accusations were a ruse—an attempt to expel ICMP from the country because they were exposing an atrocity committed by Russia. It didn't mean they wouldn't make an example of her, though. The threats they'd made had been very real.

Alec had pulled political strings and got her out of the

country in record time. After what had happened to Ivy in Palau, her cousin didn't mess around.

"It's possible," she said. "But I'm not dreaming of the men who detained me like I am about the kids."

"Your brain might be protecting you by having you process the trauma you can handle. I would think the fear you felt in Ukraine was a sort of terror entirely different from the heartache triggered by your work. One you are used to processing, the other is unknown. In our next sessions, I think we should delve deep into those thirty-six hours. Maybe through hypnosis, if you're comfortable with that."

"I suppose…" Even as she said the words, revulsion rose inside her. Yeah. She was resisting thinking about Ukraine. The doctor could be on to something.

"Delving into that event, like exploring the loss of your friend at a young age, are the long-term strategies for relief. If we can root out the source, we can maybe put an end to the panic attacks and make the anxiety manageable, maybe even disappear."

Lord, how she wanted the anxiety to disappear. But she was under no illusion there would be a quick fix, much as she wanted one.

"In the short term, we can discuss antidepressants and anxiety meds, as well as exercises to use when you feel an attack coming on."

"Yesterday, in the lake, there was no warning. I just…fainted."

"But you said you were seeing children's bones and confusing the locations. Those were the warning signs that your anxiety was ratcheting up. If you can learn to identify those and do a few simple exercises, you might be able to stave off an attack, or at least lessen the severity. The fainting is really alarming, but given that the attack had a trigger—the strong

association of the bones in the lake to the bones in Croatia—
the sudden drop in blood pressure makes sense. What you are
suffering from is different from a simple panic attack. It's more
like a phobic trigger—some people see blood, and their phobia
makes their blood pressure drop so fast, they faint."

"I can't do my job if I faint at the sight of bones."

"Exactly. But unlike a person seeing blood without warning, you know when you're going to see bones. So you need to
learn mechanisms to ground yourself. You should share these
techniques with Isabel and your cousin, and anyone else you
spend time with, so they can help you in the event of another
attack. Are you seeing anyone? Is there anyone with you
when you can't sleep?"

The point-blank question startled Hazel in that she realized she had to lie to her psychotherapist, which didn't seem
like the best thing to do. But Sean had spent last night with
her, so it wasn't so much of a lie. "Yes. It's a new relationship,
though." Really, really new.

The doctor frowned. "Generally, I wouldn't recommend
starting a new relationship right now, but it can be beneficial
to have someone talk you through the panic, and it sounds
like your worst episodes—with the exception of yesterday—
happen at night."

"Yes. Except now I need to examine the bones during the
day." She shook her head, realizing Alec's ridiculous fake-
boyfriend idea actually could help her here. "Although my
boyfriend is taking time off work so he can be with me while
I'm examining the bones. I'm setting up a lab on the estate.
It's just across the yard, an easy commute, and a place where
he can hang out. He'll be with me if I have problems during
the analysis."

"That sounds perfect—exactly what I would have recommended if possible."

"I think it will be fine. though. I've never had an issue in a lab situation. It's always the field. Seeing human bones discarded like garbage…" All at once, the image of a small skull peeking through dirt came to mind. A tiny red tennis shoe. A stuffed frog, once green but now grayish brown from dirt and age.

Another skull, staring up at her from a shallow, fake lake. Rust-colored water filled the eye sockets like dark bloodstains.

Her breathing went shallow.

"Hazel, focus on my words. Spread your hands on the arms of the chair. Feel the texture?"

"Yes."

"Describe it."

"Leather. Cold."

"Feel it warm beneath your hands. Send your warmth into it. The warmth is the flow of energy through your body. Take a deep breath in."

Hazel did as instructed.

"Hold for a count of four. Now exhale. Focus on the outbreath. Make it long and slow. Again now."

She followed the instructions and the images faded. All she could think of was breath and the energy her hands exchanged with the armchair. She opened her eyes, which she hadn't realized she'd closed, and took a normal breath.

"That was a pretty basic technique that helps if you catch the anxiety build up right as it starts," Dr. Parks said. "If you'd been sitting at a table, I'd have had you put your hands on the flat surface. Texture is important to grounding yourself. So is breathing. You can do that exercise alone or guided, as I just led you. But there are other techniques you can use as well, and you'll want to try them all to see what works best." She leaned forward, staring into Hazel's eyes. "How do you feel?"

Hazel took another slow breath, and considered the question. And strangely, she felt…good. The simple technique had worked to refocus her thoughts before they spiraled out of control. She smiled. "Good. Like I can do this."

Dr. Parks smiled broadly. "I'm so pleased. You *are* going to work through this, Hazel. I'm so glad you didn't waste any time coming to see me. So often, people resist seeking help in the early stages of anxiety, but this is perfect timing to begin the work."

"It was Isabel's idea." Isabel had recommended Dr. Parks because the woman had helped her after her ordeal in Alaska and to process her grief from losing her brother.

By the time the session ended, Hazel felt revitalized. For the first time, she had real hope she could work through this. With the coping mechanisms, she'd have a way to deal with the physical manifestation of her anxiety while she processed and worked through the mental issues.

Of course, the quickest solution would be for Sean to hold her every night. He could be her therapy. She shook off the thought as she stepped into the waiting room where he sat. He might be handsome and charming and hot and have an unexpected caring side, but he couldn't cure her. She needed to do the hard work herself.

As they left the office, Sean said, "I called Ian. We're all set for the weekend."

"So it's official. We're dating."

"We are. Also, my mom wants to meet you."

Good Lord, how would they navigate that? "I'm sorry you had to lie to your mother."

He shrugged. "It's not like the time I told her I was sleeping over at a friend's but really was planning to take my girlfriend to a hotel so we could lose our virginity together in something other than the back of a car."

"And you got caught?"

"Yeah. Most kids get busted for using a fake ID while buying beer. I was using it for the hotel room. Except, at seventeen, I really did look like I was twenty-one, but my girl-friend, who was also seventeen, looked like she was about fifteen. The clerk called the cops, figuring he was saving a young girl from statutory rape. So that was fun."

"Oh my God. Were you arrested?"

"No. Because we were the same age—and we hadn't even gotten our room—the only thing I was guilty of was having a fake ID. The police took it and called my mom and my girl-friend's mom. Not surprisingly, we were both grounded for two weeks."

"Did you end up losing your virginity together?"

"Ah, so we're already to the sharing our sexual history part of the relationship."

She smiled. "Hey, you brought it up."

He laughed. "True."

They descended the stairs. The staircase was wide and sweeping with an old, carved railing. She ran her hand down the smooth, dark hardwood. Taking in the texture. Feeling grounded.

"To answer your question," Sean said, "sort of, but not then. Our parents conspired to keep us from being alone after that—and eventually we ended up getting in a big fight and broke up." He shrugged. "High school."

They reached his SUV in the small parking lot behind the doctor's office. Hazel climbed into the front seat and said, "I'm still trying to figure out what 'sort of' means."

"Well, when we finally had sex, I was a virgin and she wasn't. You asked if we lost our virginity together." He shrugged. "I was home on my first break from the Navy. I ran into my ex-girlfriend at a party and…might have made a point of letting her see that the muscles she'd liked before had multiplied."

Hazel laughed. "Your shirt was accidently ripped off?"

"Something like that. Anyway, we ended up having sex in a car after all." He fixed her with a look. "How about you?"

"My story is boring in comparison. Sophomore year of college with my first real boyfriend. We dated for about a month before having sex in his bed in his apartment. We continued dating for a couple of months until I came home one day to find him banging my roommate on our couch."

"Ouch. That the guy Ivy took cyber revenge on?"

"Yep. Although I don't think she ever did anything. Honestly, after the initial heartbreak passed, I was more devastated by my roommate's betrayal. She was all teary and claiming it only happened the one time, saying it was an accident. I asked what that even meant—had he tripped and his dick fell inside her? She was pretty damn sorry, though, when I demanded she move out. Alec's dad owned the condo, so I wasn't leaving. Her rent was only a token amount too—just enough to cover utilities. So really, she's the one who paid the biggest price for sleeping with him. He was such an ass, I doubt he even cared."

She cocked her head. "This was quite a tangent, but I suppose it's good to know some of these details about each other. It will add authenticity. But really, I'm sorry you had to lie to your mom about us. That doesn't feel right."

Sean shrugged. "You'll be lying to your sister, and if this goes on for any length of time, probably your parents too. Don't they live in the area?"

"They live in the Eastern Shore region of Maryland, in a tiny town in Dorchester County. They visit the DC area far more than I go there, so yeah, if this goes on for too long, they'll get wind of my new boyfriend." She smiled. "After what happened to Ivy in her first marriage, they would ask Alec to have Raptor run a background check on you—they were so relieved by Raptor's report on Matt—and they'll be unabashedly thrilled to know you're pre-vetted."

"Not the usual way I go about impressing my girlfriend's parents, but I'll take it." Sean put the car in gear. "Okay, what's next? Do we need to get you a dress for the wedding?"

"Nah. I've got plenty of dresses. Let's head back to Alec's so I can set up the lab and get to work."

As Sean pulled out into traffic, she felt calmer than she had in months. Partly it was feeling good about her conversation with Dr. Parks, but more than anything, it was the ease she felt with Sean after he'd held her last night. Something had changed. But if she wasn't careful, she could easily make the mistake of falling in love with him.

*S*ean helped Hazel set up four eight-foot banquet tables in the conference room in the annex that had been cleared to be Hazel's lab. He knew this room well. In the early days, when Rav had first purchased Raptor, he'd run the company out of the estate annex while both the DC office and Virginia compound were overhauled to get rid of everything the previous owner, Robert Beck, had his corrupt fingers on.

There'd been a biological weapons lab in the Virginia compound, forcing the entire compound to close for six months as it was carefully searched by the FBI and then cleaned by a federal hazmat team. When he wasn't on assignment, Sean and a few other operatives had worked with Rav in the annex during those months, planning the trainings they now ran at the Virginia compound and Anderson Lake property in addition to providing feedback on the operational structure of the private security company moving forward.

He and Rav had a connection in that they'd both left the military to spend time with dying parents. The job had been a lifeline for Sean.

As the company came together, he'd felt a renewed energy. It had been an exciting time, working with Rav as Raptor reformed into a company to be proud of, and being in the annex triggered a bit of nostalgia.

Hazel bent over to pick up one of the large metal trays they'd stacked just inside the door last night, and thoughts of Raptor past whooshed out of his head as he took in her ass.

She stood, large, heavy metal tray in hand, and placed it on the nearest table. He shook his head to clear away the haze of lust and crossed the room to help her. It only took a few minutes to set out all sixteen trays she'd borrowed from Talon & Drake. She then took bags of bones that had been collected from the lake and set one in the center of each tray.

"How can I help?" Sean asked.

She looked up, and he could tell she was about to brush off his offer, but then she bit her lip and said. "There's one thing you can do. Put a strip of masking tape across the bottom of each pan and label it with the bag number and all the other information written on the bag. That would save me a lot of time."

"Are these the coordinates for the location where the bones were collected?" he asked as he studied an extra large zipper top bag that contained a skull and an assortment of other bones.

"Yes. UTM coordinates. If I determine the bones are from a legit burial ground of some sort, they'll be returned to the same spot."

He stared into the empty eye sockets. This had been a person once. Flesh had covered these bones. This person had once had hopes and dreams. Now they were a skull in a bag.

He'd seen his share of death when he was active duty. He'd killed for his country more than once. Yet this was different. Hazel wasn't casual with her handling of the remains, but at the same time, there was a professional indifference to the bags and numbers.

He thought of his sister's medical tests. For her, the results were life and death, but to some lab technician somewhere, she was a series of numbers. One number estimated her odds of beating cancer. Another number predicted whether or not the cancer would return in five years.

And there was nothing he could personally do to change those numbers.

He placed a strip of tape in the bottom of the pan and tried to remember what Hazel had said. Something about returning the bones to the lake if she determined it was a legitimate burial ground. "And if the burial ground isn't legit?"

"We'll collect all the bones, and I'll group these with bones from the same area, hoping to sort out the individuals."

Sean had seen the piles of bones when he scooped her from the lake. There was no way they could all be sorted into individuals—not without DNA. "Are the bones going to be sent off for DNA?" he asked.

"If it looks like there is any. Most of these bones are calcined—burned. They could still contain DNA, but it might be hard to get, and there is no way every single bone could be tested for sorting."

"How do you know they're burned?" It wasn't as if they had scorch marks.

"The bright white color and the fragile, friable ends of the long bones. Have you ever thrown a chicken or rib bone into a campfire after eating, then noticed how white the bones were the next day, when the fire was out?"

"Come to think of it, yeah."

"The calcination process turns bones white."

As he labeled the trays, she set to work on the first one,

starting by clipping a microphone to her collar. The digital recorder, he noticed, was hooked to her waistband.

She donned surgical gloves, then pulled bones from the quart-size bag one at a time and described each one into the microphone. She used words like distal, lateral, proximal, left, right, fragment, friable, and several other terms he didn't catch.

He'd just finished labeling all sixteen trays by the time she moved on to the second tray, which was more interesting because it included the skull that had distracted him. She spent a long time studying it, describing the sutures, measuring the nasal opening and eye sockets.

He waited for a pause in her examination, so as not to disturb her flow, and asked if there was more he could do.

"Sorry, no. I'm afraid this is going to be very boring for you. I need to be the only one who handles the bones. It's a chain-of-evidence thing."

Sean wasn't the least bit bored; he was fascinated. This was Hazel in her element. She was supremely competent and knowledgeable. That shouldn't come as a surprise given that she had a PhD in the subject, but in all the years he'd known her, he'd never seen this side of her. He'd only seen the sexy, fun party girl. Now she was the intensely focused, expert-in-her-field scientist.

She wore the thick glasses, and again her long auburn hair was pulled back in a high ponytail, which brought out her cheekbones. She gazed down at the bones in the metal pan and the ponytail shifted, exposing the back of her neck. And now he had a new favorite part of Hazel to stare at. He wanted to run his lips over that sensitive patch of skin. Would she shiver when he did that?

Damn, now he was lusting after a woman as she analyzed death. But he couldn't forget how it had felt to hold her last night. He hadn't been aroused then, and he wasn't necessarily aroused now. It was more a notion of what he could explore if they took a dangerous leap.

She pursed her lips as she stared at the skull, her brows furrowing.

"What's wrong?" he asked.

"Just thinking about how race and gender are going to be a statistics game. It's going to come down to measurements of different elements and averages. Were I to guess at a glance, I'd say this skull is African American." Her mouth scrunched to one side. "I'm sorry. The forensic anthropology term is 'negroid,' which I hate using as much as I hate the term 'mongoloid.' From here on out, I'll just say Black, and if I mean Native American, I'll say Native, and Asian if I mean Asian, and European or white instead of Caucasoid."

Sean nodded. "Cool." He studied the skull. "You can tell race from a skull?"

"To a certain degree. Age is, of course, what we can identify with the most accuracy. After that comes gender, then race. For race, we look at things like the nasal aperture. In Black skeletons, it tends to be wider, but again, it's statistical. For gender, we look at the frontal bone—the forehead—for the slope and the thickness of the superciliary arch and supraorbital border, which make up the brow ridge. Men tend to have more sloping foreheads with thicker brow ridges than women. We also look at the mandible. Men are more likely to have squared jaws, where women have more pointed chins."

He glanced at the skull on the tray. "That one doesn't have a mandible."

"Correct. Doesn't mean it isn't in the lake. The rising and lowering of the water table or fish activity, among other things, could have separated the different cranial elements."

"So what, exactly, are you doing here?"

"This is all preliminary, to determine if more work needs

to be done or if this is a prehistoric burial ground we're disturbing. If it's prehistoric, we'll return these bones to their final resting place and won't disturb them again."

"But you said that skull looks Black, so it wouldn't be prehistoric."

"Exactly, but it could be historic. It remains possible it's a slave burial ground. In which case, I have questions, like, why were all the remains burned? It's possible these are all victims of a fire, but how did the remains end up in the reservoir?"

"You think this is evidence of a crime?"

She glanced at the bones laid out in the metal trays. "This is such a small sample of what's out there, it's hard to say. One or two burned individuals could easily be explained away in an historic or prehistoric context. But this many? Not so much."

"How many do you think are in the lake?" he asked.

"Yesterday, I counted twenty-six skulls. But it could easily be more—those were just the intact craniums. There could be shattered skulls mixed in the piles of bones. Given the fact that they were all burned, I think these people were murdered. The real question is, *when?*"

Chapter Nine

*H*azel hung up the office phone. She took a deep breath, enjoying a moment of privacy. She and Sean and spent every minute together yesterday until he'd gone home at seven to spend the evening with his mom. This morning, he'd arrived at seven sharp, and they'd shared breakfast in the main house before crossing the yard to the annex, where he sat in the corner while she worked, talking to her bones.

Sean was good company, but she wasn't used to constant companionship, especially not from someone she needed to hide her feelings from. When it came time to call the Virginia medical examiner to share her preliminary assessment, she'd glommed onto the call as a reason to retreat into Alec's old office and use the phone in private.

This would be so much easier if every moment spent with him didn't make her just want him more.

She stood from the desk and stretched. Time to get her game face on. She had a fake boyfriend she needed to shower with disinterest.

Her life had gotten really weird of late.

She stepped out of the office to find Sean standing over one of the trays, looking at the bones. His hands were clasped behind his back, likely to prevent himself from touching the bones in a moment of forgetfulness.

He was so wonderfully responsible and conscious of the rules and boundaries she'd set. Did he have to be so damn perfect?

He glanced up. "What did the ME say?"

"She'll forward my preliminary assessment to the proper authorities—Sheriff Taylor, the FBI, the utility company, district attorney. She wants me to go back and collect all the bones I can today, given that inundation is supposed to start tomorrow. There's no way we can collect them all and get three-point provenience, but at least I can get the skulls and pelvic bones and other diagnostic elements. I've only done a preliminary evaluation of what I collected so far, and she wants me to do an intensive exam—scanning every surface under magnification to look for wounds or anomalies that could give us a cause of death. The specialist she has in-house is busy and wouldn't get to this case for a month or more." She shrugged. "I've got the bones and the time."

Hazel hadn't been surprised by the request; it made sense for her to continue the work. She had the expertise and was known to the ME. As a grad student, she'd interned at the ME's office, and later, after she had her PhD, she'd provided expert testimony at a few trials in the Commonwealth of Virginia. Transferring the analysis to someone else would only waste time at this point. What she wasn't sure of was if she was happy with the request or not.

Her client was no longer Talon & Drake, it was the medical examiner's office, and she couldn't say no without risking her reputation. This would be intensive work, and she had to do it whether she was ready or not.

Her gaze scanned the trays of bones. "I'm afraid this will

mean several days of babysitting me while I work. You'd have to take more leave from Raptor like Alec suggested." Officially, Sean had already taken personal days yesterday and today.

"There's another option we haven't considered. It will keep you protected and we'd both be able to work. And I think Rav will be onboard with it."

"What's that?"

"Move the bones to the lab in the basement of the Raptor compound. The security there is even better than here. It's a large space with plenty of tables to lay out the trays. Plus the cameras and other equipment are state-of-the-art, mounted on tracks above the table so you can record everything. You can work in the basement, and I can go back to helping out with the trainings, and no one would wonder why I'm suddenly glued to your side like a possessive boyfriend."

She considered the idea. Her commute would get a lot longer, but it would be much kinder for Sean, who had upended everything to do this job. Plus, with more room to work and better camera systems, documentation would go much faster. "What's security like? Could anyone in the compound just walk in and mess with the bones?"

"No. The lab is heavily restricted—which is why it hasn't been used in the five years Rav has owned the place. Frankly, the bones would be safer there over the weekend while we're gone than they would be here."

"Sold. If Alec says okay, let's do it."

Less than five minutes later, they had permission, and Hazel began loading trays in the back of Sean's SUV. "After we drop these in the lab, we need to go back to the reservoir and collect what we can before dark." She'd planned to start the intensive analysis today, but that would have to wait, which was probably for the best. Tomorrow, they'd head for

West Virginia and the wedding. She'd get three days off to clear her head before she needed to immerse herself in the missing skin of the dead.

*S*ean watched Hazel collect the bones in the shallow waters. They'd gotten off to a rocky start with the bodyguard thing in this very spot, but in the last two days, they'd settled into a working relationship that was much smoother. Now that he'd spent days watching her in her element, he almost couldn't reconcile this Hazel with the party girl.

He'd liked the party girl just fine—too much, really. But this Hazel, she fascinated him. He could watch her all day… He couldn't help but grin. Good thing, because that was exactly what Rav was paying him to do.

He was starting to forget the reasons he'd kept his distance from her over the years. But the job thing had been front and center and very valid that first night they met. No way could he hook up with the boss's cousin in the garden just hours after meeting her—and he'd known that was exactly what Hazel had wanted.

Part of him had been a little angry with her that night, that she didn't consider what it could mean for his job.

One did not bang the boss's cousin hours after meeting her, especially when the job itself was brand-new. But for Hazel, he'd just been a guy her cousin brought home. There were no consequences for her beyond failed birth control or risking exposure to STDs.

On the flipside for him, she'd been the first person to make him *feel* in those first weeks after his father died. She'd made him laugh that night. He'd felt warm and excited and experienced a rush of joy and pleasure that had seemed impossible in the well of grief.

She'd been a light in the darkness. And a temptation he'd barely managed to resist, if only because a tryst in the garden would have been another way to forget his grief.

But she didn't know any of that. He hadn't told her that night that his father had passed away just weeks before. He'd avoided all conversation about his family so he wouldn't have to mention the grief that nearly choked him, but strangely, that had led to him always avoiding the topic of his family with her. It was as if the subject was forbidden in his mind, or he'd have to explain the complicated emotional landscape he'd wandered the night they met.

Telling her about Katrina's cancer had felt weird. Foreign. Katrina was the part of his life he'd walled off from this one particular woman for a reason he wasn't sure he quite understood himself.

Proof Hazel wasn't the only one who needed a psychotherapist. He'd never really worked out his issues surrounding his dad's death. Might be time to actually deal with that. He wasn't sure he'd ever quite realized he'd somehow managed to wrap Hazel into the pain at that time. Her only crime was being the sexy, sweet, fun emotional break he'd so desperately needed, and the pleasure he'd felt at meeting her had become a source of guilt.

He shook his head. He needed to focus on the reservoir and the woman he was guarding and not take these mental breaks that served no purpose. He was looking for an excuse to drop his rules. To make a move he'd only end up regretting.

He scanned the water and the shoreline, looking to the north end of the lake where Raptor had acreage. He'd spent many hours there in the last four years in simulated war games designed to train operatives and military personnel.

His gaze traveled south to the property adjacent to Raptor land and the large house that overlooked the lake. The boundary between the two properties was defined by dozens of No Trespassing signs on both sides. Reasonable, considering the trainings Raptor conducted.

But who was the mysterious landowner? In all the time Sean had been coming here, he couldn't remember seeing any activity at the house. The large veranda overlooking the lake had, to the best of his knowledge, always been empty.

He returned his attention to Hazel and the bone garden. He wasn't to touch the bones, but he had free rein to walk the area and drop pin flags if he saw something interesting. All he saw were bones, piles and piles of bones. But he marked the skulls and pelvic bones and anything else he thought she might want to collect.

"The sun will be setting in about forty-five minutes, Haze. We need to wrap this up."

She nodded and carefully placed yet another zipper-topped bag with a skull inside into a large mesh bag that held her gruesome collection of plastic-wrapped humans. "Twenty-seven skulls total, not including the fragments we're likely missing in our hurry."

"And they're all male?"

"There's one that might be female. Even the long bones in the vicinity are gracile, so I collected those too. But all the other bones are…shockingly similar." She met Sean's gaze. "I don't like what happened here. This is so much like many mass graves I've seen before. We want to think the US is above this. But here we are, in Virginia, just miles from our nation's capital. It does happen here." Her voice trailed off as she stared across the lake. After a lengthy pause, she said, "Did you know ICMP is still searching for three hundred and twenty-eight prison inmates who 'disappeared' during Hurricane Katrina?"

He frowned. "No. Never heard of that."

"It's true. And no one is talking about it. People—massive groups of people—can disappear even here in the US, and no one talks about it, no one does anything about it, if they're in a marginalized group. Prison inmates, who cares, right?"

He looked at her and for once could answer that question. Hazel MacLeod cared.

As if he needed another reason to fall hard for the woman.

Chapter Ten

The fake boyfriend charade started in earnest at nine a.m. on Friday, several hours earlier than Hazel would have liked. She'd wanted the four-hour drive alone with Sean to prep herself for looking her sister in the eye and lying to her, but no such luck.

The problem was, Ivy was more than a sister. She was Hazel's best friend. They were only fourteen months apart in age, one year apart in school. When no other kids could tolerate their nerdiness, they'd had each other.

Their oldest sister, Laurel, was five years older than Hazel. While she and Laurel were close, their relationship wasn't the same. Hazel could fool Laurel in a heartbeat. But Laurel wasn't the sister who would be in the caravan heading to the Mountain Lakes region of West Virginia today.

They'd arrived at the Raptor DC office parking lot at nine as instructed. Three cars were already in the lot. Sean parked several spaces away, presumably to give her a chance to collect herself before they stepped into their roles.

She closed her eyes and took a deep breath. *Here goes.*

He took her hand, bringing it to his lips. "Everyone here is going to be happy to see you, you know."

She spotted Matt and Ivy's SUV pulling into the lot with Matt at the wheel. Her stomach clenched. This was about to get hard. "I hate this," she muttered.

"Is it so hard to pretend you're into me?" Sean asked softly, his mouth against her fingers.

Her gaze flew to his at his use of a warm, almost seductive tone. Heat flooded her as if he'd flipped a switch and turned on the furnace.

She gave him a stiff smile, not wanting him to see exactly how much she wanted him, not when they weren't putting on a show for others. She would be acting twenty-four seven for the next two days. Alone with Sean, she'd be pretending she didn't want him. In front of others, she'd be pretending he was all hers.

Good times.

"You know that's not the issue," she said softly.

"Then what's the problem?"

"I'm not comfortable with lying." And yet even those words were a lie. The real reason she dreaded this farce was simple: She couldn't stand the idea of being close to him, of pretending, but not having him. It would be all too easy to mistake his words and touch for the real deal, and she feared making an ass of herself again.

He placed a hand behind her neck and tilted her head back, bringing her face to his. She knew Ivy was in the car that pulled into the spot beside them, but her back was to it as she faced him. He was performing. "Then leave the lying to me," he whispered. His lips caressed hers. Soft. Sweet.

At some point this weekend, they'd likely share a deeper kiss in front of an audience. That it would be fake already broke her confused heart.

He lifted his head. His eyes were warm. More than warm.

Hot. He was good at deception. "Let's do this," he said, then released her and pushed open his door.

Hazel took one more deep breath and climbed out of Sean's SUV. No sooner were her feet on the pavement than Ivy was climbing out of her car, her expression one of confusion and surprise. "Hazel? What are—?"

"Surprise!" Hazel said as Sean rounded the vehicle and slipped an arm around her waist.

"Hey, Ivy. Matt," Sean said, nodding to her sister's new husband. "Hazel agreed to be my date for the wedding, and we thought it would be fun to surprise you."

Ivy's gaze bounced from Hazel to Sean. Definitely surprised, a little confused—which made sense, considering Hazel usually told her everything—but happy. She spread her arms wide, and Hazel stepped into them. She squeezed Hazel tight and whispered, "So, Sean, huh? I *knew* it. It was obvious you were interested in Grand Cayman."

She said the last part louder than Hazel would've wanted.

Sean's laugh was relaxed and smooth. "I was working in Grand Cayman, so I had to play it cool." Ivy released Hazel, and Sean put his arm around her again and added, "But this weekend is all fun."

Hazel nearly choked. That was the most blatant lie yet. She looked up at Sean and narrowed her eyes, but a laugh escaped, ruining the stern look. He flashed an innocent grin and dropped a kiss on her nose.

And with that gesture, her nerves settled. This was *Sean*. Warm, funny, fascinating Sean. Smart, sexy, objectively perfect. Pretending to be crazy for him wouldn't be difficult because it wouldn't be pretend. And he would make it easy for her. He was showing her now he would do all the heavy lifting in the acting department. After all, he had to pretend to be infatuated with *her*. That required Shakespearean training.

She wasn't objectively attractive, not like Sean. She didn't have enough curves. Her face was too broad and her thick hair had a tendency to frizz in humid air.

She appreciated Sean's acting abilities. He'd make this work. She relaxed against him and, as she had when he held her the other night, she felt safe.

She hadn't realized how unsafe she'd felt until he held her and her fear lessened. And that was the beauty of Sean Logan: he was her bodyguard, protecting her from some mysterious threat she didn't believe existed, but really, she felt safe with him in a way that had nothing to do with threats or politics.

She slid her arm around his waist and gave a light squeeze. His hand on her shoulder squeezed back, a gentle communication. They were a team.

"Where's Julian?" she asked. The five-going-on-six-year-old was nowhere to be seen.

Matt smiled as he held Ivy's hand. "Mara's mom is insane and offered to pick up Julian from kindergarten this afternoon and keep him overnight. She's also watching Colin and Grace tonight and will drive all three kids to the inn tomorrow morning."

Hazel wasn't sure how old Colin Dominick was, but she was pretty sure he was less than a year. And Grace Scott couldn't be much more than a year and a half. "She's doing a sleepover with a baby, a toddler, and a kindergartener *by herself*?"

"Mara's aunt is helping, so she's not alone," Ivy said. "But I'm sure the babies will be a handful. Julian was excited to stay at Catherine's for the night—she lives in a condo with a pool, and after his summer on the boat, he's been going through water withdrawal."

Ivy and Julian had spent the summer on Matthew's yacht, cruising the Caribbean. Hazel had enjoyed the frequent photos Ivy had sent of their family adventures as they made their way to south Florida, where the boat was now.

"We should join the others," Sean said, nodding to where Erica and Lee were chatting with Trina, Keith, Curt, and Mara.

She couldn't help but brace herself. Her connection to this group was tenuous. A few of the men, like Sean, she'd met several times over the years through Alec and Raptor functions, while she'd met the women through Ivy, Isabel, and her work in helping identify the remains of submariners for Naval History and Heritage Command—where all except Isabel worked—last year.

In spite of her hesitation, everyone treated her like an old friend, greeting her with warm, welcoming hugs. It brought a rush of emotion to her eyes, really, this pure acceptance from a tight-knit group, and for the first time since Alec had suggested it, she was glad to be here. This weekend could even be...*fun*.

Honestly, it hadn't crossed her mind that she might enjoy this weekend. She'd been certain it would push her out of her comfort zone on fifteen different levels. But now, it was sweet to see Erica and Mara drape their arms around each other as they shared the joy—and worries—of having a full day and night without their babies. For both moms, this would be their first twenty-four hours away from their babies since birth.

Alec and Isabel arrived and had just finished their hellos and hugs when the bride and groom drove into the lot to hoots and hollers from everyone. The level of joy was palpable.

"I can't believe my little girl is getting married," Trina said as Cressida climbed out of the car.

Cressida laughed and gave her matron of honor a hug. "You're only four years older than me."

"Yes, but you'll always be that little girl I took in as intern."

"Thanks, Mom," Cressida said as she draped an arm over Trina's shoulders, looking at least five years older than the shorter woman, but then, Hazel would bet Trina still got carded regularly.

Cressida was one of the most naturally beautiful women Hazel had ever seen. Flawless skin, big brown eyes. She bore a striking resemblance to the actress Natalie Portman. And her joy today made her absolutely radiant.

Cressida's gaze landed on Hazel. She beamed and released Trina. "Hazel! I was so excited when Ian told me Sean was bringing you!" She gave Hazel a squeeze and then released her to Ian, who also hugged her.

"Thank you for letting me crash your wedding," she said.

"Wouldn't have it any other way," Ian said. His eyes were warm as he studied her. "Heard you had a rough time in Croatia." His words were low, under the din of excitement as Cressida hugged the other guests.

She nodded.

After her ordeal in Ukraine, she'd had a lengthy conversation with Ian about working in Eastern Europe, the Middle East, and the Balkans. He was one of the few people who really understood the ramifications of her detainment, one of the few she'd been able to open up to about how utterly terrified she'd been. He also loved that part of the world with all his heart but was unlikely to ever return. It wasn't safe for him after he'd been outed as a CIA case officer. She'd decided to take the Croatia assignment after that conversation. She'd been determined to reclaim the job that meant so much to her.

Perhaps Dr. Parks was right, and her panic attacks had more to do with Ukraine than she'd realized.

Ian's face was solemn as he said, "I'm glad you're with

us." Then he smiled. "Because it's time to play." He then hugged Sean and said, "Nice job, man. Smart move. *Finally*."

"I have my moments," Sean said, squeezing Hazel to his side again.

Trina clapped her hands to get everyone's attention. "Okay, you might all be wondering why we've gathered here—"

"Treen, that speech is for tomorrow," Erica said with a snicker.

Trina flashed a devilish grin. "C'mon. You didn't think we'd all simply *drive* for four hours to the inn, did you? When we can make it a competition?"

"What kind of competition?" Mara asked, suspicion in her voice. "I'm not a fan of road races."

Meanwhile, all the men were standing a bit taller, more alert. But then, half of them had trained for high-speed chases, evasion, and fancy maneuvers.

Trina burst out laughing. "Oh, goodness, the looks on your faces! Ian's certain he can make it to the hotel in three hours, while Mara and Erica are ready to bail. No. Not *that* kind of competition. A scavenger hunt." She pushed her glasses back on her nose, then pulled a stack of envelopes from her purse. "Each of these envelopes contains an identical list of the types of places we'll pass on our route. Every couple is a team. When you find a place that fits the scavenger hunt, stop and take a selfie—both of you must be in the shot—proving you were there. Ten points for every stop. The team with the most points wins a fantastic prize. But—"

"You sure this is a good idea?" Mara said. "I'm still imagining lots of speeding to make as many stops as possible."

Trina laughed. "I was just getting to that. First—no team can make more than seven stops, and second, a point is deducted from each score for each team that visits the same place."

"So it's a maximum of seventy points, as long as you don't go to any of the same places as the other teams," Ivy said.

"Exactly. If five teams visit the same site, the stop is only worth five points each. There are also some bonus points possible—if a site fits the bill for two categories, it's worth twenty-five points instead of ten or even twenty."

"So, what's the prize?" Ian asked. "Besides bragging rights?"

Trina hit a button on her car key, and the trunk popped open, revealing a beautifully wrapped gift bag in silver and black. "That."

"Trust me, you want it," Keith said.

As Trina's husband, he would know the details. The men looked at the gift bag with renewed interest thanks to the former SEAL's endorsement.

Trina was just about to pass out the envelopes when another car pulled into the lot. Her eyes widened, and she squealed with excitement. "Oh my goodness! They made it!"

It took Hazel a moment to recognize the couple in the sedan. Undine and Luke. The couple lived in the Pacific Northwest, but she'd met them at Alec and Isabel's wedding last year. Luke had gone with Ian to rescue Ivy in Palau. Hazel was forever grateful to both men for bringing her sister back from that nightmare.

"When your flight was delayed, I didn't think you'd make it in time," Trina said as Undine jumped out of the car and hugged her.

"They got us on a red-eye," Undine said.

Luke embraced Ian.

"Glad you could make it," Ian said.

"Wouldn't miss it. Congrats, my friend."

Luke and Ivy hugged, then Ivy glanced sideways at Hazel before she said, "Luke, this is my husband, Matt."

Matt held out his hand. "Nice to finally meet you. Ivy's told me about what you and Ian did for her."

Luke's gaze also flicked Hazel before he shook her brother-in-law's hand. His face transformed into a broad, warm smile. "Pleasure to meet you, Matt."

Sean's hand at the small of her back pulled her attention away. She looked up at him, and he grinned down at her. Dimples and all. He whispered in her ear, "I'm glad you're on my team."

The warmth in his eyes said he meant it. This wasn't acting. Was it?

Then his lips brushed over hers again, and she tried to keep her brain from blanking out. It wasn't even a real kiss and she was going all swoony. But it was Sean. Real or fake, he was potent.

After the round of hugs for Undine and Luke were completed, Trina then explained the scavenger hunt rules again. "Okay, so we have seven cars with seven teams of two. Keith and I will be in the convoy, but we aren't competing. We'll meet you all for lunch, which is listed on the sheet. Don't be late for lunch, or I'll deduct points."

"You need to spot Luke a few points," Ian said. "He's just taken a red-eye, and everyone knows SEALs aren't good for much when they haven't gotten their beauty sleep."

Matt and Alec snickered. Alec had been an Army Ranger, Ian, Delta Force. Matt hadn't served, but according to Ivy, he and Ian had bonded immediately upon meeting.

Undine laughed too, then shrugged at her husband's side-eye. "He's the groom. We *have* to humor him. For the next two days, we'll pretend Delta Force guys are actually badass."

Keith—a former SEAL like Luke and Sean—laughed and held up his hand for a high five from Undine.

"Children, please," Trina said. "We're wasting time when we could be having champagne." From her open trunk, she grabbed a bottle of champagne. "Keith, grab the glasses."

Keith handed out pretty plastic champagne flutes as Trina popped the cork. With sixteen people, it took two bottles until everyone had a glass.

"Can I make the toast?" Cressida asked.

"Of course," Trina said.

Cressida smiled at Trina. "Thank you, Trina, for everything you've done in helping with the planning these last months, and thank you so much for this, for starting the party here in DC, so we can celebrate every moment of this journey." Cressida's eyes moistened, and she glanced at her fiancé. He squeezed her hand. "If I start to cry, you'll take over?"

"Always," Ian said.

"'Kay." Cressida took a deep breath, then resumed. "It's been a helluva journey that started on a plane in Turkey—"

"In a nightclub for me," Ian said. "That's when I first saw you. And was captivated." He grinned. "She dropped a guy with one punch. It was hot."

Hazel laughed. She knew parts of their story—Ivy's ex-husband was a key player in their ordeal—but she'd never heard that detail before.

Cressida flashed a toothy grin. "Our journey continued through Syria and Iraq." She met Sean's gaze. "Where Ian met Sean for the first time. Trina, Keith, Curt, Mara, Erica, and Lee all worked so hard to get us home. And in the time since, we've been blessed with a growing group of friends to share our ongoing journey. Ian and I debated long and hard about whether we should just elope like Trina and Keith, have a massive wedding like Alec and Isabel, or something in between. In the end, we realized we don't know enough people for a massive wedding." She smiled as everyone chuckled. "But the people we *do* know, the people who matter—

everyone here, right now—we wanted to share this with you. We're all so busy. I can't remember the last time we were all together for wine-tasting night.

"The only thing we were certain of is the last time we were all together was for Alec and Isabel's wedding. And we wanted that, an excuse to spend time with all of you. So we decided on a weekend at one of Ian's favorite places in the world with the people we love most. Tomorrow, there will be more guests at the wedding—people who are also important in our lives—but they aren't you. Thank you for carving these days out of your lives to share this moment with us."

Cressida's eyes teared again, and Ian raised his glass. "So here's to all of you. Thank you for your friendship, thank you for joining us on this journey."

Everyone raised their glasses and drank. As Hazel sipped her champagne, she felt guilty for intruding. She was drinking some other woman's champagne, with some other woman's date at her side. But still, Cressida's heartfelt words affected her. She liked these people. She wanted to belong.

Hazel watched Matt, the other newcomer, as he drank his champagne. Did her new brother-in-law feel as out of place as she did? He didn't look like it. But then Matt always exuded a calm competence that she'd liked.

He was nothing like Ivy's ex, thank God. It was weird for Ivy to have gotten so involved with someone so quickly, and she'd had Julian to consider. But Matt had never triggered any red flags. He was quiet, but not cold. Charming without being smarmy, and he always looked at her sister like she was the center of the universe.

Sean had run a background check on him when they were still on Grand Cayman. Sean was there as Ivy's body-guard, after all. Matt's unhesitant acceptance of the investigation had been a mark in his favor. Now Hazel and Matt were the odd ducks in a group of close-knit friends. But of course,

Matt had Ivy as his reason for being there, and Hazel had…a fake boyfriend.

Sean took Hazel's flute and set it with the other empty glasses. "You ready to win this thing, Haze?"

"Nah, this one's ours," Curt said.

Ian scoffed. "As if Cressida and I won't crush you all."

Hazel laughed at the guys' ability to boast when they had no idea what the challenge was. Trina wouldn't let them open the envelopes until they were all in their cars and ready to go.

She smiled at her fake boyfriend, getting into the groove of the moment. "Sweetheart, we've *so* got this."

Keith clapped Sean on the back. "Good luck."

"We'll see everyone at the lunch rendezvous," Trina said, scanning the assembled group. "Good luck! And speeding tickets will nullify all points. Be safe and sane, people."

Before heading for their car, Sean took her hand and approached Alec. "You and Isabel leave quickly," he said softly. "We'll hang back. I'd aim to be the last out of the lot, but my guess is that will be Keith and Trina."

Alec nodded. "Use the radio if you see anything."

"Will do."

Alec paused. "And Sean, have fun. You heard Cressida. This is a celebration for all of us."

"Will do, boss."

They climbed into Sean's SUV. Hazel noted that none of the other couples had left yet; they were all studying Trina's list. She ripped open the envelope that had "Sean" written in neat script on the outside.

The game was straightforward. There were more than a dozen types of sites that could earn them points, but they could only make seven stops. "Do you want to play to win?" she asked.

"Honey, I always play to win."

"Okay, then, we need to choose seven places, preferably ones no one else will choose."

"Where are we headed?"

"Museums—"

"That's easy. We can just go to the National Mall and go to the least popular ones."

"But none can be a Smithsonian," she finished.

"Tricky Trina. What else?"

"National Parks—but again, the Mall doesn't count. Civil War battle sites. The Appalachian Trail. A National Historic District. Keep in mind there are bonus points if a site fits two categories."

"This is the nerdiest scavenger hunt ever."

She laughed. "This is the *best* kind of scavenger hunt."

"Well, obviously. So where do we start?"

She smiled. "There's a tiny national park in southwest DC. I'd be shocked if anyone who didn't grow up in the area knows about it. It's right by the entrance to 395. Easy ten points on our route."

"That the one that's basically a roundabout? Near the fish market?"

"Yep."

He watched Alec and Isabel leave the lot, followed by Luke and Undine. Only Trina and Keith were left. "Let's grab our first ten points, then."

Chapter Eleven

It wasn't until they were circling the park that Sean realized how clever Trina had been to require them both to be in the selfie. Hazel couldn't just jump out of the car and snap a picture. Sean needed to find parking. They got lucky and found a spot on the street to L'Enfant Plaza and ran down the road to Benjamin Banneker Park to snap a picture with the fountain and the official NPS park sign.

They arrived in time to see Erica and Lee snapping a picture of themselves with the sign.

Sean laughed. "I didn't think anyone else knew about this park."

"Same," Erica said. She pointed to a condo building two blocks east. "I lived in that building my first year in DC. I had a view of this park from my living room."

Sean pointed to a building a block south. "My sister and her kids live there." He stared at the building, wondering how she and the girls were doing today. His mom was there, probably sitting on the floor with the girls, building castles out of blocks, which the girls would crush like Godzilla, giggling the whole time.

He loved those kids so much, it made his heart ache.

They said good-bye to Erica and Lee and took their selfie, then ran back to the car to hurry to Manassas, a Civil War battlefield they hoped only a few other teams would visit, but odds were they all would. It was directly on the route.

In minutes, they were back on the road heading toward the battleground, and Sean tried to shake off worry for his sister. He was on a silly, nerdy, wonderful scavenger hunt heading to his best friend's wedding while watching for a tail and protecting his boss's beautiful cousin whom he'd lusted after for years.

Just another normal day.

They crossed the Potomac and passed the Pentagon and Arlington National Cemetery before merging onto the interstate that would take them to Manassas.

Beside him, Hazel let out a contented sigh. "They're a fun bunch. Your friends."

"They're your friends too. You know every one of them."

"More acquaintances. Except Ivy, Alec, and Isabel, of course."

"And me," he felt a compulsion to add.

"I'd like to consider you a friend, but it's not like we ever talk unless forced together. You've never emailed me because you read a book you thought I'd like, and I've never texted you just to say hi. Friends communicate when they aren't face-to-face."

He considered her words and knew she was right. The strange part was, there'd been plenty of times when he'd read a book or seen a movie or visited a place he wanted to tell Hazel about, but he'd always stopped himself from reaching out because she was the boss's cousin and he knew deep down they could never keep it "just" friends.

Then there was the guilt he'd felt over enjoying her so much—because he'd wanted her—in those early weeks after

Dad died. Any time he'd reached for his phone to text her, he'd felt a twinge and, without quite understanding why, he'd set the phone down and filed it away as something to say to her the next time he saw her at Rav's.

Maybe he could let that go, but the timing was shit. Hazel was dealing with issues that were beyond him, and he couldn't wait until his sister was better so he could return to his work abroad.

Each round of chemo made him more eager to flee. He wanted to go back to Greece, Dubai, Saudi Arabia, or Morocco. He wanted to provide security for wealthy clients who were cutting business deals with a ridiculously high number of zeros. He wanted to run ops to recover kidnapping victims or to provide security for art and artifacts being transported in the Middle East. Every job was different, and in every one, the enemy was corporeal. It wasn't a disease that could only be fought by poisoning your own body. Or as with his dad, a cancer that couldn't be fought at all, no matter how many toxins he took in.

Shit. He'd thought being a SEAL had been hard, but that was nothing compared to chemo. His sister was the bravest person he knew.

Something about Hazel's vulnerability triggered that same discomfort in him. He couldn't fix her. Acting on the attraction between them, given her vulnerability, given his desire to flee at the first opportunity, would be taking advantage. Sure, he could make her feel good in the moment, but he had no intention of being there for the long haul. As soon as his sister gave him the green light, he was telling Keith to send him back to Dubai. Or Egypt. Anywhere but here.

Acting on this thing with Hazel would be the ultimate dick move.

He cleared his throat and chose his words carefully.

"Okay, when this is all over, we'll stay in touch. I'll text you from Dubai, or wherever I am."

"It's okay," she said. "It should happen naturally. Either we'll stay in touch or we won't."

He rolled his palms on the steering wheel. He could give her a truth. "I've wanted to text you lots of times since Grand Cayman. I wanted to know how you were. I wanted to share funny cat pictures I saw on the internet."

"Why didn't you?"

He shrugged. "I didn't think you wanted to hear from me, and I didn't know if you like cat pictures."

"Cat pictures are good, but if you'd sent pictures of baby goats, I'd know you really get me."

"Noted."

They settled into silence. His mind drifted from Hazel to his sister, to his mother. She'd been full of questions about his new girlfriend and had insisted that he bring Hazel to a family dinner next week.

He didn't mind the lie of the fake relationship because he genuinely liked Hazel, and in an alternate universe, he could imagine them being together, but getting his mother's hopes up that her thirty-eight-year-old son might finally settle down was a different story.

He'd said it was too new to know if it was serious; there was no need for a family gathering to introduce Hazel, not yet. But Mom would have none of that. *Are you ashamed of your family?"* she'd asked. She'd been teasing, but there was a note of hurt in her voice.

"I just think it would be too much for Kat right now."

"Kat can be the judge of what she can handle. That girl has always been tougher than you."

He couldn't argue with that. Kat was a powerful force. She was facing her cancer head-on, powering through the blows, while all Sean wanted to do was run. *"Okay. But we'll do it here, in my home. Otherwise you know Kat will spend days cooking and cleaning. And we'll order takeout."*

From the look in his mother's eye, he knew he was going to lose the battle over takeout versus a home-cooked meal, but at least he'd set the parameters of where and when. He cleared his throat. "I, uh, suppose I should mention… My mom wants to meet you. We're having dinner at my condo with my family next week."

Hazel sat bolt upright. "Shit. I'm so sorry, Sean. Maybe this will be all over by then and you can tell your mom the truth."

"Tell her I lied to her? Hell, no."

"It's not like you had a choice. It's your job."

"Still no. She won't understand. She'd probably ground me for a week."

Hazel laughed. "And take away your video games?"

"Yep. Dinner with my family is happening no matter what."

"Should I be nervous?"

"Nah. They'll love you." They would. With her PhD and work for ICMP, she would have Katrina's awe and his mom's respect. Katrina was a social justice warrior, and his mom had been a middle school history and government teacher for thirty-five years.

"Do they know I'm white?"

He nodded. "And they know we've known each other for years. My mom is reading a lot into me bringing you to the wedding."

"Which is understandable. Especially since you already had a date lined up." Hazel paused. "Is she…going to be at the wedding tomorrow? Your date?"

"Yes."

"Shit," she muttered. "Is she going to hate me?"

"No. She's cool. Tricia's an operative, a friend of Ian's. I asked her to be my date because I knew Trina was planning something for the caravan, and it was a couples' thing." Hazel didn't need to know that Tricia had admitted she'd hoped something would happen between them this weekend, and he certainly wouldn't tell her he'd considered making a move if it felt right. Hazel felt guilty enough as it was.

And the real truth was, if he'd been granted the ability to choose any woman in the world for his date this weekend, crazy as it was, the woman sitting next to him was the person he'd have chosen.

"Tricia. I've met her. Tall, gorgeous, African American? Former cop?"

"That's Tricia."

"I'm sorry, Sean."

"Stop with the apologies, Hazel. I chose this. I could have said no. I didn't. This isn't your fault."

"It *feels* like my fault. You could have a gorgeous, kickass operative as your date, but you're stuck with me."

"I have a gorgeous, brilliant, kickass scientist as my date. I'm not complaining."

"I wasn't fishing for that."

"And I don't take bait."

She was silent a moment, then said, "I'm sorry. Thank you. That was a lovely compliment, and I'm being rude. I just feel like I usurped Tricia's place, and I'm a little envious because your friends are really great. I *want* to belong here."

"Sweetheart, you aren't a usurper. You're Ivy's sister. Alec's cousin. Isabel's friend. And I like you. Very much." He released the wheel and threaded his fingers through hers. "I'm glad you're my date this weekend."

She squeezed his fingers. "Thank you." After a short stretch of silence, she asked, "Is it weird, being the only Black person in the group?"

"Not really—this is only a fraction of my world. An

important fraction, but still just a sample. Raptor is a pretty diverse company overall. Tomorrow at the wedding you'll meet several Black, Hispanic, and Asian operatives. My guess is the people of color make up about forty percent of the staff—it's a rough mirror of military and law enforcement, where most employees come from. Frankly, at events like this it's harder being the single guy than being the Black guy. Trina has been trying to fix me up with everyone under the sun since we first met."

"Have you gone on any dates?"

"Nah. I don't do blind dates. Especially not ones arranged by my boss's wife."

She snickered. "Good point."

They fell into a companionable silence. He took the exit for Manassas and spotted Undine and Luke as they drove out of the main parking lot. They traded waves, and he parked as close as he could to the sign. Another nine-point stop. Less if others had chosen this battleground as well.

Not that he really cared about winning. This was all about the game. The time with Hazel. The strategy. He liked winning, but more than anything, he wanted her to have fun today. To lose the shadows from her eyes.

He snapped a picture of the two of them in front of the sign, and they were back on the road in minutes. "Where to next?"

"We've got eighteen—maybe less—points so far. We need some ten-point stops if we want to win."

"Of course we want to win." It was what she'd expect him to say, plus it would make her smile.

On cue, she did, and his heart warmed. "My bad," she said. "I forgot SEAL pride was at stake."

"The only easy day was yesterday."

She laughed. "I'm sure this compares to dropping into a hot zone on an op."

"Unmarried best man at a wedding? Hell, yeah. Thank goodness I have you as my shield."

"I'll protect you from all the matrimony-starved guests who see you as fresh meat."

"Thank you. So where are we going next?"

She studied her phone. "There's an historic district that's also a Civil War battle site on the route—Moorefield Historic District, in West Virginia. That'll be twenty-five points, but it's after lunch. We should probably hit some museums en route. Lunch is in Front Royal—about forty-five minutes from here. Ha! There's a beer museum in Front Royal. That'll be another ten pints—I mean points."

Sean laughed. "Sixteen pints, but only three points, I bet, considering everyone will stop there."

"It's near a Confederate museum. I'm good with skipping that."

"But no one else would dare go there. We can take a photo outside the museum. Get the points without giving them our money."

"Works for me. Lunch is at a tap house and grill a few blocks away."

"There's an Appalachian trailhead near Front Royal, right?" he asked.

"Yes. It's near Shenandoah National Park. If we went to the trail inside the park, we'd get twenty-five points."

"Doubt we'd have enough time to drive from the park entrance to the trail and still make it to lunch on time."

"Then we should go to the trailhead on 522. It's just…" She tapped her phone. "Seven minutes from the beer museum. If everyone else does the trailhead that's just off the interstate, we'd get the full ten points for going a little out of our way."

"Sounds good. Trailhead first. Then the two museums. Five stops before lunch, with a twenty-five-point historic district lined up after lunch. All we need is to figure out our last stop."

They drove in companionable silence until they reached Front Royal. He took the exit and headed toward the trailhead south of town.

"Have you ever hiked the trail?" she asked.

"Only day hikes in a few sections. I've always wanted to do the whole thing."

"Same. But I've never had that kind of free time. And… I'll be honest, I've examined the remains of a few women who were dumped in the woods—so I'm not keen on doing something like that by myself."

"I can see how that would get in your head."

"It's bad enough knowing what knives do to bones. The damage to soft tissue, the pain those women suffered… I have to put myself in their skin—when they had skin—and reconstruct it. Each case has stayed with me, especially the two who couldn't be identified. The women who will never have a voice."

The trailhead was little more than a small dirt lot where the trail crossed the road. But the sign was there, and a boardwalk section of trail disappeared under a canopy of green and yellow leaves.

He parked in the empty dirt lot and faced Hazel, cupping her cheek. "Your work is important. I know it's hard when you can't have closure with a case, but it's pretty fantastic that you try."

He pressed his lips to her forehead and breathed in her scent. It was a good thing he hadn't seen this side of Hazel in Grand Cayman, or he might've found her irresistible.

"Thanks. Sorry I went there. It creeps up on me at times."

"Totally understandable. Remember, I was in the military for fifteen years. I work in private security and operate in war zones at times. I know the darker side of the job. I know how easy it is to get sucked in."

She looked out the windshield. "Thanks. For understanding. And this is a beautiful trail. Maybe what I need is to take a break and do the trail. I could probably find a friend to do it with me. There are a few guys I worked with in Croatia who are due home soon and who will have two or three months off and the same need to escape."

He didn't like the idea of her hiking the trail with a guy who wasn't him, but that was his problem to deal with in silence.

He took her hand as they walked the short distance to the sign. It was a crisp fall day; the bright yellow leaves glowed in the sunshine. A crisp breeze shook dry leaves, and with her hand in his, he suddenly felt…lighter.

This was a fun day to celebrate and play with a group of friends. He was with a beautiful woman, in a beautiful place. It really didn't get better than this.

They positioned themselves in front of the trail marker, and he pulled out his cell phone. They put their faces together. His other arm cradled her waist, holding her to his side. Before he hit the button, he said, "We should kiss for the photo."

He didn't plan it. Didn't even know where the words came from, but she turned her head to meet his lips. He hit the button on the screen. He still had one arm in the air with his phone in his grasp as he tightened his arm around her back, pulling her flush against him as her mouth opened under his.

He wasn't sure who deepened the kiss. Under oath, he'd say it was simultaneous. Spontaneous. All he really knew was he was kissing Hazel. His tongue stroked hers, and she tasted sweet and crisp—just like the fall day.

He slid his phone in his back pocket and wrapped his

arms around her on autopilot. He couldn't name the moment when her arms slipped around his neck and her fingers ran over his bare scalp.

How many times had he fantasized about this? How many times had he imagined what it would be like to make love to her? One thing he knew after finally having a taste, his fantasies could never compare to the real thing.

She made a small sound in the back of her throat, a soft moan that would have him pinning her to a wall if they weren't outside, next to a road at a trailhead.

A car approached, and he raised his head, glad to see it wasn't one of their group. He wanted no mistake on her part. This kiss—their first real kiss—hadn't been for show. It might've started that way, but he put the camera away the moment things got real.

He looked down at her face and saw the confusion in her eyes, and all at once, he remembered how vulnerable she was. How she'd just been talking about the worst aspect of her job. And he felt like a shit for taking advantage.

He gave her a smile and released her. "Sorry," he said. "I didn't plan that."

She shrugged. "It's okay. I'm just as guilty as you of getting carried away. I shouldn't have—"

"No. It's fine. You're fine. That was—" He had no clue what to say. The truth? *That was fucking amazing. I want to lift you up and pin you to a tree and screw your brains out. I want to go down on you and make you come apart. I want to spend days exploring your body until I've catalogued every freckle and know how to make you come hard and fast, then again in a slow, sustained release that goes on and on until your body quakes at my slightest touch.*

Want hit him with a new intensity. But then, he'd wanted Hazel for years and he'd finally gotten a taste. He should have seen this coming. He cleared his throat. "The kiss was great, but probably a bad idea."

She nodded and looked away.

He stepped back. "On to the museum?"

"Yes, please."

He didn't even remember the drive to the Confederate museum. Their photo in front of the sign was perfunctory. No foolish suggestion of kisses. What had he been thinking?

They arrived at the beer museum to see the bride and groom with Luke, Undine, Trina, and Keith. He shook off the fog that had surrounded him from the moment his tongue slid inside Hazel's mouth. This was why they were here. To play with friends. Win a prize. Celebrate Ian and Cressida.

He was not supposed to get distracted by his fake girlfriend.

He was her bodyguard, nothing more. It didn't help that he was starting to agree with Hazel. Isabel was the obvious target. But that didn't mean he wouldn't do his job and do it well.

He held her hand as they approached the others, who stood in front of the museum entrance. Trina greeted them with a grin. "You've got twenty minutes to go through the museum before our lunch reservations in the taproom down the block."

He smiled at Ian. "You going inside or heading to the restaurant?"

"Going in," Cressida said, looping her arm through Hazel's and pulling her away. "We'll see you inside."

Sean laughed and released Hazel. "Don't forget, we need to get a picture at some point, Haze." He turned to Trina. "You saw us here, in case she forgets."

Trina shrugged. "Rules are rules."

"And you're making them up as you go along," Keith said.

She grinned. "Only a little bit."

Ian glanced toward the door, then lowered his voice. "We need to talk about Hazel and what she knows. About Matt."

Sean had been expecting this. Of the sixteen people on this road trip, Hazel was the only one who had no idea Matthew Clark was actually Dimitri Veselov, her sister's abductor and former Russian spy and assassin.

Hazel had played an unwitting but important role as the person who'd witnessed Ivy and Matt's "first" meeting. Now, her presence could complicate matters, given that Luke and Matt had been friends in one of Matt's previous lives.

"To the best of my knowledge, she knows nothing," Sean said.

Luke gave a sharp nod. "Good. We don't want anything to happen that could screw up the adoption. It would crush all three of them if Julian were sent into foster care. And if the GRU gets even a hint that Dimitri is still alive, it's all over."

Ian clapped Sean on the back. "We're counting on you to keep Hazel distracted. Probably best to keep her away from Ivy and Matt while Luke is here."

Considering Hazel didn't want her sister to know she was lying about her relationship with Sean, that wouldn't be too hard. He nodded. "Don't worry, I've got it under control."

Ian's gaze fixed on the door his fiancée and Hazel had stepped through. "I like Hazel. Always have." Then he frowned. "Don't screw this one up."

"This from the guy who needed relationship coaching the night we met."

"Just returning the favor, man."

Another car pulled up. Ivy and Matt had arrived. They joined the group in front of the museum. "Shocking that of all the museums between DC and West Virginia, everyone is going for the beer museum," Ivy said.

"It's all about priorities," Luke said.

"Where's Hazel?" she asked Sean.

He nodded toward the door. "Inside with Cressida."

Ivy smiled and took his hand. "I'm so excited to see you two together."

A lot of people were going to be crushed when he and Hazel staged their breakup. That didn't sit well with him. Worse, he might be one of the crushees.

"I've been waiting for this since Grand Cayman," Ivy added.

"She was in Croatia the whole time," he couldn't help but point out.

She laughed. "Yeah, but that didn't mean I wasn't still hoping for this."

"No pressure or anything," Luke said with a laugh.

Ivy rolled her eyes. "You guys didn't see what I saw in Grand Cayman."

Matt draped an arm around her shoulder. "When did you have time to spy on Hazel and Sean? If I remember correctly—"

She elbowed him in the ribs. "We were there for a few days before you showed up. Sean and Hazel bickered the entire time. It was adorable."

Adorable wasn't exactly how Sean remembered it, but he'd let Ivy have her rose-tinted memory.

They all entered the museum together, and no one was surprised when the rest of their group arrived over the course of the next twenty minutes. They took turns grabbing selfies in front of the museum, and then found a passerby to take a photo of the entire group together, with Ian and Cressida in the middle. Sean put an arm around Hazel after steering her away from Ivy and Matt.

He felt guilty for lying to everyone—even Hazel wasn't safe from his lies. But still he smiled for the photo because his heart felt strangely light every time he had Hazel MacLeod in his arms.

Chapter Twelve

They sat at a long table in the taproom for lunch, Hazel squeezed between Sean and Mara. Years ago, Mara had worked for the Joint POW/MIA Accounting Command, which, in the way of the US military, now had a new name and acronym, Defense POW/MIA Accounting Agency, or DPAA. Mara had been a forensic archaeologist for DPAA and traveled the world to recover the remains of servicemen and women who had been lost in past conflicts. Prior to that, she'd done a stint in Bosnia excavating a mass grave, victims of the genocide.

Hazel had always felt a kinship with Mara, knowing the woman had faced the same kind of atrocity Hazel had seen in the field. Today, Mara had grabbed the seat by Hazel's side and taken her hand. "I heard you had a hard time in Croatia. I just wanted you to know I'm always available if you want to talk. Or not talk. Whatever you need."

All at once, the woman's kindness made her eyes tear. "Thank you. I might take you up on that later."

Mara smiled and grabbed her menu, then she said in a whisper, "So you and Sean…?"

"I can hear you, Mara," Sean said.

"I'm just asking what everyone is wondering. Hazel has only been back for what, a week?"

"Twelve days," Hazel said.

"I work fast," Sean added. "I wasn't about to let anyone else swoop in."

That sounded a lot better than he was being paid to be her boyfriend. But then, the kiss in front of the trail marker had told a different story. It had been spontaneous and real. He hadn't been putting on a show for anyone, and neither had she. She'd had some pretty spectacular kisses over her thirty-five years, but that one was in a class all its own.

Sean Logan had kissed her as if he wanted nothing more than to take her against a tree.

Then afterward, he'd retreated. Awkward. Nervous. Regretful.

When this ridiculous charade was all over, she would download an online dating app and find a guy and get laid. She'd do whatever it took to get over the heartache of Sean Logan not wanting her.

Two waiters delivered their drinks, and they all shared another toast to friends and love, and she returned her focus to where it belonged, this gathering of people who were so touchingly welcoming.

The group energy was vibrant, and she was lucky to get to witness it, even as an outsider. Even better, no one here was making her feel like an outsider. And she knew what ostracism felt like. She was a nerdy MacLeod sister, after all.

She watched her sister at the far end of the table on the opposite side. Sitting next to Matt, her eyes lit with laughter, her cheeks flushed with joy. A few years ago, Hazel had feared Ivy would be swallowed whole from the grief of her broken marriage and then the horror of learning her ex was a monster who trafficked weapons with terrorists. Then she'd gone through an ordeal in Palau that she still hadn't fully shared.

That Ivy had found love and joy after all that was a gift Hazel hadn't dared to believe would come true. She was thankful to Matt for his part in putting roses in her sister's cheeks, and grateful Ivy had their soon-to-be-adopted son, Julian, to love.

Plus it wasn't lost on Hazel that Ivy was drinking sparkling water, not beer. Ivy had wanted a baby for years, and that she might fulfill that dream with Matt made Hazel bloom with happiness for her sister.

Ivy's transformation gave Hazel hope. If Ivy could survive her ordeals and come out on top, surely Hazel could overcome a few nightmares.

Across the table, Alec was looking at his phone, his brow furrowed.

"You promised you wouldn't work today," Isabel said.

"Checking email isn't work."

At least three people snorted.

"Nice try," Curt said.

"Oh, hell. That prick Small is hosting a rally today."

"Senator Small?" Isabel asked.

"Yeah."

"Is he the one who used to be a"—Lee held up his fingers in air quotes—"'correspondent' for the white supremacist conspiracy theory website? What's it called?"

"Voigt Forum," Sean said.

"Yeah, that's him," Alec said.

Curt stiffened. "I can't believe the Justice Department dropped their investigation of him."

Alec gave Curt a look that spoke volumes, and Hazel wondered if Alec had initiated some sort of secret investigation of his fellow senator.

"What's the purpose of the rally?" Isabel asked.

"It's a variation on the 'white lives matter' theme."

"Where is it?"

"In a small town down the road from Moorefield, West Virginia."

Hazel perked up. There were a lot of points to be had in Moorefield, with their Civil War battle site and historic district. "So it's on our route."

"Sort of. Off the main road a few miles, but close. It starts in two hours."

"Hey, Treen, how many points for crashing a white supremacist rally?" Lee asked.

"Twenty-five."

"We're heading to Ian and Cressida's wedding. We can't stop and counterprotest," Erica said.

"Hey, there's nothing I like more than punching Nazis," Ian said.

"I'm in," Cressida said. "Just promise no bruises on your face."

"I'll protect him, Cress," Matt said. "My face can take it." Matt had scars along one cheek and a lump on the bridge of his nose, souvenirs from a car accident he'd been in a year before he met Ivy.

Trina laughed. "Best. Wedding. Ever."

"Does the rally count as one of our seven stops?" Undine asked.

"Sure," Trina said, "if you haven't got all seven already."

"Wouldn't going to the rally be a Hatch Act violation for you, Alec?" Lee asked.

"Nah. It's not a campaign rally. I'm sure there'll be some sort of censure from the Senate, but frankly, I don't really give a damn. They can censure me all they want, but Small is the one with ties to white supremacist groups."

Hazel looked at Sean. As a Black man—who was currently very publicly dating a white woman—he risked the most in showing up at the rally, and fear jolted through her at the thought of him being the target of a mob. "Do you want to go? We can skip it."

"And let Ian get twenty-five points ahead? No way." He smiled at her. "I'll be fine, sweetheart." He glanced across the table and met Alec's gaze. They shared some sort of silent mental exchange, then he gave his secret boss a sharp nod.

Whatever that meant, she knew one thing for certain from the way the muscles in Sean's jaw bunched. There was no dissuading him from making this stop. And now she wondered if the senator had anything to do with the heavily redacted letter Alec had received.

They picked up their twenty-five points in Moorefield —the other teams had already made six stops, forcing them to bypass the historic district in favor of the rally. Sean figured this clinched the win for Hazel and him.

After snapping their photo, they continued on to the town where the senator was holding his rally. Sean had been surprised at Rav's decision to go, given the hint he'd allowed that Senator Small could be connected to the threatening letter. He'd pulled Rav aside when they left the restaurant. Rav confirmed he wanted to rattle the other senator. The last thing Small would expect was for the junior senator from Maryland to crash his rally. Odds were Rav would draw more headlines from the act than Small would get from headlining the event.

Rav was playing spoiler, pure and simple. He wasn't up for reelection for another three years, and he wasn't dependent on campaign donations to fund his run. He wasn't in politics for money or power. He really just wanted to make a difference.

Meanwhile, Small was facing a difficult primary next year and there were questions about some of his business deals. Rav showing up at his rally and drawing attention to the negative aspects of his top supporters while tossing attention to Small's challenger would steal some of the shine from the old racist's day.

Sean was all for making racists unhappy.

"What's the deal with Senator Small?" Hazel asked. "Does Alec think he's behind the threat?"

Rav had been insistent about keeping Hazel in the dark, and Sean had no idea how his suspicions of Matthew fit in. "I don't know. He dislikes the man. He mentioned him a few times at the gym. He's had suspicions about some dirty deals and organized crime."

"He sounds charming."

"I don't suppose I can convince you to sit in the car?"

"Hell, no."

He reached across the console and took her hand. "Then you'll stay close to me at all times. Okay?"

"Sean, being by your side will put a target on you."

"And I don't give a damn about that. I'm not going to let a bunch of racist assholes dictate where I can go, what I can do, and whom I can be with. Every time we play their game, it gives them more power. But I understand if you're afraid. If you don't want to be by my side, then you'll have to stay in the car. I'll ask one of the other guys to wait with you."

"No! I'm not afraid for me. I'm afraid for *you*. I don't want to see you get hurt."

"You should be afraid for you. You're just as likely to be a target for being seen with me. As far as being safe, we've got Luke Sevick, Keith Hatcher, and myself, all former SEALs. Ian Boyd, former Delta Force and CIA, Alec Ravissant, former Army Ranger, then there's Lee and Curt, who both have studied karate since they were kids. They might not know weapons and battle, but I'd never count them out in a fight. And I know because I've sparred with—and lost to—both of them. And then there's Matt, who can also hold his own."

Hell, Matt had more training than all the men in their group. Sean had collected stories about the Hammer ever since he'd first learned of Ivy's abduction by the man, and didn't doubt Matthew Clark could take Sean without breaking a sweat. And Sean didn't admit that about anyone.

"Matt? What makes you think he can fight?"

"We've sparred a few times at JT's gym." This wasn't exactly true. Matt refused to spar. He never gave a reason, but Sean suspected some of those training sessions in Mother Russia had been particularly brutal. Matt saved all his aggression for punching bags. He lifted weights and beat on the bags and basically worked out alone, never quite joining the group of men who gathered a few times a week during the hours JT reserved his gym just for them.

Raptor had a full gym at the Virginia compound, but JT's gym was closer to both Sean's home and the DC office. He'd been honored when he'd been included in the select group given free access to the private training times, and it was there his friendship with the men in this caravan had fully developed.

"My point is, we've got a badass group of men here. We'll be fine."

"Badass doesn't save you from being mowed down by a car."

"Which is why I want you to stay in the car if you are afraid. You'll be safe there."

"And I will never let a bunch of racist assholes control *me*."

He lifted her hand, bringing the back to his lips. "Okay, then. It's settled. We'll join the counterprotest. Together."

She nodded.

"I won't let anything or anyone hurt you, Hazel. I'm your bodyguard, remember?"

"Bodyguard, boyfriend. I'm forgetting which one is the lie."

She was joking, he knew, but after that kiss, he'd thought the same thing. One felt far more real than the other.

They reached the turnoff and drove the final miles to the town where the rally was being held on Main Street. The outskirts of town hadn't aged well, but not surprisingly, the backdrop for Senator Small's rally was a postcard-worthy historic district. They found parking with the others about two blocks from the main rally and gathered in the lot to discuss their approach.

"There's a counterprotest across the street from the rally," Rav said. "It was organized by a group that's been mobilizing to fight Senator Small's bill to shift county jail management to private corporations in economically depressed areas. My assistant is on the phone right now with the leader of that organization to let them know I'm here. We're hoping they can send someone our way with signs for us to carry so we can march down the street as if we planned this and grab the spotlight from the senator in the middle of his speech—which is supposed to start in five minutes."

Sean didn't know the protocol of one senator crashing another's rally, but he really liked the fact that Rav didn't give a damn about politeness when it came to making a statement to white supremacists.

He'd always been proud to work for Raptor, but now, as he looked at the owner of the company, his boss, Keith, and his coworker Ian, he was glad these men were true allies, doing the right thing simply because it was the right thing.

Not that he'd ever doubted it, but it wasn't often he witnessed friends taking a stand when they could have quite literally driven by and looked the other way.

And on the way to Ian's wedding, no less.

Minutes later, a car pulled into the lot and a Black man and two Black women jumped out. One of the women approached Rav, while the others pulled signs from the trunk of the sedan. "Senator Ravissant, I'm Hayley Hayes with the End Private Prisons Political Action Committee," she said in a soft West Virginia accent. "We're thrilled y'all are here and willing to march with us today. We figured our small counter-protest would get no coverage—which is one of the reasons the senator placed his rally in this overlooked part of the state. It was hard to get counterprotestors to show up on such short notice." Her grin broadened. "And the fact that you have such a large entourage is, frankly, amazing."

Rav shook her hand. "My assistant alerted me once she realized the rally was happening not far from our route. We don't wish for the press to know our destination, so as far as interviews go, we'll say we drove here specifically to attend the counterprotest."

The woman nodded. "Your assistant let me know. We haven't spoken with the press yet. We figured your entrance would draw the cameras and do the talking for you."

"Perfect," Rav said. "Ms. Hayes, this is my wife, Isabel." He glanced around at the group and said, "It will take forever if we introduce everyone."

The woman smiled at the group. "Hey, y'all. Just call me Hay Hay. With me are Donovan and Annelise."

Donovan handed Sean a sign with the words RESIST HATE and said, "Thanks for showing up."

"Same," Sean said, shaking his hand.

Once the signs were passed out, they were ready to march.

Hay Hay called a protestor at the scene and asked if five more protesters could meet them in the lot to march with them. That would bring their number up to twenty-four. Rav, Hay Hay, and Isabel would lead. There were only two news vans and one satellite truck to cover the rally. Once Rav was identified, the cameras would turn to him. The story of one senator crashing another's rally was certain to be more newsworthy than the rally itself.

"As the only Black person in the senator's entourage, are you willing to be interviewed on camera?" Hay Hay asked Sean.

"Yes. I'm a Raptor employee. I served in the US Navy for fifteen years and was a SEAL for ten."

Keith dropped a hand on his shoulder. "Sean is our senior field operative. We keep offering him jobs in management, but he keeps refusing because he likes to be in the field, rescuing hostages and fighting terrorists who prey upon Americans abroad."

Hay Hay's eyes widened. "The press is going to *love* you." She glanced at Rav. "You aren't being paid by the company owner to attend this rally, are you?"

Sean laughed. "Hell, no." His gaze flicked toward the street. They couldn't see the rally, but he could hear the crowd and a distorted voice on a loudspeaker. He couldn't make out the words, but he could guess at what the man was saying. "I believe in fighting terrorists who prey on Americans at home too."

Hay Hay grinned. "You're going to be perfect. Thank you for showing up."

Sean nodded. "Thank you for everything you're doing." He wished his mom and Katrina were here. Katrina especially would love this, but healthwise, it would be a few months before she could handle this sort of event.

Additional marchers arrived, and they assembled by the

road, waiting for their cue from the group assembled for the counterprotest across from the rally.

Once they received word the senator was at the podium, they set off down the street in a tight group. Security was light. Not a lot of people had been given advance warning of the rally, and given its remote location, few had been expected to attend beyond the buses of people the senator had arranged. Sean had noted the buses parked well out of view of the news vans and satellite truck.

They rounded the corner, at last coming into view of both the rally and counterprotest. The assembled protesters —at least fifty people, a better turnout than Sean had expected—let out a cheer that momentarily drowned out the crowd of two hundred who gave the senator their rapt attention.

Reporters' heads turned and, a moment later, so did the cameras.

The senator droned on into his microphone, but he'd lost the attention he'd been aiming for—that of the press. Rav led the march straight to the area cordoned off for the counter-protest and took a place in the front with Isabel at his side, while the rest of their group tucked into the back, behind the protestors who'd given up a sunny fall Friday to be there. Sean also headed for the rear of the crowd, but Donovan caught his arm. "Nah, man. You should be up front."

Hazel would have gone to the back with the others, but he threaded his fingers through hers. "You okay with being on camera?" he asked.

"With you? Of course."

He smiled and leaned down and kissed her, not sure if he was playing a role in that moment or not. All he knew was it felt natural. Like breathing.

He took a spot by Rav's side as the reporters flocked, ignoring the senator who'd paid for this gathering in favor of the one who'd crashed it. "Senator Ravissant, what does it mean that you're here?"

He held up his sign that said, "WHITE SILENCE IS VIOLENCE." "It means I'm exercising my right to free speech as an American citizen. It means I'm adamantly opposed to Senator Small's efforts for expanded privatization of American jails. African American communities are targeted by police the most and unjustly incarcerated the most. Senator Small's policies are tantamount to modern slavery in which officers round up citizens on trumped-up charges, courts set bail rates impossibly high, ensuring citizens who have yet to be convicted of anything remain locked up. Then the owners of the jail force them to work for nothing in chain gangs to 'pay for their upkeep.' This happens to citizens who, more likely than not, have committed no crime. We need prison reform. We need bail reform. We do not need more privatized jails."

"Thank you, Senator." The reporter then turned to Sean and asked his connection to Rav.

They did a replay of his conversation earlier with Hay Hay, except Rav was the one who talked up his credentials.

The reporter's eyebrows rose. "Mr. Logan, are you calling Senator Small a terrorist?"

"No, ma'am. I'm saying rallies like this are terrorist breeding grounds. This kind of rally emboldens bigots to commit hate crimes against people of color, LGBTQIA, and those of non-Christian faith. This country was founded on many different freedoms, among them freedom of association and freedom of religion. Senator Small advocates limiting those freedoms for those who are not white, male, straight, and Christian. I will not sit back and be silent when a man who has never served, whose wealth was built on the backs of slaves, seeks to reinstate slavery in the country I've fought and bled for."

The reporter was in the middle of a follow-up question when someone off-camera said, "Is that former US Attorney General Curt Dominick?"

The reporters abandoned Sean and dove through the crowd to the back, where Curt and Mara held signs with the others. When questioned, Curt said he wasn't hiding from the cameras, he merely didn't want to draw attention away from the rally organizers and make the narrative about him. But since they insisted on placing a microphone before him, he asked that instead of running a "where is he now?" sort of piece on Curt's presence at the rally that they focus on the issues raised by Senator Ravissant and that of concerned citizens like himself who'd taken time out of their day to show up and exercise their freedom of speech.

Follow-up questions on the Justice Department's investigation into Senator Small's business dealings were met with a stiff "I'm not at liberty to discuss investigations that occurred during my tenure as US attorney general."

They were still interviewing Curt when the senator finished speaking, and not a single news camera had recorded the second half of his speech.

Sean couldn't help but grin, knowing that had been the goal of this intervention in the first place. He slipped an arm around Hazel's waist and twirled her around. It was such a small success, but satisfying nonetheless.

They returned their signs to Hay Hay. On the walk back to their cars, Senator Small glared at Rav. From the look on his face, it was clear he wanted to say something, but cameras were rolling, so the man said nothing.

It wasn't until they were halfway down the block that Isabel slipped between Hazel and Sean. "Did you see him, Hazel?"

Hazel nodded. "He was next to the senator when we

walked by just now. I was too focused on the interviews to see where he was during the speech."

"He was next to the stage, on the steps to the side. Looking like he was providing security, but he has no jurisdiction here."

"See who?" Sean asked. "What are you talking about?"

"Sheriff Taylor. He's here, along with the deputy who was at the reservoir on Monday."

Chapter Thirteen

After the rally, everyone was eager to keep moving and get to the inn, which was little more than an hour away. Hazel was tired but happy. She'd attended several of Alec's campaign rallies when he ran for the Senate three years before, but hadn't been to anything in the intervening years, having spent much of that time overseas. It was exciting. Exhilarating even, to be with like-minded people who were trying to create positive change. She'd forgotten what it felt like.

The people she worked with at ICMP were also trying to make a difference, but the work was the darker side of justice, where you only saw the horror humans commit, not the ways in which activists tried to make a difference by making their voices heard.

"I'm really glad we did that," she said.

"Me too," Sean said. He pointed to his phone in the console. "Since I'm driving, can you text my sister and tell her to turn on the news? She'll get a kick out of it."

"Sure."

"Pass code or thumbprint?" She held out the phone to him.

He kept his eyes on the road and gave her the six-digit code. It was ridiculous that she got a little rush at the idea he trusted her with his pass code, but she did. *Pathetic woman takes great joy in tiny signs of man's interest. Click to read more.* Her life was certain to become a hit limited series on Netflix.

She opened the address book. "Her name is Katrina?"

"Yes."

"Found her. Tell me what you want to say."

"Just say it's you because I'm driving and to look for the rally on the news."

She typed out a message and hit Send. A moment later the reply came.

KATRINA

> Thanks for letting me know! I'll tell our mom too. So are you and Sean serious? I can't remember the last time he introduced a girlfriend to the family, and I hear we're all having dinner next week.

She laughed and tried to figure out the best reply.

"What?"

"Oh, nothing. Just chatting with your sister."

"Crap. I really should have thought that through. I should've used voice commands."

"Yes. Yes, you should have."

She typed a reply that wouldn't set up any big expectations.

> I'm not sure about serious. Just seeing where this goes.

> Can't wait to meet you. It's about time Sean moved on after the fiasco in Grand Cayman.

Hazel jolted and let out a small gasp.

"What?" Sean asked.

"Nothing." Her voice was a little higher pitched than usual. She stared at the screen. How to respond?

"I should probably mention that Kat is my twin. We're close. But she tends to…overshare."

Sean's voice was nervous. She liked that. But still, she looked at him askance. She hadn't even known he had a sister until Monday, and now she found out Katrina was his *twin*?

> I feel like I should tell you my full name. I'm Hazel MacLeod.

Odds were, even if Katrina hadn't known her first name, she knew the fiasco had been Ivy MacLeod's sister.

The reply was immediate.

> Oh shit.

> I'm going to claim chemo brain. Yes. Definitely chemo brain. Sean, when you read this, it was the chemo. Or, Hazel, maybe you can be a sweetheart and delete?

> I think you're fine playing the chemo card.

> Finally chemo is good for something.

Hazel couldn't help but laugh. She liked Katrina already.

> Hope you are feeling better.

Much. Only one more round and I *should*
be done. I can't wait.

I'm so sorry you're going through this.

It sucks. But Sean has been amazing. Really.
He's a great guy. And OMG, you are HER.
Looking forward to dinner next week! (Now
I'm REALLY looking forward to dinner…)

Me too.

Have fun at the wedding! I'm going to watch
the news now. Looks like they're about to
talk about the rally. Ohh. Love your hair. I can
see why Sean is obsessed with you.

Really? Tell me more.

I think the baby's crying. Gotta run. See you
next week.

"How old are your nieces?" Hazel asked.

"Three and five."

She smiled. Not exactly a baby, but close enough. She set the phone in a slot on the center console and turned in her seat to stare at the handsome man driving the large SUV. She was fascinated by everything about him. Was it possible he'd harbored some kind of crush on her?

She doubted it, but it sounded like she'd at least made an impression. A fiasco of an impression, but the words "move on after the fiasco" were strangely encouraging.

Katrina thought what had happened in Grand Cayman had been holding Sean back. Why? What had Sean told his sister?

he hotel room was going to be a problem. Not that it wasn't perfect. It was. For a couple. But for Sean, who was on bodyguard duty for the next forty-eight hours, it would be a nightmare. At least the bed was big enough to share. It was a giant four-poster with gauzy curtains. Romantic. Made for sex.

And then there was the huge Jacuzzi tub adjacent to the bed. The tub could be in the bathroom, but no, this tub was in the center of the room so a couple could relax together in the hot, bubbling water and watch the sunset through the huge west-facing picture window that overlooked the lake.

Hazel oohed and aahed over the bed, tub, and window. "I think this might be the most gorgeous room I've ever stayed in."

And the way the afternoon sun hit her hair, she was the most gorgeous thing in the room. He wanted to scoop her up, drop her on the bed, and finish the kiss they'd started several hours ago. He wanted to hear her call out his name as he made her come repeatedly. Then he wanted to soak in the tub with her before lifting her to the ledge, spreading her legs, and going down on her.

He wanted this weekend to be real and the bodyguard part to be a charade. But she wasn't his girlfriend and he would be on duty. And he didn't fuck around on the job.

She bent over her open suitcase, which sat on a low rack at the foot of the bed.

Her ass in the air like that made him hard. But then, after the kiss today, all she had to do was breathe and he got hard.

He needed to get out of this room before he forgot himself and violated one of Raptor's main rules for operatives: no screwing around with the client while the job was ongoing.

"We can unpack later. Trina wanted us to gather in the garden for the results of the scavenger hunt."

"We have twenty minutes. Did you send her our selfies?" Hazel asked.

"Shit. I forgot." He pulled out his phone and tapped the message app. Hazel's conversation with his sister was on top. He glanced at the thread, and his stomach dropped.

He looked up to see Hazel's crossed arms and a satisfied smile on her face. "Don't worry. I sent them to Trina while you were driving." Her words and tone were innocent sounding, but her smile was anything but.

He set the phone aside and advanced on her. Screw the rules. She was too damn irresistible when she smiled like that. In two steps, he'd scooped her up and dropped her on the bed, then crawled up over her. He had her pinned between his hands and knees, even though he didn't touch her. He could feel her body heat, a warm caress on his exposed skin. The fresh scent of citrus and mint clung to her hair, and he wanted to eat her.

"I bet you have some questions for my sister," he said.

"I do."

"Ask me. Not my sister."

"I don't think so."

"Please?" He wasn't above pleading.

"No."

"You're a beautiful woman, Hazel."

She smiled and licked her lips. "Thank you."

His cock thickened at the sight of her tongue. "I never said I didn't want you."

"You never said you wanted me either."

"Wanting and having are two different things."

"I'm well aware of that." She reached up and stroked his cheek. "I'm going to lay it all out now. One hundred percent real. I want you. I've wanted you since the first dinner party at Alec's house four and a half years ago."

He knew that. He'd always known that. "I'm your bodyguard. What you want, even what I want, is irrelevant. Raptor has rules against fooling around with clients."

"Yet here I am, pinned beneath you."

He started to pull back, to do the right thing, but she grabbed his shirt, keeping him above her. "You aren't working for Raptor right now, and I'm not a client."

"You are—"

"No. Alec is your client. I don't even think I'm in danger."

"We can't, Haze. Not while I'm protecting you."

"You think Alec and Isabel won't be having sex this weekend because he's protecting her?"

"I really don't want to think about Rav's sex life, thank you very much."

"And I'm calling bullshit on your rules. I'm not in danger. I'm not your client. And you aren't working for Raptor. Those are all excuses. And you know it, or you wouldn't be pinning me to this bed."

He stared down at her. His body throbbed with need. She was everything he wanted, and he *could* have her.

But want had nothing to do with it. This wasn't *right*. Not when she was vulnerable and he was ready to bolt. He wouldn't stick around, and that would hurt her. Worse, they could have weeks ahead of them stuck in their roles of fake relationship. If he fooled around with her now, things could get damn awkward when it was clear he didn't want more. "Maybe I don't want to have sex with you."

It was his biggest lie in a day filled with them, and he suspected she knew it.

"And maybe you do."

There was no "maybe" about it.

"We'll finish this conversation later," Hazel said. "Let's go meet the others and collect our prize."

He climbed off the bed and offered her a hand to pull her up. As he did so, he said, "We could be stuck in this charade for weeks. Sex is a bad idea."

She stood and patted his cheek. "You can tell yourself that, Sean. But what you're really doing is running scared."

She crossed the room to the couch where she'd set her purse and scooped it up. "Let's join the others and get our prize. Then I'll claim exhaustion and retreat in here so you can hang with the guys without having to pretend for a while. Deal?"

"Hazel—"

"I'm trying to make this easier for both of us. I'm mindful of the fact that this is your best friend's wedding and you should be here to have fun. Let me give this to you, okay?"

He nodded. Anything else would be a dick move, considering he was the one who'd just refused her blatant offer. He'd hurt her, yet she wasn't making this weekend about her.

Two things were certain. Hazel MacLeod was too good for him, and he sure as hell was running scared.

Chapter Fourteen

Hazel couldn't believe she'd said it straight out. She wasn't even drunk this time. And yet she'd still crashed and burned. The way he'd pinned her to the bed, then hadn't touched her had created aches in places she hadn't known existed.

And now she'd put Sean in an awful situation. It wasn't his fault Alec had screwed everything up by forcing them together. When this was all over, she was going to kick her cousin's ass for his sheer cluelessness.

She wanted to hide in their room as she'd promised, but the rest of the day was planned, and it would look bad if she spent the time sulking in the room. So she had to suck it up and put on a happy face. In the last week, she'd discovered that she liked pretty much everything about Sean Logan. His looks had been the draw at first, but damn, what wasn't to like about a man who carried her to safety after being injured in the lake—*twice*?

And then there was the way he'd held her when she couldn't sleep, convincingly faked being infatuated with her, and kissed her like he was desperate to have her. And she could be stuck playing his pretend girlfriend for weeks.

She was definitely going to kick Alec's ass.

Ian stepped up beside her and draped an arm over her shoulders. One thing she'd noticed today, this was a touchy-feely bunch. She liked it but imagined it was hard for Ivy, who'd always had more social boundaries.

The groom leaned down and whispered in her ear, "I'm glad Sean finally got off his ass and asked you out."

She smiled. "What makes you think he's the one who made the first move?"

Ian's brow crinkled. "Uh, the fact that he's had the hots for you for years?"

"Has he now?" Much as she wanted to believe him, she couldn't let herself hope. Not in the face of Sean's rejection just minutes ago. The word "fiasco" sounded less promising at this point.

"Yeah, it's been obvious."

She couldn't help but laugh. "Right. I thought spies could read people."

"Technically, I was never a spy. I ran spies."

"Yeah, whatever. I've read enough books to know that when you write your memoir, you'll call yourself a spy in the title."

"Well, it sells better that way."

She looked up at him in shock. "You aren't really writing your memoir, are you?"

He smiled. Ian Boyd's smile was a beautiful thing. "Nah. The CIA would redact too much. It would be horribly boring."

Redacted. At this point, she seriously disliked that word. Alec was holding information back from her.

Sean joined them and handed Hazel a champagne flute. "What are you up to, Ian?"

"Telling Hazel all about that time in Jakarta."

Sean rolled his eyes. "Go ruin someone else's love life. I think Luke and Undine look too happy."

Ian laughed and walked off, while Sean put an arm around her and kissed her temple.

"What happened in Jakarta?"

"Absolutely nothing."

"Right."

Sean flashed an innocent smile she didn't buy for a second.

She rose on her toes and kissed his lips. Might as well enjoy this while she could.

He placed a hand behind her head as she dropped to her heels, and followed her, making the kiss something more lingering.

She forgot how to breathe.

It's an act. All an act.

Trina tapped the side of a glass with a spoon. "Before I announce the winner, I have to say, I'm sure no one thought I'd let our bride and groom lose, right? Even though they came in third, they get the same prize as our top scorers." She pulled two identical gift bags from a box on the floor. She must've hidden the second bag so Ian and Cressida would believe they had to compete to keep the game interesting. It was clear Ian had a competitive streak, but then most of the men did.

Trina handed one bag to Ian, then turned and handed the second bag to Sean. "Our top scorers were Sean and Hazel with a score of eighty-nine. Congratulations and"— her voice deepened with a wicked edge—"*enjoy.*"

Sean took the bag and glanced into the package. His eyes widened, and his gaze jerked up to Trina.

She grinned. "You're welcome."

"What's in the bag?" Luke asked.

Sean and Ian exchanged a look. They both shook their heads, mute.

Now Hazel was curious. She hooked a finger over the top of the bag and tilted it in her direction so she could peek inside.

Oh good Lord.

A few feet away, Cressida peeked into the bag in Ian's hands. She let out a squeal of laughter. "Trina!"

Trina shrugged innocently. "Hey, I told you there was a reason this was a couples thing."

"I think—" Hazel cleared her throat when her voice broke. "I think I'll go put this in our room."

"I'll come with you," Sean said.

That's what she said. Laughter bubbled up at the joke she didn't dare say aloud.

On her way to the hotel lobby, Hazel finally remembered her manners. She turned on her heel and smiled at the day's game maker. "Thank you, Trina. It's exactly my color and size."

Trina and Cressida both snorted. Ian and Keith laughed. Sean let out a strangled groan.

A minute later, they were climbing the stairs to their second-floor room. Now in addition to having a massive king-sized bed made for sex and a hot tub made for sex, they also had a bag full of toys all made, quite specifically, for sex.

Sean held up a giant blue dildo, marveling at the molded veins and testicular details. "*This* is your color and size?"

"Yes. Want me to demonstrate?"

God, yes. But he didn't dare say it aloud. "At least it's blue.

I don't know how I'd feel winning a dildo that looked like a white guy's dick."

Hazel studied a box that held a U-shaped vibrator. "This one's for stimulating the G-spot. You can download an app on your phone and control the settings."

"I don't think I want Apple or Google to know when I'm using my sex toys," Sean said.

"I'm pretty sure they already do. At least, Facebook probably knows."

"And that is why I'm not on Facebook." He shook his head, then pulled flavored lubricant from the bag. "I'm sorry Trina did this. It's…awkward."

"Are you kidding?" She held up an oddly shaped small purple vibrator. It was probably meant to mimic a tongue and had been in the box with the U-shaped toy, part of a set. "I've been wanting one of these since my last one quit. They're the *best*. And, sadly, expensive."

He closed his eyes, imagining all too easily how fun it would be to play with the toy and Hazel. It was waterproof, so they could play with it in the hot tub. He could slide deep inside her body as water sloshed over the sides of the tub and he stroked her clit with the small, powerful vibrator.

She dug in the box and pulled out the charging cable and plugged it into the USB power port on the desk. "Do you mind if I keep this one? You can have the dildo."

"I don't *want* the dildo." *Not without you to use it on. In. With.* The preposition didn't matter as long as the noun was all Hazel.

"Fine, then you can have the wrist and ankle cuffs with the under-mattress straps. I've always wanted to try bondage but haven't ever been with someone I wanted to try it with." She shrugged and gave him a slight smile. "You've got to really trust a guy, you know?"

And there was another mental image. Hazel splayed on

that king-sized bed, arms and legs wide, strapped tight as he went down on her. Down on. Two prepositions he very much enjoyed giving and receiving. And, if she were game, he'd fuck her mouth while her arms were bound, sliding as deep as she could take him.

Was deep a preposition? Probably not, but it seemed like one. Who knew prepositions could be his favorite part of speech?

He wanted to curse Trina and her scavenger hunt, but at the same time, he had new fantasies of Hazel to enjoy. He'd put the blue dildo to work as his cock slid in her mouth while she was tied to the bed.

Oh, the things he wanted to do to her…

With the bondage kit, he could tie her on her stomach and use the U-shaped vibrator. It was made to stimulate her clitoris on the outside and her G-spot—along with himself—on the inside. He touched the silicone-covered device. "You can have the other vibrator, but this one is mine."

"I thought you didn't want Google up in your business?"

He studied her from head to toe, his gaze lingering on the good parts—which was pretty much all of her—and smiled. "Sweetheart, this is for getting in *your* business. And it works offline." He pressed the power button and it began to buzz and vibrate—weakly. "Better charge this one too."

Jesus. He was a fool for playing her game. Much safer to share the room—and bed—*without* a bunch of powered-up sex toys.

But damn, the challenge in her eyes, the defiance in her posture, was hard to resist.

"You can have the lube," she said. "I'll take the massage oil candles."

His eyes narrowed. He didn't mind her taking the vibrator and even the dildo. Both could be used solitary. But who was she hoping to use the massage oil with? "Which one of us gets the sex dice?"

"There are two dice. We can each keep one."

He shouldn't play this game but couldn't help himself. He stepped forward, backing her toward the dresser where the vibrator was charging. "It's not a good idea to break up the set."

"I could say the same thing about the two-part vibrator kit."

"So maybe we should keep them together."

"Fine. You get the dice. I get the vibrators."

He laughed. His dick throbbed. That body part wanted to have a say in the equitable division of toys. Or at least testing the toys. What sort of sound would she make if she was tied up and he made her come with the vibrator? She wouldn't be able to pull away when it got too intense.

She'd be at my mercy…

Her lips parted. The air between them was thick with heat. He had no doubt her thoughts ran parallel to his. He traced her full bottom lip with his thumb. "What would your safeword be, Hazel, if I tied you up? What would you say if you wanted me to stop?"

Her tongue ran over her lips. "What makes you think I'd want you to stop?"

Heat surged. He wasn't sure if it was ignited from the region near his heart or his cock. Probably both. The only confirmed fact was her words set him on fire in a way he hadn't expected. Somehow, she had the upper hand in this flirtation, with her teasing words and sexy smile.

The hellcat was coaxing him to a hard-on with her seemingly guileless admissions. She was a master at manipulation and the innocent, sexy lure. The words that left her lips were pure enticement. Playful. Fun.

And a damn land mine.

He wanted to blurt out all the things he would do to her. How he planned to make her his, how he would use Trina's considerate gifts.

But there was a knock on the door, and he had to get a grip on his lust. They were here for a wedding. A weekend with friends. He was the best man, and they were supposed to do a rehearsal in thirty minutes.

Much as he was annoyed, he was thankful for the interruption. He swept the toys into the top drawer of the dresser and took a deep breath, willing his erection to fade. "Who is it?"

"Alec and Isabel." Rav's voice was muted. The old inn had nice, thick walls and doors, he noted.

"I'll get the door," Hazel said.

He nodded, then he caught the back of her neck and pulled her to him. His lips brushed hers. "We'll finish this conversation later."

A slow, somewhat wicked smile spread across her features. "Yes. Yes, we will."

Chapter Fifteen

Hazel sat between Isabel and Sean at the small circular table in their suite. Across from her, Alec held up a tablet displaying the official portrait of Sheriff Carl Taylor on the county website. "You're both sure this is the guy who was standing next to Small?"

Hazel nodded in unison with Isabel. Sean shrugged. "I was too focused on scanning the crowd to pay attention to the dais. I figured if there was any threat coming at Isabel or Hazel, it would be from someone in the crowd, not at the front."

Alec nodded. "Yeah, that's where I wanted you to focus. I was watching Small and the stage, but I'd never seen Sheriff Taylor before, so it didn't register."

"You think Taylor and Small have something to do with the threat?" Hazel asked. Once again, she wondered what was in the redacted parts. She had no doubt Alec had a very specific list of suspects. "If you think Small is dangerous, why bring Isabel there?"

"I don't know if there is a connection. I just find it interesting that a sheriff who was trying to shut you down on the same day the threat came in is a Small supporter. And I wasn't worried about bringing you both to the rally because I knew Small would never expect us to show up."

"To be fair, Sheriff Taylor's attempt to shut down Hazel's examination of the remains isn't entirely out of line," Isabel said. "Processing the remains can be a pain in the ass and, if it were a known burial ground or cemetery, entirely unnecessary. And it would anger local tribes. Before the dam was built, that reservoir was a lovely narrow valley. It *could* be historic or prehistoric and totally innocent."

Alec turned to Hazel. "But you said it's not."

"No, I don't think so. My preliminary exam raised enough questions that I contacted the Virginia ME and advised her this could be a criminal investigation. She requested I collect as many bones as I could from the reservoir before inundation began again today. She's working on paperwork to halt inundation and a work order for me to do an in-depth examination of the bones.

"It'll take days to get them to stop refilling the lake, so I collected all the skulls and other diagnostic elements I could find yesterday afternoon. We're at twenty-seven now. One is potentially female. The rest appear to be males, twenty-five to thirty-five years old. It's the uniformity and the evidence all the remains were burned I find most suspicious. There also aren't any clothing fibers or jewelry."

"What about dental work?" Alec asked.

"The lower mandibles were all separated from the craniums. I managed to find a few in the lake yesterday and haven't examined any of them yet. The skulls I have examined appear to have some dental work, but not a lot. Metal fillings were first used in the US in the 1830s, which means while the remains aren't prehistoric. It's still possible— however unlikely—the remains could be from a legitimate historic cemetery. We'd have to test the metal to be certain in that regard."

"But if it were an historic cemetery, there would be clothing. Metal. Other items to help date the remains," Isabel said.

Hazel nodded. "Exactly. I don't think the remains are historic, but a definitive determination requires a more intensive exam than I've been able to do so far."

"Were they burned alive?" Isabel asked.

"It's possible. I haven't found knife cuts or bullet fractures in the bones, but my examination was preliminary." She shrugged. "Again, further analysis is needed."

Alec frowned. "Are you okay to do more forensic analysis?"

She gave a slow nod. "I have to. If I turn down this work, it would kill my reputation with the Virginia ME." She took a deep breath, then added, "And I do feel okay with it. Dr. Parks taught me some techniques to help calm the anxiety before it builds."

Sean's gaze turned unfocused with thought. "If Sheriff Taylor has anything to do with those remains, your work will be for nothing. The county sheriff is the only law enforcement with jurisdiction."

"We need to get the feds involved," Hazel said.

"That might be easy," Isabel said. "Even though it's a private utility company, it's a federal contract—Federal Energy Regulatory Commission required the dam repair, which makes it a federal undertaking. The energy produced goes to West Virginia, Maryland, and Virginia—it's only ten miles from the West Virginia border and seven and a half from Maryland. We can use the federal permit to claim the FBI has jurisdiction."

"I'll run that by Curt, see what he thinks," Alec said. "The sheriff will fight it."

"But once the remains are in the FBI's possession, there

won't be anything Sheriff Taylor can do about it," Hazel said. "It would be a hard fight for him to get them back, and I certainly have no intention of turning over the samples I've collected to his office."

"I'll go through channels to get an investigation going on him," Alec said.

"I've been wondering who owns the big house on Anderson Lake," Sean said. "The one next to Raptor land. That's the landowner who managed to delay your fieldwork, right, Isabel?"

She nodded. "I've been wondering that too. If there's some connection between the landowner and Sheriff Taylor."

"All you have is the name of a holding company?" Hazel asked.

Isabel nodded.

"I'll get an investigator on that," Alec said. "I've already got a team looking into Senator Small—"

Isabel jolted. "Seriously? You're investigating a fellow senator?"

Alec shrugged. "Of course. The voting process isn't as good at vetting people as we'd hope. The guy is a racist prick and might as well have a price tag on his votes. But there's more to it. He's got shady deals going on the side with the for-profit prison lobby—and now we know he's buddies with a local sheriff who uses the county lockup for chain-gang labor. I'm going to get proof of Small's dirty deals and force him to resign, but the US attorney for the Northern District of West Virginia is a crony of his. It's unlikely he'll face charges unless what I find is bulletproof."

"Sometimes I really wish Curt was still attorney general," Isabel said.

"Alec, why do you think Small is connected to the threat?" Hazel asked.

He shook his head. "I don't know if he's connected, and I can't give you more details than I already have. I'm sorry."

"You know I'm not the target. You're putting Sean through this ridiculous farce for no reason."

"Hey, we won a prize," Sean said. "Too late to change our story now."

Isabel tossed Hazel a sly gaze. "So what was in the bag?"

Hazel felt her face heat. Stupid complexion that made her prone to blushing. "It was a big box of my favorite chocolates, and I'm not sharing."

"Not even with Sean?" Isabel asked, clearly not believing the lie.

She flushed deeper, thinking of their conversation, divvying up the prizes. "He can have a few. Maybe."

Sean laughed. "Don't worry about me, Iz. I will make sure I get my favorite pieces."

Isabel's grin turned wicked. "Oh, do you like the ones with nuts?"

Sean snorted. "Nah, Haze can have that one."

Hazel rolled her eyes, thinking of the royal-blue balls attached to the dildo. "Are we done here? Don't we have a rehearsal to attend?"

Alec's gaze went from Hazel to Isabel before he said, "You two go. I need to talk to Sean alone for a few minutes."

Isabel stood and leaned down to Alec for a kiss. Hazel circled the table, passing behind Sean to grab her key card from the dresser on the way to the door. If anyone else had been in the room, she'd probably have leaned down for a kiss too, and the strange part was that *not* kissing Sean felt unnatural. Walking behind him without a touch didn't feel right.

"Don't forget, we're here for a wedding," Isabel said to Alec in a lecturing tone. "And Sean is needed for the rehearsal."

"He won't be late. I promise," Alec said.

"Riiiight," she said, then followed Hazel to the door. In the hallway after the door closed, Isabel paused to listen. "Damn," she said softly. "The walls are thick and so is the door. That's the problem with these old hotels. Too much privacy."

Hazel chuckled. "The nerve. Take off a star when you post your review." She stared at the door, also wondering what was being said on the other side. "What do you think Alec is telling Sean?"

"I don't know, but it bothers me Alec is telling Sean things he refuses to tell us. I trust Alec with everything, he's my whole world, but I don't understand why he's not telling me what's going on."

"Doesn't Sean have some sort of security clearance because he works with government clients?"

"He does, but still. You and I are the ones who were threatened. It would be nice to know what we're dealing with."

"You were threatened. I'm merely collateral damage."

"Don't be so sure, Hazel. If this has anything to do with the sheriff, you're the bigger threat than I am. You're the one who suspects homicide and has the education to argue the point."

"Fair point, but Alec received the threat before I even arrived at the site."

They headed down the corridor toward the curved staircase. They passed Curt in the hall, and he gave them a nod and a smile. A moment later, Hazel heard a knock on a door and turned to see Curt standing in front of her room.

She frowned at Isabel and whispered, "They asked Curt to join them?"

Isabel's eyes narrowed. "Well, he definitely has security clearance as a former cabinet member. And we know Alec wanted to ask him about FBI jurisdiction, but I bet he also has questions about the Justice Department's investigation of Senator Small.

"I wish we were still in the room."

Isabel sighed. "Me too."

The rehearsal was short and simple. Ivy's son, Julian, and Erica and Lee's daughter, Grace, were ring bearer and flower girl, but neither was present, and Grace was so young, she was more likely to be in her mom's arms than sprinkling flower petals down the aisle between chairs set up in the garden. Matt stood in for Julian and promised he'd pass on the complex and vital instructions for ring bearing to Julian first thing when the boy arrived tomorrow.

Cressida, who had never known her father, surprised Curt by asking him to walk her down the aisle. His eyes crinkled at the corners as he hugged her and said, "I'd be honored."

The ceremony would be performed by a judge, the father of one of Ian's Army buddies. The judge also wasn't present for the rehearsal, so Luke stood in for him. The walk-through of the ceremony was full of jokes and teasing as Luke delivered his part as the Impressive Clergyman from *The Princess Bride*.

Hazel sat with the others who were not part of the ceremony, laughing. Matt knelt next to Sean to approximate Julian's height, holding a plate because no one remembered to grab a pillow, while Luke misquoted the Impressive Clergyman and Cressida corrected him. Somehow they morphed from *The Princess Bride* to *Monty Python and the Holy Grail*, and the debate over the airspeed velocity of an unladen swallow was on.

To end their antics, Ian pulled Cressida to him and said,

"When do I get to kiss the bride?" then kissed her, deeply, without waiting for permission.

Catcalls followed. Hazel felt another rush of envy. Not for the love between Ian and Cressida and their obvious happiness—although that looked pretty great too—but for the warm friendships that filled this room. She wanted to be a part of this.

Ian finally came up for air, and Cressida laughed and leaned into him, as if swooning. "If I'd known you had that in your arsenal, we'd have done this whole wedding thing sooner."

Ian grinned. "I had to hold something back. You don't buy the cow if the milk is free."

Everyone laughed.

"On that note," Luke said, "I think this rehearsal is a wrap."

On cue, the hotel manager announced. "If you'll all return to the patio, an open bar has been set up for cocktail hour. Dinner will be served in the dining room in an hour."

The open bar and dinner were Alec's wedding gift to Ian and Cressida. Alec had told Hazel once that one of the perks of handing Raptor over to Keith to run was that it gave him a chance to develop friendships with the people who worked for Raptor in a way that hadn't been possible when he was both calling the shots and paying the bills. Now it was on Keith to manage the business. While Alec still owned the company, he didn't make any management or contract decisions. Those were all on Keith.

It didn't appear Keith had a problem being both boss and friend, but then he was from the same ranks as the rest of the employees—former SEAL with over a decade of service but no college degree, let alone Ivy League like Alec. It was easier for Keith to straddle the worlds than it was for Alec.

Like any attentive date, Sean walked with Hazel to the

patio for cocktail hour, even though it really wasn't necessary. Hazel felt very welcome in this gathering. Her body hummed with the fun energy of the assembled guests. If she ever married, this was what she'd want. Simple. Small. With people who genuinely enjoyed being together. Envy struck again, but not so strongly it overshadowed the pleasure.

Cocktail hour flowed into a casual dinner, eaten inside because the insects came out when the sun went down. After dinner, the group split along gender lines, Trina having arranged for the women to enjoy facial masks and manicures in the main lounge while the men went off to chop wood, then drink beer around a bonfire on the shore of the lake.

Seriously, they were chopping wood for fun. She would never understand men.

There was much laughter and a few scary photos taken as they all wore their masks and had their nails done by a fleet of manicurists. Hazel studied the other women, who all looked like they were from those horror movies with the hockey mask guy. She couldn't remember the name. She'd never paid much attention to horror films when she was in her teens and early twenties, but after she'd examined the remains of a woman knifed thirty-three times, she'd lost any appetite for that kind of entertainment. But that didn't mean she couldn't appreciate the jokes and general fun as they all donned masks that promised to make their skin clearer, tighter, and younger.

If only fifteen minutes under a coconut mask could really deliver a time and beauty machine. But tonight, she would believe. She'd let go of her cynicism, drink her chocolate martini—made to Trina's specifications—and enjoy this buzz of stolen friendship.

She watched her sister, Ivy, as she laughed and chatted with her friends, and a different kind of happiness settled in. After a nightmare marriage and painful divorce, followed by a traumatic experience in Palau, Ivy had it all: a job she loved, a husband who was crazy about her, and a child to love and nurture. Hazel hadn't known how deeply Ivy wanted a child until she began fostering Julian.

That the adoption wasn't complete yet remained a concern, the fear that a court could yank him away from a mother and father who loved him intensely loomed over everything. But soon those papers would be signed, and Julian would be Ivy and Matthew's son for all time.

Julian's parents had died a year and a half before in an accident that happened right as Ivy returned from Palau. Hazel had no idea that Ivy had gone through the process of being approved to be a foster parent. She would have taken on a child sooner, but she'd known the Palau project was coming and had deferred until her return.

Julian's loss of his parents was devastating, but he'd been lucky to land in the arms of a woman who'd insisted she wanted to adopt him from the start. Julian's mother had been bilingual—Russian and English—and in another stroke of fate, Matthew was fluent in Russian as well. He spoke to the boy solely in Russian while Ivy spoke English to him. Hazel loved that her nephew wouldn't lose his Russian heritage along with his Russian-American mother.

She was incredibly happy for her sister, who finally had everything she'd ever wanted.

Facial masks and nails complete, the group of women settled around a table to play bridal shower games, but the moment the stockpile of toilet paper came out for making wedding dresses, Cressida rose to her feet. "I love you, Treen, but I think everyone here—including you—would much rather join the men by the bonfire than dress me in toilet paper."

Trina winked at her. "Don't underestimate my toilet-paper-dress-designing skills. But I figured you'd feel that way.

There's a stack of blankets by the door. It's cold, and snuggling under a blanket is pretty much the only way all sixteen of us will fit around the bonfire."

Hazel's belly fluttered as Trina's meaning became clear. The women would invade the men's party, joining them by sitting on their partners' laps.

The fake-boyfriend thing was about to get too real.

Chapter Sixteen

Sean placed himself to Matthew's left so he could hear the quiet conversation between the former Russian spy and assassin, and Luke Sevick, a former SEAL and current NOAA lieutenant who had been friends with Matt when the spy was deeply embedded in the US Coast Guard. This was the first time they'd seen each other since they'd crossed paths in Palau.

Around the campfire, they could relax. Hazel wasn't here. There was no reason to pretend they didn't know each other.

It was vital Hazel remain in the dark, as that was the only way to keep Ivy and Julian safe. Tomorrow, a slew of guests would arrive, none of whom knew the truth. When that happened, it would be easier for everyone involved. It was harder when the only audience for a charade was a single person.

Not that Matt had any trouble navigating his new backstory. A lifetime in espionage had turned him into a chameleon, ever adaptable. It was Ivy who was the wild card. Her face was eminently readable, every emotion laid bare.

She was a terrible liar and worse actress, but her fierce love for Julian gave her performance strength and credibility. She was determined not to shatter her son's life by slipping.

But now there were new suspicions about Matt. Suspicions strong enough to warrant the fake-relationship charade with Hazel. So Sean chose the seat next to Matt in order to eavesdrop. Not that he'd pick up on anything interesting. Matt was too well trained and Luke an absolute straight arrow.

"So, Sean, what's the deal with you and Hazel?" Ian, seated to Sean's left, asked, his voice just loud enough to be heard by everyone.

He looked at his friend. "I'm going to plead the fifth here."

Curt perked up at the weak legal defense. "How does that apply?"

He should have chosen his words more carefully. There was nothing Curt loved more than picking apart a legal argument, even when it was just a group of guys talking around a campfire. "Uh, the guy who signs my paychecks—who happens to be her cousin—is five feet away, and I'm sitting next to her brother-in-law who, rumor has it, is something of a badass. I'm saying nothing. Ever."

Ian came to his rescue, if you could call it that, when his words were a different kind of indictment. "I always knew you had it bad for her. Glad you finally got off your ass and did something about it."

There was nothing he could say to that. As far as everyone here but Rav knew, he *had* gotten off his ass, and he certainly couldn't deny an infatuation without raising questions. "Shut up and get me another beer," he ordered the groom.

Ian laughed and reached into the cooler at his side,

grabbed a cold microbrew, popped off the cap, and handed it to Sean. Then he held out his bottle in a toast. "Thanks for standing up with me, man."

Sean smiled at the heartfelt tone behind the words. He'd first met Ian when he'd orchestrated Ian and Cressida's exfiltration from Syria. "I wouldn't miss this for anything," Sean said. "Cressida is an amazing woman. You are a lucky man."

Ian's gaze shifted across the fire, toward the historic inn. He grinned. "Yes, yes, I am."

Sean followed his gaze and saw Cressida leading the charge of women crashing the fire-pit party. Eight women, each beautiful in her own way, but there was only one who'd haunted his fantasies for years. He'd finally kissed her earlier today. Tonight she would share his bed in a room full of sex toys.

She made a beeline for him, holding a wool blanket in her arms. She looked tentative, nervous. And it only took a moment to realize why. None of the women had chairs, and one by one, they settled onto their husbands' laps.

Like the others, Sean scooted his beach chair back from the fire to make room. He spread his legs and held out his arms in invitation. It was the only option, and hell, having Hazel in his lap wouldn't exactly be a hardship. But he would get hard. Epically so, if past history of having Hazel in his proximity was any indication.

She cocked her head and gave him a wry smile, then dropped into his lap without a word. Her sweet ass nestled against his groin as she settled between his spread thighs. She tilted her head back and he pressed his mouth to hers in a quick kiss, as would be expected.

It was weird how all this felt so natural, and yet it was fake. He wanted to know how much she was performing in this moment, because sure as hell, his erection against her ass was real. He liked Hazel MacLeod way too much, and now she knew exactly how much she turned him on.

"Hope you don't mind we invaded your guy time," Cressida said as she snuggled on Ian's lap to Sean's left.

"Hell, no, I don't mind," the groom said. "What could be better than sharing this beautiful night with my best friends and the woman who makes my life complete?"

"Ohh. Good one," she said with a laugh.

"I finally got the hang of the boyfriend thing," he said in a teasing, smug tone.

Erica snickered. "Too bad now you have to master the husband thing. It's a whole new ball game."

"Already got it covered." He kissed Cressida's nose, then said, "Wanna know what the guys and I were doing down by the lake before we built the fire?"

"Knowing you, after you finished chopping wood, things probably devolved into a hatchet-throwing contest or some other guy competition," Cressida said.

"Accurate," Sean said. Some men wanted bachelor parties; Ian had insisted they all chop wood, both for the weekend's celebration and for his honeymoon. Tomorrow night, after the reception, he and Cressida would take off for a quiet cabin on a private lake about fifteen miles from here. He'd told Sean he'd wanted to bring Cressida to that cabin on that lake since they'd been on the run for their lives and had spent a night by a lake in Turkey.

While Trina had outdone herself and arranged the scavenger hunt, Sean got off easy when it came to best man duties. His major task involved making sure there would be bolts ready for splitting and all the men had gloves and axes. Ian wanted firewood, he'd get a full damn cord. Like Trina, Sean had turned it into a game, and he'd had prizes—growlers of microbrews, not sex toys—for winners. For some reason, it never crossed his mind to shop for sex toys.

"Who won the hatchet-throwing contest?" Mara asked.

"Guess," Keith said.

"Don't do it, ladies. It's a trap," Trina said. "If you don't guess your own husband, you'll be in trouble, but we all know who the winner had to be."

In unison, six women said, "Matt."

Sean felt Hazel's body stiffen with surprise. "Why Matt?" She turned to her brother-in-law and laughed while asking, "You have some mad ax skills I haven't heard about?"

Matt chuckled, and Sean wondered what sort of answer he'd give. He needn't have worried. Matt was always in character. "In my early twenties, I lived in the Pacific Northwest and worked as a logger on the Olympic Peninsula. On the side, I started competing in the lumberjack competitions around the state. I was good at the log roll, speed climb, underhand chop, and springboard chop, but axe throwing was my best event." He kissed Ivy's cheek. "I'm guessing you shared that story at a wine-tasting night?"

He was smooth, the way he named events lending credibility to his story. But Matt had lived on the Olympic Peninsula, so he was probably familiar with the competitions.

Ivy nodded.

"Believe me, if *I'd* known about Matt's crazy axe-throwing skills," Sean said, "I'd have come up with a different contest."

Ivy laughed. "Sorry, Sean." Her tone said she wasn't sorry at all. To Matt, she whispered, "What did we win?"

Sean laughed and tightened his arms around Hazel as relief settled in. She'd been given a reasonable story for why the women had all guessed that Matt was deadly accurate with a hatchet, and probably wouldn't think twice about it. But the truth was, Matt had begun his spy training at the age of fourteen and was deadly accurate with *everything*. And tonight, he'd crushed them all in the axe-throwing competition—as Sean had guessed he would. But it sure was fun watching the guy throw, and the competition to match his accuracy had been fierce.

Ian cleared his throat. "So anyway, can we forget how awesome Matt is for a moment and get back to *me* and how I'm going to kick ass at being a husband?"

Cressida laughed. "Honey, we agreed not to talk in public about all the ways in which you excel."

Ian laughed. "Don't worry, sweetheart. I'm an ex-spy. King of discretion."

She snickered.

"Now," Ian said, "as I was saying when we were throwing axes around, I noticed a field of fall wildflowers at the edge of the forest. There were sunflowers, goldenrod, asters, and phlox—I might've looked them up on my phone—and it reminded me of—"

"Turkey," Cressida said, her voice whispery with emotion.

"Yeah. So I was thinking, tomorrow, instead of carrying some fancy, boring, sterile bouquet that was put together by a florist, it would be more special if you carry flowers I pick for you myself."

Cressida sucked in a sharp breath. "Yes, please."

He reached behind his chair and plucked a bundle of flowers he'd picked earlier and had tucked into a plastic water bottle with the top cut off—they'd used one of the saws to create the impromptu vase. "I'm going to pick a fresh bouquet for you tomorrow right before the ceremony but cut these tonight so you'd have an idea what they would look like."

Cressida took the bouquet into her hands and pressed her face into the blooms. "Oh, Ian," was all she managed to say.

"Wow," Erica said. "That's pretty romantic."

"Damn you, Boyd," Luke said. "Did you have to give her the flowers in front of everyone?"

"How are the rest of us going to live up to that?" Curt added.

"Seriously, Ian. She's already agreed to marry you," Sean said. "No need to set the bar so high for everyone else."

"Sorry, guys," Ian said. "But when you've found the love of your life, you just want to let her know in every way possible what she means to you."

Laughter was building among the women, including Hazel, who was shaking with it even as her chuckles were almost silent. The quakes were physically arousing, while the soft sound was even more enticing. "Isn't that what sex is for?" Sean asked, playing the role of dumb single guy.

As he'd hoped, laughter exploded around him, including from the woman who was settled firmly on his lap.

"Lucky Hazel," Erica said. "Still in the 'sex is the only way I can show my feelings stage.' I loved that stage."

"*Hey,*" Lee said with exaggerated offense.

"Don't worry, sweetie, I love the 'we've been together forever and I haven't slept for more than four hours since the baby was born' stage too. It's just…different."

"We don't have Gracie tonight," Lee said in a low voice.

"I know. No way am I staying by the fire past ten o'clock."

"Hear, hear," Mara said. "I think I'm going to turn into a pumpkin at nine thirty."

Everyone laughed, and the conversation drifted. To Sean's right, Mara gave Curt, Lee, and Matt an update on a call she'd received from her mom, who was babysitting all their children for the night. To his left, Ian and Cressida chatted with Trina and Keith about a work project Trina and Cressida were collaborating on. And on his lap, Hazel relaxed, seeming content in her role as the couples around them conversed. She shivered when the wind kicked up, and Sean draped her wool blanket over both of them.

He nibbled on her neck as he did so. Playing his role to the hilt. Yeah. That's what he was doing. He was holding a beautiful woman in his arms and nibbling on her neck for a *role*.

Forget the fact that if they stayed sitting at this campfire for too long, he'd have to consider calling a help line to deal with his four-hour erection.

For her part, Hazel tilted her head to the side, giving him better access to her neck as she wiggled her ass against him. Hidden as they were under the blanket and in the shadows beyond the fire, no one could see the small action.

But damn, he could feel it. And if she did it a few more times, he wouldn't have to worry about a four-hour erection because he'd embarrass himself right here under the blanket. He nipped at her neck. "Cool it, hellcat," he whispered.

She increased the friction.

He clamped a hand around her waist to hold her still, but her shirt had ridden up under the blanket, and his hand landed on bare midriff. And hell if his fingers didn't have a mind of their own and slide over the soft skin of her belly.

His fingers skated down to toy with the waistband of her jeans. He dipped below, to the first knuckle, just enough to let her know the action was no mistake, then he slid upward. He could take her breast in his palm right now.

He stopped just shy of the goal. What if he'd read the situation wrong? Given that this was all an act and she was pretending to be his girlfriend, she wouldn't object. But he'd be a man taking advantage.

The way she wiggled against his erection was a green light, but that could be as involuntary as his hard-on. That she wanted him wasn't in doubt, but she didn't want a fling, and that was all he had to offer her. She could be physically reacting to his touch, but mentally, he could be the last thing she wanted.

He slid his hand down to her bare belly. Neutral ground. Sweet soft skin he wanted to explore, but safe. He'd just have to be content with having Hazel in his arms and leave it at that.

Chapter Seventeen

Sean leaned his head against the closed hotel room door. He was a little drunk and a lot horny. He hadn't planned to drink tonight. He was on the job. But Rav was drinking with the rest of the guys, and he'd ordered Sean to enjoy being best man.

But still, Sean wouldn't have had so much to drink, but the beers went down easy as the hours slipped by. Then he'd had Hazel on his lap, and he'd drunk to numb the erection that told her in no uncertain terms he wanted to fuck her.

Now it was almost one in the morning, and he was buzzed and hard. The couples with children had left the campfire first, followed by the women about an hour later. But Ian had wanted to stay and feed the flames, so Luke, Keith, Rav, and Sean had stayed to enjoy the starry night, hot fire, and good company.

Now Hazel waited in his bed. He should head to the bathroom next to the lobby and stroke one out. It was the only safe choice considering his room was fully stocked with sex toys, massage oils, and—oh damn, the mental image was killing him—bondage straps.

The idea of Hazel strapped to his bed, legs spread wide, unable to resist as he went down on her... His dick was so hard, he could steal Matt's assassin moniker, the Hammer.

And fuuuck. He must be drunk if he found that joke funny. Assassin jokes weren't ever funny. He should drink water. A lot of it.

Or Hazel. Drinking Hazel would be a few thousand fantasies come true. He'd spread her legs and stroke her with his tongue. Her thighs would cradle his face, the soft slide of skin against stubble.

Yeah, baby. He'd make it so good for her.

This was all Ian's fault. Sean couldn't say no to a drink when the groom insisted, right?

Nah. Trina and her sex toy gift-a-thon were to blame.

Hazel's words from earlier flitted through his brain. *"I've always wanted to try bondage but haven't ever been with someone I wanted to try it with. You've got to really trust a guy, you know?"*

She'd said it so innocently, but she'd known what those words would do to him.

Oh, baby, trust me. *I will make it so good for you.*

No. No. No. No. No.

He couldn't go there with her. She wanted a relationship. She was broken. He couldn't wait to leave. As soon as Kat's chemo was over, he was gone. Back to Dubai. Back to Saudi Arabia. He'd return to the job he loved, where he was in control. Where he could protect people.

Fuck cancer. Fuck genocide. Fuck whatever it was that Isabel had found in that reservoir. That was nasty shit, and he was done with it. All he wanted was to go back to the life he had before his sister's diagnosis. Before his father died.

In his life before cancer, he dealt with death. Hell, he'd faced it daily as a side effect of ops. But dammit, he knew what he was dealing with in combat and the world of private security. There were risks. IEDs, bullets, and bombs to name a few. There were enemies he could fight. Disarm. Disable. Defuse. But fucking cancer…he couldn't do a damn thing to help his sister. Just like he couldn't help his dad. He was nothing to cancer cells or chemo, where the cure hurt more than the disease.

He wanted to escape this place where he couldn't do a damn thing to save the people he loved.

All at once, his brain filled with images of him buried deep inside Hazel MacLeod. That would be an escape of a different sort.

No. No, no, no.

She wanted love and babies. He wanted a screw. He was drunk. She might be too.

Did that rhyme?

He shook his head. Drunk poetry was the worst poetry.

He fished his key card out of his pocket. He couldn't stand here all night. People would ask if he and Hazel were fighting or would wonder why he'd brought her to the wedding.

He entered the room and saw Hazel sleeping in his bed, and his belly churned and he wondered if he was passing on the best thing that would ever happen to him. He liked Hazel. She was sexy and fun and smart as hell. In the last few days, he'd discovered there was a lot more to the party girl. In fact, he'd begun to wonder if the party girl was a persona she'd put on just for him.

Could this thing between them work? He was Black, middle-class, former military. His uncle had married a white woman in the late seventies, when it had been a helluva lot harder to be an interracial couple.

Hazel was white, and while not rich herself, she had family that was firmly part of the one percent. She'd never known financial insecurity, food insecurity. Her safety net had been vast and deep. She had a bachelor of science, a master's degree, and a PhD in forensic anthropology, and no student debt, he presumed, as albatross after all that hard work.

She was currently residing in her cousin's mansion while she figured out her next career steps. That was one hell of a safety net.

Knowing his parents couldn't afford to help them both with school, he'd joined the Navy right out of high school so his twin sister could go to college. No regrets. He'd loved serving, and when he passed BUD/S and became a SEAL, he'd truly found his calling.

He rubbed a hand over his jaw, watching the rise and fall of Hazel's breasts in the dim light that spilled from the mostly closed bathroom door. She was so fucking sexy. Her lips had been soft against his. Warm and welcoming.

He made a beeline for the fridge and grabbed a cold bottle of water. He drank a half liter before he came up for air, then set the bottle down. His gaze landed on Hazel's now wide-open eyes.

"You coming to bed?" she asked in a husky voice.

He wanted to bury his mouth between her thighs and make her scream with orgasm. Make up for the lost months —no, years—he'd wanted but not had her.

But he had two heads, and the one that rested at the top of his spine was in control. "Nah. I'll sleep on the couch."

She cocked her head. "So when you were handsy by the campfire, that was…?"

"Me playing a role and letting it get out of hand."

"Out of hand? Hm. That's not what it felt like. I distinctly remember you taking things in hand."

"I'm sorry. I got caught up in the heat of the moment. I shouldn't have done that."

She deflated. There was no other word for it. He'd rejected her, and her whole body shrank in on itself.

"I like you, Haze, it's just—"

She waved him off. "Forget about it. I know you're working for my cousin." She flopped down and rolled to her side, her body stiff with hurt and tension.

"Hazel—"

"It's late, Sean. Can we please go to sleep? Tomorrow is a big day of flower picking and axe throwing and whatever else you guys have planned before a sea of guests arrive, and we have to lie to everyone about how long we've been dating and how much we mean to each other. Frankly, I need a solid night's sleep before I spend a day lying."

And there was nothing left for Sean to do but agree and turn out the light. He knew Hazel wouldn't object if he shared the king-sized bed with her, but for sanity and safety's sake, he opted for the couch.

Chapter Eighteen

Cressida looked stunning in her simple, elegant gown, holding her handpicked wildflowers. The emotion on Ian's face as he said his vows was as romantic as anything Hazel had ever witnessed.

And then there was Sean, who looked so damn handsome in his tux. Something had shifted this week—probably after he held her all night long—and this was no longer simple lust. Her feelings had gotten much more complex, and his rejection hurt that much more because of it.

The way he'd touched her by the campfire, she'd been sure they were about to take the next step, but instead, he claimed his acting had gotten out of hand.

She got it. The man didn't want her. She was done throwing herself at him and wouldn't make this weekend any more awkward than it had to be.

Goddamn Alec and his stupid need for secrecy. She didn't need a damn bodyguard.

Thankfully, the ceremony only lasted about fifteen minutes—it only felt like an eternity, with Sean up there, looking so hot, he should be a fire-code violation—and then the party began.

Much as she wanted to, she couldn't escape into their hotel room when the ceremony ended. As the best man's date, she would be dining with the bride and groom at a table that faced the rest of the guests. Her absence would be noted, and there was no way in hell she'd allow her heartache to be felt by the couple on their day. Or even Sean, for that matter. This wasn't his fault.

She didn't even blame him for teasing her by the fire. He'd been turned on by female proximity and was playing a role. It happened. She would let him have this day without making it about her. But come tomorrow when they left the inn, there would be strict no-touching rules. Her emotions were being jerked around like a yo-yo, and she would break if it continued beyond today.

Seated at the end of the table as she was, there wasn't anyone for her to talk to as Sean laughed and chatted with the groom and bride to his left. She stared at the guests, who were sorted into neat tables. NHHC employees here, Raptor operatives there. Bored, the anthropologist in her began to categorize the living guests in the same way she did bones: age, gender, and race.

At least fifty people were in attendance, and more than a third were Raptor operatives who worked either at the Virginia compound or the DC office. As Sean had said, this group was much more diverse. She estimated that nearly forty percent of the Raptor operatives present were Black, Hispanic, Asian, Native American, or East Indian. And she knew from meeting many of Alec's employees over the years they were gay, straight, trans, and one was gender noncon-forming.

After the meal, the band began to play, and Ian and Cressida had their first dance, followed by Curt claiming a dance with Cressida as the stand-in for father of the bride, while Ian danced with Cressida's mom.

Hazel toyed with the idea of asking Sean to dance, but if he didn't want to, that would be awkward. He hadn't spoken a word to her since Ian and Cressida left the table to dance, his attention on his conversation with Trina and Keith, who were seated on the other side of the bride and groom.

"Hazel!"

She turned to see JT Talon approaching her. "I wanted to thank you for saving T&D's ass this week."

She smiled at the engineering firm's CEO and stood to hug him. "Hey, JT, I was hoping you'd be here."

He kissed her cheek. "When Isabel told me you were on the job, I was relieved. We're in the middle of negotiating an on-call engineering contract for FERC relicensing projects. It's worth big bucks, and delays in the current projects will have a negative impact, even when it's not our fault. So basically, I owe you. Big."

"Good to know," she said, once again glad she hadn't let little things like mental health issues stop her from answering Isabel's cry for help. "If I end up hanging out a shingle and starting my own forensic consulting business, I could use a glowing endorsement."

"Done," JT said. He then turned to Sean, who'd stood to greet JT when she did. "Didn't know you and Hazel were a thing." He clapped Sean on the back. "Smart move."

"I have my moments," Sean said, shaking JT's hand. He leaned closer to Hazel but didn't touch her. Yesterday he'd have put his hand on the small of her back, but today, he'd kept his distance. It might be because her dress was backless, and the skin-to-skin touch would be intimate. Or he was done playing the boyfriend game and was phoning it in.

The reason didn't really matter. She wasn't going to ruin this for him because she was upset he'd rejected her again. That would be a crappy thing to do when he'd agreed to this assignment even knowing it would interfere with his ability to enjoy this party.

JT stayed and chatted for a bit, then he wandered off after extracting a promise from Hazel to visit the Bethesda office next week while he was in town. They'd just settled back into their seats when Ian and Cressida returned from the dance floor, faces flushed and happy.

The band's lead singer announced it was time for the garter and bouquet tossing, and Hazel groaned. As a single woman, she hated bouquet tosses with a passion, hated the idea that she was supposed to want to catch the bouquet. It always felt like her denials were assumed to be a lie.

It was one of the reasons she'd been thankful Ivy had eloped with Matt while Hazel was in Croatia. Otherwise, she'd probably have been maid of honor again, and there was no ducking the toss when you were in the wedding party.

Beside her, Sean let out his own groan. "You aren't really going to toss the garter, are you?" he asked Ian.

"I think it's a state law or something," Ian said. "But we're skipping the raunchy ungartering ceremony. I refuse to undress Cressida in front of an audience." He pulled the frilly white garter from his pocket. "Ready to fly. Let's go, best man. I'll fling it at you."

"No, thank you. Toss it to JT."

"JT's a no-go unless I want my ass kicked at our next sparring session. Shit, did you hear Alexandra has a baby? JT...he isn't dealing well."

Sean frowned. "Is Alexandra...with anyone?"

Ian shrugged. "Not really sure. Last I heard, she was in Europe on some sort of research grant. But Erica said she has a kid and is coming back to be near family. No word on if the dad is coming with her."

"Fine, toss the garter to Chase, then. I'll stay here and guard your drinks, like any good best man."

"No way. State law also requires single best men participate in the garter toss."

Hazel couldn't help but snicker.

"Just you wait, the bouquet toss is next," Sean said, rising from his seat.

"State law doesn't cover the date of the best man," she said.

Ian didn't even bother to turn his back before the toss. He pointed the elastic garter and shot it right at Sean's chest. Sean didn't catch it, but when it landed at his feet, he grudgingly picked it up to peals of laughter from all the married people in the room.

Married people thought this shit was hilarious. They should try being in their midthirties and being single at a wedding. It wasn't the least bit funny when the smell-of-desperation jokes started flying.

Hazel stayed firmly in her seat as the unmarried women assembled for Cressida's toss of her wildflower bouquet hand-picked by the groom. That gave Hazel a moment of pause. If she caught the bouquet, she could've given it back to Cressida so she could dry and keep the flowers.

But wouldn't you know it, Sean's real date for the wedding caught the flowers. Tricia laughed when the flowers landed in her hand, but her smile in the joint photo with Sean was something of a grimace, and Hazel felt guilty once again for stealing the woman's date, even though it hadn't been her fault.

The band started playing again, and Sean and Tricia, being at the center of the dance floor for their photo, started dancing.

Shit. If she'd caught the bouquet, that could be her dancing with Sean instead of her having this unsettling feeling that he belonged with the beautiful operative and not her. Tricia worked in the same field. She probably didn't have nightmares about murdered babies. She was athletic and smart and was probably everything Sean was looking for in a woman.

Ivy dropped into the empty seat beside her. "It's just a dance, Haze. He's here with you."

Oh hell, did her face show everything she was feeling? Had anyone other than Ivy noticed?

"I'm fine," she lied. "You having fun?"

Ivy nodded. "I am. But this is also making me so glad Matt and I eloped." She leaned in and whispered, "Erica dragged Cressida's mom up to a hotel room because she was getting ready to go full-on narcissist and cause a scene."

Hazel watched the bride, who beamed as she danced with her husband. "Does Cress know?"

"Nope, and we'll keep it that way."

She leaned on her sister. "I love how all of you take care of one another."

Ivy put her arm around Hazel. "Who would have thought the dorky MacLeod sisters would end up with such a cool group of friends?"

Hazel watched Sean dance with Tricia and knew her spot in this group would expire soon, but still, she'd enjoy the feeling of belonging, even if she was jealous of the beautiful operative.

Her gaze scanned the room, and she noticed a white man staring at the dancing couple, his eyes narrowed.

Was his problem with Sean, Tricia, or both?

He was handsome in a rugged sort of way, with long, sun-streaked hair pulled back in a ponytail. He didn't look like a

Raptor operative, but he was certainly buff like one. She leaned toward her sister and whispered, "Who's the guy in the burgundy shirt to the right? Long hair."

Ivy followed her gaze. "That's Liam Gibson. He's the new underwater archaeologist at UAB."

"They finally replaced Undine?"

"I'm irreplaceable," Undine said, dropping into Ian's vacated seat. "My position is still open. Liam replaced Erica around the time you left for Croatia. They've been filling in my spot with short-term interns. Greg is being really weird about the whole thing—but then, it took him nearly a year to replace Erica."

Dr. Greg Mulholland was the underwater archaeologist for the US Navy and the head of the Underwater Archaeology Branch within Naval History and Heritage Command. He was noticeably absent from the gathering, even though he was Cressida's direct supervisor.

Mara was head of NHHC, while Greg ran UAB. Ivy had told her that during Mara's maternity leave, Greg had gotten a little too comfortable as acting head of NHHC.

"Liam's hot," Hazel said. Then she remembered she was supposedly in a relationship. But then, that didn't mean she couldn't notice when other men were good-looking. She was in a fake relationship, not fake dead. "What's his issue with Sean and Tricia?"

Ivy frowned. "No clue."

As if he sensed their scrutiny, Liam turned and met Hazel's stare. Her instinct was to look away, but something about the way he cocked his head kept her gaze locked with his. A slow smile spread across his face, and he rose from his seat and made a beeline for her.

"Well, this should be interesting," Undine whispered.

He nodded to Ivy and Undine, then reached out a hand

to Hazel. "I'm Liam, and given the family resemblance, I'm guessing you're Ivy's sister."

She took his hand as she nodded. "Hazel MacLeod."

A corner of his mouth quirked. "Hazel and Ivy. Is your other sister Heather? Willow? Myrtle?"

She laughed as he released her hand. "Nah, you're way off. Laurel."

He chuckled. "What was I thinking?" He nodded toward the dance floor and raised a brow. "Would you like to dance?"

She considered saying no—it was a slow song, which could be awkward considering her fake boyfriend and the fact Liam was a complete stranger—but Sean was dancing with someone else, and Ivy worked with Liam, plus he wouldn't be here if he wasn't a friend of Cressida's. After all, not even Cressida's boss was here.

"Sure," she said, rising to her feet. With a nod to Undine and Ivy, she followed Liam to the dance floor.

He took her hips in his hands, pulling her an inch closer than necessary for the dance, but not so close as to be inappropriate for complete strangers. "Ivy said you're a forensic anthropologist."

"And she said you're an underwater archaeologist."

He smiled. "I am. Usually that's how I impress women, but not with this crowd."

She laughed. "Yeah. You're a dime a dozen here. Who do you want to impress?"

He looked down at her with a curious expression. His hands slid from her hips to the small of her back, pulling her a half inch closer. "I thought that was obvious when I asked you to dance."

"Well, this is awkward, then, because I'm here with another man."

"Here, maybe. But not with him. He's dancing with

another woman and hasn't so much as looked your way since you sat down to dinner."

Was Sean's distance that obvious? How embarrassing. She couldn't even keep the interest of a fake boyfriend.

"He's busy best-manning," she said in Sean's defense.

"That's fine, but while he's busy being best man, I'm doing my best to steal his date."

She cocked her head. "Why?"

"I'm familiar with the work you did for the Navy to identify the *Wrasse* seven, and Ivy has told me a lot about you. I've been looking forward to meeting you."

Her role in identifying the remains of the sailors who died on *Wrasse* in 1962 hadn't been in the documentary, but it wasn't a secret either. Plus he worked for UAB, so he'd know more details than most.

"Well, I hope I live up to your expectations."

He smiled, and his dark eyes crinkled at the corners. He really was handsome. Deep creases lined his face—the product of a life spent on the water, most likely—and gray peppered his long hair. She wouldn't do anything to embarrass Sean, but part of her wished she could lean into this moment. It was a heady feeling to have a mature, handsome man look at her that way.

It was a shame it was the wrong man.

The moment the asshole's hands landed on Hazel's bare back, Sean lost the ability to think. The guy was holding her too close, and if his fingers slipped a few millimeters lower, they'd be touching her ass. "Who's that guy dancing with Hazel?" he asked Tricia.

She narrowed her gaze. "I guess it was too much to hope I'd have your undivided attention for an entire song."

"Shit. I'm sorry. I—"

Tricia laughed. "I'm kidding! Mostly. Jeez, Sean, if you have it so bad for Hazel, why have you been avoiding looking at her all night? I figured you two'd been in a fight."

He frowned at her, utterly confused. "What?"

She raised a brow. "You can't be that clueless."

"I guess I must be. What are you talking about?"

"Wow. You've just made me very happy I'm not your date if you've no idea how you've been acting."

He furrowed his brow. "How have I been acting?"

"During dinner. You spent the entire time chatting with Ian. You practically had your back to Hazel. The first time you glanced in her direction was when JT Talon was talking to her. I figured there was trouble in paradise."

"I haven't—" He stopped himself, thinking back over dinner, trying to remember his conversation with Hazel, but all he remembered was talking to Ian and Cressida. They'd chatted about a few of Ian's Army buddies who couldn't make it, and Cressida's friend Suzanne, who was running a project on the other side of the world but had watched the ceremony in live stream.

Hazel hadn't been part of that conversation.

Had he really ignored her the entire meal? The small wedding party had been seated on one side of a banquet table that faced the rest of the guests. Hazel had been on the end, just as Keith had been seated to Trina's left on the other end of the table. If he'd ignored her with his back to her through the entire meal, she'd been forced to sit and stare at the assembled guests, saying nothing for…twenty, thirty minutes?

He was a complete asshole, and now everyone here knew it. Worse, Hazel had to be embarrassed and hurt.

He turned Tricia so he was facing Hazel and her dance partner. She laughed at something the guy said, and her smile was genuine. His gut clenched. He didn't like seeing her with another man. Especially when the guy was looking at her like he hoped she'd be his dessert.

The song ended, and he thanked Tricia for the dance and debated what to do. The next song was a faster number, and Hazel and the guy broke apart as Ivy, Matt, and Julian joined them on the dance floor. Hazel took Julian's hands and began to dance with the boy. She laughed as they twirled, and Sean went back to his seat, not wanting to interrupt her happy moment.

Seeing her dancing with such exuberance, as she had in Grand Cayman, made his heart feel lighter. She suffered from nightmares and feared losing the career that meant every-thing to her, but right at this moment, he could see the flush of joy on her skin and the light of pleasure in her eyes.

He'd seen her as a party girl without understanding her flip side, the intensely serious forensic anthropologist. Now this joyful woman made sense, and had far more depth than he'd ever given her credit for.

She danced with all of her body, unselfconsciously. She wasn't shy and danced with everyone—men, women, chil-dren, and gender nonconforming alike. The guy who'd danced with her for the slow dance remained in her orbit, but she didn't show him more or less attention than the others.

Most of the guests were on the dance floor. The energy of the room was electric, the bride and groom in the center of the happy dancing mass. But his eyes were fixed on his beautiful date. He'd lusted after her for years, and now, when he could finally have her, he was sitting on the sidelines.

She must've felt his stare because she turned and met his gaze. She stopped moving, then slowly, she smiled. A broad, happy, warm smile. Beckoning, even.

The weight on his chest lifted. Being with Hazel made

him feel good, and, like a dumbass, he kept pushing her away.

He rose from his seat, rounded the table, and crossed the room to the dance floor. It was time to claim a dance with his date.

She smiled as he danced up beside her, and bumped him with her hip, letting out a playful laugh. They danced side by side in a group that included Ivy's family, Erica, and Lee, who was at the edge of the floor where it was less crowded, dancing with his daughter in his arms.

The song ended, and everyone paused to catch their breath. Julian dramatically pressed his hand to his forehead and said, "I'm exthausted!" The word came out with a lisp because he was missing his top front teeth. "Can we have cake now?"

Ivy laughed. "Not now, but probably soon. Let's get you some water."

She held out her hand, and he took it, grabbing Matt's with his other hand. He then leapt up and swung between his parents. "Aunt Hazel said there are two kinds of cake! Chocolate and lemon. Can I have both, Mom?"

It was the first time Sean had heard Julian call Ivy "Mom," and his heart squeezed. He hoped to hell Matt was the man they all believed him to be, because if Julian was hurt in the fallout, Sean would have to beat the crap out of the Hammer.

The first notes of the next song began, and this one was a slow tune. Lots of guests left the floor, but couples stayed, including Ian and Cressida. Sean turned to Hazel and pulled her into his arms without asking. She was stiff against him for a moment, then looked up at him in confusion as she draped her arms around his neck.

"You're an impossible man to read, Sean Logan." The

words were said softly, close to his ear. Only he could hear them under the music.

"Tricia pointed out to me what an ass I was during dinner, and I'm sorry. I shouldn't have ignored you."

She held his gaze as she swayed against him, then slowly, she gave him the slightest of smiles. "Have I mentioned that I really like Tricia?"

He gave her a soft laugh, then cupped her cheek and leaned down to whisper in her ear, "I do too, but I like *you* more." His lips brushed her ear, and it wasn't an accident. He wanted to suck on the lobe and then slide his lips down her neck to her collarbone.

Clavicle, he mentally corrected. Hazel would call it by the proper name. Maybe she'd teach him about bones as he explored her body.

He pulled her closer to him, tucking her in the crook of his arm as he twirled with her. Tricia came into view. She was dancing with the guy Hazel had danced with earlier, and he didn't feel the slightest stir of jealousy.

He pulled Hazel tighter, spreading his hand across the bare skin at her back, and gave in to an urge and pressed his lips to her neck and breathed in her scent. Again he caught that nutty, almost chocolaty, scent that was so familiar. This time it clicked. Before he'd left the room to give her space to get ready for the wedding, he'd seen a bottle of essential oils beside the big bathtub. He met her gaze and smiled. "Hazelnut?"

She nodded. "It's my signature scent." She winked at him. "And my nominal one."

"I like it." He leaned forward and whispered, "It makes me want to dip you in chocolate and eat you."

Her eyes flared with heat. "I think the champagne has gone to your head."

He grinned and shook his head. "Not even a little bit."

He cupped her cheek, tilting her head back. He brushed his lips lightly over hers, then shifted his arms so she was cradled against him as they swayed to the music.

He wanted to kiss her here, now, but she would assume this was fake, part of their cover story, and he didn't want her to think he kissed her only for show, so instead, he held her as they swayed to the music and simply enjoyed the feel of her pressed to his body.

Chapter Nineteen

$\mathcal{S}$ean Logan held her like he wanted her, and Hazel thought she might melt into the dance floor. She'd be nothing but a puddle of chocolate sprinkled with ground hazelnuts. Sultry lyrics enveloped her along with Sean's arms. This was the place she'd wanted to be for so damn long.

She was lost in a dreamy haze when the last notes faded and Sean cupped her face and lowered his mouth to hers. His kiss was soft, sweet. Intimate and just a bit lingering. He took her hand and led her back to their seats.

Their table was empty as Ian and Cressida remained on the dance floor. Under the table, out of sight of anyone who might be watching, Sean held her hand, his thumb lightly stroking her knuckles in a touch that was only for her benefit.

The cake was cut and served, followed by more dancing and then the toasts. Sean and Trina teamed up and took turns reading a speech they'd cowritten. It was funny and touching, and Ian, Cressida, Trina, and Sean all had tears in their eyes at the end.

After that, they danced to the live music until neighborhood ordinance required quiet and the band packed up their equipment. The flower girl was asleep in her mother's arms, and the ring bearer valiantly fought to stay on his feet by the time Ian and Cressida climbed into their firewood-filled SUV to take off for their honeymoon. The vehicle was pelted with birdseed as they drove away.

Guests not staying at the inn piled into cars to head to the larger chain motel a mile down the road. A few guests had snagged the remaining rooms at the inn, including Raptor operatives Josh, Tricia, and boyishly sweet Chase.

Chase had played a role in whatever happened in Alaska to Isabel, but Hazel remained in the dark as to what it was. She knew Isabel was fond of the young man, but she worried about him too.

After seeing the bride and groom off, they entered the inn again to find the remaining Raptor operatives and their partners gathered in the front sitting room. Sean held her hand as he entered the room. Keith held up a beer in offering.

"Nah," Sean said. "Not staying. Just saying good night. Today was a blast, but I'm beat." He bent down and kissed Trina's cheek. "You did an amazing job making this weekend special for all of us. Thank you for your help with best man duties."

Trina beamed. "Thank you, Sean. You were great too."

Hazel said her good-nights as well, and, with her hand firmly in Sean's, she followed him from the room and up the stairs. She didn't know what to expect tonight, given all the hand-holding that hadn't been for show. But no matter what, Hazel would not make a move on Sean.

Been there. Done that. Had the rejections to prove it. If this was going to happen, it was up to him.

Sean fished his key card out of a pocket and unlocked the door. He whisked her inside, closed the door, and pressed her against it. "That dress is too damn sexy. All night long, I've been imagining yanking up the skirt and burying myself deep inside you."

Oh my. "Are you sure you haven't had too much to drink?" She had to ask again, because that was the most un-Sean-like thing he'd ever said.

He shook his head, piercing her with a hot gaze. "Oh, Hazelnut, if you only knew how many fantasies I've had about you over the years." He smiled slowly. "Have you ever had fantasies about me?"

"Hazelnut" was the sort of nickname that could be an insult, but coming from Sean in that sexy voice, as she remembered what he'd said earlier about dipping her in chocolate, it turned her knees weak. She wanted him to call her that again and again and again.

"Not even one?" he asked as he nibbled on her neck.

It took her a moment to remember his original question. Her brain had pretty much exploded when he mentioned fantasies about her. Ahh, yes. He wanted to know her fantasies. "Maybe." She ran a hand over his shoulders and down his chest. He'd removed his jacket and bow tie hours ago, but he still wore the smooth white shirt. She wanted it off so she could see the muscles she'd gotten to ogle in Grand Cayman, when he'd accompanied them to the beach, dressed in swim trunks and an open Aloha shirt, like any tourist.

"How do your fantasies start?" he asked. "Mine always start with me threading my fingers through your hair." As he spoke, he cradled her head in one palm while his other hand slid into her hair, which she wore up in a braided bun. He plucked out a hairpin and then another, and the braids and loose strands fell, giving him something to slide his fingers through.

She closed her eyes and enjoyed the feel of his nails on

her scalp. She let out a soft purr and said, "My fantasies usually start with a kiss." Her voice was husky to her own ears. "Pinned to the wall, like now, your mouth on mine, showing me how you plan to possess me."

"I think we've been having the same fantasy."

And then his mouth was on hers. His tongue slid inside without hesitation as he kissed her deep and hot. Carnal. Intense. It was the kind of kiss that could make her forget how to stand. Or breathe.

He lifted her, sliding up the skirt of her dress to free her legs. She wrapped her thighs around his hips. His arm under her ass and the door at her back supported her as his thick erection pressed her center. He rocked his hips, teasing her, driving her insane with arousal.

"Yes, this is definitely one of my fantasies," she said into his mouth.

"In your fantasies, do I fuck you against the door, or do we make it to the bed?"

She loved that he used the word fuck, because that was how this felt. Wild. Carnal. Dirty. Just like her fantasies. "Depends."

Right now, the hot-and-wild-against-the-door fantasy topped her list. But slow-and-sensual-on-the-bed was another favorite.

"Hazelnut. Witch Hazel. Beautiful, mesmerizing Hazel." His tongue dipped into her mouth between each phrase. "You drive me so fucking wild. Always have."

"Then why haven't we been here before now?" she asked.

"You're my boss's cousin," he said matter-of-factly.

She supposed she understood, but at the same time, they didn't live in an era where male relatives had a say in their female relatives' love lives, and having known Alec since the day she was born, she knew without a doubt that her cousin could separate business from family. "Keith's been your boss for the last three years," she said.

"Not today." He again thrust his hips, causing her mind to momentarily blank. He kissed her again, cutting off any response she might've made if she could think.

He raised his head and met her gaze. "Taking you against the door is a waste of a very good bed." He slipped an arm behind her back and carried her to the big four-poster. He set her down in the center and smiled. "Especially when I want to explore all of you."

Her dress had hiked up to her hips, exposing her tiny red thong. He cupped a bare butt cheek and squeezed as he held her gaze. "Have I ever told you how fucking hot you are in those glasses?"

She laughed. "Um…no?" She wasn't about to point out he'd never called her hot at all.

"What the hell is wrong with me? Those glasses are so damn sexy. Say one of your technical bone words."

"Technical bone word? Like when I was describing the skeletons?"

"Yeah." He leaned down. "Wait!" He slipped a hand beneath her neck and unhooked the single fastener that closed her dress's collar and held up the bodice. He pulled the front down, exposing her breasts. The backless dress had required her to go braless. "Oh fuck. So beautiful. Now say something technical."

She reached up and unbuttoned his shirt as she said the first words that came to mind. "Nasal, maxilla, lacrimal, ethmoid, sphenoid."

"What are those?"

"The bones of the eye socket from medial to proximal."

"I didn't know there were so many eye bones."

"Did you know that the jaw is the only joint in the body that's a hinge *and* a sliding joint?"

"Not even a little bit."

"Come closer," she said, "and I'll demonstrate." She stroked his erection through his slacks, letting him know with her hand exactly what she meant.

He took her wrists in each of his hands and pinned them to the bed above her head. "In due time," he said, then kissed her. This kiss was slow but deep, and she melted into the mattress. His body above hers, his hands trapping her as he kissed her hot and urgent. This definitely matched one of her many fantasies of Sean Logan.

He released her wrists and supported his weight by planting his fists on either side of her head. His mouth withdrew from hers slowly, and he pushed up, extending his elbows until he was upright and straddling her. His mouth was wet from her lips, and his eyes burned with desire. "Before this goes any further, I need to tell you something."

Shit. What STDs were deal breakers? Most could be prevented with condoms if they were careful. But oral sex would be out unless they had a nonspermicidal condom and dental dams. She mentally braced herself. "Okay."

"As soon as I can, I'm going back to the Middle East. I don't want to lead you on, and this can't go anywhere, relationshipwise."

That was…not what she was braced to hear. And from the ache it triggered in her chest, she realized an STD reveal wouldn't upset her like this did. At least if he'd been warning her about a sexually transmitted disease, she'd know it was because he cared about her health.

But no. He didn't care about her. He just wanted to get laid.

She scooted back on the bed, shifting up on her elbows. Her dress rolled as she moved. She was practically naked and didn't care. "So you're…dumping me before we even have sex?"

"No." He shook his head in confusion. "I just… I wanted to be clear about my plans."

"So basically, all that stuff you were saying about how much you want me…you meant you want me *now*. This minute. But have no interest in tomorrow."

"Well, we're stuck together for as long as you need a bodyguard, so I was sort of thinking we could have tomorrow and even the next few weeks. But after that, I'm leaving, and I don't do long-distance."

Nice. Sean wanted to get laid, and he'd decided that after rejecting her multiple times, he might as well take her for a spin. After all, as long as he was stuck guarding her, she was the only vagina available to him.

She was *so* not game.

She scooted back farther, pulling up the top of her dress to cover her breasts. "So you want a fuck buddy until it's no longer convenient for you. And then you want to be able to walk away because I don't mean anything to you."

"What? No! I care about you! That's why I'm telling you this now."

"Right. There's just one problem. We've known each other too long to be no-strings fuck buddies. I'm not saying I expected this was the beginning of a relationship, but I at least thought it had a *chance* of evolving into one. But if you're shutting that door before we've given it a try, what's the point? Five feet from here is a drawer full of devices that can give me an orgasm without making sure I know they need to be free to try other pussy across the ocean at the first opportunity."

"That's not what I said, Hazel."

"Really? Then what did you mean?"

He opened his mouth to protest, but nothing came out.

"Yeah. I thought so." She climbed off the bed and straightened her dress over her hips. "Congratulations.

You're just another asshole who got drunk and horny at a wedding."

His jaw tightened. "I had one glass of champagne today."

"Well then, sober Sean is even worse than drunk Sean. At least drunk Sean had the courage to admit he'd gotten carried away last night. What's your excuse tonight? Tricia didn't want you?"

"No! Dammit, I want *you*. I've always wanted you."

"You have a bizarre way of showing it, rejecting me at every opportunity. And if you wanted me, you wouldn't throw out caveats to push me away, right before you're about to have me. I'm sorry, Sean, but I liked you too much to accept your terms."

"Liked?"

She shrugged. "Good news, maybe you've cured me of my infatuation. And bonus, I can guarantee I won't throw myself at you and make you feel awkward again." She turned to the closet to grab a coat and sneakers. She needed to walk. Outside. Her head might explode if she didn't get outside fast.

"Hazel—"

She slipped on her jacket.

"You can't leave. I'm your bodyguard. Twenty-four seven."

"You really should have thought of that before you told me how much I don't mean to you, but that you want to fuck me anyway."

"I never said—"

"Listen, I'm trying to hold my shit together and not start crying. I'm about ten seconds from losing it. I. Need. Air." Her voice wavered.

He grabbed the room key and his tux jacket from where he'd dropped them on the floor and began buttoning up his shirt. "You're not allowed to be more than ten feet away from me."

Oh, sweet hell. As if crying over his rejection wasn't painful enough, he would have front-row seats to her humiliating breakdown.

None of this would be happening if she'd just sucked it up and stayed in Croatia.

Chapter Twenty

Sean followed Hazel at a short distance. He wished he could give her more space, but he was a dipshit and an ass and hadn't foreseen this scenario. Why hadn't he realized how his words would sound to her? Or worse, that it wasn't so much the way they *sounded* as what they'd actually *meant*?

He'd wanted to have his Hazelnut cake and eat her too, and then walk away without any messy emotions. But as she'd said, their friendship had passed any friends-with-benefits possibilities months, maybe even years ago.

Hell, wasn't that why he'd rejected her in Grand Cayman, because they couldn't have sex and expect things to go back to the way they'd been before? Because he hadn't wanted Rav to fire his ass for breaking his cousin's heart?

And now here he was, following her down the stairs as she raced toward the exit so she could have space from him to cry with a veneer of privacy.

He was a complete asshole.

She took a sharp turn at the bottom of the stairs so she wouldn't pass by the salon where the Raptor operatives were gathered. He could hear Keith's laughter and was glad for her discretion.

How could he have put her in this situation?

She headed toward a side door that led to the garden that backed up to the national forest. She passed another salon and tucked her head down but didn't break stride. When he passed, he knew why she'd tried to slip by unnoticed. Matt sat with his body hunched forward, elbows to knees, engaged in intense conversation with Chase.

That was an odd combination. Sean didn't know if the two had ever met before today, but the young operative looked at Matt with rapt attention.

Unease trickled down Sean's spine, but he didn't pause as he passed the arched opening. Hazel had reached the French doors that led to the garden, and he had to follow her. Once she was outside, she broke into a run, heading for the woods, forcing him to do the same.

In all his thirty-eight years, he didn't think he'd ever hurt someone this deeply. That the person he'd hurt was Hazel, a woman he cared about more than he wanted to admit, and who was fighting anxiety because of her work to identify victims of genocide, made him question everything he believed about himself.

What is wrong with me?

This was Hazel. Beautiful, sexy, brilliant, amazing Hazel.

My Hazelnut. My sweet, seductive Witch Hazel.

He'd just made the worst fucking mistake of his life.

She reached the woods and slipped between the trees. He followed her winding path until they were deep in the forest. "You need to stay in my line of sight," he said when she kept ducking behind trees.

She turned to face him. Moonlight penetrated the branches, and he could see she'd managed to stave off tears in favor of anger. She was well and truly pissed. And he had it coming. "Why, because you want to see me cry? Because it makes you feel powerful to see me humiliated?"

"That's the last thing in the world I want."

"No, Sean. I think what you meant to say is *I'm* the last thing in the world you want."

"Oh, sweetheart. That is so far from being true. I've wanted to fuck you since the first night we met. I had fantasies of pulling you into the closet by the entryway and fucking you between the coats. When you took me outside to see the Milky Way, I wanted to pull down your panties and go down on you as you watched for shooting stars. My fantasies about you are endless. Wild. And very dirty." He took a step toward her. "Filthy, even."

Her chest rose with a deep breath, and he was thankful for the full moon that allowed him to see her eyes light with heat. "I like filthy," she whispered. Tentative.

"Yeah?" he asked, inviting her to say more.

She held his gaze in the darkness, her skin bright in the milky glow of the moon. Finally, she said, "That night, I wanted to escape into the woods with you and take you into my mouth. I'd just met you, but I wanted to be wild. Dirty." She paused, then added, "Filthy, even."

His cock hardened as he remembered that night and how sultry she'd looked in a low-cut green silk cocktail dress. Her auburn hair had shimmered in the moonlight just like now.

She continued in a husky voice, "I wanted you to plant my hands against the rough bark of a tree and take me from behind. I wanted to feel you thrusting inside me as you cupped my breasts." She took a step toward him now.

"If I'd taken you in the woods at Rav's," he responded, "we couldn't have returned to the party without everyone knowing I'd just banged my boss's cousin in the yard mere hours after we met." That was only part of the reason he hadn't acted that night—his dad's recent passing had also loomed in his mind—but it was the major reason he'd held back.

"I know. So instead when I got home, I fucked myself with my favorite toys and imagined your cock, your fingers, your tongue. It was the first of many times I've fantasized about you. I've wanted you for four and a half long years. Until this week, except for that embarrassing night in Grand Cayman, I pretty much accepted you don't want me in the same way."

"Oh, Hazel, that has never been true. I've always wanted you. I want to lick you. I want you to come against my mouth. I want your mouth on my cock, your hands on my body. I want your sweet, hot pussy tight on my cock." He'd never dared talk dirty with Hazel before. But he'd imagined it, saying filthy things to her as he claimed her body. "You've been front and center in my fantasies since that night in Rav's garden."

She put a hand on his chest. "Show me, Sean. Take me. Here. Now."

He wanted to, desperately. But she'd given him a very clear no to a no-strings screw just fifteen minutes ago, and nothing had changed since then. "I don't think this is what you want."

"Maybe this will get you out of my system."

"What if it just makes the ache worse?"

She smiled. "That confident, are you?"

"I've wanted you for four and a half years, so yeah, I will satisfy all your filthy fantasies."

"That's a tall order considering right now, in this forest, is the only time you can have me."

She'd just turned his own limits on him. He'd asked for temporary—until he returned to the Middle East—but she would only give him right here, right now.

And he was just enough of an asshole to accept her

terms. He planted a hand on the back of her bare thigh and slid upward, under the skirt of her dress, until he cupped a bare cheek of her sweetly rounded ass. His mouth was just inches from hers. "You want me to fuck you, right now. Under this tree?"

"Yes."

"Will you let me push up your skirt and go down on you, make you come against my mouth?"

She licked her lips. "Yes." She ran her hand over his out-of-control erection. "As long as you give me this. Tonight, *this* is mine."

His mouth hovered above hers. "All yours." He kissed her, his tongue stroking deep. He cupped both ass cheeks and squeezed. Fuck, she felt good, and he was finally going to have her.

"We have one problem, Hazelnut. I left the condoms in our hotel room."

"When was the last time you were tested? Are you clean?"

He considered the question. Raptor required annual checkups, mental, physical, the works. He always had the doctor run the full battery of STD tests. "About three months ago. I'm clean. I haven't been with anyone since before Grand Cayman." It was rare for him to go so long without even a casual hookup, but since that night, he hadn't wanted anyone but Hazel.

"I haven't been with anyone since my last round of tests before Croatia. I'm clean, and birth control is covered—I had the three-year implant eighteen months ago."

"You want me to fuck you bare?" His cock thickened even more. He couldn't remember the last time he'd had sex without a condom. He rarely dated women long enough to reach the no-condom stage.

"Yes. Tonight is all we get. Might as well have the full fantasy."

He should tell her he wanted more than right now, but the words wouldn't leave his mouth. He was such an asshole to take what she was giving him without offering her more. But he didn't know how to give more. He could—and would —satisfy her now.

He dropped to his knees and pushed up her skirt, just like he'd fantasized so very long ago. Her tiny thong was hardly in his way, but he ripped it off anyway, breaking the thin straps and shoving the scrap of satin into his pocket. She gasped as he spread her legs and licked her clit for the first time.

She'd trimmed but hadn't shaved, and he wished the moonlight would let him see just how red her curls were. She moaned as he licked from clit to labia. He spread her folds and slid his tongue inside. She was tangy and slick and so fucking good. She bucked as he focused on her clitoris, licking and sucking, grazing his teeth over the bundle of sensitive nerves.

Her legs wobbled. He pushed her back against a tree to stabilize her, then stroked her with his tongue until she came to a shuddering orgasm against his mouth. Her moans rang through the forest, and he hoped no one else had opted for an outside tryst. These sounds she made were his and his alone.

She cupped his shaved head as she came, both holding him to her, then pushing him back when the pleasure got too intense.

He released her and stood as she flopped back against the tree, breathing hard. He needed to be inside her slick, wet heat now. He turned her around and peeled off the coat she wore. He wanted to see her bare back in that sexy dress as he fucked her. The cool air on her shoulders triggered goose bumps, but he'd warm her from the inside out. She wouldn't feel the chill in just a moment. He pressed her palms into the rough bark of the tree, then unzipped his fly and freed his cock.

He raised her skirt and looked at her bare ass in the moonlight. Holy fuck. She was giving herself to him, letting him take her bare. He stroked his thick erection as he looked at her beautiful ass. "You ready for this, babe?"

"God, yes."

He placed the head of his cock against her opening and slid deep in one hot, slick stroke. "Holy hell." He groaned at the sensation of being deep inside Hazel MacLeod. He placed his right hand over her right, pressing it into the bark. His left hand slid under the halter of her dress and cupped her breast. He kissed her neck as he fucked and squeezed.

Taking Hazel exceeded his fantasies, a feat that shouldn't be possible given the years he'd had to perfect them.

"Sean." His name was a moan. A perfect, sexy breath of sound, drawn out because he was making her feel wild. Dirty. Filthy, even.

He thrust into her, taking her hard, going faster than he'd intended, but it felt too damn good to stop. He moved a hand to her clit and stroked, determined to make her climax again before he got his own orgasm.

She tightened around him, and her breathing changed. She was almost there. And she was pulling him with her. She let out a guttural cry at the same time his orgasm overtook him. He pulsed into her, letting out his own grunt as he came.

He held her still against the tree, his heart pounding.

He knew only one thing in that moment. One time with Hazel would never be enough.

Chapter Twenty-One

*W*ell, that was one way to stave off a panic attack. Hazel had a feeling Dr. Parks wouldn't approve, but then, whatever works, right? And she'd been so close to a full-blown panic attack when Sean said those sexy words that pulled her from the brink.

Definitely not something that would be found in psychology texts. Or would it? Hazel's ology expertise was of the osteological variety. She knew nothing about studies of the mind, which was probably why hers was so messed up.

She let out a soft whimper as Sean slid from her body, his fingers stroking her clit on the dismount. He kissed her neck and whispered, "Don't think this is over, because we're just getting started."

She wanted to sink into those words. She could have Sean. Today. This week. Even next. He'd give her that if she asked. But then he'd leave for the Middle East, taking her heart with him.

If she was to have any dignity left when it came to her feelings for Sean Logan, she had to be the one to end this. She had to be the one to walk away.

So far, she'd done all the begging and he'd done all the rejecting. Time for a role reversal.

Always leave them wanting more, right?

She'd said yes to wild, dirty, outdoor sex. She'd even agreed to no condoms, because if she was going to have Sean only once, it would be as perfect a connection as she could make it. A memory to last until her heart found a way to quit him.

But now, for the first time in the four and a half years of their pathetic association, she was calling the shots. She pushed away from the tree and scooped up her jacket from the ground where he'd dropped it. She patted the pocket and was thankful to find the bandana she always stored there.

She used it to wipe between her legs, cleaning the evidence of Sean's ejaculation so the walk back to the inn would be more comfortable. Sean reached out, offering to help with the intimate task, but she refused. "No, thanks."

She shoved the dirty cloth back into her pocket and met his gaze. His brow furrowed. He probably expected her to want to kiss and cuddle.

And she did want that. But if she gave in to it now, it would be that much harder to push him away later. Thankfully, they were in the woods, not entwined in a bed. Really, she couldn't have planned this better. She'd had her taste of Sean Logan in a way that fulfilled her very first fantasy of him, but without the intimacy that would allow him to see how utterly broken her heart was that he didn't want more than a passing fling.

She'd known for years she could fall in love with Sean. What she'd never quite realized until this week—maybe she'd just figured it out tonight—was that she was already in love with him, and had been for a long time.

There was no way she could continue with this charade

of fake boyfriend/real bodyguard. Her heart would shatter like calcined bone under pressure.

She took Sean's shirt in her hands. This would be their last kiss. Her goodbye to all the hope she'd had of sharing her life with this man. "Thank you, Sean. That was just what I needed." She kissed him. His lips were stiff against hers at first, wary. He knew she was withdrawing, and he didn't understand. Of course he didn't.

For him, this was the simple start and end of a fling, while for her, she was losing a friendship that had mattered a great deal to her. Hell, she was losing this entire group of friends except her sister and cousin. She'd never belong in this group once she and Sean officially broke up. These were his friends, not hers.

A shame, because she really liked everyone.

All at once, Sean's mouth relaxed and he deepened the kiss. Showing emotion with his mouth that he never gave her with words. He knew this was a good-bye as much as she did.

Finally, she ended the kiss. Sean's arm was a tight band around her back, holding her against him, but when she pushed back, he released her.

"Tomorrow, I'll tell Alec that we no longer require your services. If he still insists I need a bodyguard, he'll have to hire someone else."

"It doesn't have to be this way, Hazel."

"Don't worry about your job. I'll make sure he knows it's my fault. Not yours."

"I don't give a fuck about my job. I'm talking about us."

"There has never been any *us*. It was all a charade."

"But it doesn't have to end this way. Now."

"Yes. It does." *It's the only way I can protect myself from completely falling apart.* "I told you before we screwed, this was all we'd have. I meant it."

His nostrils flared. "I guess I didn't believe you."

Frankly, she hadn't believed herself either. She was rather proud she'd followed through, considering he was the one thing she wanted in the world. But she was taking care of herself, which should have been her focus all along. "You don't want me, Sean. I'm more broken than not." She glanced over at the tree she'd held on to as he thrust inside her. "I was about three steps from a full-blown panic attack. This method of dealing with it wasn't…conventional, but I'm thankful just the same."

Sean's eyes widened, and he stepped back. "I took advantage of you while you were losing it?"

She shook her head. "No. You helped me. But I really need to take it from here if I'm going to get better. Can't always count on you to be there to fuck me back to my senses, can I? Not when you're heading to the Middle East. I've got to figure this out on my own."

"I'm sorry—"

She waved him off. "Don't be. I enjoyed it. A lot." She leaned forward and stroked his cheek. He'd shaved right before the wedding, and his skin was silky smooth. "You are every bit the amazing lover I knew you'd be. I'm glad I got a sample."

That last part might've sounded insulting. She couldn't really tell, but she meant it. What she didn't say was how much she would cherish the memory of their hot, dirty, fantasy-fulfillment screw.

He caught her wrist when she would've turned to walk away. His eyes burned with remorse and anger, as if he didn't know which emotion to go with. "Don't do this, Hazel."

"Do what? Walk away from you after fucking you? Isn't that what you'd planned to do to me?"

His eyes widened, and he stepped back. "So this was revenge? To put me in my place?"

She shook her head. "No. It was just a screw. Because I wanted to try you at least once." Then she turned and walked away.

Sean couldn't quite believe what had just happened. One moment, he had everything he wanted in the world, and the next, she was walking away from him.

And once again, it was his own stupid fault.

He never reacted rationally to Hazel, because she'd spun him up and tied him in knots for years. The woman he'd always wanted but never thought he could have.

And now he'd had her, and she was rejecting him. He wanted to hold on to anger, but how could he? He'd screwed her as she was fighting a panic attack? What kind of asshole did that?

He should have recognized what was happening. After her appointment with Dr. Parks, Hazel had explained the techniques he could employ to help her. And nowhere on the list of grounding exercises was banging her in the woods.

He followed her through the trees. A chill breeze licked through the leaves, making a soft rattling sound. The air smelled of crisp, dry earth, but he still had Hazel's scent on his body and the memory of the sweet, chocolate nutty oil that permeated her skin and teased him as he'd kissed her neck and thrust inside her.

All at once, a gust whipped through the leaves, the cold portent of fall. Hazel wore her skimpy dress, sneakers, and a lightweight coat. She shivered as she marched ahead of him.

A loud crack sounded, the unmistakable sound of a bullet. He dove for Hazel, pushing her to the ground, covering her body with his own. The only protection he could give her.

A moment later, a massive boom rang out as light flared beyond the woods, illuminating the dark night.

That could be only one thing. An explosion. Inside or near the inn.

Chapter Twenty-Two

Sean patted Hazel down to be certain she hadn't been hurt by the gunshot. Relief swept through him. She was fine except for possible bruises when he'd shoved her to the ground.

She pushed at his chest. "We need to check on the others," she said.

He shook his head. Much as he wanted to, his job was to protect her, and taking her to the inn and the site of the explosion would break that first rule. "We can't. Not until we know more." He pulled out his cell and dialed Rav, who answered immediately. "Hazel's fine. With me in the woods. Isabel?"

"Safe. In our hotel room."

"Where was the explosion?"

"The parking lot. Looks like a vehicle blew up."

"I heard a gunshot. You can't blow up a car by shooting the gas tank."

"Yeah, someone must've set up an explosive that could be ignited with a bullet."

His phone beeped, and he could see it was Keith, initiating a group call for all operatives. Ian's name was omitted from the list of recipients, thank goodness. The guy had left for his damn honeymoon less than two hours ago.

"We gotta take the call," Rav said. "Reminder: the threat to Isabel and Hazel is still classified."

Sean didn't need to be told, but he understood why Rav had to say it. He accepted Keith's call. "Logan. Outside. Fifty yards east of the inn in the woods with Hazel. No injuries."

All operatives, including Rav, checked in, giving their location and status. No one was injured. All but Sean and Hazel were inside the inn.

Keith summed up the situation. "Some sort of explosive was set off under Chase Johnston's Prius. I'm sending Chase, Matt, Tricia, and Josh to search the woods for whoever fired the shot, but odds are the person is long gone. Lee, Curt, and JT are rounding up fire extinguishers to put out the spot fires ignited by the flying debris. Fire department is on its way to deal with the Prius, but the fire's mostly out there—big flash, little burn. Car's toast. The Prius parked nearby is also damaged. That one yours, Rav?"

"Yes," he answered.

Interesting. Two Priuses, both blue, one an older model, the other less than a year old. Was Chase's car targeted by mistake?

Either way, it would be a warning to Rav. And maybe a sign Isabel was the target.

"Sean," Keith said. "I want you to search the inn with Luke."

Sean was glad for that order, because it wasn't in direct conflict with his orders from Rav, which were to protect Hazel. He could leave Hazel with Rav as he searched the hotel.

"Send everyone who is not actively searching or dealing with the fire to my suite," Rav said. "I'll talk to the hotel manager. We need a head count, make sure no one was hurt or is missing."

Sean hit End. "I'm taking you to Rav's suite."

She nodded. "We need to stop at our room on the way. I need underwear. And a change of clothes. I can shower in Rav's room."

He nodded. He didn't relish the idea of her smelling like sex for the next few hours as they investigated the blast either. No point in rubbing it in his boss's face how badly he'd messed up with Hazel.

She grabbed her clothes and toiletries, and they hurried to Rav's suite. Others had already gathered, including Erica and Mara holding their sleeping children. Julian was asleep on the couch in the far corner of the large room as Ivy and Rav shared what was clearly an intense conversation. The moment Hazel entered the room, she abruptly stopped speaking, and Sean guessed she'd been discussing whether or not it was possible this had anything to do with Matt's past.

"Where is Catherine?" Sean asked, referring to Mara's mother.

"She's packing up the babies' bags," Mara said. "She, Erica, the babies, and I are going to drive back to DC as soon as we can."

Ivy bit her lip, then said, "Will you take Julian too?" Her gaze flicked to Hazel, then she added, "Matt needs to stay and be interviewed. He saw the explosion. And frankly, I'm worried about Julian overhearing too much and this becoming a traumatic memory for him. He still dreams about the car accident that killed his parents as if he'd been there."

"Of course," Mara said. "He can stay with us for as long as you need."

Sean took that as a coded offer to protect the boy should Matt have been compromised. Curt and Mara had a state-of-the-art security system that rivaled Rav's. The guy was a former cabinet member, and his name had been floated more than once as a potential presidential candidate. That brought out the crazies.

"Thank you," Ivy said.

"I need to search the hotel," Sean said to Rav. "You good here?"

"Yes," Rav answered as more people arrived, including Undine and Luke.

Sean didn't look at or say good-bye to Hazel, much as he wanted to. Others were watching, and he and Hazel needed to work out their issues in private.

Sean led Luke to his room, where he picked up his gun and holster from the room safe. He'd worn a small gun at his ankle during the wedding, which he now passed to Luke, along with an extra radio headset, as he donned his own.

"You always travel with your gear?" Luke asked.

He did, but it was usually in the back of his SUV. He'd put it in the room safe because this was a working vacation, but he couldn't tell Luke that. "Yes."

"Did you expect something to happen this weekend?" Luke asked, a note of concern in his voice.

"No, but after we visited the rally yesterday, I wondered if we were waving a red flag in front of a bull." This was true enough.

Luke nodded. "Good point. You think that's what this is about?"

"It's possible. Rav's car is also a Prius, and it was damaged too."

They got a passkey from the hotel manager and methodically searched the entire inn, starting with the ground floor and working up. The two security guards Rav had embedded with the staff maintained their cover as Sean questioned them, even though they knew he was aware of their roles, but Luke was there, and they had orders not to reveal their role to anyone. Even the hotel manager played along.

Frankly, he was impressed by the security guards' professionalism in light of this bizarre turn of events, and he'd tell Keith to get both operatives on Raptor's payroll when this was all over.

Search complete, Sean and Luke headed to the parking lot, where a police officer was interviewing Keith as firefighters inspected the shattered remains of Chase's Prius. Curt, Lee, and JT were gathered on the far end of the large veranda, out of the way of the first responders. Luke and Sean joined them.

"The FBI is on their way," Curt said. "The use of a bomb —and the fact that Alec's car could have been the target— could make this a domestic terrorism investigation, which means this is a federal case." He nodded to the pair of officers questioning Keith. "Locals are unhappy that feds will be taking over. They're fishing for reasons this wouldn't fall under federal jurisdiction. Keith's humoring them and going along."

Sean guessed they were interviewing Keith and not Curt because the former attorney general knew federal laws and applicable precedents better than the officers knew their mothers.

It was unwise to get into a legal argument with the attorney who'd once been known as the Shark. He'd been the head of the Department of Justice for nearly four years, spanning two presidencies. He'd been a midterm replacement when the previous attorney general retired due to ongoing health issues, and he'd been asked to stay on when administrations changed. He would still be AG if he hadn't opted to step down three months before his son was born. Now Curt was a stay-at-home dad while Mara worked full-time for NHHC.

Keith left the officers and joined their group. "Sean, they want to talk to you next."

Curt stopped Sean with a hand on his shoulder and said in a low voice, "If you've got your phone on you, record the interview."

"This is a one-party consent state?" Sean asked.

"Yes, if there's no reasonable expectation of privacy. You're outside, in public. Stay outside and talk loud so your voice will carry to us. No expectation of privacy."

Sean tapped the headpiece he'd donned to search the inn. "This is a better recording device than my phone." Not to mention that Keith, Luke, and the team searching the woods would all be able to listen in. But he'd let Keith tell Curt that good news.

He flicked the record button as he pulled the headpiece off, leaving it to rest around his neck, readily visible, as he crossed the veranda to the officers. Both were white men, one in his midtwenties, the other maybe on the other side of thirty. Neither man looked happy. The glow of the porch light highlighted the tight jaw of the older officer and the cold glare of the younger one.

Sean decided to go with congenial, pretending he didn't notice the hostility, to see where it would get him. He smiled wide and offered his hand to the officer on the left. "Sean Logan. Raptor field operative. Best man at the wedding." When the officer didn't move to shake his hand, Sean shifted to the younger man on the right.

Nothing. Just disdainful glares as the men attempted to stare him down. He knew this type. They wanted to make him feel awkward about the ignored handshake, but instead, they'd revealed exactly who they were. He met their gazes in turn and planted his fists at his hips, his right hand a few inches above his holstered weapon. The stance opened his shoulders, letting both men see he was neither intimidated nor weak.

Sean had two inches in height and probably thirty pounds of muscle on both men. The younger officer flinched. "You going for your gun, boy?"

"No. And I don't take kindly to being called *boy*. I'm guessing I've got ten years on you, son." He projected his voice, as Curt had suggested.

There were situations in which he'd be forced to ignore the racist term and "sir" the young cop as a precaution against getting shot for being Black while living. But tonight, he had a crowd of people watching and listening. He did *not* have to put up with this racist shit.

The young man's lip curled at being called son, but he said nothing.

"You got a permit to carry that weapon?" the older officer asked.

"Considering West Virginia allows concealed carry without a permit, I fail to see how that's relevant, but yes, I do. I'm a licensed security specialist, and I have a concealed carry permit for every state that allows it along with the foreign countries I work in."

"Where were you at the time of the gunshot right before the explosion, b—Mr. Logan?" The man's gaze wasn't fixed on Sean. He looked over Sean's shoulder, toward Curt and the others. The older officer, at least, was aware of their audience.

"I was taking a stroll in the woods."

"Alone?" the younger one asked.

"No. I was with my girlfriend."

"She can confirm your story?"

"Of course."

"We're going to need to talk to her. Where is she now?"

"While I'm sure she won't mind answering your questions, this isn't your investigation. Your role here is to make sure the crime scene is secure and wait for the FBI."

"Don't you tell me how to do my job, boy," the older cop said.

"I have a name. It's Sean Logan. And you have yet to tell me yours or explain your authority in this matter."

"Surrender your weapon, Mr. Logan. We're going to have it tested to see if it's been fired in the last hour. We also need to swab your hand for gunshot residue."

"I will surrender my weapon to the FBI when they arrive, if they ask for it."

Footsteps sounded behind him, and he turned to see Curt approaching. "Mr. Logan is correct, and I'd hate to have to file a report with the Justice Department about how you interfered in a federal investigation."

The officers both glared at Curt, and Sean guessed they were calculating how far they could push this with the former attorney general watching.

Rav stepped outside, accompanied by a freshly showered Hazel along with Isabel, Undine, and the owner of the inn. Rav's headset was also around his neck. Sean took that to mean he'd been listening. "The FBI team is in the air and will land at the helipad by the fire station in about thirty minutes," he announced. He turned to the officers and offered his hand. "We haven't met yet. Senator Alec Ravissant."

Each officer shook Rav's hand in turn, mumbling a greeting. Rav also wore a gun open carry, but not surprisingly, they didn't question him, try to confiscate his weapon, or request a gunshot residue swab. Granted, Rav had been inside at the time of the shooting, but still, Sean knew the suspicion cast his way had more to do with skin color than his location at the time of the shooting. What were all those "boys" for if not to put him in his place?

Hazel approached him and slipped an arm around his waist. Rav had probably told her about the questioning, and she was establishing herself as his girlfriend and alibi. He draped an arm around her shoulders and kissed her temple. He'd screwed up so badly earlier.

"You okay?" she whispered.

"Fine. Just angry."

"Me too."

An hour later, after the FBI arrived, everyone who didn't have an alibi for the time of the shooting and explosion had gunshot residue tests done on their palms. Sean offered his palm for a test as well, to show he had nothing to fear, and Hazel insisted on being tested too. "If you're under suspicion for being outside, so am I."

"Sean is not under suspicion," Rav said flatly.

After being interviewed, Mara and Erica were cleared to drive home. They loaded their kids into Mara's mom's minivan. The passengers included Ivy's son, Julian, who would go home with Mara. Sean watched as she and Matt kissed the boy and promised to pick him up from the Dominick home the following day.

Sean's heart ached a little bit, wondering if they'd be able to keep that promise to the child who'd lost so much already.

After the minivan left the parking lot, everyone retreated to the front sitting room to await one-on-one interviews with the FBI Deputy Special Agent in Charge who'd flown out to personally oversee this investigation.

Sean confirmed with Rav that this was the same DSAC who was aware of the threatening note directed at Isabel and/or Hazel and that the threat might be the reason for the explosion. But the DSAC didn't know about Matt's GRU past, and Sean hadn't had a chance to tell Rav about seeing Matt talking to Chase before the explosion. It was a tangled web of who knew what, and a fine line prevented Sean from telling the DSAC everything.

"Luckily, the only damage to our Prius is shattered windows," Rav said. "We can get a mobile repair truck out here tomorrow to replace those." He turned to Chase. "Would you be willing to stick around and drive our car back?"

Chase nodded. "Sure." Then he shrugged. "Any chance I could borrow it for a few days?" He nervously ran a hand through his hair. "I…don't think my insurance is going to cover this."

"It's yours until we get this all sorted out. It's possible your car was mistaken for ours and targeted. I'll cover your costs, insurance or not."

Chase's shoulders slumped in relief, then he gave a wry smile. "I'm starting to think working for Raptor is bad for me."

Sean snorted, having a pretty good idea of what the boy had endured in Alaska. "True, but you're here for a wedding, not for work."

Chase laughed. "Good point."

"Isabel and I will catch a ride back with you and Hazel," Rav said to Sean. "If you don't mind."

"Of course." He figured they'd be cleared to go around five or six in the morning. No point in spending the rest of the night at the inn and trying to sleep. Hazel and Isabel wouldn't be safe until they were back within the walls of Rav's estate. They'd be in Gaithersburg by midmorning and could sleep all day.

He wanted nothing more than to hold Hazel tight and guard her as they slept. But odds were she'd shove him away. Hell, she intended to tell Rav to fire him, and he had no reason to think that had changed.

"Is there any way we can make sure Ian and Cressida don't hear about this?" Trina asked. "At least not until they're back from their honeymoon?"

Keith put his arm around her in support. "I was thinking the same thing."

"If we can confirm they're safe and sound at their destination, I don't see why they need to be bothered," Curt said. "They were gone for at least an hour before the explosion. They aren't witnesses."

"Cressida texted me about twenty minutes after the blast," Trina said. "It was just a quick note telling me they were at their cabin, and she asked me to thank everyone for making the weekend so special."

"Perfect," Alec said. "No reason to bother them, then."

Everyone staying at the inn was safe and accounted for. There'd been no injuries and only the two cars damaged because once all the wedding guests left, those two vehicles had been the only ones in that part of the lot.

The way it played out had Sean convinced it was meant to be a warning to Rav. A shot across the bow—or hood—so to speak.

Sean was interviewed early, but because he had more knowledge of the situation than most, he and Rav were asked to stay until after all the interviews were completed. Neither Hazel nor Isabel were asked the same, but then, neither of them were operatives.

Even knowing Hazel had been released, Sean was caught off guard when she returned to the sitting room with her suitcase and Ivy and Matt. "I'm beat. I'm going to catch a ride home with Ivy." She gave Sean an innocent look, but he could see the calculation in her eyes. She knew neither he nor Alec could raise a reasonable objection to her riding home with her sister.

She'd outmaneuvered them, and she had no idea how much danger she was placing herself in, because she had no fucking clue who—and what—Matthew Clark was.

Chapter Twenty-Three

Sean followed Hazel to the car, his entire body radiating anger, but Hazel didn't care. She wanted to leave and hadn't been looking forward to a four-hour car ride with Sean. She'd screwed up. She never should have indulged in a quickie in the forest, but part of her didn't want to be forced to regret it so soon. She wanted to savor the memory for a little while.

The best way to do that was to get the hell out of Dodge. Or in this instance, get the hell away from Sean. The last thing she wanted was to drive back to Gaithersburg with her dreamy-in-love cousin and his wife when her heart had just been ground to bits. Add to that Alec's unwillingness to accept that Isabel was the target and it would be excruciating.

She absolutely understood why Alec had a deep-seated need to believe Isabel wasn't the one in danger, but Hazel was done being bent into a pretzel to feed his denial. She was done with bodyguards. Done with playing along. This wasn't about her, and she wouldn't lie anymore to make her cousin feel better.

Sean insisted on carrying her bag and loaded it in the back of Matt's SUV before turning to kiss Hazel good-bye, keeping up the charade of fake boyfriend. His jaw was tight and the kiss perfunctory.

Hours ago, he'd kissed her neck as he thrust inside her, and she'd felt like the universe was hers for the taking.

Now, at least, they wouldn't have to go through a long-drawn-out breakup charade. Anyone watching would know their new relationship was on the skids. She hated that she was even thinking about this crap, when really, she was worried about Isabel.

She'd managed to pull Isabel aside. She was putting on a good show, but Hazel knew the explosion had shaken Isabel. *"I hate that Chase is caught up in this,"* Isabel had said. *"It feels like Alaska all over again, and I'm not even sure why. A memory I can't quite reach."*

Isabel had shared few details over the years about what happened to her when she was abducted in Alaska. Once she'd mentioned she didn't remember most of it, but sometimes memories would surface, like an elusive déjà vu.

Alec needed to focus his energy on protecting Isabel. By leaving with Ivy and Matt, Hazel was freeing up Sean to help Alec where it really mattered.

Before she pulled away from Sean's fake embrace, he touched her cheek and said in a whisper, "We're going to talk as soon as I get back to Gaithersburg."

"Fine," she said. She didn't know if she was going back to Alec's or not, but she wasn't about to tell Sean that. He didn't need to know she planned to ask Ivy if she could stay with her for a week or two while she apartment-hunted. She had money in savings and could afford a studio while she picked up consulting jobs and waited for the Virginia ME work order to be authorized. Plus, JT might have more work for her, and maybe she could line up some guest lectures with a few local universities. Her work for ICMP always drew a wide audience. People were interested in the intersection between forensics and the aftermath of genocide and how it reshaped the political landscape. It was a history, politics, and science lesson all in one.

"Be careful," Sean said, his eyes burning with intensity. He then turned and gave Matt a hard stare, which was odd. He'd seemed to like Matt from the moment Ivy met him in Grand Cayman.

Yet Matt returned Sean's look with a hard stare of his own. What was the deal with that?

She was too exhausted to try to decode their looks. A Vigenère cipher would be easier to crack, with or without the key.

She climbed in the backseat and flopped her head against the headrest, closing her eyes as they pulled out of the parking lot. She didn't look back or wave good-bye. Her fake relationship—and even the almost real one—was officially over.

"She never believed she was the target," Sean said to Rav once they retreated to the hotel room recently vacated by Hazel.

Their hotel room. The one with the fantastic king-sized bed in which he should have made love to her. But he'd fucked up, and instead, he'd taken her in the forest at a time when she was vulnerable.

She'd never forgive him. But then, he'd never forgive himself.

He walked over to the dresser and pulled open the top

drawer. All that remained inside was the remote-controlled G-spot vibrator, the dildo, the bondage kit, the lube, and one of the sex dice. He closed the drawer and planted his fists on the dresser. He dropped his head and laughed and cursed at the same time.

She left the dildo but split the dice.

Hazel made a statement even when she walked away.

"What's going on?" Rav asked.

"Nothing. I just fucked up." He turned and met his boss's gaze. "You aren't paying me for this weekend. I screwed up. That's why Hazel took off. This is all my fault."

Rav was silent for a long moment. Finally, he said, "Does she know how you feel about her?"

Sean leaned back against the drawer that was half-empty of sex toys. "No. And if I told her right now, she'd never believe me." Hell, he was just figuring it out himself. "What's your gut saying on Matt? He doesn't have an alibi, and he's the only person to witness the explosion."

Rav's jaw tightened. "I want to think Matt's one of us, but it's hard to know what to believe. For years, he was embedded in the US Coast Guard without any hint of what he really was. Deception is like breathing for him."

"He loves Ivy and Julian. He lights up every time he looks at the boy."

"He loves *Julian*. No question there. Everything he's done has always been to protect him. I'm worried Ivy is the only way he can adopt Julian."

"Bullshit," Sean said. "They fell in love before they knew it would ever be possible for Ivy to adopt Julian."

"Sure, Ivy fell in love. But she doesn't have the best track record there. She married Patrick Hill, after all."

Sean understood Rav's concerns, but it bothered him that Ivy's first marriage was being held against her. But then, Hill had manipulated her. Who was to say Matt hadn't done the same? Matthew Dimitri Clark's training was beyond that of a grifter like Hill. Matt was an absolute master at deception.

And Hazel was in a car with him right now. If Matt was somehow involved in this mess, Hazel had just walked into a trap.

They'd been on the road for thirty minutes when Ivy said, "Spill, Haze. What's up with you and Sean? You breaking up already?"

Hazel didn't bother to open her eyes. She'd wanted to sleep since leaving the inn, but was caught in a strange combination of exhaustion and adrenaline, heartache, and confused lust. She'd mentally been reliving the moments in the forest, when Sean had been on his knees before her, making her forget everything but the feel of his mouth.

She was half-asleep, lulled by the hypnotic, intense daydream. "He was never my boyfriend," she murmured, mostly to herself so she could live with her decision to walk away.

"*What?*" Ivy asked.

Hazel's eyes flew open, and she sat up straight.

Oops.

Part of her wondered if she'd meant to let that slip, and she realized she probably had. It was ridiculous that Alec insisted she couldn't trust her sister with the truth. She was family and Hazel's best friend. Plus, the whole national security thing was moot—Hazel didn't know anything about that, so there was absolutely *nothing* she could reveal.

And Matt had been investigated by Raptor about ten minutes after he'd met Ivy. He was certified fresh.

She'd hated lying to Ivy. How would she feel if the tables were turned and she discovered Ivy didn't trust her enough to share something as important as a death threat or that she'd lied about a relationship?

Hazel would be devastated her sister didn't have faith in her. "He was never my boyfriend," she repeated.

"I heard you, I just don't understand. You both just spent the entire weekend acting like a couple. So you're saying it was just a hookup? That's fine, but why pretend it was more?"

"No. It wasn't just a hookup." At least not until a few hours ago, but Ivy didn't need to know what happened in the forest. "It was all a lie."

Ivy gave her a confused look. "You lied about being a couple because Sean needed a date for the scavenger hunt? That's a little weird. And unnecessary."

"No. I came to the wedding with Sean because Alec was convinced I needed a bodyguard."

"*What?*" Ivy said with alarm. "Why would you need a bodyguard?"

"I love our cousin, you know I do. But he's being irrational, and I think it's because Isabel was threatened. He's just not thinking clearly."

"You've lost me, Haze. What are you talking about?"

"Isabel was threatened?" Matt asked. "When? Does the explosion have to do with the threat?"

She rubbed her temples. She was so frigging tired. A glance at the clock explained why. It was five in the morning. She'd gotten up at seven yesterday, and they'd had a full day before the late-afternoon wedding.

She was so thankful Matt was driving. He looked wide-awake, while there was no way she could operate a motor vehicle right now. "It's a long story, which began a week ago. Monday, to be exact." She dove in, telling them everything she knew—which wasn't much. Alec would be pissed, but his objections to telling family made zero sense. If there was something he hadn't told her, it was his own damn fault.

He'd made her lie and pretend to be involved with a man she very much wanted to be involved with. This part was her story to tell, and she would confide in her best friend. When she finished, Matt and Ivy were silent for a long time. Finally, Ivy said, "There's really only one reason why Alec wouldn't tell me any of this. Why he'd put Sean through this charade in front of all our closest friends."

It took a moment for Hazel to realize she was talking to Matt, not her. She was about to ask what that reason could be, when Matt nodded.

"What's going on?" she asked.

"Alec's being pigheaded," Ivy said.

She'd known Ivy would be hurt, but from her tone, the stiffness in her shoulders, and her tightly clenched fist, this went far deeper. She was angry. Fiercely angry.

"If it makes you feel better, he's not trusting me with any real information either. In one sentence, he tells me someone might've threatened me, and in the next, he shows me a heavily redacted letter that explains *nothing*."

"I get that he's worried about Isabel, but to suspect *you*? What the hell is wrong with him?"

Again, it took Hazel a moment to understand who Ivy was talking to and what her words meant.

Matt let go of the steering wheel with his right hand and took hold of Ivy's. "It's okay, sweetheart. He has good reason to wonder about me." He met Hazel's gaze in the rearview mirror and added, "I showed up out of the blue and fell hard for your sister. Alec doesn't know me, and given Ivy's background and the fact that pretty much all foreign intelligence agencies want her mapping AI drone, it's perfectly reasonable for Alec to wonder about me." His focus remained on the road, but his next sentence was directed at Ivy. "He's worried because he loves you and Julian, and he's scared for Isabel. Cut him some slack."

"I can't believe he made Sean work during a wedding in which he was best man!"

Hazel sighed. She'd been struggling with that one all week and hated it that she was just a job to Sean. A job he couldn't wait to leave behind. After all, Dubai was calling.

Good thing she had a new vibrator, because she was giving up men. She wished she'd taken the dildo too.

"Hazel, I think you're being a little too quick to assume you aren't a target," Matt said.

She crossed her arms and glared at him in the mirror. "You going to take Alec's side on everything?"

"Actually, I am. Here's how I see it. Yes, Isabel was probably the prime target, but with you there, with less obvious but still red hair, they've got more cards to play. Anyone going after a wealthy sitting senator who was an Army Ranger and also happens to own his own private army isn't fucking around. These guys mean business, and your cousin knows it.

"First, they set him up so he can't tell *anyone* by tying it to a national security concern—and the fact that they know details about national security means they're connected, which is even scarier. With the need for secrecy, they've removed the private army. Boom. Then they word the note in a vague way that means Alec's got to protect two flanks. And again, he can't tell anyone, except, say, one trusted employee, a man who was in Alaska and knows the shit that went down there. I bet you anything the national security issue that has Alec worried is the cover-up the FBI, CIA, and DIA managed to arrange."

"Cover-up?" Hazel asked, her head spinning at Matt's wild speculation.

"Yes. Cover-up. You don't really think it was as simple as the FBI made it sound, do you?"

Ivy frowned at Matt. "Simple? Isabel was abducted and held for ransom."

"It was more than that," Matt said. "She was tortured and very likely brainwashed."

A chill spread through Hazel. How did Matt know this? He'd been an analyst of some sort for the NSA before he inherited a crap ton of money from an uncle around the same time as the car accident that scarred him. Perhaps he was higher up and better connected in the NSA than he'd hinted at? But then, employment by the NSA was usually kept quiet.

Did he know for a fact that Isabel had been tortured, or was this all speculation?

"If I wanted to go after a wealthy senator with a seventy percent approval rating," Matt continued, "one who doesn't need campaign donations and who lives in a fortress, I'd remove his army—which was neatly done with hints that the cover-up has cracks—and go after what he loves the most. Isabel, yes, but the rest of his family too. Everyone knows this, especially after what Ivy went through in Palau.

"Then I'd really screw with him by staging an incident that makes it look like Isabel was the target. Blow up a car that's just like hers. Even better, their car is damaged in the blast. The goal being to scare Isabel at a time when she's surrounded by operatives. A time when she should be safe even though she's not ensconced in the fortress. Then, the moment Alec's attention is on Isabel and not you, that's when I'd strike, but not at Isabel. That's when I'd go after you."

Now she broke out in a cold sweat. Just like in Croatia. But then, it had been from nightmares. This…this was real. She took a deep breath and rubbed her hand on the seat cushion, feeling the texture, trying to ground herself, as she should have done in the forest by touching the tree and listening to the wind and the leaves, instead of screwing Sean.

Now she had the sound of the tires on the road. The hum of the engine. The sound of the madman in the driver's seat, telling her she was in danger.

Had Isabel really been tortured?

What did Matt know, and how did he know it?

Who is Matthew Clark?

The SUV's headlights cut through the darkness, illuminating a tunnel of roadway. She stared at the extent of the light where it faded, unable to penetrate the dark morning ahead.

Was Matt right? Was she in danger? She'd ditched her former SEAL bodyguard and former Army Ranger cousin to catch a ride with Matt, who might be as fit as the rest of the guys, but his only special skill that she knew of was throwing hatchets, and he probably didn't have one of those in the car.

"Matt…" Ivy said, drawing out his name in an alarmed tone.

"I see it," he said.

"See—?" But then Hazel turned and saw it too. A car barreling down on them. Her breath left in a rush, taking away her ability to scream. The car was coming up the straightaway very fast. Like…a hundred miles per hour kind of fast. Matt pressed the accelerator, and they shot forward down the state highway, avoiding being rear-ended by the speeding car. But then she wanted to scream because they were coming upon vehicles in front of them.

Traffic would be light on Sunday morning at normal speeds, but they were going—she glanced at the speedometer and would have blanched if there was blood left in her body to expel—a hundred and ten.

Matt darted from lane to lane, maneuvering between the slower vehicles like a race car driver, staying just ahead of the speeding vehicle behind them, who darted and weaved in a similar fashion.

Someone was going to make a mistake, and people were going to die.

As part of her training, she'd examined the bones of high-speed-accident victims. She could see the shattered pelvises, crushed skulls. Femurs splintered into a dozen pieces.

She finally got air in her lungs, but instead of screaming her fear, she let out a low moan of terror. Her heart pounded and her whole body shook. Meanwhile, Matt was calm in the driver's seat, shifting from lane to lane without any outward sign of stress.

Ivy gripped the handle above the door and made a small squeak as they nearly touched a bumper in front of them with a close lane change. Then the road opened up before them, no visible cars ahead. Matt pressed the SUV to go even faster, and shockingly, it did. But then, it was a Porsche Cayenne and built for speed.

All at once, Matt changed lanes and slammed on the brakes, and then the car that was chasing them passed the Cayenne, and Matt was in pursuit.

"Call Alec. Give him the license plate," Matt said.

Ivy did as instructed. How was she holding herself together? Hazel was pretty sure she was about to puke.

"Alec, we're being chased by a black Audi sedan. Virginia license plate." She read him the numbers.

"Sync to my Bluetooth, Ivy, so I can talk to him," Matt said, tucking a headset around his ear, then returning his hand to the wheel. "Shit! Gun."

He slammed on the brakes.

In an instant, the windshield became a web of cracks, and Hazel thought the bullet might've passed by her head on the way to the back window.

The Cayenne slowed to a less rocket-like speed, and Matt exited the four-lane highway with a sharp turn to the right. Hazel was pretty sure two wheels left the pavement, but they made the turn and then several more, until they were deep in the industrial area of a medium-sized town.

Matt found a boarded-up old gas station next to a chained-up factory of some kind and pulled into the station lot and drove around the building, out of sight of the main road. He put the car in Park before speaking into his earpiece. "Alec, we need to talk."

Sean ignored all speed limits as he drove to pick up Hazel. Keith and Trina followed in another SUV. They would pick up Matt and Ivy and bring them back to DC. Curt had given Rav and Isabel the keys to his car. The former attorney general would catch a ride back to the city with Lee.

Sean, Rav, and Matt had a lot to discuss, but right now, Sean wanted to get Hazel to a safe house, to hell with the rest.

If anyone with less skill than Matt had been at the wheel, Sean had no doubt Hazel would be dead or taken hostage. Maybe even tortured as Isabel had been.

Sean had seen the videos. He'd heard her screams. No one had touched her, and yet she screamed as if she were being ripped in two. Just before Sean left the inn, Rav had admitted to him and Isabel that there had been references to Alaska in the threat.

This time, it could be Hazel strapped to the table. Hazel's screams.

He hit the accelerator, wishing he also had a Porsche so he could get to Hazel that much faster. He'd used ten precious minutes at the inn, packing and planning, but still, he reached the abandoned gas station less than an hour after the gunshot had sounded.

Fifteen seconds after that, he had her in his arms. She pressed her face to his chest and sank into him, sort of like she had the other night, when he'd held her as she slept. After a long moment, he released her, and she climbed into the passenger seat of his SUV. After grabbing her bag from the back of the Cayenne and putting it in his vehicle, he shook Matt's hand. "Thank you."

"Next time, a little warning would be nice."

"That wasn't my call to make," he said.

Matt nodded.

Ivy hugged Sean and said, "Take good care of her. She's reeling." Then she whispered in his ear, "She still doesn't know about Matt."

Did Ivy think they were going to be able to keep their secret from her? He hoped to hell not. It was keeping secrets that had gotten them into this mess, and Hazel would be devastated when she learned the extent of the lies. But all he could do was nod. "I'll tread carefully."

Gravel crunched behind him as Keith and Trina pulled into the lot. Sean waved and jumped into his vehicle. In minutes, they were back on the road.

He reached across the console and took Hazel's hand. She squeezed his fingers, then said, "Mind if I sleep?"

"Not at all. We've got about three hours to the safe house."

"We're not going to Gaithersburg?"

"No. You need time to sleep. Regroup. I've got a place lined up that isn't connected to Rav. No one will know where we are. It's only for a day or two, but it will give us some time to think. To plan instead of just reacting."

"A day or two, just you and me?"

"Yes, do you mind?" This was the part he'd worried about, that she'd balk at being alone with him. He couldn't blame her if she did.

"No charade, no bombs, no car chases?"

"Not if I can help it."

"Sounds heavenly."

The tight band around his heart loosened a fraction. "Sleep, then. We'll be there before you know it."

The adrenaline crash on top of twenty-four hours without sleep must be hitting her hard, because a minute later, she was out.

Sean watched the road, vigilant for a tail. He took a long, twisting route to the cabin nestled in the Virginia woods about twenty minutes from the reservoir where she and Isabel had been working last week. At last, he pulled into the carport and shut off the engine. He found the key—it was right where Chase had said it would be—and carried Hazel inside.

She stirred as he scooped her from the car, but dropped into sleep again as he crossed the dirt driveway. He settled her on the bed in the only bedroom, then went back to grab their bags and food—leftovers from the wedding, which the staff at the inn had packed for them.

As they'd given him the food, they'd expressed the hope he wouldn't believe all West Virginians were like the cops that had interviewed him earlier in the night. Sean had thanked them and assured them he knew many wonderful West Virginians, and racist cops could be found in all US states and territories.

Between the leftovers and supplies stored in the cabin, they had enough provisions for two or three days. After the food was put away, he stripped down to a T-shirt and boxer briefs and climbed into bed with Hazel. It had been twenty-seven hours since he'd slept, and he needed sleep as much as she did. He pulled her into his arms and breathed in her hazelnut scent.

She was alive. Safe. And in his arms.

He'd do everything in his power to keep her that way.

*H*azel surfaced from a deep sleep, disoriented. It took her a moment to figure out where she was. She had a vague memory of Sean carrying her inside. Now she was curled against his side. He was asleep, and she wanted to stay here forever.

But her bladder had other ideas. She carefully extracted herself, trying not to wake him, but he was an operative, so it was no surprise when his eyes popped open. "Sleep," she ordered. "Everything's fine. I'm just getting up to use the bathroom."

He nodded and closed his eyes.

The clock on the nightstand indicated it was two twenty-one, and she deduced from the light that penetrated the closed blinds that it was p.m. Her internal clock was so screwed up from the crazy night that she'd needed the cue. It wouldn't have surprised her if she'd slept the entire day, but it had only been about eight hours since she'd fallen asleep in the car.

In the bathroom, she splashed water on her face, then decided to take a quick shower to wash the cobwebs from her brain. The shower had generic shampoo and conditioner, for which she was thankful. She tried to remember what Sean had told her about the cabin. Who did it belong to? And was there food?

Please let there be food.

She was starving.

Hunger kept her from lingering in the shower, and after a

quick wash, she dressed again in the clothes she'd put on after showering in Alec's room, not wishing to wake Sean by returning to the bedroom to grab her bag.

Thankfully, there was a comb in the medicine chest. Not great for getting the tangles out of her wet hair, but better than nothing. She put a dab of toothpaste on her finger and swiped her teeth so her mouth at least felt fresher.

Feeling clean and marginally human, she entered the kitchen. In the fridge, she found hummus and naan along with other Middle Eastern dishes that had been served at the wedding. Oh, bless Sean for thinking to grab food before breaking land speed records to pick her up after the most terrifying car ride of her life.

She nibbled on the bread with hummus while heating up a half-dozen lamb meatballs—her favorite köfte—in the oven. The sound of footsteps and the creak of the bathroom door told her Sean was up. She put several more meatballs in the pan. He was bound to be starving too.

The shower turned on, telling her he'd be a few minutes, so she decided to make coffee. She didn't usually indulge in caffeinated beverages in the afternoon—especially now that she battled insomnia and nightmares—but today was an easy exception.

She was too hungry to wait and ate more naan, a cold meatball, and several bites of sliced fruit as the coffee brewed. She was filling her mug when Sean entered the kitchen. He wore clean sweatpants and nothing else, his skin bare from his waist to the top of his head, which he'd shaved yesterday before the wedding. A fine layer of stubble on his jaw and the crisp curls on his chest were the only hair to be seen.

She leaned against the counter, holding a hot mug of coffee in her hands, and stared at the expanse of dark-skinned muscle. He was so damn beautiful. Her gaze lifted to his face and caught his smile.

He'd noticed her ogling him, but she didn't care. It was his fault for not putting on a shirt. She lifted her mug, offering it to him. "Want some coffee?"

He crossed the small space and stopped before her. Taking the mug from her hands, he set it on the counter, then tilted her head up and pressed his mouth to hers. The kiss started out soft and sweet, but when she responded, he took it deeper.

His tongue was a hot stroke against hers, igniting her entire body. She let out a mewing sound of need she was pretty sure she'd never made before. His mouth remained on hers as he cupped her face in his wide palms.

He raised his head, and she opened her eyes. His gaze was intent. Hot. "The only thing I want right now is you."

She didn't really give a damn if he wanted her for now or forever. She didn't care about the limit she'd placed in the forest. She could have died this morning. She could have been hit by that bullet or mangled in a wreck. They could have been run off the road and she could have been kidnapped. She could right now be going through what Isabel had endured in Alaska.

But instead, she was here with Sean. Safe. Alive. She was going to give him what he wanted while taking what she needed. She cupped his face and pulled him down to meet her mouth. Giving her answer without words.

He groaned, scooped her up, and carried her back into the bedroom.

"Wait! The meatballs."

"We'll eat later," he said, not breaking stride.

"They're in the oven. I don't want to burn them."

He set her on the bed. "Be right back." A moment later, he returned. "I turned off the oven but left them inside to keep them warm for later." He grabbed his bag from the floor and pulled out the gift bag they'd received from Trina. He dumped the contents on the bed.

She laughed at the sight of the bondage kit, dildo, and other treats. He grabbed the single sex die she'd left him and gave her an irked look. "I told you we shouldn't break up the set."

She shrugged, trying to present innocence. "I left you the dildo."

He picked up the blue silicone penis from the bed. "Without you to share it with, I didn't *want* the dildo."

"We can reunite the dice and share the dildo." She ran her hand over the erection that strained inside his sweatpants. "But right now, all I want is this. You. Just you."

"We'll probably be here for a few days. Plenty of time to experiment with the toys."

"Works for me."

He set the die and the dildo on the nightstand. "Before we do this, I need to tell you something," he said.

She pulled back. Holy hell. He was about to do it again. Dump her, or put a time limit on their sexual relationship.

He grabbed her cheeks and kissed her. "No! Not that." He held her face inches from his and stared into her eyes. "Rav had Matt's call on speakerphone. I heard everything. The interval between Matt shouting 'gun' and hearing the shot to the moment Matt said you were fine was the longest four minutes of my life. I couldn't breathe. You were in danger, and there was *nothing* I could do. Worse, I hadn't admitted the truth about my feelings to you, and that omission was what drove you away, putting you in that situation. When Matt said you were uninjured, I promised myself I wouldn't squander this second chance." He paused, taking a slow breath, then he said, "I'm in love with you, Hazel. I have been for some time."

*H*e held her face, staring into her eyes. She said nothing. Hell, he wasn't sure she was even breathing, but that made two of them. Then a tear spilled from her left eye and raced down her cheek, followed by another sliding down her right cheek.

His heart pounded so hard, it might explode as he waited for her to tell him what the tears meant. Was she happy, or ready to flee in terror? He had, after all, pushed her away repeatedly. She might not believe him or, even if she did, not trust him.

Finally, she said, "I've been in love with you for…I think a year? Before Grand Cayman, certainly."

With those words, his heart did explode. But in a good way. He grinned and picked her up and twirled her around, their laugher combined in a way that made the whole room lighter.

Hazel loved him. In spite of all the ways he'd screwed up in the last week and in Grand Cayman, she was going all in with him.

He set her feet on the floor and kissed her again, this time taking her mouth slowly as he cupped her face. Later, he'd take her fast and wild, like he had in the forest, but this time, he would make love to her.

She ran her hands over his chest as he kissed her. He was glad he hadn't bothered with a shirt because he loved the feel of her hands on his skin. And he needed to touch her in return. He released her face and grabbed the hem of her shirt, breaking the kiss to pull it over her head. He heartily approved of the fact she was braless, just like she'd been last night.

He cupped one breast and took the other into his mouth.

As he sucked, he released her breast to unfasten her jeans. He slid them open at her hips, surprised to see she wasn't wearing panties either. He cupped her bare ass cheeks as he had last night, and as he'd desperately wanted to do in a hotel room in Grand Cayman all those months ago.

He pulled back and looked at her. "In Grand Cayman, I thought you came on to me because you'd been drinking and wanted sex and decided I would do."

She shook her head. "No. I drank for courage to make my move, but I was so nervous, I drank too much."

"You were still too drunk to consent that night, but if I'd realized it wasn't just a convenient vacation hookup thing, I probably would have asked you out when we returned stateside and I wasn't on duty."

"I guess we just weren't ready for this yet."

He squeezed her ass again. "But now we are." He kissed her neck, nibbling along her throat, and whispered, "I wasn't about to let anyone else have the job of protecting you. The moment Rav said you might be in danger, I was in, one hundred percent."

She pulled back and held his gaze, her eyes wet again. "I've wanted you for so long, this terrifies me a little."

"I'm scared too," he admitted. "Fear is why I kept turning you down." There were so many ways he could and had already screwed this up. "But we'll figure it out together. No more hiding from my feelings. No more pushing you away when all I want is to be as close to you as humanly possible." He pulled her to him, his hands still on her bare ass. "And by the way, going commando? I approve."

She laughed. "I didn't want to wake you by grabbing my bag with clean clothes from the bedroom."

He finished sliding her jeans off, and she stepped out of them, completely nude and all his. Last night, he hadn't gotten her naked. He'd only seen parts of her. But now she was completely exposed to his avid gaze. Her body had changed in the months since he'd found her naked in his bed in Grand Cayman. She was toned in a way she hadn't been back then.

"You've been working out," he said as he ran a hand over her faintly defined abs.

"Yeah. Stress relief in Croatia. I figured if my muscles were exhausted, I'd be able to sleep. It worked for a while. And then it didn't."

He kissed her, wishing there was something he could do to help her deal with the mental pressure of her work. But all he could do was make love to her and hope she'd get lost in the pleasure and forget for a bit.

He scooped her up and set her on the bed and stared down at her naked body. Hazel soft or Hazel toned, he didn't have a preference. She was beautiful and perfect no matter what.

He pushed down his sweatpants, freeing his erection and revealing that he too had gone commando. When he'd pulled the pants on after his shower, he'd hoped he wouldn't remain clothed for long, and now here he was, all his wishes granted.

She smiled as she gazed at his body. His cock thickened just from the raw heat in her eyes. She licked her lips. "You're so beautiful, Sean."

"I was just thinking the same thing about you." He climbed on the bed and stretched out beside her. She shifted her left leg to rest on his hip, opening her thighs. His hard length pressed against her from clitoris to abdomen as they lay on their sides, facing each other, his balls resting at the juncture of her thighs. He rocked his hips, rubbing the base of his penis over her clit, and she made a soft, sexy moan.

How had he resisted this for so long?

Why had he resisted this for so long?

He kissed her again, taking her mouth. Claiming her

tongue. He ran his hands over her smooth skin, loving the feel of her in his arms, flush against his body. Different from the wild urgency of last night, when all he'd done was unzip his fly.

Last night was hot as hell. A memory worth reliving. But now he wanted a deeper connection with her. And touching her wasn't enough. He needed to taste her again too.

He slowly slid down her body, his tongue tracing each inch of skin on his path downward, lingering in a way he hadn't last night. He paused on her breasts, enjoying her moans as he sucked on her nipples. Then he moved on, nibbling on her abs, tracing her belly button with his tongue, until finally he reached her clitoris and gave it a slow, hard caress with his tongue. Her whole body jolted as she sucked in a gasping breath and made a wordless sound of approval.

He circled her clit with his tongue, then grazed it with his teeth before sucking on it.

"Sean!" His name was a gasp, a moan, and a plea, and it was just about the sexiest thing he'd ever heard from her mouth.

She bent her knees and opened her thighs wide, and he settled in to pleasure her, his tongue and fingers exploring her tight, slick vagina and then stroking her clit until she was shaking and on the verge of release.

She let out a mewing sort of moan and said, "Don't make me come yet. I want to come with you inside me." She scooted up the bed, breaking his contact with her clit, and sat up. "And before that, I need to have you in my mouth."

Who was he to deny her that?

He climbed from the bed as she scooted to the side and reached for him. She wrapped her hand around his erection and stroked him from base to tip, then licked him the same way.

She took the tip in her mouth and sucked. He groaned.

Hazel going down on him was about ten thousand fantasies coming true.

Her wet, hot mouth stoked his erection to new heights, and she moaned with pleasure as she sucked on him. He revised his take from a few minutes before, deciding that the sound she made while taking him deep into the back of her throat might be the sexiest thing he'd ever heard from her.

She sucked and stroked, and he forgot everything but the feel of her hot mouth. This was his Hazel. His beautiful, brilliant Hazelnut. He watched his penis slide between her pink lips as her thick auburn hair fell over her pale cheekbones. He wrapped his fingers in her hair as he slowly thrust his hips, taking her mouth and losing himself in the pleasure of this moment.

On the verge of coming, he pulled back. Like her, he wanted to come while inside her. Later, she'd come against his tongue, and he'd do the same in her mouth. But this time, he wanted to kiss her as he came, to feel her inner muscles tighten around him as she climaxed.

She scooted back on the bed as he climbed on again, crawling until his hips were settled between her spread thighs, the tip of his cock pressed to her opening.

He met her gaze as he held himself on the brink of entering her. Her eyes were hooded with pleasure and burning with sultry need he was pretty sure his own eyes mirrored. "I love you, Hazel."

He slid his tongue into her mouth at the same time he thrust into her body. One smooth stroke and he was in deep, her tight heat wrapped around him. Joined in the most intimate way possible, and the pleasure of it was even more intense than last night's joining had been.

He went as slow as he could, drawing out the pleasure as long as possible, but this was too insanely powerful to hold back for long. She tightened around him, and pleasure pulsed. She let out soft gasps and moans as she kissed his neck and gripped his back. She was coming hard and fast, and she took him with her.

He kissed her as she let out a cry of release, taking the sound into his mouth as his own orgasm overtook him, his body pulsing with pleasure so intense, he let out a guttural growl.

Replete, he rolled to his side, pulling Hazel with him, still inside her body. He tucked his head into her neck and breathed her in as his heartbeat gradually slowed.

This was better than his fantasies. Sex with her was a deep, powerful, soulful connection. Beautiful, brilliant Hazel. She made him laugh. Made him feel. Made him think. Now she was safe, and she was his. This wasn't a charade. This was the real deal, and he wouldn't ever let her go again.

Chapter Twenty-Five

*A*lec paced Keith's suite in Raptor's Virginia compound. Keith never used the CEO suite—he and Trina preferred their condo in DC—so it wasn't a problem for Alec and Isabel to take over the large suite until they had a grasp of what was going on. The security here was even tighter than at the estate, and here he had a mercenary army to protect her.

Isabel sat in the corner of a plush couch, her arms wrapped around her knees. "I think I need to watch the videos, Alec," she said. "I need to see if that unlocks my memories, like going into the cave unlocked yours. The key to all this could be in my own brain."

He knew she was right, but the idea of her watching them scared the hell out of him. He'd spent the last three years feeling grateful she couldn't remember how she'd suffered. Her screams still haunted him.

He'd saved one copy of the videos on a thumb drive that was stored in a safe in his office at the estate. The FBI, CIA, and DIA all had copies as well, but this was his copy, which he'd held on to in case Isabel's nightmares became unbearable and she needed to watch so she could face what happened head-on. Once his memories had returned, his nightmares had ceased. It might be the same for Isabel.

But she hadn't wanted to see the videos in the aftermath, and her nightmares had faded over time. There'd been no reason to revisit the agony she'd suffered. No reason to rip open that wound.

And he'd contorted himself and everyone around him to keep her from learning the truth about this latest threat. The last thing in the world he wanted was for her to rip away the barrier in her memory. He knew from experience she'd feel the pain anew, as fresh as the moment the infrasound waves cut through her body like a laser.

"Maybe there's another way," he said.

"Stop it, Alec. You know there isn't. That's why you lied about the threatening letter."

"I didn't lie. It was redacted."

"*You* redacted parts that weren't related to national security because you knew I'd choose to watch the videos." Her voice was hard and angry, and he deserved it.

"I can't stand the idea of you going through that again," he said softly. Memories of that day and night as he and his team searched for her still haunted him. Three years later, he was even more in love with her than he'd been then. They'd had three years to learn every facet of each other, their lives so completely knit together that she made him whole.

"You can't hide the truth from me either. Give me some credit. I survived it once. I'll survive it again."

He paused before her and pulled her to her feet, taking her into his arms. "I'm the weak one here. I'm afraid *I* won't survive it. I will lose my shit watching you suffer—both on the video and now."

"Do you want children?" she asked.

"You know I do."

"You'll have to watch me in pain then."

"Yes, but that's pain with purpose. We'll have a child to raise and love together. This pain serves no purpose. All it will do is hurt you."

"But what if watching the video opens up my memories? What if we learn something we can use?"

"I've seen the videos, Iz. It's you screaming until you're hoarse." He didn't share the part that haunted him, when she sobbed and begged for death. "Please, let's exhaust all other avenues first. I've got a team of investigators. We've got a private army for protection. Hazel is safe with Sean. Let's not do this unless we have to."

She leaned her forehead on his chest, and he tightened his arms around her. Eventually, he'd give in and show her the videos, but he intended to put it off as long as possible, because he couldn't voice his biggest fear: what if watching the video activated something planted in her brain? When Isabel first began therapy, he'd had lengthy discussions with Dr. Parks about the techniques Westover had used. Parks had been assigned Isabel's case because she'd analyzed the effects of infrasound for the CIA. Dr. Parks had agreed it was possible—however unlikely—Westover had planted a time bomb in her mind.

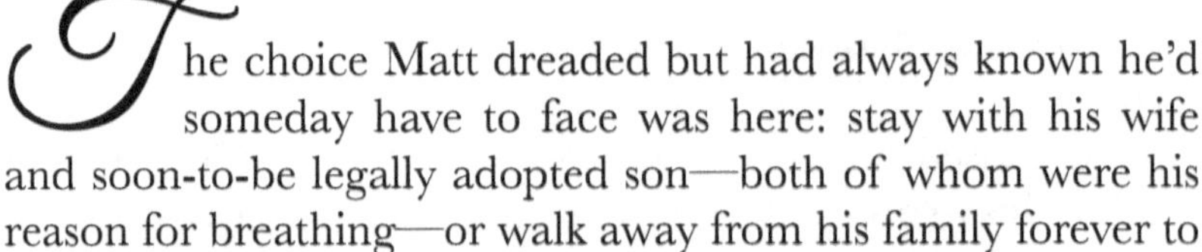

The choice Matt dreaded but had always known he'd someday have to face was here: stay with his wife and soon-to-be legally adopted son—both of whom were his reason for breathing—or walk away from his family forever to keep them safe.

He could hear Ivy preparing an early dinner in the kitchen of the small Airbnb they'd rented under a false name. Knowing it could come to this, he'd acquired a few fake identities even the CIA didn't know about, and had Bitcoin and other electronic currency he could access to fund a new life, if necessary.

Ivy and Julian would keep all of Matthew Clark's assets, which were quite extensive thanks to years of being sent on dirty ops in the service of Russian oligarchs and the government. He'd been well paid as the Hammer and had never touched a dime of that income until it was time to claim a new life. He could ensure his wife and son never had to worry about money.

But before he made his decision, he needed answers. Was it time to flee to protect everyone, or stay and fight?

If he left, there would be no coming back. But if he stayed, not only were Ivy and Julian in danger, but also Ivy's family: her sister, her cousin, and her cousin's wife.

Right now, Julian was safe with Mara and Curt. But it would devastate the boy to lose another parent without notice. It would devastate Ivy. They'd finally gotten to sail off into the sunset after months of not knowing if they'd ever see each other again.

It would devastate Matt to be without the two people who gave his heart a reason to keep beating. But he'd do it if it meant keeping them safe.

The trick was reading the landscape. He needed to time the action so it wasn't too late to do any good.

He needed to dig deeper into the GRU's infiltration of the US intelligence community. He'd seen the explosion, knew exactly who was behind it. Then he'd heard Hazel's story of threats and lies.

The question was why?

Why had Isabel and Hazel been targeted now?

He had five pieces of a hundred-piece puzzle. To protect everything that mattered, he needed to figure out what the other ninety-five pieces were.

The GRU had infiltrated and compromised the DIA years ago, and he'd spent ten months sharing intel with the CIA to ferret out all the traitors. Now he searched his memory for missing pieces.

Isabel and her brother, Vincent, had both been victims of infrasound experimentation. Now he suspected Chase Johnston was another victim. But as far as anyone knew, the human testing had been confined to Alaska and ended three years ago.

Was everyone wrong about the end date? Had the experimentation that had started in Alaska continued unchecked in Virginia?

He opened his laptop and clicked on the portal that would take him into the dark web. He'd been trained by the most corrupt and elusive operators in the world and could navigate the dark web like a cipher. Matt had one question, the answer to which could change everything: why hadn't Chase Johnston been killed three years ago?

Chapter Twenty-Six

Hazel pressed her face into Sean's neck, hardly able to believe this was real. But it was. Every wonderful moment. The feel of him between her thighs. The look on his face as he said he loved her.

Sean Logan was hers. No limits. No boundaries.

The joy of it made her light enough to float. "You know what would make this moment perfect?" she asked.

"How could this possibly be more perfect?" He nibbled on her neck as he gripped her ass.

"This moment needs meatballs. Lots of meatballs."

He laughed. "Hungry?"

"Starving."

"Well then, let me get you some meat."

She snorted but refrained from making the obvious joke. "And don't forget the dipping sauces."

"My woman likes her meat with sauce. Good to know."

She groaned even as her heart floated higher at his possessive words. She ran a hand down his side and cupped his ass as her lips followed a line up his neck and to his ear, where she whispered, "And I want bread. And fruit. And maybe some couscous with lentils."

He chuckled. "No more sex until I feed you?"

"A girl needs to keep her strength up."

"All right, then."

He rose from the bed, and she enjoyed watching his perfect ass as he left the room. While he gathered food, she grabbed her bag and cleaned up in the bathroom. She returned to the small bedroom wearing satin panties and a camisole she'd packed for the weekend in a moment of hope. The scarlet ensemble was tiny and pulled her breasts together, giving her a respectable amount of cleavage, thanks to the wonders of padding.

She planted herself in the center of the bed, with one knee bent and both legs just slightly spread. Sean returned with a large tray laden with food. He took one look at her and halted midstep. The food on the tray slid to the edge, threatening to tumble off before he righted it. He set the tray on the dresser and turned to her. "I think you've made a miscalculation," he said.

"How so?"

"You look so fucking sexy. Now I want to go down on you. In fact, I want to break out the bondage kit, strap you down, and fuck you with my tongue."

Her body flooded with heat—something that shouldn't be possible considering how hot he'd already made her. "I don't see how that's a problem."

"I thought you were hungry?"

She cocked her head. "I suppose it would be hard to eat tied up."

"You'd have to take whatever I put in your mouth," he said with a wicked grin.

She jumped from the bed and grabbed the bondage kit

from where it had fallen to the floor. "How does this thing work?"

He walked up behind her and cupped a breast while his other hand slid between her legs. His mouth found her neck. "Tell you what. We'll play with that later. I promise. Right now, I'll go down on you while you eat your meatballs and sauce." His fingers found the edge of her panties and slipped beneath, separating her folds. He dipped a finger inside her while his thumb played with her clit. He stroked, and she leaned back against him as intense pleasure rendered her incapable of anything except breathing. And even that involved a lot of gasping.

He steered her toward the bed, then released her. "Sit with your back to the headboard, legs spread. I'll get you a plate."

She obeyed, loving the command in his tone. But then, she had zero objections to his orders.

He handed her a plate covered with meatballs and dipping sauces. They smelled so good, she groaned again, and this time, Sean wasn't even touching her. "Eat," he said as he settled between her thighs.

He waited until she took a bite, then he dipped his head down and stroked her clit with his tongue. The flavorful food in her mouth combined with the pleasure of his hot tongue had her groaning.

His mouth was slow and sensuous as she ate, making her feel good, but not taking her to the edge. After she'd managed to eat three meatballs, she set the plate aside. He grinned, then sucked her clit, causing her whole body to jolt.

She'd known he'd be this kind of lover. Playful. Fun. Attentive. Caring. He was the full package.

And with his thick biceps and prominent pecs, *oh, what a package*.

He skillfully licked and stroked. She didn't come easily

with oral sex, especially a second time, but Sean took his time and listened to the cues of what worked for her, and she found herself tipping over the edge, coming slow but hard.

He held her there, his tongue pressed to her clit, his fingers inside her. As she came, she demanded, "Get inside me."

He laughed and slid up on the bed, and then he was in her again, before she'd finished plateauing. Pleasure coursed through her as he slid inside, and she let out a low purr at the feeling of completion.

"I think that's the sexiest sound I've ever heard," he said. His ongoing thrusts continued her post-orgasm pleasure. He came again, growling with release. A sound that was low and sexy and fulfilling all by itself.

He stilled, braced above her, his back arched, as deep inside her as he could get. His eyes opened, and the deep brown orbs held a warm, satisfied light. His chest rose with the ragged breath of exertion as he lowered himself to rest his weight on his forearm. He cupped her cheek with one broad hand. "I don't think I'll ever get enough of you, but this is a good start."

He kissed her, a slow, lingering, tongue-filled kiss as he rocked into her, no longer fully erect, but still joined in a satis-fying way.

He ended the kiss and rolled to his side, pulling her with him so he remained in her body. She pressed her forehead into his neck. "This is really happening, isn't it? I'm not having the most amazing dream of my life?" she asked.

"Oh, sweetheart, this is real. I've finally stopped being a dumbass and am going after what I've wanted for a long, long time."

When she would have protested the name he'd called himself, he pressed a finger to her lips. "I've been a fool when it came to you. I couldn't take you up on your offer in Grand

Cayman, but nothing but my own messed-up head was stopping me before or after. I feared getting involved with Rav's cousin could bite me in the ass, and for a lot of years, my job was all that mattered to me."

"What do you mean?" She understood superficially, but he clearly had family he cared about, friends that meant the world to him.

He ran his fingers over her cheekbones, traced her jawline and lips with a thumb. "I want to tell you this, but it's a long story. I'm going to clean up and grab coffee. You want some?"

She smiled and kissed him. "Yes, please." After he was done in the bathroom, she took her own turn. This was different, being lovers with a man she'd known for years. They weren't getting to know each other through sex, as she'd done with past lovers. They were deepening their existing connection with sex.

She'd already told him that she'd never tried bondage because she'd never trusted a partner enough, but with Sean, the trust was already there, and she couldn't wait to explore her kinky side, which she'd always kept locked down tight except in fantasies.

She returned to the bedroom and settled onto the bed, this time with the platter of food. Sean ate a few meatballs and had naan and hummus before answering her question about his job with Raptor.

"Being a SEAL was all-encompassing," he said. "I left the Navy and the Team because my dad was diagnosed with pancreatic cancer. The initial prognosis gave him four months. He managed to stretch it to eight. I was able to get out at the three-month mark, so I had five months to help out my mom and spend time with my dad. To say good-bye. My parents lived in DC then—Mom moved away after Dad died —so I rented an apartment in the city to be nearby and help out. But Dad didn't want me to see him in his weakened state, and my mom is stronger than any woman I know. It was pretty clear I was intruding on their long good-bye, and they didn't want any kind of role reversal in which I was taking care of them.

"I understood, but it didn't give me a way to process losing my dad. I was shut out, unable to do anything but be a son, and after years of being a SEAL, where we swooped in to save the day, it was hard to deal with. I'd given up my military career to be with my parents, and they didn't want me present twenty-four seven. They needed to face Dad's passing in their own way. And it was his death—I wasn't going to make it about me."

"But it was about you too. You were losing your father." Hazel couldn't imagine being shut out of her dad's life in his final months.

He nodded. "Yeah. But I'd been gone for almost fifteen years in the military, visiting rarely. I'd given up my spot, and they'd learned to live with my absence. I don't resent either of my parents' reactions to my sudden return home. I get it. I should have discussed my plans with them instead of just trying to take charge. I know my dad loved me. I know he was proud of me. He and my mom wanted my memories of him to remain intact. To see him as the larger-than-life father I'd worshipped growing up. And the best thing I could offer him as he was dying was to give him that. To only show up announced so he would be clean and dressed and seated on the couch in the living room, not in the rented hospital bed, wearing a gown.

"But for me, I was adrift. I didn't belong anywhere. About six weeks before Dad died, Rav hired me. It was a lifeline. And Rav, he *needed* me. He was trying to rescue a company most thought was unsalvageable. The previous owner had been involved in so many dirty deals. The FBI managed to keep Beck's biological weapons lab in the Virginia compound out of the news, in spite of what happened to Curt and Mara—"

"*What?*"

Sean looked at her, confusion on his face. "Rav didn't tell you about that? I was sure you knew."

She shook her head. "No. My cousin is pretty tight with his secrets."

His brow furrowed, and she felt a wave of discomfort. But then, Sean probably knew a whole lot more than she did about the threatening letter that had gotten them into this situation.

He cleared his throat. "Sorry. He has his reasons."

She stared at the platter of food, wondering how much Sean knew that he wasn't telling her, and if any of it would hurt when she learned the truth. Because she would demand the truth from Alec. After being chased down the road and shot at, she deserved the truth. She might've taken the threat seriously if her cousin had been honest with her.

She hadn't taken it seriously, and that had put Ivy and Matt at risk. She might never forgive herself for that.

Sean placed two fingers under her chin and raised her gaze to his. He leaned down and kissed her, slow and sweet. "I'd tell you if I could. You know that, right?"

She nodded.

He ran a thumb over her lips. "Good." His hand dropped, and he returned to his story. "My job with Raptor was…everything. The first time I met you was just weeks after my dad died, and I was a mixed bag of emotions. On one level, the attraction I felt was crazy strong that night. When you invited me outside to stargaze, I knew exactly what you wanted, and as I've already told you, I wanted it too. But with the loss of my dad, it felt…inappropriate. Wrong. Or maybe even like I was reacting out of grief. Looking for a distraction. You were hot and funny and a flirt…and I just wanted you.

"And then there was the fact that I needed the job with Raptor and no way was I going to fuck it up by getting involved with the boss's sexy cousin. And both of those mind-sets—that the attraction was triggered by a need to escape grief, and getting involved with you would be a bad move careerwise—stayed with me. Every time I saw you, I just wanted you more, but I didn't know if it was because you were associated with being the thing that had made me feel alive when I was deep in grief, or if it was because you were forbidden fruit in my mind."

She moved the plate of food aside and straddled him. She ran her hands over his shaved scalp, then cradled his face in her hands. "I'm so sorry about your father."

"Thank you."

His arms encircled her, and they held each other. She tucked her forehead against his neck. After a long interval, she broke the silence. "Losing your father to cancer must make your sister's illness so much scarier."

He nodded. "At least she's letting me help her. But crap, I'm terrible at it. I feel so help*less*. None of my skills are any good when it comes to cancer."

"You've been taking care of your nieces. That must be a huge relief for her, to know they're in good hands during her treatments."

He nodded. "The girls are a light in my world. But even so, I hope I'm what *they* need right now. What if they're picking up on how worried I am? What if I'm only making everything harder?"

"You can only do your best and give them the love they need." She paused. "I can't wait to meet them." She smiled, remembering Katrina's text messages. "And your sister and mother."

His mouth quirked. "Uh. Yeah. About that—"

She lifted her head and kissed him. "No way. I'm waiting for Katrina to tell me."

They kissed for a long time. It was sweet and hot, but not the kind of kiss meant to go anywhere. Just a joining. An acknowledgment of their new relationship.

Less than twenty-four hours ago, someone had blown up a car at the inn, then she was chased down the road at high speeds and shot at. In spite of that, she would always rank this as one of the best days of her life.

Chapter Twenty-Seven

A loud buzzing jolted Alec awake. The meaning of the signal registered slowly—it had been years since he'd slept in a Raptor facility, and the codes were no longer second nature—this one was a call from the front gate.

"Ravissant," he said, hitting the button on the console next to the bed.

Beside him, Isabel sat up. "What's going on?" she asked in a sleepy voice.

"Mr. Ravissant," the security guard said, "Mr. Clark is here, insisting he needs to speak with you."

Matt.

He'd wonder how he guessed Alec and Isabel were in the compound, but that was likely simple logic. What place was available to Alec that was safer than the estate?

"Is his wife with him?"

"No. He's alone."

"Fine. Let him in. Tell the front desk to escort him to an interview room."

After Matt's heroics with Hazel yesterday, Alec was ninety percent certain they were on the same team, but he wouldn't take chances. The interview rooms were little better than a cell.

To Isabel, Alec said, "Go back to sleep. I'm going to talk to Matt."

Even in the dark room, he could see she was fully alert. "I think I should be there too."

"No."

"What aren't you telling me, Alec?"

He couldn't lie to her and he couldn't tell her the truth. "I need to talk to him alone."

"Alec Ravissant, you made vows to *me*. One of them was that you'd never lie to me."

"I'm not lying to you, and I've made a lot of vows and oaths. I'm trying to keep all of them right now. Let me talk to Dimitri alone, and then I'll figure out what I can tell you."

"His name is Matt, not Dimitri."

Shit. It wasn't a good sign that he was thinking of him as Dimitri again. He pulled on a pair of jeans and grabbed a clean T-shirt from his bag, saying nothing to acknowledge his slip.

He leaned down and cupped a hand behind Isabel's head, kissing her hard and fast. "I love you, Iz. All I want is for you to be safe."

"And all I want is for you to be honest with me. You know I love you. You know I trust you. I need you to trust *me*."

"Oh, Iz. There is no one on the planet I trust more than you. I will tell you everything, once I'm certain of what everything is. Please. Keep trusting me. Have faith that I'm doing all I can to keep every oath and vow I've ever made, to you, to my country, to our friends, and to my family."

"Why do you suspect Matt? He saved Hazel yesterday."

"He did, and for that, I'm eternally grateful. Now go to sleep. I'll be back as soon as I can."

He was thankful when she didn't argue. He locked their

suite behind him and made his way to the room where Matt would be waiting by now. Yesterday morning, he'd agreed with the former spy that they needed to talk, but he'd been more concerned with getting everyone to safety, and there hadn't been an opportunity for a private discussion.

Clearly, Matthew Dimitri Clark had decided it was time. Alec just wondered if he'd be fed Russian lies, or if the man truly played for Team USA.

The Russian spy sat calmly in one of the four chairs in the small room. He slowly stood and said in a heavy Russian accent, "Nice cell. And the body search was most fun. What is your game here, Senator Ravissant? Have you decided I am no longer worthy of your support? Of your family? Do you expect me to start chasing after a damn moose and squirrel like this is some ridiculous cartoon?"

"Cut out the accent. This isn't a melodrama."

"Do you not want to be reminded of who I really am?"

"I know damn well who you really are, and I know your accent is effortlessly invisible. I sat in on your hypnosis sessions."

"You don't think I can beat ridiculous tests?" The accent faded with each word. "You forget my training and my desperate drive to survive."

"Whose side are you on, Dimitri?"

His eyes narrowed. "It's Matt, thank you very much, and I'm on the side that keeps my wife and son safe."

Alec believed him, but maybe it was only because he *wanted* to believe him. "Why are you here in the middle of the night?"

Matt stared him down, unflinching. He was nothing like the guy who'd helped flip burgers at the family Labor Day barbecue a few weeks ago. This man was colder. Harder. A formidable enemy.

Or a worthy ally.

After a long silence, Matt dropped back into the chair. "Three years ago, the Hammer was ordered to kill Chase Johnston. I never knew why the young man was targeted, but I suspect now it was because no one knew how well his memory barriers would hold up under CIA scrutiny."

Alec felt the blood drain from his face. Chase was one of Raptor's most trusted employees. He wasn't the most valuable, but he was absolutely above suspicion, given all he'd gone through. "If that's the case, why is he still alive? I thought the Hammer never failed."

"The Hammer had a few failures. One in Morocco. Another in Budapest. But failures like that aren't the sort of thing one likes to advertise in the assassination business. Reputation is everything for a contract killer."

"I'll keep that in mind," Alec said dryly. "So you failed to kill Chase? A defenseless boy who was deep in the throes of a mental breakdown triggered by psychological and physical torture?"

"No. The order to kill him was rescinded. I assumed because it wasn't the sort of job usually given to the Hammer. Innocent children were a bridge too far."

Alec noticed that Matt never openly claimed the Hammer's deeds. But then he'd always maintained that he'd been an unwilling assassin, and polygraph and a dozen other tests bore out that statement. Not that Matt couldn't beat the tests. He'd just stated as much.

"And why didn't you tell me this before? Why didn't the CIA tell me?"

Matt frowned. "The Hammer wasn't given his name. Just a picture and location, with more details to come."

"Was that unusual?"

"Yes and no. Information is always limited to a need-to-know basis, and I have a feeling the Hammer's handlers knew —" Matt paused and then sighed. "They knew *I* would balk.

Chase was such a young kid. It was unlikely he was connected to any Bratva groups, or I'd have seen him before. Chase wasn't the Hammer's usual demographic, so to speak. Plus he was in DC at the time, and most of the Hammer's assignments were out of the US. They wanted to keep my Coast Guard cover intact, and hits within US borders were risky. At the time they sent me the photo, they probably knew the hit was likely to be reassigned. The less I was told, the less I could reveal, should my cover ever be blown. A good choice on their part considering I spent months telling the CIA everything but never mentioned that assignment because, frankly, I forgot all about it. After all, there was nothing I could tell them about a kid whose name I didn't know and who'd probably been dead for a while."

He leaned back in his chair. "I assumed the job went to someone else and never thought of it again. Until Saturday." He crossed his arms. "I have a good memory for faces. It's part of the training. I only saw his photo for five minutes before I burned it, but I remember the face well. Imagine my surprise when I saw Chase Johnston, still breathing, at Ian and Cressida's wedding."

"And why did you show up at my compound at two in the morning to tell me this story now instead of telling me then?"

"I was too stunned in the moment, and I didn't want to risk Ivy and Julian. Any threat to my cover is a threat to them."

"So why now?"

"Two reasons. One, I've now had a chance to research and know who Chase Johnston is and how he's connected to what happened in Alaska. Two, Hazel told me about the threat."

Alec swore, even though he'd suspected. In Matt's description of the car chase, he'd never questioned who the target was, even though it was more likely to be Matt or even

Ivy. As Matt's wife, she would be the key to controlling Matt as much as threatening Isabel was a way to get at Alec.

Alec remained quiet, waiting.

Finally, Matt sighed. "I think Chase Johnston's life was spared because the barriers in his mind held up under interrogation. I think those barriers are still there. I believe Chase Johnston is an unwilling sleeper agent. And he blew up his own car under orders."

"What makes you so certain Chase was behind the explosion?"

"Because I watched him do it."

Alec stared at the man, stunned into momentary silence. Finally, he said, "Yet you didn't tell the FBI that."

"They'd have taken him into custody without understanding the risks. He could be programmed to shut down under pressure. I did some digging last night, and I was right to hold back that information. I found Chase's hospital records from three years ago. In Fairbanks. He went into cardiac arrest."

Alec closed his eyes, remembering the young man's pale, unconscious face as Isabel performed the CPR that saved his life. "He resisted the commands of his programmers. He was supposed to abduct Isabel. When he wouldn't do it, he collapsed and his heart stopped."

"And what do you think being arrested for domestic terrorism would do to him, if indeed he's still under mind control?" Matt asked.

"Point taken. But why not tell me yesterday? Or at any point before now?"

Matt closed his eyes. When he opened them, Alec realized he wasn't wearing the contact lenses that disguised his intense blue eyes. "I needed to make a decision first. Ivy and Julian are my world. If I'm a danger to them, I will walk away and never come back."

"I think Ivy would rather go into hiding with you and Julian."

"I know she would, but I wouldn't take them from everyone who loves them. Not when staying with me means they'd never be safe." His eyes were intense, pained. "I've spent a lifetime looking over my shoulder. I don't want that for my wife and son."

Alec nodded.

"I needed to decide if revealing what I know about Chase could in any way compromise me. If this meant it was time to disappear. But except for an order received by the Hammer, this has nothing to do with me, so I will do everything I can to help you sort this out, but none of what I reveal can get out that it came from me. If the CIA learned I played a role in this, they might try to force me into witness protection. Or simply expel me from the country. I need your promise that the only people who will know of my involvement are the handful of people who already know who I am."

Alec nodded. It was an easy promise to make. He didn't want Ivy to lose her husband or Julian to lose his father any more than Matt wanted to be lost.

He leaned in to ask Matt another question, when his phone buzzed. Phone calls at this time of night were never a good thing.

He frowned at Caller ID before answering. "Ravissant," he said to the head of security at his estate.

"Mr. Ravissant, there's been an explosion."

Chapter Twenty-Eight

Sean didn't know what had woken him. A footstep? A car engine? Whatever it was, it wasn't natural. Instinct told him their mini-vacation was over. He touched Hazel's shoulder. "Sweetheart, we gotta go."

"Hmmmmm?" The sound was soft and drawn-out. Sleepy.

"Sorry, babe. We need to grab our stuff and get out of here. Quietly."

He slid from the bed and grabbed their bags, dumping the items they'd left on the nightstand and dresser inside, then he pulled on jeans and a shirt as Hazel did the same. She was sleepy and sex tousled, and he wished this wasn't how their first full night together as lovers had to end, but his instincts were pinging like crazy. They had to get out of here. Fast.

Dressed with bags in hand, he led her to the front door, then came to a dead stop. Something moved past the window. A silhouette that wasn't deer or coyote. Human.

Instinct took over, and he grabbed Hazel, pushed her to the floor, and covered her body with his. The window crazed, then shattered. As if it had collapsed under a high-pitch frequency.

Shit, were they about to be hit by infrasound? It couldn't pass through windows, and in Alaska, both Rav's and Isabel's windows had shattered before they were hit with the sonic weapon for the first time.

But whoever was outside the cabin had opted for old-school terror tactics. A Molotov cocktail smashed against the hearth to the right of him with a loud crash. There was a flash of flame, but the stone hearth meant there was nothing to catch fire. The flames disappeared as quickly as they'd erupted.

A second Molotov cocktail lit the shrub beneath the front window. The branches, capped with dry autumn leaves, caught instantly. Flames flared outward, licking the window ledge and curtains. In a few minutes, the entire cabin would be ablaze.

He rose to his knees, his body still blocking Hazel's from the window. "Crawl to the bathroom. We'll go out that window."

It was small and therefore an unlikely exit point, plus it faced the carport.

In the bathroom, he raised the window. The size meant Hazel would have no problem, but it would be a squeeze for him. He turned to her. "I'll go through first, then I'll pull you through. If the path is clear to the carport, we'll go that way; otherwise, we'll head into the trees." If they had to hide in the forest, he had a satellite phone and could call Raptor. They'd make their way to a road for pickup. The compound was about forty minutes away.

He kissed her hard and fast, then climbed on top of the toilet seat. He wrenched the window open and dropped their bags. Then he launched himself through, diving as if he were stretching to catch a football. He rolled on the hard grass as he landed, a maneuver he practiced on a regular basis.

He sprang to his feet and turned back to the window after doing a quick scan to make sure they were covered. A storage shed protected one flank, the carport was behind him, and they were sheltered by the rear wall of the kitchen on his other flank. They were as protected from view as they could be.

Hazel had no such experience with diving out windows, so he reached up and pulled her through the opening. He set her on her feet, scooped up their bags, and they ran for the carport.

In seconds, they were inside the big SUV and he was backing out of the carport. No other vehicles or people were in sight, but the front of the cabin was fully engulfed in flames.

The sound that woke him was probably accelerant being poured on the wood structure. The flames had spread unnaturally fast.

He tossed Hazel his cell phone. "Call 9-1-1 and report the fire. They need to get this under control before the entire forest lights up."

She made the call, asking Sean for the address. He gave her the information, and she relayed it to the operator. They asked her to stay on the phone until emergency services arrived, but he nixed that idea. By the time fire trucks got there, they'd be long gone. They'd sort it out with the arson investigators later. Right now, he needed to call Rav.

Hazel's hands were shaking badly, and she dropped the phone in the process of trying to end the call. It slipped between the seat and the center console, and he could hear her heavy breathing as she dug it out from under her seat.

Finally, she placed it in the phone holder mounted to the dash, her hands still wildly shaking. They made it to the main highway with no tail in sight. He needed to call his boss, but right now, Hazel's state of mind was more important. "You okay?"

"I don't know. Freaked out, I guess. But I think it's sort of normal to freak out about someone trying to burn us alive, so that's good?" She pressed her hands to her knees and leaned forward a bit. He guessed she was trying to even out her breathing. "I close my eyes and all I see is calcined bone. Like the men in the lake who were burned. That could have been us."

"But it wasn't. We're here, and the fire is behind us."

She was silent for a long moment, then said in a quavering voice, "Talk to me. Whose cabin was that?"

"Chase Johnston's."

"Oh no!"

"Yeah." He rubbed her back with one hand, his eyes on the road, scanning the mirrors for a tail. She wanted him to talk, so he did, his voice low and calm. "Chase purchased the cabin with a bonus he received after what happened in Alaska."

She took a long, slow breath. "I can see Alec doing that. Especially given the bond between Chase and Isabel."

Her voice no longer shook, a good sign.

"He said he comes here at least once a month for the solitude, a chance to quiet the noise in his head."

"And now it's gone."

Yeah. He probably shouldn't have mentioned the last part, when the goal was to calm her. *Dumbass.* He rubbed her back some more. "He'll get through this. And so will you."

"I feel guilty. Freaking out with my stupid panic attacks. Fainting in a lake because of bones. Chase and Isabel had to deal with so much worse. I'm such a crybaby."

"Someone just set the cabin you were sleeping in on fire, Hazel. And even if they hadn't, you have every right to all your emotions. You face some evil shit in your job. That it affects you means you're an empathetic human being. Your empathy and sense of humanity are two of the reasons I love you."

He felt the muscles of her back relax at his words. This was the right track.

"Thank you," she said softly.

"*Thank you.* For sticking around for years while I figured out my shit. For not giving up on me each time I pushed you away."

She sat up slowly. "I kept trying to give up. But I was too crazy about you to ever quite let the idea of us go."

He slipped his hand from behind her back and returned it to the wheel. "I need to call Rav now, and put him on speaker. You ready?"

She nodded.

His call was quick and to the point, informing Rav of the attack on the cabin and letting him know they were on their way and would arrive at the compound in thirty minutes. He wasn't wasting time with taking a surveillance detection route as he'd done going to the cabin. Whoever lit that fire knew he'd go straight to the compound like it was a safe base in a game of tag. No point in trying to hide it when he needed to get Hazel safely within the compound walls.

He asked Rav to talk to the local fire department and police to explain why they'd fled the scene. He suggested arson investigators look for accelerant under the living room and bedroom windows, then added, "And tell Chase I'm sorry."

"We'll talk about that when you get here," Rav responded cryptically. "Actually, we've got a lot to talk about."

He probably hoped to continue keeping Hazel in the dark, but Sean was done with that shit. Twice, Hazel had been targeted. Rav would tell her everything. Even about

Matt. And Rav would spell out why he was suspicious of Hazel's brother-in-law.

No more damn secrets.

They drove through the security gate at the compound just as dawn was breaking over the night sky. Sean led Hazel to his rarely used suite to drop their bags. As the top operative in the company, he had a posh set of rooms. He punched in his security code, and the door swooshed open like the doors on the spaceships in *Star Trek*.

It amused him every time.

Inside the cozy living room, he used the same code to close and lock the door, then pulled her into his arms. This was the first time he'd held her since they'd fled the cabin. She melted against him, and he cupped the back of her head. "I will protect you," he whispered.

She raised her head to meet his gaze. "I know you will. You already have."

"I'll do a better job of it. Hell. I thought we were safe there. I'm still trying to figure out how they knew where we were."

"I know how." The man's voice came from the bedroom doorway.

Sean jolted, shoving Hazel behind him, blocking her from the line of fire, and turned to face Chase Johnston.

Chapter Twenty-Nine

Hazel had nearly gone into cardiac arrest at the male voice. What was Chase doing in Sean's quarters? His *locked* quarters?

"Yeah," Sean said. "I thought it was you."

He did?

All at once, Sean launched himself at Chase. He pinned the younger man to the ground and then rolled him over, pulling his arms behind his back. "Hazel, grab my cuffs from the cabinet by the door."

She did as instructed, tossing them to Sean's outstretched hand. He caught them and slapped the metal bands around both wrists in a practiced motion, then patted Chase down, removing a handgun and two knives.

Search complete, Sean stood and pulled Chase to his feet. The younger man hadn't resisted, but now he started to twitch, almost like he was fighting a battle within himself. His gaze went from Sean's to Hazel's. His eyes were bleak. Lost. "Help me. Please," he said in a low whisper. "I—I don't know…w—what's happening to me… Again."

"Who did you tell about the cabin?" Sean asked.

Chase opened his mouth to speak, but then his body convulsed. He passed out as if a light had turned off. Sean caught him before he hit the floor. He laid him out and checked his pulse. "Pulse is rapid, but he has one."

"He's still breathing too," Hazel said, seeing his chest rise in a nonconvulsive way.

Sean lifted Chase from the floor, positioning the heavy man over his shoulders, using a fireman's carry. "He needs a doctor, and we need to find Rav."

She followed Sean down the winding corridor, wondering how many twists this day would take.

It was barely dawn.

The Virginia compound offered only a bare-bones medical clinic that wouldn't be staffed this time of morning. As Sean carried Chase to the facility, he radioed for a medic and for Rav to meet him at the clinic.

"Why is he handcuffed?" the medic asked, his voice hostile when he entered the clinic to see Chase deposited on his side on an exam table.

Of course, the man knew Chase. They all did. He was the company puppy. Everyone looked out for the kid. Everyone wanted him to get better.

"That's need-to-know," Sean said. "Clear it with Rav."

"You mean Hatcher."

"No. Rav's our boss on this." Although it was probably time to call in Keith too.

A moment later, Rav arrived to back up Sean's claim. The medic remained angry, but he examined Chase, whose vital signs had returned to normal. He was no longer handcuffed behind his back but to the hospital bed.

"We've been quietly searching the compound for him for

the last hour," Rav said. "Keep him here under guard. Let me know when he wakes." He turned to leave. "Sean, you're with me. Hazel, go to Sean's quarters and lock yourself in."

"No!" Sean and Hazel said at the same time as they followed him into the corridor.

"You don't have the clearance for this, Hazel," Rav said as he walked at a brisk pace.

"Bullshit! Twice someone has tried to kill me. You will tell me everything, or I will leave this compound and go straight to the press."

Rav looked to Sean for help, but he shook his head. He wouldn't take the boss's side this time. "*Everything*, Rav. Even the stuff about Veselov." He used Matt's Russian last name so Hazel wouldn't pick up on his meaning. They needed to tell her this story in order, or she'd never understand why everyone had lied to her for so long.

"No. This is not open to discussion."

Anger spiked. "If you don't tell her, I will." He'd be fired, but so be it. There were other jobs, but there was only one Hazel MacLeod.

Rav came to a dead stop and stared Sean down. They'd disagreed a fair amount in the early days as Rav learned his job as CEO, but nothing like this. Never once had Sean considered walking away from Raptor. He'd never been this angry at the boss he respected and considered a friend.

"We'll discuss this in a conference room in private."

"Fine, but Hazel isn't leaving my side." He reached out an arm and pulled her to him, letting Rav see the change in their relationship. He'd said he didn't have an issue with Sean dating his cousin. Time to live up to those words.

Rav's gaze went from Sean to Hazel, and he must've noticed the way she leaned into him, all barriers gone. Finally, he gave a sharp nod and, without saying a word, turned and continued down the corridor.

Sean released her but took her hand in his as he followed Rav to the main conference room on the second floor. When Sean stepped into the room, he understood why Rav had wanted to speak alone first. Matthew Dimitri Clark sat at the table.

"Matt?" Hazel said. "What are you doing here?"

Matt's gaze went from Rav to Sean to Hazel. When his gaze met Sean's again, Sean gave a sharp nod. *Tell her.*

After a long pause, Matt rose to his feet. "I think it's time for me to formally introduce myself." Did Sean hear a trace of a Russian accent? Matt circled the table and approached Hazel. "My name is Dimitri Veselov." Now his accent was thicker, more pronounced. "I first met your sister in Palau, when I needed her help to find stolen Russian spy equipment for my handlers in the GRU." He offered Hazel his hand.

She stepped back, her face drained of all color, then she flushed a deep red. Shock, outrage, and horror were etched into her features. She looked at her cousin. "You knew about this?"

"Yes."

She turned to Matt. "Does my sister know?"

"She knows everything," he said in his usual American-accented English. "She's known exactly who I am since the day after we met. Julian is my nephew. She agreed to raise him when his parents died."

She turned to Sean. "You knew about this too?"

He nodded.

"And you didn't tell me?"

He nodded again.

She glared at all three men in the room, but she saved the biggest look of hurt for Sean. Her eyes widened as new understanding dawned. "You knew in Grand Cayman."

"Yes."

"Your job… It was to distract me, wasn't it? The night

we…I… I thought maybe we could really happen because of the way you danced with me, the way you looked at me. I drank for courage to make my move, and you…you were just fulfilling…an assignment?"

He didn't know how to answer that, because it was the lie he'd told himself at the time. But now he knew it wasn't true. He'd been lying to himself as much as to her.

She stared at him with that stricken look and took another step backward. "Can't. Breathe." The words were pushed out of her, as if she could barely muster the air to make the sounds. She turned for the door.

"This isn't the time for a tantrum, Hazel," Rav said.

At those words, she bolted down the hallway.

"She's having a panic attack, asshole," Sean said, heading for the door to chase after her.

"Panic attack? Why? This has nothing to do with Croatia."

He stopped short of the door. "For a smart man, you can be really stupid. Especially when it comes to your family. You, Ivy, and Laurel are the most important people in her world, and you lied to her, continually for months, and made sure I and all your friends lied to her too."

"It was the only way—"

Sean didn't have time for this. "Get Isabel and Ivy here. We need to talk. *All* of us." Then he turned and ran after Hazel.

*H*azel was suffocating. She ran blindly down corridors, searching for an exit. She needed air.

Outside, she would find oxygen.

She turned down another blind corridor, having no idea which way led to an exit.

"Hazel!" Sean shouted behind her.

She ran harder.

He'd said he loved her, but he'd lied. Repeatedly. If he really loved her, how could he have lied like that?

Her sister—her best friend—had lied to her. Duped her. How could Ivy have kept such a massive secret from her?

It had cut Hazel to lie to Ivy about Sean. To pretend a relationship that wasn't real. But her sister had blithely lied about a *life* that wasn't real.

Ivy had married a spy—the man who had abducted her, Hazel presumed—and she'd lied to Hazel about who he was. She'd pretended to meet him and have a whirlwind romance, a charade performed only for Hazel's benefit, because Sean had *known*.

She rounded a corner and came to a dead end. She let out a low sob. She hated this stupid compound with all its twisting corridors. Alec had said it was Robert Beck—the previous owner—who'd insisted on the maze layout, and Hazel hadn't visited enough to learn her way around.

She kicked the walls that seemed to be closing in. So much for finding air.

Arms wrapped around her, and she let out a guttural cry and shoved them away. She couldn't see. Couldn't think. Couldn't breathe. The walls were closing in, and now she was cornered.

This was like her nightmares, but with fewer bones and more walls. She was stuck in a labyrinth of death.

"Hazel. Sweetheart. Let me help you." Warm hands gripped her shoulders. "You're having a panic attack."

She tried to break out of his hold. "No shit!"

"Breathe, Hazel."

"I can't!"

"Listen to my voice, then. Tell me three things you can hear."

This was one of the techniques Dr. Parks had taught them. She tried to draw in a breath.

"Three things, Hazel."

"Your voice," she said. Then a moment later added, "The air conditioner. Me. Gasping for air."

"Good. Okay. Now tell me three things you can see."

She couldn't see anything. The world was blurry and horrible.

"Breathe," he said calmly. "Three things you can see."

She tried to focus. Her eyes fixed on a small circle in front of her. "A button on your shirt."

"What color is it?"

"White."

"What else do you see?"

She followed the line of buttons upward. "You have stubble on your jaw." She remembered how that stubble had felt against her skin last night when he'd kissed her. Gone down on her. Made her feel like she was the prize he'd been waiting for his whole life.

He stroked her cheek. "Tell me one more thing you see."

She continued scanning up and finally met his gaze. His deep brown eyes held hers. She took another breath, and this time, she felt air enter her lungs. Fill them. She was no longer gasping. "Your eyes."

"What color are they?"

"Brown, with flecks of yellow." She'd never really noticed the yellow before, but she'd never stared quite so intently into his eyes. When they'd made love, she'd closed her eyes, lost in the feel of him.

He stroked her cheek again. "I love you, Hazel. Nothing changes that. I love you."

She felt her eyes tear but refused to let them fall. "I love you too. That's why this hurts so damn much."

"I never wanted to lie to you. But I was hired to do a job."

"That job being to lie to me. To romance me to distraction because you needed to sell the story of Ivy and Matt's whirlwind romance to me."

"The night we danced… I thought I was distracting you, yes. But it was more than that for me. I was hiding behind an excuse. And yes, your playing witness to their 'first meeting' was to make it real. Someone had to play that role."

"Did Ivy pick me?"

"No. Ivy didn't know Dimitri would show up in Grand Cayman. We couldn't tell her, in case the CIA didn't release him with a clean cover. The GRU had to believe he was dead, or Ivy and Julian would be in danger."

It helped—a little—to know her sister hadn't chosen to lie to her. "Alec chose me, then."

"Yes."

"I'm going to kick his ass."

He cupped her face. "I'll do it for you if you want."

She let out a laugh, then her eyes teared again. "You lied to me too."

"I'm sorry. Sorry I was complicit. Sorry I maintained the lie this weekend. Once Rav hinted he suspected Matt, I should have insisted we tell you everything."

"You suspect *Matt*? You think he tried to kill us tonight?"

"Not anymore. C'mon. We need to go back to the conference room. There's a lot we both still don't know. Like what Matt is doing here now. Or why Chase revealed our location —and who he told."

She leaned into Sean and took another deep breath, then voiced the question that haunted her. "Yesterday…wasn't a lie? You weren't doing your job? Like a good soldier?"

His eyes widened with alarm and maybe a spark of anger. "First of all, I was in the Navy. Not a soldier. Second, yesterday was real. I've never slept with a woman for a job and am not about to start now. I *love* you. I've wanted you for years. I will never get enough of you. I would never lie about that."

"Is this going to work? Us, I mean?"

"I don't know. We've got a lot to figure out first. But I want to give us a chance."

"You have to promise you won't lie to me again. Ever."

He nodded. "Done. No more lies, not even for the job." He leaned down and kissed her, a soft brush of his lips over hers. "Now, can we please go back to the conference room?"

She nodded. She very much wanted to know what Dimitri Veselov had to say. And she really wanted to kick her cousin's ass.

<h1 style="text-align:center">Chapter Thirty</h1>

Sean returned to the conference room, holding Hazel's hand in a clear message to everyone present. Isabel was seated at the conference table and looked approvingly at their joined hands.

Sean met Rav's gaze, his jaw tight. Sean would keep his vow of never lying to her again, and Rav would respect that or he would walk.

Hazel released Sean's hand and crossed her arms, her posture defensive and hurt. "I'm not five, and I don't throw tantrums. I'm struggling with mental health issues and don't appreciate being belittled for it."

"I'm sorry," Rav said. "I was out of line. I didn't realize that was a panic attack, but that's no excuse. I was an ass."

Sean wouldn't have known either, except he'd sent her into a similar attack after the wedding without realizing it. She'd used the same words today that she used then. She couldn't breathe.

This time, he'd understood. She'd been suffocating and needed grounding. He would stick to orthodox methods of staving off panic attacks moving forward. No more wild sex in the woods. Not unless Hazel specifically asked for it.

This was the worst possible time to start a relationship with her—she was so vulnerable. But he'd managed to help her through this panic, to talk her down. That meant something.

He didn't know how to deal with cancer, how to help his sister, but he could help Hazel. He *would* help her. He would ground her, give her a reality to hold onto. He would love her and be by her side as she found her bearings.

He draped an arm around her shoulder and pulled her close. She lost her defensive posture and relaxed into him.

Isabel grinned. "It's about damn time you two got together. I've been watching you circle each other the entire time I've known you."

"All it took was a car chase and Hazel being shot at for me to get my head out of my ass," Sean said.

Hazel laughed, then slapped a hand over her mouth. "I can't believe I laughed at that."

"If we couldn't laugh, we'd all lose our minds," Rav said. Then he flushed, realizing what he'd said and who he'd said it to. "I'm sorry. I didn't mean—"

This time Hazel's laugh was full, unrestrained. "Oh my God. The look on your face! That's almost enough payback for the crap you put me through. *Almost.* I'm still incredibly pissed. And hurt."

"I'm really sorry about that, Hazel." This came from Ivy, who stood in the open doorway. "It was vital that we have some believable story to introduce Matt to the family, or his cover would fall apart. I didn't know you would be used that way, but I went along in the moment, without ever considering what it would mean to you if the truth came out."

She stepped into the room. "I know you're mad at Alec, but

please understand, everything he did was for me." She reached Matt's side, and he put an arm around her shoulders and she leaned into him, much as Sean held Hazel. "Because he understood how much I love Matt. How much I need him. Plus, we're Julian's parents. He needs us, and we need him. There's so much I can tell you now, that I couldn't before. But first and foremost, no one wanted to hurt you. Everything Alec did, he did because he loves all of us and wants us to be happy."

"I did it for Julian too," Alec said. "So he'd have a father, a man who loves him completely. Someone had to sell the story of Ivy and Matt's first meeting, and who better than Ivy's sister and best friend? If you believed it, everyone would. And that's exactly what happened. But I never really considered how you'd feel, and for that, I'm sorry."

"I get it," Hazel said. "I know eventually I'll be able to forgive you, but right now, I'm a little raw and feeling betrayed." She looked at Matt. "And I have a lot of questions for you."

"I'll tell you everything you want to know later," he said. "Right now, we need to figure out exactly what's going on with Chase Johnston, and why the cabin was set on fire."

Rav cleared his throat. "And why the annex at the estate blew up."

Shock coursed through Sean. He didn't think anything else could surprise him today.

"*What?*" Hazel and Ivy said in unison.

Rav nodded. "It happened about fifteen minutes before you called to say the cabin was on fire. Far as we can tell, no one was hurt. The annex is far enough away from the house and garage that it's the only structure damaged. I was about to go to the estate when you called."

"It blew up. Not Molotov cocktails?" Sean asked.

"No. It's made of concrete brick. It wouldn't burn. My guess is they'll say the gas furnace blew, but let's face it, someone was after one of two things: to scare the shit out of Hazel or to destroy the bones. Probably both."

Hazel gave a pained laugh. "Well, they succeeded on the first part."

"But not on the second?" Ivy asked.

Sean allowed a wide grin as his arm around Hazel tightened. "No. On Thursday, we decided to move all the bones here."

"Oh, thank God," Isabel said.

"So this is about the bones after all," Hazel said. "The threat. It was to keep Isabel from finding the bones, and me from examining them."

"It's looking like that," Rav said. "But given the site's location, in a reservoir adjacent to Raptor land, and given what's going on with Chase, we need to examine all the angles." He pulled out a chair at the head of the table. "It's past time we all talked."

Everyone took a seat at the large table, the six of them clustered at one end. Sean took the seat to Rav's right, across from Isabel, Hazel by his side. Matt and Ivy sat next to Isabel across the table.

"I think it's time to call Keith in as well," Sean said. "For the same reason. Raptor land. Chase's involvement. This is a Raptor issue, not just a political one."

"Agreed," Rav said. "I called him while you were talking to Hazel. He's on his way. We'll bring him up to speed when he gets here." He cleared his throat. "First, we should start with the threats and timeline."

Ivy jumped to her feet and went to the whiteboard, picking up a dry-erase marker from the tray. "It will be easier to organize the data if we map it out. Tell me the dates and locations, and I'll draw the timeline."

"We can project a map onto the second board and mark the location of the reservoir and where things have blown up or been torched," Isabel said, rising to use the conference room computer that was hardwired into the projection system.

Sean smiled. The mapping expert and archaeologist wanted visuals. Worked for him. They needed to take an analytical approach to this mess, because his emotional reaction to the danger Hazel was in was messing with his focus.

Right now, he was the one who needed grounding.

Isabel found a satellite map and zoomed in. A rectangle that included northeastern West Virginia, northern Virginia, and Gaithersburg, Maryland filled the whiteboard. She grabbed a marker and approached the board.

First, she circled the estate on the outskirts of Gaithersburg. "Our house, where the annex blew up." Next she drew an X at the location of the inn in West Virginia. "This is where Chase's car blew up." She moved just over the state border and circled a lake. "This is the reservoir." Just inside that circle, she drew another circle. "This is Raptor's property that abuts the reservoir." She looked at Sean and raised a brow. "I don't know where Chase's cabin is. Can you locate it?"

He stood and studied the contours of the landform, following the path of the two-lane highway he'd driven yesterday morning. He found the approximate area and circled it. "Right around here." He stared at the circle in relation to the others. The cabin wasn't on the reservoir, but it was close. Less than fifteen miles from Raptor land. "Chase said he spotted the For Sale sign on the property on one of his trips out to the wilderness training area. The quiet of the place spoke to him. He used the signing bonus he received when he took the job at the Virginia compound to pay for it."

Everyone, even Chase, knew the signing bonus had really been reparations. Rav paying him for pain and suffering.

"Okay. Now we have the locations—" Ivy began.

"No. Two locations are missing," Rav said. "The compound should be included, along with Senator Small's holdings on the reservoir."

"Senator Small has property on the reservoir?" Ivy asked.

"Yes. It took some digging to identify the true owner, but it appears Small has the parcel adjacent to Raptor land."

"Small is the property owner who forced the delay in fieldwork?" Hazel asked.

"Yes," Isabel said.

Rav stood and crossed the room and circled another parcel on the map. "Twenty-five years ago, Small and Beck had plans to go into business together, to build a private jail and rent out the prisoners as cheap labor—fighting fires, road maintenance, that sort of thing. Raptor was supposed to provide security, and Small would handle the labor contracts. But Lawrenceville and GEO Group got the contract, and Beck decided to use the parcel of land for wilderness trainings instead. Their collaboration dissolved, and the jointly purchased parcel was divided—presumably to pay Small back for his investment. Small's portion was transferred into a holding company." Rav tapped the circle on the map with the red marker. "This parcel has belonged to him ever since. He's the one who built the large house that overlooks the lake."

"The holding company," Hazel said. "It was hiding Small all along."

"Yes," Rav said.

"And Small is still pushing for more privatized prisons through legislation," Ivy said.

"Also true," Rav said, returning to his seat. "My bid to stop it is one of the reasons he and Voigt Forum targeted me. Which brings us to the timeline and the threatening letters." He looked at his wife and cleared his throat. After a long pause, he said, "I get threatening letters all the time. It's a hazard of the job. While most are toothless, I take them all seriously and have staff who regularly check Voigt Forum and other sites for threats. Voigt Forum pretends their anonymous users are the ones who post threats, but I have no doubt their own staff or bots generate most of them. They want to appear to have more users than they do, when in truth, they're little more than a fringe site.

"A few weeks ago, a threat appeared on Voigt that was pretty generic. It said I should resign, I'm a traitor and baby killer—which is one of their standard attacks on my military service—and if I didn't, my family would pay the price." His gaze fixed on Isabel. "I always take threats to family seriously, but considering it appeared to be bot generated, it went into the 'monitor and move on' pile. But then I received a similar threat via email, no longer a random post I wouldn't necessarily be expected to see. So it moved up on the threat assessment index. I discussed with Isabel whether or not she should lay low while it was investigated."

"I refused," Isabel said. "I won't let my life be controlled by racist assholes. A hate site like Voigt Forum doesn't get to decide where and when I work. Hell, even pro-Ravissant groups don't get to control me. I'll wear what I want, say what I want, and I won't soften my image or change my last name to appeal to whatever demographic they want me to court. Alec is the politician, not me. That's the deal we made when we first got together."

Rav smiled. "It really drives them nuts that you won't play the game."

She flashed a toothy grin. "I'm nobody's token." She returned her attention to the map. "And at the same time that threat came in, the dam relicensing project was finally a go for fieldwork. Talon & Drake had bid on it the minute Raptor, as a landowner adjacent to the reservoir, was notified about the repair requiring a deep drawdown. I gave JT the heads-up myself. We already have an on-call with FERC, so it was an easy contract mod. Our timing for the survey was limited because the drawdown would be so much deeper than usual. They wanted a short window with the lake that low. Archaeological survey is standard practice during drawdowns, especially when previously recorded sites will be exposed for the first time in decades. We'd been all set to start fieldwork a week earlier but were delayed when one of the reservoir property owners objected to the survey." She pointed to the circle Rav had drawn, marking Small's property. "That property owner, to be exact."

"Small didn't want you on his land," Hazel said.

Isabel grimaced. "No, he did not. It took a few days to sort out—Small's objections were irrelevant. His property line is well above the reservoir high-water zone, to give the utility the right to raise the lake several feet if needed. But we had to sort out the exact boundaries of what we were allowed to survey, to make it clear we wouldn't encroach on Small's property. He dragged it out as long as possible—he was slow to reply or 'misunderstood' the communication. And of course, this was all done through attorneys. I had no idea Small was the landowner until yesterday, when Alec received the report with the details."

She studied the map, then turned back to her audience. "With the lost days, we had to hurry the fieldwork. The repairs were nearly complete by the time we were out there. Including the weekend, we had nine days to finish before lake refill began Friday."

"Important to the timeline," Rav said, "I received another threatening email the day before Isabel went into the field. This one again repeated that I should resign, with more veiled threats to family."

"But...no one really wanted you to resign at all, did they?" Hazel said. "Small was trying to stop Isabel from going into the field."

Rav nodded. "Yeah. I think so. Two days later, another threatening letter arrived. It was also vague on who was being threatened—again, saying 'family,' but this one also included 'redhead'—a pretty strong indicator that they were referring to Isabel. Looking back, however, it was four days after Hazel moved in with us."

Rav pulled a page from the file on the table. "But on Monday, things stepped up a notch, taking the threat to a whole new level. It was no longer a low-grade concern. It's time I share with all of you the threat that came in Monday."

Tension left Sean in a rush. He'd still feared fighting Rav on that point. Maybe he wouldn't be losing his job anytime soon after all.

Rav frowned at the paper in his hands, then began to read. "*Resign Manchurian candidate. We know what you covered up in Alaska. You harbor spies in your home. Resign, or the redhead will pay the price.*"

He glanced up from the letter. "Before I continue, I want to give everyone some context. The part about harboring spies was alarming on two fronts. Matt, Ivy, and Julian had stayed with us for several days when they flew back from the Caribbean and discovered their house wasn't ready for them to move in yet. So the reference could be to Matt. Which is scary as hell, because if he's been compromised, we're in a world of trouble.

"That meant the spy reference had to be redacted—and not just from Hazel. I couldn't share the full letter with the US Capitol Police. Only a handful of individuals in the FBI know the truth about Matt. But there was also another possibility, which was alarming in a different way. It also could have meant Hazel. And I hate to say it, but that was my hope, because then it means Ivy and Julian don't need to disappear into witness protection."

"Wait. How could it have been referring to Hazel?" Matt asked.

Sean was glad he asked, because he was wondering the same thing.

"Nine months ago," Hazel said, "ICMP sent me to Eastern Ukraine to examine bones that had been found in a mass grave—the remains of refugees who had been fleeing contested and occupied towns in Eastern Ukraine in the aftermath of the annexation of Crimea. I was detained and interrogated by pro-Russian separatists who accused me of being a spy."

"Not a lot of people know about the incident," Alec added. "Relations with Russia are bad enough without that becoming a headline, and ICMP wanted to keep it quiet. It's already difficult for them to gain entry into certain countries without false rumors of espionage circulating. But my staff and certain members of the Senate know because I pulled strings to get Hazel out of the country, fast. After what happened with Ivy in Palau, no one wanted to take chances with slow diplomacy."

Hazel let out a soft shudder. "I thought they were going to kill me. They threatened as much—to make an example of me, in an attempt to scare ICMP into dropping the investigation of Russian atrocities."

Sean took her hand in his. She was icy cold. He knew Eastern Ukraine had been a bad trip for her—it had preceded Grand Cayman, and she'd said some things that indicated it had been an ordeal, but she'd never shared details.

She squeezed his fingers. "It was the scariest day of my life—until yesterday's car chase and this morning's fire. Dr. Parks thinks I have PTSD from that incident, but I'm dreaming about the kids' graves because it's the safer stress to face."

"Why have you never told me any of this?" Sean asked.

She shrugged. "I really don't like to think about that day. I'm doing my best to forget it." She glanced up and met the gazes of the other women in the room. "And after what Isabel and Ivy went through, it seemed pretty whiney for me to freak out about it when no one hurt me. I was just scared."

"You were terrorized," Isabel said. "It scars you. No one will rank what happened to you versus me or Ivy or Mara or Erica. Part of our bond is that we've created a safe place to share as much or as little as we want and everyone listens and supports."

"Thank you," Hazel said softly. "Maybe I'll join you for the next wine tasting."

"We'd all love that," Ivy said.

To Sean, Hazel said, "After a horrible thirty-six hours, I was released and put on a flight for the Netherlands, where ICMP is headquartered. I was told if I ever returned to Ukraine or entered Russia, I would be taken into custody and tried for espionage." She met her cousin's gaze. "Remembering how much you did to get me out of that situation makes me feel a little shitty for being so pissed at you today."

Rav smiled. "I love you, Hazel. I love Ivy and Laurel too. I do whatever it takes to protect my family."

Hazel swiped at her eyes. "Love you too, cuz. You're forgiven."

"You should have worked it longer, Hazel," Isabel said in a stage whisper. "He gets very generous when he feels guilty."

Hazel laughed. "He already bought me a microscope. I'm good."

"It didn't blow up?" Keith asked from the doorway. They all turned toward the door as he entered and stepped toward the map on the wall, staring at it as if drawn like a magnet.

"No," Hazel said. "We brought it here along with the bones on Thursday. They're locked in the basement lab." Her gaze flew to Rav's. "Unless Chase could get in there? He was in Sean's locked room."

Rav frowned. "The lab is locked tight and unused most of the time. After Alaska, I had Lee change all the codes so only a few of us have access. Sean. Keith. Ian. Me. Anyone else?" he asked Keith.

"Josh and Ethan, when he's in town. He's in Hawaii right now."

Ethan was a firearms instructor who rotated between the Hawaii, Alaska, and Virginia compounds.

"Is Josh in the compound?" Rav asked.

Sean nodded. "He's living here full-time."

"Send him to check the lab and have him report back."

Keith called Josh and gave the instructions. Call complete, he took the seat at the table next to Hazel and said, "What else did I miss?"

It took a few minutes to bring the CEO up-to-date. When told about Sean's fake relationship with Hazel, Keith let out a bark of laughter. "How'd you like Trina's prize package?"

Hazel snickered.

Sean kept a straight face—barely—and said, "Your wife has very good taste. Tell her I said thank you."

Keith laughed again. "You're welcome." His phone buzzed, and he answered it, all traces of humor gone, back in operative mode. After a moment, he said, "Lab checks out. Bones are fine."

Hazel let out a relived sigh.

He met Rav's gaze, a brow raised, and nodded toward the phone. Rav somehow understood the unasked question and nodded.

Into the phone, Keith said, "Yeah. Park yourself outside the lab and guard it until we head down. Take names of anyone who enters that corridor who shouldn't." He hit the End button and set down the phone.

"I'm very sorry about the annex, Alec," Hazel said, "but I'm so relieved the bones are fine."

"Me too, Haze," Rav said. "We'll deal with the mess at the estate later. Right now, this is all that matters."

"Anything else I need to know?" Keith asked.

They went over the maps and Hazel's detention in Ukraine, bringing Keith fully up to speed with what had been shared so far, then they came back to the letter.

Finally. Sean was beyond desperate to know what else it said.

"Okay. So the spy line could indicate Hazel or Matt," Isabel said, "But the 'Manchurian candidate' part is, frankly, what alarms me the most."

Rav nodded. His gaze went from Hazel to Ivy to Matt. "You need to know, there *was* a cover-up of what happened in Alaska, and part of what was withheld from the public could have led to Manchurian candidate kinds of speculation, as I was running for the Senate at the time. Sean and Keith know most of the details because they were there at the end, but even they don't know everything Isabel and I went through." He frowned. "I was abducted for several hours and tortured." His jaw snapped shut, then he took a deep breath and said, "And during that time, I overcame and killed one of my abductors, but I didn't remember that until several days later, when we found the place where I was tortured and the memory blocks dissolved."

Chapter Thirty-One

Holy crap.

Hazel had known Alec had undergone something big, but she'd never guessed anything like that. He'd killed a man and didn't remember it for days? She could see why that would raise questions for voters.

What did it take to make a man forget he'd killed someone?

"I want to be clear," Alec said. "We didn't cover up the events in Alaska to protect the campaign." He grimaced. "That was just a…side benefit. If it had only been about the campaign, I would have insisted on the world knowing everything. For Isabel and for Vin." He glanced at his wife, and she nodded. Her eyes took on that sad yet proud look she always got when her brother was mentioned.

Hazel had always wished she'd had a chance to meet Vincent Dawson. She grieved for him in a way that was similar to how she grieved for the souls of the bones she'd examined. The men, women, and children she met in death, but never in life. Every single one stayed with her, whether she observed an anomaly in their femur or zygomatic arch, she remembered and mourned them. The ones who had names, and the ones who would never be identified.

Especially the nameless, because if she didn't mourn them, who would?

"The cover-up was about national security," Alec said, pulling her wandering brain back into the meeting. "The CIA and DIA were convinced that if Russia knew Westover had been successful in his infrasound tests, they would do everything they could to replicate the results. A method of torture that broke a person down in a matter of hours but didn't leave a mark on the body, and in which the victim didn't remember the interrogation, is too powerful a weapon to let any country have in its arsenal. So the CIA and DIA cleaned up the mess, and the FBI put out the cover story you've all heard."

"But clearly, Russia found out anyway," Ivy said. "Wasn't the attack on the US Embassy in Cuba an infrasound attack?"

Alec gave a noncommittal sort of nod. "It was similar, for sure, but it might've been microwaves. It's possible Westover was sharing his data and inspired Russian scientists, or it could be the other way around. Russia would have an easier time getting human test subjects. Westover was limited to people like Chase—a man no one knew well, so his odd behavior was taken as normal for him. To be truly successful with experimental weapons like Westover was using, he'd need a lot of humans to run experiments on."

Alec had one hundred percent of Hazel's attention now.

Test subjects.

While some medical studies required diversity of the human sample, for others, having multiple people of the same age, race, and gender was ideal. Perhaps with an outlier here and there to act as a control.

All else being equal, did two individuals have the same

reaction to infrasound? Many studies had shown that women have a higher tolerance for pain than men. From what she'd read, most forms of torture relied on terror combined with pain to break the subject, so a study that only included men would have different results from those conducted on women.

"What's up, Haze?" Sean asked.

She looked up sharply and realized everyone was staring at her. She must've made some sort of sound when the idea hit her. She shook her head. "Nothing. Just a theory. Something I need to consider when I'm in the lab." She looked to Alec. "What else was in the letter?"

He looked at her with concern, then lifted the paper again and resumed reading. "*Resign, or the redhead will pay the price. You are a traitor who doesn't deserve your seat. Killer of men and babies. We will tell the world what we know. The bones in the cave will be identified. The redhead will expose you. The spy will strike. No one is safe. Do the right thing, or your family will get smaller.*"

He paused in the reading and met Hazel's gaze. "The reference to the redhead exposing me along with the line about bone identification seemed like a reference to you, even though there's no need for you to examine those bones. Isabel and I found the remains of the man I killed in Alaska in the back of the cave where both Vin and I were tortured. As far as I know, once the case was closed, the remains were released to next of kin for burial or cremation."

"I can see why you weren't ready to rule me out as the target," she said.

"Yes. Add to that the line about the spy striking, and Matt was back in play and a suspect. Or again, they were referring to you with the idea you would expose the cover-up in Alaska. But really, it's the final line in the letter that prevented me from sharing everything with you and Isabel."

"What is it?" Isabel asked.

Alec closed his eyes for a long moment. He took a deep

breath, then focused on the paper. His voice was hard and flat as he read the last sentence. "*Resign, or we will wake the sleeping monster with the ring of a silent bell.*"

Isabel gasped.

Alec set the paper down and took her hand. "Silent. That's the word that had me on the phone to Sean, sending him to the reservoir to pick up Isabel. Infrasound is inaudible to the human ear. Some animals communicate with it, but humans aren't among them. It's sound that's *felt* by humans. A bell that's silent must be referring to infrasound."

"Wake the sleeping monster?" Ivy asked.

"Chase Johnston," Sean said. "The way he's behaving. He's still in their control."

"I think so," Alec said. "When I first read it, I thought it referred to Isabel, that Westover had planted something in her mind that last day." He met her gaze. "But I also knew it could be an empty threat, to freak us out. To freak *me* out. I didn't want you terrorized again when it might not be true."

"Holy shit, Alec." Isabel had turned white. Even her many freckles appeared to have lost their pigment.

"I'm sorry, honey." He closed his eyes and took another deep breath. He opened them again, his focus entirely on Isabel. "I will find these motherfuckers and destroy them. It's not simply someone who knows what happened in Alaska. Whoever wrote this note, whoever is messing with Chase, they *worked* with Westover."

Hazel slowly stood from her seat. "I think it's time I examine the bones and see if I can figure out why they didn't want Isabel to find them—or me to examine them—so badly they risked everything by coming after me and blowing up the annex."

Chapter Thirty-Two

They stood as a group in front of the locked steel door to the lab. Josh had reported that no one visited the corridor under his watch, and was dismissed. Now, they were ready to enter.

"The large incinerator and hazmat disposal system is built in and can't be removed. There are sprinkler systems for decontamination and other state-of-the-art equipment. I didn't want to destroy it, but given the experimentation Beck was running down here," Rav said, "and the secret lab room we found in Alaska, access to this area is granted only to our most trusted personnel."

"Any chance there's another secret lab here?" Matt asked.

"Five years ago, the FBI scoured every inch of this building before I was allowed to take possession of the compound. Three years ago, after we found the Alaska lab, we did another search here and of the other compounds and didn't find anything. Under Beck's ownership, only the Alaska and Virginia compounds had labs. The other facilities are much smaller, mostly housing for operatives working for our bigger security clients. We've reviewed blueprints and measured and pounded on walls, finding some hidden storage spaces but nothing like the hidden lab in Alaska."

"You should get Ivy's mapping equipment in here," Matt said. "CAM can see through walls."

Ivy shook her head. "CAM can't see through steel. Plus there's no way to calibrate to the natural landscape when nothing is natural here."

Rav punched in the security code on the number pad next to the door, pressed his thumb to the biometric scanner, then pulled out his set of keys. "The lab requires a code, thumbprint, and a key."

"Which I'm thankful for right now," Hazel said. "Chase had no problem entering Sean's quarters, locked with just a code."

"Yeah," Rav said. "I'm going to ask Lee to go over the system and see if Chase has access to one of the master bypass codes."

"Good idea," Sean said as Rav pushed the heavy door open. No whooshing Star Trek door for the lab. In the event of a catastrophic power outage, all electronic doors in the compound unlocked and could be easily slid open. This door had old-school hinges that could only be accessed from the inside. Rav hadn't messed around when sealing off the lab.

The lights came on automatically, and Hazel let out another sigh of relief as she approached the bones laid out on the big metal trays. As far as Sean could tell, everything was just as they'd left it Thursday night.

She made a beeline for the stool in front of the microscope and flicked the switch to light the bright light bars that hung from the ceiling above that table. She ran a hand over the neck of the microscope. Sean recognized the touch as a caress, one he'd felt several times from that same hand, and he smiled.

She liked him at least as much as she liked her fancy new

microscope, and with Hazel MacLeod, that was saying something.

She lifted her glasses, letting them rest on top of her head, then leaned down and put her eyes to the lenses. Her dark auburn hair slid down, curtaining her face. She tucked a lock behind her ear and adjusted something on the scope. The bright light above haloed her, bringing out the deep red lights in her hair, and Sean felt a kick in the gut and a fierce male pride.

His.

That long, slender neck. The narrow chin. Those soft, sweet pink lips.

His. All his.

Her incredible, magnificent brain. Her compassionate soul that guided her to choose a line of work in which she gave a voice to long-silenced victims.

He was absolutely crazy about her.

When this ordeal was over, he was going to take that vacation Rav had talked about as part of his cover, but for real. He'd take Hazel to a cabin or a beach or wherever the hell she wanted to go, and they'd spend a week experimenting with all the toys they'd won.

He'd wasted a hell of a lot of time these last few years. He wasn't about to squander another minute.

Isabel, Ivy, Alec, and Matt asked questions about the bones on the table, while Sean stood back from the group, watching Hazel.

"Doesn't look so fake now," Keith said softly, stepping to his side. "Given the way you look at her."

Sean kept his gaze on her as he smiled and said, "I'm thinking when my sister is done with chemo, I won't be going back to Dubai after all."

Keith nodded. "The client will be disappointed, but your replacement will be glad for the extension."

"You upset that Rav didn't bring you in the loop on the threat sooner?"

He shook his head. "Nah. It's all part of the job. And given that Chase is involved, it's good he didn't bring Raptor in officially." He glanced toward the door. "Speaking of. I'm useless here. I'm going to check on Chase, see if he's woken up."

Rav turned. "When you're done there, I want to meet in your office. Isabel needs a computer to research forest or other fires in the vicinity of the reservoir in the years since Beck and Small purchased the land, and Matt's going to do some dark web searching for us."

Keith gave a sharp nod and left the lab. The others followed, as there was nothing they could do to help Hazel. Only Sean would stay in the lab with her as she worked.

The thick door closed, and Sean engaged the dead bolt. He turned to face her. "Alone at last."

She laughed. "If you think I'm fooling around with you in this creepy biohazard lab in front of a bunch of human remains, you're nuts."

He circled the table and pulled her into his arms. "The biohazards were cleaned years ago." He winked and pressed a kiss on her lips, then cradled her head against his chest. "But no fooling around when you have work to do. I'm not a fan of skulls watching either. Might give me performance issues."

She snickered, then pulled back, meeting his gaze. "I should get to work."

He ran his knuckles over her chin. "You going to be okay? Examining the bones?"

She nodded. "This feels right." She let out a deep breath. "I think a lot about bones that are entrusted to me. It's sacred to handle human remains, no matter what the circumstance." She waved her hand over the table. "We didn't meet in life…

and the person they once were would never have wanted or expected to end up in my care in death. But regardless, here we are. And *these* bones... Someone tried to destroy them, but they didn't. I don't think I've ever felt so protective of bones, so connected, as I do to these now. We will find out what happened to them. We will tell the world who they are. They will be counted. Justice will be late, and it won't be easy, but there will be justice."

She spoke fiercely, the fear and anxiety gone from her eyes. Competent, confident Hazel was in control. "You are so damn amazing," he said softly. Reverently.

She shook her head. "I'm not special, but I love that you think I am."

"You are special, Hazel. And not just because you're good at your job. You're special because you give more than lip service to empathy. You go to hostile, foreign nations and hold them accountable for the atrocities they commit. You care about *all* the victims. Even the inconvenient ones that yank you from your much-needed break. I've always been impressed with your job, but I never understood the emotional toll it took on you. I know you aren't 'fixed.' There will be more panic attacks and nightmares in the future. But you won't face them alone. I will be right by your side, if you'll let me."

"There's nothing I want more. But I'm afraid it will wear you out, because one thing I've figured out today, in the midst of all this crazy, is how important my job is to me. I don't want to give it up. I can't give it up. So I need to find a way to cope so I won't have to. This could be a very long haul."

"I don't care if it takes the rest of our lives. I'm not a basket full of rainbows and puppies either. I'm terrified of letting my sister down. My nieces down. I feel helpless if I can't muscle my way through a problem, and let's face it, few problems require muscle."

"Oh, Sean, you are the best man I know, and I can honestly say I know some pretty great ones. But in all the years I've known you, I've never seen you actually use muscle to defuse a situation. You use logic and calm and your crazy-good people skills to talk people down when tensions rise, like when you were protecting Ivy during Patrick's trial and that guy cornered her in a restaurant and started screaming she was a traitor. You were amazing, the way you spoke to him and kept him calm until the police arrived. And I bet you're amazing with your nieces too. I can't wait to see what Uncle Sean is like."

He smiled, his chest feeling warm at Hazel's words. "He's pretty goofy."

"I bet he's super hot."

He laughed, cupped her face, and kissed her deeply. They both needed this break. In a way, it was just as grounding as describing buttons or sex in the forest. After a long, enjoyable moment, he raised his head and said, "I love you." It surprised him, how easy the words were to say. He'd never been able to do it before. But then, he'd never felt for anyone like he did for Hazel.

She kissed his neck and whispered, "I love you. I'm still a little amazed this is happening. Us, I mean."

"Oh, honey, it's happening. I'm just kicking myself for waiting so long." He released her. "But now I need to let you work. Like before, I'll be planted in the corner watching you."

"I wish you could read a book or something. This is going to be pretty boring."

"Even though we should be safe locked in here, I can't allow getting distracted by a book. Don't worry about me. I'm good." He nipped her earlobe. "And watching you is no hardship." He stepped back and took his seat in the corner.

This part of the job—vigilant watching, in a relatively

safe space—could get tedious, but not today. He had a beautiful woman to watch and a major puzzle to solve.

After clipping the microphone from the digital recorder to her lapel, Hazel slipped on a pair of magnifying goggles over her glasses and plucked a bone from the first tray. As before, she described the bone, noting marks and breaks that were pre- or postmortem. It took her thirty minutes to go through the first tray of seven bones.

A knock on the door and Sean checked the monitor for the door camera, seeing Ivy and Matt. Ivy held up a coffee carafe and two mugs. Sean jumped from his seat to admit them.

"Bless you," Hazel said upon seeing the coffee mugs.

Ivy poured her sister coffee and sat at a stool across the table from Hazel's workstation. "I wanted to ask what the idea was that you had when we were all in the conference room. You said it was something to consider when you were in the lab."

"I was thinking about the human testing that was done in Alaska. Westover was severely limited in his test subjects. It was a small town in remote Alaska. Not exactly a large population to draw from."

Ivy cocked her head. "Unlike, say, Virginia. Where Raptor had another lab."

"Yeah. Exactly." She waved an arm toward the bones filling the trays. "I only did a preliminary examination last week, but what I saw was…somewhat uniform. It's hard to determine race, but several are likely Black. The thing that I find interesting is all except one skull are male. And all are in the twenty-five-to-thirty-five age range. Even a similar height based on the long bones."

Sean slid from his seat and moved to the table, wanting to see both sisters' faces as they discussed Hazel's theory. Matt had the same interested look.

"You think these men could have been test subjects?" Ivy asked.

Hazel shrugged. "It's possible. Where might you find twenty-six men, all of similar size and age?"

"A privately owned jail?" Sean said, his belly churning at the idea.

"But Beck and Small never got their venture. The private jail wasn't built," Ivy said.

"No, but that could have been the plan," Hazel said. "When that fell through, maybe they got their prisoners from somewhere else. Like, from the local sheriff."

"We need to look up how long Taylor has been sheriff," Matt said.

"And look for news stories of missing prisoners in the same time period," Ivy added.

Hazel took a sip of her coffee. "While you do that, I'll examine every micron of the bones and look for whatever the hell it is they're afraid I'd see."

"You're certain there's something to find?" Matt asked.

"No. But being chased down and shot at, combined with the annex blowing up, makes me think they're worried I *could* find something."

"We'll leave you to it, then," Ivy said. "Isabel's looking for news accounts of fires. We'll start digging into Taylor and missing persons."

"Thanks, sis. And thanks for the coffee."

"No problem. The kitchen is working on breakfast. Someone will deliver a tray when it's ready."

Sean locked the door behind them, then settled at the table with his coffee to watch Hazel. "You think these guys were experimented on, like Chase and Vincent Dawson?"

It was likely Vincent Dawson, Isabel's brother, was the first test subject at the Alaska compound. Sean knew Isabel had moved to Tamarack to prove her brother had been murdered. In the end, she did prove it, but Vin's death had been part of the cover-up insisted upon by the CIA, to prevent other countries from attempting to replicate Westover's work.

"My gut says yes. It's unusual to find bones like this in the US. If this were Rwanda or Bosnia, I'd assume from gender and age they were soldiers. But then there would be bullet holes. And clothing."

"The flow of water sifting the bones couldn't have removed clothing fibers?"

"It would remove some—even a lot, certainly. But the clothes would still be there, in the silt bed, just not on the bones. Cloth preserves really well in water. These men were stripped before they were burned."

Sean studied the remains laid out on the table. Who knew what they'd been through before they were stripped and burned?

He thought of the torture Vin had suffered. Sean had met him once, when he'd been sent to Alaska to fill in for a week-long training two months before the soldier died. Vin had been one of those charismatic people you couldn't help but like. Quick with a joke, friendly. A natural teacher.

Westover had tested his infrasound weapon on Vin and later applied what he'd learned from torturing Vin to brainwash Chase.

Had these men undergone the same thing?

Hazel pulled her goggles back over her glasses and returned to work, recording the details of a skull, staring into the empty eye sockets. She turned the skull and described the sutures and bumps and cracks. She frowned, looking at a spot just below where the right ear would be, if the skull were covered in flesh.

She examined the spot and then removed the goggles and placed the skull beneath the microscope, all the while speaking into the microphone, describing a deep groove in the bone that he gathered wasn't natural.

"At magnification, the eight millimeter groove is consistent with a scalpel blade. Cut is one point five millimeters wide in the center, tapering at the ends to point seven five millimeters. Groove is four millimeters deep at the apex."

She placed the skull back on its tray and slid from the stool to reach for another skull on a tray just out of her reach. Sean would hand it to her, but she'd explained the first day that for chain of evidence and the integrity of the police investigation, only she could touch the bones.

She examined the second skull, only checking the spot behind the ear. She pulled the magnification goggles over her eyes and flicked on the light bar at the top. She returned that skull and then grabbed another. This time, she cursed upon looking at the spot behind the ear.

Sean wanted to ask her what she saw, but he didn't want to break her concentration. She went from one skull to the next. Finally, on the ninth one, she said, "Gotcha, you son of a bitch!"

"What is it?"

"Several of the skulls have a cut in the mastoid process of the temporal bone. And the ones that don't have the cut, the mastoid process is missing—and one of those is broken along the same cut line. But this one"—she held up the skull with the right side facing him—"has a small fragment of plastic embedded in the groove. The bone healed around the plastic, holding onto a piece when the implant was removed."

Chapter Thirty-Three

Hazel called everyone down to the lab. She turned on the projector that attached to a magnifying camera and showed her findings on the large screen. It might be a creepy biohazard lab, but it did have excellent camera equipment.

On the screen, she pointed to the small piece of what she believed to be plastic. It held a hint of red. The plastic had probably absorbed some rust from the lake bed, discoloring the item.

She then used the camera to show the scalpel cut grooves in each of the skulls. Many of the cuts showed signs of healing, indicating the subject was alive when the cut had been made.

"So you think someone performed surgery, implanting something behind the right ear?" Alec asked.

"I do. My guess is it's a chip of some sort, but we'll need more than a tiny fragment to be certain."

Isabel touched behind her ear. Her eyes held a haunted look. "What would that do?"

"There could be any number of things, but given the consistent placement of the groove, it could relate to hearing, with wires that stimulated the cochlea or auditory nerve. A transmitter of some sort."

Isabel frowned. "Or a translator," she said softly.

"What do you mean?" Alec asked.

"Not a language translator, a sound wave translator. Or… an infrasound translator." She continued to rub the spot behind her ear. "I don't remember much from…my experience in Alaska, but there was one conversation they let me remember. It had to do with the timing of being zapped, or maybe it was the frequency. It's all a little fuzzy. But the thing I *do* remember is they wore masks, and I was told it was because the mask translated their speech into a sound wave I could hear and understand when they were zapping me. It could be bullshit, the masks could have been worn just to be disorienting and scary, but…I don't think so. They were pretty specific and changed their voices even when I wasn't being subjected to infrasound waves."

"So it's possible Westover was working with masks," Keith said. "While in Virginia, they were perfecting the technology to deliver infrasound without the need for a big, bulky mask."

"With a transmitter, they could dial in on a victim," Alec said. "Focus the sound wave right on them so no one else would feel the effects. Hell, they could use an implant to trigger nausea and vertigo. And they wouldn't need to wear masks to deliver orders in public."

"Manchurian candidate," Matt said softly.

"Chase," Isabel said.

Hazel stared at the skull before her. "We need to look for a scar behind Chase's ear."

As one, they stood and headed to the door. Sean locked the room behind them. No one had the patience for the elevator, and they ran up the three flights of stairs to the medical clinic, where Chase Johnston was asleep and still handcuffed to a bed.

The medic examined Chase at Alec's request, while everyone else waited outside the room. After a moment, Alec stepped to the door, his face blank. "Hazel?" He nodded toward the hospital bed, and she stepped into the room.

"Take a look," Alec said. "We need your opinion."

She paused to look at the man on the bed. Chase was pale, his skin slack with slumber. The monitor showed a strong heartbeat. She wasn't a medical doctor, but she'd taken classes after earning her PhD to have a better understanding of how the skeletal system worked with the other systems of the body in life.

She grabbed a pair of latex gloves from the box on the counter and slipped them on before approaching the bed. Before touching him, she turned to the medic. He nodded his permission, and she turned Chase's head slightly to get a better view of the area behind his right ear. The scar, if it was there, would be just above the hairline. She ran her fingers over Chase's short hair and felt the hard ridge of a scar, even through the latex.

She let out a soft gasp and reached for the magnifying goggles in the holder mounted to the wall along with the sphygmomanometer and stethoscope. She flipped on the high-powered light above the lenses and examined the spot behind his ear up close. She could see the space between indi-vidual hairs and the puckered skin of a suture scar.

She stood and flipped off the light. "The FBI will want to shave the spot and take photos. But yeah. He's been cut there. Same place. The length of the cut is what I would expect on the skin's surface, longer than the groove in the bone."

"Westover didn't do that to him," Alec said. "He was

thoroughly examined, X-rayed, MRIed, you name it, after what happened in Alaska. When he was medically cleared to work for Raptor again, we were given his records. If he'd had a chip in his head, we'd have known. *He'd* have known."

"It appears someone picked up the testing where Westover left off, after Chase started working for Raptor again."

Chapter Thirty-Four

Hazel spent the next hour on the phone with the Virginia medical examiner and then with a forensic specialist in the FBI. The medical examiner agreed to sign a release, acknowledging that Hazel informed her that the remains collected from Anderson Lake would be released to FBI forensic analysts. This was officially an FBI investigation.

Paperwork went back and forth via computer, and at last the proper signatures gave Hazel permission to hand the bones over to the FBI. They agreed to send a team to the compound, to be accompanied by the Deputy Special Agent in Charge who was in charge of the investigation into both explosions. She would bring a doctor with her who would examine Chase and arrange for him to be admitted into a DC hospital under guard—for his protection, not because he was a prisoner. Once safe in the hospital, medical professionals would begin the difficult task of determining how to remove the implant.

Of course, first they had to determine if it was there, but Hazel had no doubt about what they'd find.

But who was behind it?

The FBI would be getting search warrants for Small's—and Raptor's—property along the reservoir. Raptor had a few buildings—storage, mostly—that had been scoured along with the rest of Raptor's holdings. Small had the vacation home that overlooked the reservoir.

Hazel rubbed her temples. She was exhausted. She still needed to eat breakfast. And shower. But everyone was gathered in the main conference room, and she wanted to know what the others had learned in the hours she'd been dealing with legalities.

She was alone in Keith's office, with Sean outside, guarding the door. She stood and stretched, joints popping and cracking. She met Sean in the hall.

"You okay?" he asked.

"I think so. Tired. Hungry. Angry."

"Yeah. Me too." He took her hand. "There's food in the main conference room. And Ivy has some news to share."

A buffet had been set up along the interior wall of the conference room. Hazel had missed breakfast, and the chafing dishes were filled with chicken, fish, rice, beans, vegetable soup, and green salad. She was so hungry, she loaded her plate with everything and filled a large bowl with soup.

When she took her first spoonful of soup, she let out a happy sigh and remembered Dr. Parks's warning not to load up on caffeine and forget to eat when she was working. She hadn't meant to do that today. It had simply felt too urgent to speak with the ME and FBI. She wouldn't have been able to eat before making those calls.

She frowned, thinking of Dr. Parks. She was supposed to see her this afternoon. She pulled out her phone and texted the woman with one hand, because she couldn't stop eating and needed the other to cram food in her mouth.

Ivy laughed. "God, I haven't seen you eat like that since high school. But then you weren't using a smartphone. You had your nose in a book."

Hazel managed to swallow a bite of fish and rice and wiped her mouth as she said, with her focus still on her phone, "I still eat while reading, just not when people are around."

"What's so important on your phone it can't wait?" Sean asked.

"I just remembered I was supposed to have a follow-up appointment with Dr. Parks today. Canceling, but I should reschedule. I want to talk about panic attacks that are triggered by stress other than work. That's been…new. I think I have a grip on it, but still. And then there's work stuff to talk about."

"You can't talk about Chase," Alec said. "Even though she was his doctor, she's not with the CIA anymore."

Hazel nodded. "I know. I would never talk about the specifics of any homicide investigation I'm working on."

Her phone pinged with a response from the doctor's assistant. "I can reschedule for tomorrow afternoon, or Friday morning." She looked up and met Sean's gaze. "Is tomorrow good for you?"

Sean nodded. "My schedule is yours to command."

"Hopefully, you won't need a bodyguard much longer," Alec said. "With the bones being turned over to the FBI, it negates the reason to go after you, but for now, we hope whoever was after you doesn't know the bones survived the blast. You're still in danger until the search warrants are served."

"So Friday, then?" she asked.

"Next week would be even better," Alec said.

She considered the request. "I can wait."

"Good. I want you to stay here while the FBI gathers

evidence for the search warrants. Will that be a problem?" Alec asked.

It wasn't like the estate was her home anyway. Living in the compound was fine for her. "Will that be a problem for you, Sean? What about your mom and sister?"

"I'll explain the situation as much as I can. We'll reschedule dinner for next week. They'll understand."

"But I'll be safe here. You can spend time with your mom."

Sean gave her a look that was both confused and irritated. "Did you forget that Chase got inside my quarters?"

"But Lee is going to update all the lock codes this afternoon—"

"This is my job, Hazel."

"But your m—"

Sean cut off her protest with a kiss that was probably deeper than it should be in a room full of people that included both his bosses. But if it didn't concern him, she had no complaints. She liked the way he wasn't shy about making it known they were really a couple now.

He raised his head. She opened her eyes to find him staring down at her with an intense look in his deep brown eyes. With yellow flecks.

"You done arguing now?" he asked.

She nodded, no longer sure why she'd objected to begin with.

Keith laughed. "Trust me, Sean, that doesn't work once you're past the honeymoon stage."

"Right?" Matt said. "I haven't won an argument since Grand Cayman."

Ivy snickered. "You didn't win even then, sweetheart."

"Let me keep my illusions."

Hazel returned to her meal and phone. She texted her reply to Dr. Parks's office, scheduling an appointment for next

Monday. She forwarded the exchange to Sean and Alec so they'd have the updated schedule.

"What about you?" Hazel asked between bites of food. "Are you and Isabel moving back to the estate?"

"Not for a few days. The FBI is handling the explosion investigation, and they're coming here to interview us. Gandalf is going to be delivered this afternoon. This is home until we know who wrote that letter."

"We, however, will be heading home shortly," Ivy said. "It appears the note had nothing to do with Matt. We're in the clear, and Julian is wondering why we didn't pick him up from Mara's last night, plus we're supposed to go scuba diving with Luke and Undine while they're in town. "

At Hazel's confused look, Matt said, "Luke and I are… old friends. Sort of." His face broke into a warm smile that was somehow different.

She fixed her brother-in-law with a look. "You have so much explaining to do."

He grinned. "I will. I promise." He looked to Alec. "In the meantime, I can't tell the FBI about the canceled hit on Chase. The agents involved in this investigation don't know about me, and the more who know, the harder it will be to maintain my identity."

"If a connection to Russia can't be found through other channels," Alec said, "I'll ask my CIA contact to interview you and pass the information on to the FBI as unsourced intelligence."

"Fair enough."

Ivy stood and moved to the computer console. "Before we go, I have some information to share." She opened a file, and a map of Virginia was projected onto the whiteboard. "A few years ago, MacLeod-Hill was contracted by the Commonwealth of Virginia to compile data for crime statistics, basically, an automated program that would scan various news sites in Virginia and pull locational data for violent crime: homicide, sexual assault, missing persons, robberies that included weapons or in which someone was injured. They wanted map layers that could be sorted in any number of different ways. Solved, unsolved. They were particularly interested in a database that could access historical data, which was one of my specialties. Rather than spending hours today searching news websites for reports of missing persons, I called my former client and asked if they could run some searches for me. It's all public information, and she was happy to do it. It took less than ten minutes for her to find and email me the information we're looking for."

Ivy tapped the mouse, and a bulleted list giving the search parameters appeared. "I asked for missing persons within a fifty-mile radius of the reservoir for the last twenty-five years —the time Small has owned the reservoir property. I didn't limit to males of a certain age. I didn't want to bias the search results. There were plenty of results that could be easily disregarded—a seventy-two year old woman with Alzheimer's was never found, children abducted by estranged parents. Runaway teenage girls.

"But there were several matches that could paint a very different picture." She tapped the mouse again, and a PDF of a newspaper article appeared on the screen. The headline read: "Cameroonian Immigrant Reported Missing." A photo of a young Black man accompanied the article.

"This is Samuel Baima," Ivy said. "He'd been in the US for five years, working as a grocery bagger in a town twenty miles from the reservoir. When he didn't show up for work for several days, a concerned coworker called the police. That's when Baima's immigrant status was discovered—he'd overstayed his visa and was living in Virginia illegally. Apparently, he'd purchased a social security number from a hacker so he could work. He had no driver's license, and he'd purchased a car without transferring the title. The registration was expired. He disappeared seven years ago. He hasn't been found."

Hazel stared at the smiling face in the photo. Was his skull down in the basement lab?

Ivy pulled up another news story. Another illegal immigrant reported missing. This one hadn't been reported for eight weeks because of fear over his illegal status.

The next slide surprised Hazel. The article was about a woman. "This is Selena Ramirez. Six years ago, she reported three men missing. All illegal immigrants from Central American countries. She faced a backlash from her community because she dared to go to the police and report the missing men, bringing attention to other illegal immigrants. Selena herself had naturalized citizen status, and she believed the illegal community was being targeted, that either these were hate crimes or modern slavery.

"Sheriff Taylor wrote the missing men off as victims of a drug war. Six weeks after Selena went public with the story of the missing men, she herself disappeared. Sheriff Taylor's investigation turned up evidence that a Central American drug cartel had removed her because she was drawing too much attention to their operation, and closed the book on the investigation without any arrests—or any body."

Hazel rose from her seat and approached the screen, staring at the woman's face. Big brown eyes, full lips. Thick dark hair. High cheekbones. Selena Ramirez had been gorgeous in life. Excellent bone structure. Was this the sole woman in the basement?

"I can do a photo overlay, see if her bone structure matches the skull we have. It's not definitive, but if nothing else, we can rule her out."

"So Taylor was rounding up illegal immigrants that fit certain criteria for human testing?" Isabel said.

"I think so," Ivy said. "Imagine how many he could pull over, arrest for driving without a license, but then…not file the paperwork. Instead of taking them to the county jail, he took them to Beck and Small's operation. And family and friends couldn't report them missing. How could they when they were in the country illegally? Or they'd overstayed their visa?"

"He's a monster," Hazel said softly, still staring at Selena. "Ivy, I want this picture. Please email it to me."

"Already done, along with pictures of the other cases that fit the criteria."

The FBI would do their own analysis, but Hazel would do this photo overlay herself. She had to know if the brave young woman had been found. Justice for Selena.

Sean stepped up beside her and slipped an arm around her waist. She leaned into him, her gaze on the projected image. "We'll get these assholes," he said.

"I know. I just wonder how many more there are. And why they were dumped in the lake."

"I know a man who can probably explain that."

Everyone looked up to see Curt in the doorway. He stepped into the room and took a seat at the opposite end of the table from Alec. "I was given the Cliff Notes version of what's going on from Alec, and then I received a call from DC US Attorney Aurora Ames, asking for specifics beyond what the FBI shared with her. She is very interested in the evidence so far because she thinks we can use it as leverage to get Robert Beck to talk." Curt glanced around the conference room. "If Beck was doing human testing in the basement lab or on the reservoir property, he might turn on his accomplices for a reduced sentence."

"Beck might be ready to deal?" Alec asked.

Curt shrugged. "Maybe. He's been in prison for four

years now. It's…not going well for him. If turning on Small reduces his sentence, he might take it."

"What do you think he can tell us?" Alec asked. "The testing on Chase happened after he'd been in prison for a year."

"He might not know about that, but he knows what they were doing in the basement here five years ago, and from what you've said so far, it sounds like someone resumed that testing. If nothing else, Beck will know who was working with infrasound besides Westover in Alaska."

"Is it worth letting him out of prison to get Small? We might be able to get Small without giving up Beck," Alec said.

"It'll be up to the Justice Department to decide how much Small is worth. Beck could just be the nail in his coffin, and all he'll get in the exchange is a move to a minimum-security facility followed by house arrest. He won't turn on his Russian compatriots because they'll kill him in prison or out. If he gives up the Russians who own him, he's a dead man. But we can get Small."

Chapter Thirty-Five

*I*t was evening by the time the last bones left the basement lab and were loaded into an FBI van. Hazel looked utterly beat after hours of explanations and documentation. Before the FBI took possession of the bones, she'd photographed every single one using the camera and light box installed in the lab. She'd also made three-dimensional scans of several bones, including the female skull and the cranium with the partially embedded chip.

Now she and Sean were alone in the empty lab as she backed up the massive files to a server Lee had created just for her. "Okay. This lab might be creepy and have bad smallpox juju, but it's also pretty damn awesome. The lighting is great and the equipment top of the line, even if it is over five years old."

"I'm pretty sure the smallpox juju is gone," he said.

"We hope."

He glanced toward the back wall. "I'm more freaked out about the incinerators. All the shit Beck was doing, it makes me wonder what was burned down here."

She turned to look at the iron door mounted to the brick wall. "Great. Now I'm afraid of the incinerator."

"Let's get out of here, then." He was more than ready to get out of the basement and retreat to his quarters.

"Upload's almost done."

He moved to stand behind her and watch the progress bar. He could stand for hours and watch a person work while he was on guard duty, but waiting for a computer that was lagging? That drove him nuts.

The moment the progress indicator reached a hundred percent, he scooped her up and tossed her over his shoulder. "Let's go."

She laughed. "What are you doing? I can walk."

He was reminded of the times he carried her from the lake. "I know you can. But I like carrying you."

Outside the lab, he paused to lock the door, then carried her to the elevator. Inside, he pinned her in the corner and kissed her. He kept his hands on her shoulder and face for the guys monitoring the security cameras. No reason to give them a show. He raised his head and smiled at her. "This girlfriend thing is kinda cool."

She stroked his cheek, staring up at him. "I'm rusty at relationships. I'll try to do it right."

"We'll figure it out together. I told Keith today I'm not going back to Dubai."

Her eyes widened. "You're not?"

He shook his head. The elevator doors opened on his floor, and he set her on her feet and took her hand as he led her down the corridor. "Nope. I'll take short-term overseas assignments if they need me, but the longer gigs are out. It's time I stop putting off life and start living my dream."

They reached his quarters, and he punched in the new code and used the newly installed thumbprint reader. His door was now biometrically coded to both him and Hazel. They entered, and he locked the door.

He'd been waiting for this moment all day. When it would be just the two of them. No responsibilities for hours. Meals weren't usually delivered to quarters, but Keith had authorized it for Sean as long as Hazel was under Raptor's protection. Even though she should be safe inside the compound, it wasn't lost on anyone that Chase had been living here for nearly three years. No matter how doubtful, they had to remain open to the idea that there were others like Chase. Or that Chase had sabotaged the facility.

Hazel wasn't to wander the building alone. The only time she could be alone was in Sean's quarters. So it made sense for them to be allowed to have food delivered.

He pulled her into his arms again. He really couldn't get enough of holding her. "*You* are my dream, Hazel. You have been for a long time. To really give us a chance, I need to stop taking off for extended assignments. Unless, of course, you go back to ICMP. Then maybe I can get jobs in the places you're sent. We can make this work."

She shook her head. "My days with ICMP are over. I should have stopped after being detained in Ukraine, but I didn't…want to let them win. To scare me away. But now, I want to start living for me. And that means being with you." She let out a soft laugh. "I actually had an interesting conversation with both the Virginia ME and FBI today. If I decide to set up my own shop, both would be interested in contracting me for either initial analysis or second opinion. It wouldn't be full-time, but I could probably get Maryland, DC, and West Virginia as clients, and JT has already promised me work with Talon & Drake. If Keith would be willing to cut a deal on the lab space here, my overhead would be low enough that I wouldn't need to work full-time."

"I love that idea. I split my time between the DC office

and here. There's always plenty of protection work for politicians and celebrities in the city, and here they need help with the trainings. If we looked at houses near here, I can deal with the commute for the city jobs. My hours aren't normal anyway, so the commute shouldn't be a big deal."

With another woman, it might seem crazy to be discussing living together on day two of their official relationship, but this was Hazel, and everything about this felt right. Overdue, actually. And Hazel didn't currently have a home, so this wasn't a conversation to put off.

She smiled and closed her eyes. "A house. Together. I like it. It feels…grounding. But then, you ground me." Her fingers tightened, gripping his shirt. "I know my head isn't going to be fixed overnight. More likely than not, I'll be up pacing half the night tonight. I've got a lot of mental work to do to sort out my anxieties, but this feels like the right path. I feel hope, where before, the anxiety was leading to depression."

"I'm in it for the long haul, no matter what path your anxiety takes you." He cupped her cheeks. "I'm going to make mistakes. I'm going to misunderstand when you are reacting out of anxiety and we'll get in fights. I'm going to say stupid things that will make you angry. But I will do my best to recognize when I'm arguing with you and when we're both fighting your anxiety."

"Thank you. I'm going to make mistakes too. A whole lot of them. But I will try to recognize when I'm upset at you or when I've been triggered by something outside of either of our control, because I'm going to keep working with bones. I want to help find justice for people like Samuel Baima and Selena Ramirez. I want Small and Taylor and whoever is working for him to pay. To suffer. To have a taste of the nightmare they inflicted on others. I don't want them to be able to hurt anyone else. To create more Chases."

"I will be by your side every step of the way. Now, we've

got sixteen hours before we need to meet the FBI at the reservoir. We can fill those hours however you want."

She closed her eyes. After a long moment, she opened them and said, "Okay. This is what I want. To shower together—not necessarily sex. Just…exploring. Comfort. Sex if we feel like it in the moment. Then I want to eat dinner in bed as we watch Monday Night Football. I don't even care who's playing. I just want to watch a mindless game and drink beer and feel safe with the man I love."

Sounded like his perfect evening. "You like football?"

"I love football. Like I said, I don't even care who's playing, but my favorite team is Baltimore. I used to like Washington, but I really can't get over the racist name."

"How did I not know this? I have season tickets to Ravens games. I give them to my sister or Keith when I'm traveling."

"I suppose this is a bad time to admit I'm only seducing you for your season tickets."

He laughed. "I don't care. As long as you seduce me. A Ravens fan." He shook his head. "You might be my perfect woman." He glanced at his watch. "Okay, we've got about ninety minutes until kickoff. Plenty of time to shower and play and then order dinner."

Hazel gave him a wicked smile. "I think we should place a bet on the game. Every time your team scores, so do you."

He laughed. "I'm not sure if I should hope for a high-scoring game or not." Then he grinned. "Then again, we've got battery-powered backup if it's a blowout."

She licked her lips. "I think I'm going to like watching football with you."

"And the guys are going to start to wonder why I don't want to watch games with them anymore."

Chapter Thirty-Six

The next three days had a strange combination of whirlwind and glacial pacing. Hazel and Isabel met with the FBI at the reservoir, and the feds began the process of getting a warrant to drain the lake again, this time bringing it even lower to fully expose the bed in an attempt to gather as many of the remains as possible.

Isabel suggested they screen the materials that had been pumped to the settlement pond in hopes of recovering a chip or other evidence, and a Talon & Drake vacuum truck was brought in to pump up the materials and deliver it to an area where it could be screened and sorted.

Hazel had done her share of screening to look for bone fragments, and she didn't envy whoever would be tasked with sorting such a massive volume of materials. But the idea that an implant might be recovered provided hope.

Chase was hospitalized under guard as doctors tried to determine how to safely remove the implant. Information on his condition was scant, but she took hope from learning he'd woken up several times—he wasn't in a coma—but was disoriented, and stress and panic caused his heart rate to spike. Considering his heart had stopped during an infrasound attack three years ago, doctors had opted to sedate him rather than risk another cardiac arrest.

Wednesday was a quiet day. Hazel spent the day in the basement lab, writing up her analysis of the bones. She submitted her report to the FBI late in the evening. She needed to write up her notes while everything was fresh in her mind, as this could become the foundation of the case against Sheriff Taylor, if evidence was found to connect him to the missing persons. If the case went to trial, odds were she'd be called to testify.

Thursday morning began normally. Or as normal as living with Sean in the Virginia compound could be. She woke to kisses and lovemaking followed by breakfast delivered by support staff.

Hazel could get used to this lifestyle, even if Sean's suite only had tiny, bulletproof windows. The lighting was high quality and mimicked sunlight as much as possible. The food was healthy and delicious, and she didn't have to cook or wash dishes. And there was Sean, at her beck and call twenty-four seven.

This was her idea of paradise.

She'd dreamed of bones in the night, but the normal kind of dream that came after an intensive day staring at photos and virtual models. The dreams were neither good nor bad. Just her subconscious continuing the work of the day.

They'd taken to meeting in the conference room at ten in the morning for an update. Hazel entered the room, feeling relaxed and a bit more dreamy than she had any right to feel considering how dangerous the situation had been just a few days ago.

She poured a cup of coffee from the ready pot and took a

cherry Danish from the platter of pastries, then sat in her usual seat at the table, startled to realize Alec was the only person in the large room. Isabel and Keith should be here, while Alec should not. He'd planned to call in to today's meeting from his office in the Senate.

His expression was tense. Angry. Concerned.

She set down the pastry that was halfway to her lips, her stomach suddenly sour. "Alec? What's wrong?"

Sean set his coffee on the table next to her, but didn't take a seat. "Something happen to Chase?"

Alec stood. He picked up his tablet and circled the table to Hazel's side. "There is something you need to see. I didn't want to tell you on the phone. I'm sorry."

He set the tablet on the table. On the screen was the Voigt Forum banner with the day's date. The headline said: *Senator Ravissant Harbors Known Spy.*

She read the subheading and cursed, but it wasn't the worst thing in the world. Apparently, they were accusing her of spying for Ukraine against Russia. "That sucks, but it will be more of a problem for ICMP than for me."

"There's more."

She reached out to scroll down and realized her fingers were shaking. But really, what could Voigt Forum do to her? It was a white nationalist propaganda site. Everyone knew it was crazy-pants bullshit.

The article attacked her integrity and her work. Not surprisingly, they claimed her testimony in a hate crime trial three years before had been false. Standard stuff for Voigt Forum from what she'd heard. She didn't read it and didn't know anyone who did besides Alec.

She kept scrolling down, and there was a photo of her with Sean at the rally last Friday. And that…was where it started to get ugly. They attacked Sean's service in the Navy.

Lied about his discharge status and implied he left after being investigated for selling arms to the enemy. It was suggested that Alec and Raptor orchestrated a cover-up, helping Sean to avoid prosecution.

The words were ugly, but they were easily refuted lies. She squeezed Sean's hand before scrolling further.

She felt a sucker punch at seeing the photo of her and Sean kissing in front of the trail marker. Their first kiss, and Voigt Forum published it with a caption calling her a race traitor and Sean a criminal.

It was vile.

"They must've hacked Trina's or Sean's phone to get the photo," Hazel said, her voice thin. But then, she could barely breathe.

"Either that, or Chase got Trina's phone. I'm sorry," Alec repeated, then he flicked the screen to bring the final photo into view.

Hazel's hands were on the tree trunk, Sean's face buried in her neck, and he pressed against her from behind, his visible hand cupping her breast under the halter of her dress. The photo cut off at the hipline, but it was obvious what they were doing in the forest.

Her vision tunneled. She couldn't breathe.

A photo of the first time she'd made love with Sean had been posted on a white nationalist website. They'd taken a sacred memory and branded it with their ugly hate.

The violation tasted like copper. Or maybe she'd bit her tongue.

She stood abruptly, spilling her coffee over the tablet. The coffee scalded her, or the mug cut her hand. She wasn't sure. There was just a sensation that wasn't pleasant.

She cradled her hand to her chest and tried to take in air. Nothing came. She kicked at the chair that trapped her next to the table.

Arms came for her, but she shoved them away. She needed air. She needed out. She twisted for the door, dodging grabbing arms to lunge for it. Her shoulder slammed into something, causing her to spin. Or maybe her vision was spinning. Her knees gave out. Arms locked around her as the world went black.

Chapter Thirty-Seven

"She didn't hit her head," Sean said to Rav as he scooped Hazel in his arms. "I think she passed out. Like she did in the lake."

"I'm sorry, Sean. But she—you both—needed to know."

Sean was already in the hall, heading for the clinic. "They couldn't get to her physically, so they went for the mental attack." He adjusted Hazel's position and noticed her hand was bleeding. Probably from when she'd smashed the coffee mug into the tablet. "Did Chase take the photo, or was someone else in the forest with us that night?"

"I think it was Chase. We're searching his quarters and Isabel's Prius again for another phone or a camera. But it could have been tossed from the car on the drive back after he sent it to Voigt. We'll probably never find it."

Sean looked at Hazel's pale face. He shouldn't have screwed her against the tree that night, but he didn't want to regret the memory. Didn't want to share it with the world. It was between him and Hazel. Fantasy fulfillment that had been his first step into embracing what he could have with her.

He sure as hell didn't know what to say to his boss. He should have been protecting her in the forest that night; instead, he'd taken her against a tree.

"I'm sorry." There really wasn't much he could say beyond that.

"Don't. It was my bright idea to put you in that situation, and I do remember what it's like to fall in love. I just hate that Voigt has stolen something precious from you. That it was probably Chase who did it."

They were halfway to the clinic when Hazel's eyes fluttered open. She groaned and clutched her injured hand to her chest.

Sean stopped midstride. "Sweetheart. Speak to me. You hurting anywhere besides your hand?"

She shook her head. She closed her eyes and took a deep breath. "I—I—couldn't breathe."

"I know. I think it was the same kind of panic you had in the lake. After you freaked out, you sort of…buckled."

"What happened to my hand? It's all a blur."

"You took your coffee mug and slammed it into Rav's tablet."

"Well, that's not dramatic or anything," she said under her breath. She tilted her head to Rav. "Sorry."

He shrugged. "You did what I want to do every time I visit Voigt Forum. I'm actually a little jealous. But glad it wasn't my laptop."

"We need to have a medic look at your hand," Sean said and resumed walking.

She didn't even argue. She just tucked her head against his shoulder and relaxed into his hold.

The medic cleaned her wounds and glued the deepest cut together—same as Sean had done with her foot a week and a half ago—and bandaged the smaller ones. The coffee hadn't been hot enough to scald, thankfully.

"I sure did show that tablet who was boss."

"Too bad it bit you back," the medic said. "I'm concerned about you blacking out. You say that was the second time in ten days?"

"I've been having panic attacks."

"But…fainting is caused by a sudden drop in blood pressure, while panic attacks tend to drive blood pressure up. As far as I know, fainting during a panic attack is rare."

That had never crossed Sean's mind, but then he wasn't a medic or a psychotherapist. "What did Dr. Parks say about that?"

"She said the same thing. But she also pointed out my panic attacks aren't random. They don't usually come out of the blue. There's a trigger. Similar to how fainting can have a trigger—whether it's seeing blood or hearing bad news or seeing something shocking. I think that qualifies today."

"You're scheduled to see Dr. Parks on Monday, right?" Rav asked.

"Yes."

"Call her. See if she can fit you in today."

"I'm pretty sure she's booked, but I'll call."

Rav nodded and stood. "I need to get back to the city." He kissed Hazel on the forehead and left the clinic.

Sean took Hazel back to their shared quarters. After leaving a message for her psychotherapist, trying to eat, and pacing, she ended up on his lap. He held her as she vented her pain at having their most intimate moment shared on a hate group's website.

"We could sue them for publishing the photo. There are laws against posting sex photos online without permission."

"You know that's what they want," she said. "There would be a media circus, and we would be at the center of it. I want our relationship to be…ours. I don't want to give them another piece of us to exploit."

He agreed. "I hate that people are going to look at that photo and either go into a racist rage or get turned on—probably both—but here's how I plan to deal with it. It captured a moment that was private. Intimate. Ours. We're the only two people who know what was going on in our heads. They might think they can guess. But it's not their moment, and they can't have it. I look at that photo and I see the sexiest woman I know, making a face that makes me rock-hard. Because it was me, inside you, that triggered that look on your face. That's what you looked like when I claimed you. When I made you mine for the first time. When you took me deep and I became yours. You were beautiful in the moonlight as you gave yourself to me. I'm going to pull those memories in. Hold them precious." He nibbled at her neck. "What I'm saying is—and I'm hoping this won't upset you—on one level, the photo turned me on. All I can do is claim that part and reject the rest."

She rubbed her forehead into his neck. "You did look pretty hot. With your mouth on my neck and your hand on my breast. I close my eyes, and I remember how your hand felt. How *you* felt. The sharp bark cutting into my palms."

He let out a breath of relief. She would've had every right to fly into a rage at the idea of the photo being titillating. But it was Hazel. He could be outraged, shocked, and horrified, but he would always find her beautiful, especially when he was giving her what they both had so desperately needed.

Her phone chimed, and she leaned forward to grab it from the coffee table. "Dr. Parks. She can see me in an hour."

"I guess it's time to venture out into the world, then. You up for it?"

"As I'll ever be. It helps to know that Voigt Forum's audience is generally the card-carrying-KKK type. Anyone who gives me funny looks or says anything will be telling me exactly who they are."

"I've always found it easier to deal with the blatant racists than the ones who pretend they're not."

"I've never really thought about how prevalent racism is. How I don't see it because I'm white and don't experience it."

"You're one half of an interracial couple now. You're going to start experiencing it firsthand."

"Voigt Forum is exhibit A. I hate how blind I've been to the harm sites like that do. I've dealt with their existence by avoiding the site. As if that's a solution."

He shrugged. "Pointing out their bullshit only drives traffic their way. In this instance, ignoring might be the only thing to do."

"I still can't believe a senator associated with Voigt could be elected to the Senate, but that's what racist election laws deliver. Black people stripped of their voting rights and a white supremacist in the Senate." She climbed from his lap. "After my doctor appointment, let's go to their DC office and make out on the sidewalk in front."

He laughed. "Now you're trying to get me fired. You aren't going anywhere near Voigt's offices. You do realize the people who tried to burn us out of Chase's cabin were probably from Voigt, right?"

"But I'll have a badass bodyguard to protect me."

He shook his head as he stood. "How about I take you out for a fancy dinner in the city instead?"

Her eyes widened with excitement. "It will be our first date!"

"I thought the wedding was our first date."

"No way. Doesn't count. I want our first date to be at a restaurant."

He grinned and pulled her to him. "Okay, then. It's our first date." He cupped the back of her head so she looked up at him. "You know what I want to do on our first date?"

"What?" Her voice was a little breathless. Excited. Happy.

He felt a male pride at being able to bring that out of her after the shock she'd had this morning. "I think our first date is the perfect time to start experimenting with the bondage kit."

Her eyes widened, then flared with heat. She grinned and said, "You're going to let me tie you up?" She pumped her fist. "Yes!"

He laughed. For her, anything.

"I want to sit in on the therapy session," Sean said as he drove to the city. "Any objections?"

"I don't have any, but I think Dr. Parks will. She'll say my answers will be different because you're there and we're involved. And she wouldn't be wrong. I might subconsciously try to impress you. Or edit my answers to avoid upsetting you."

"It's not your answers I want to hear. It's Dr. Parks. She was Isabel's and Chase's doctor when she was with the CIA, and she kept them on when she began her private practice. She was pretty much the only doctor they *could* see, considering she already knew all the classified details of what happened in Alaska."

"Yeah. Isabel is the one who referred me to her. She loves her. Says she was a huge help after what happened in Alaska. Iz was relieved she could continue seeing her when she went into private practice."

"And she might be great, but Chase continued with her too, and I'm wondering how she missed the signs that he was being tested on again."

Hazel considered the statement. Sean had a point. "It's

possible Chase hasn't been in to see her in a while. But regardless, I'm sure the FBI is looking at that. They've probably interviewed her already."

"Will you agree to let me sit in?"

"Sure. But I doubt she'll allow it, and she might get suspicious if we insist." She frowned. "God. Dr. Parks. She's the person I'm supposed to be able to tell everything."

"And she might be exactly what she seems."

She nodded. "I've only seen her twice. I'm just getting to know her. But Isabel…" She shook her head. "This will gut her if it's true." Isabel was already a wreck over Chase's condition.

"How would you feel about…wearing my headset under the collar of your shirt? It has a record function, and I could listen in in real time."

"That would be illegal, wouldn't it? She would have expectation of privacy."

"I don't really care if it's legal or not. I'm not looking for evidence to use in a court of law. I just… I want you to express concern for Chase without saying why you're worried. I want to hear what she does with that."

"Doctor-patient privilege would prevent her from saying anything."

"Exactly."

"Okay, but if I lose a great psychotherapist because she's pissed over being recorded, you're helping me find a new one." She hoped to hell Sean was wrong.

"Deal."

Several blocks from the doctor's office, Sean pulled over and retrieved the headset from his gear in the back of the SUV. He grabbed a receiver that looked like a normal pair of headphones and tucked it in his pocket, then he hid the thin gray headset under Hazel's collar, showing her how to turn on and off the record function.

"Turn it off if everything is cool and you want privacy for your session." He dropped a kiss on her lips.

She smiled. "I'm going to tell her all about my plans to tie you up and have my way with you tonight."

"Hmm. I probably should turn off the broadcast function. But then, Keith will enjoy telling Trina how much we like her prize."

The doctor's office was inside a stately old house that dated to the late eighteen hundreds. Sean parked in the small lot at the rear of the structure, and they took the stairs to the second floor, where Parks had her office.

They arrived a few minutes early, finding the waiting room empty. The office—the whole house, really—was strangely quiet. Even the receptionist was missing from her post.

Dr. Parks stepped out of her office and greeted them.

"Where is everyone?" Hazel asked.

"I don't usually take appointments on Thursdays. It's my day to do paperwork and consult with the doctors and counselors with shared patients. Plus it leaves me available to take emergency appointments like yours."

"Oh. Thank you for being willing to see me today, I didn't realize I was interrupting—"

"Not a problem. I'm glad you chose not to wait until next week. I'm concerned you had another blackout." She glanced at Hazel's bandaged hand. "And that you harmed yourself during a fugue state."

"Well, I mostly harmed an iPad. And a mug. The damage to my hand was collateral."

Parks smiled, and Hazel remembered why she'd liked her from the start. She had warm eyes, and her laugh was quick and genuine.

Sean was crazy to suspect her of anything.

"Dr. Parks, do you mind if I sit in on Hazel's session today?" Sean asked.

"I have no objections," Hazel said, before she was asked.

The doctor studied him for a moment, her brow furrowed in thought. Finally she said, "To prepare for the session, I went to Voigt Forum. Obviously, you are involved, and today's incident… It was about your relationship. I think, to give Hazel the best opportunity to gain from this session, she needs to feel free to be completely open and honest about her emotions about the incident, and your presence, no matter how supportive, would hinder that. I'm sorry."

Sean nodded. "I understand."

Before Hazel could follow the doctor into the room, he pulled her to him. It looked like he was cupping her face to kiss her, but Hazel felt his thumb slide below her collar and hit the record button.

"I'll be right here," he said. He pulled his headphones from his pocket. "Listening to an audiobook."

She smiled and followed Dr. Parks down the hall and into her office. Hazel settled into her favorite easy chair.

"Mr. Logan is quite taken with you."

"It's mutual. Has been for a long time, but we both finally stopped resisting."

"Well, it's easy to understand the resistance. Being an interracial couple can be hard on both sides."

Hazel frowned. "That's not why we were resisting. It never even crossed my mind."

"Oh, I'm sure it did, subconsciously. And look at what happened today? You're already getting a taste of the difficulties."

Had her subconscious held her back from Sean because he was Black? The thought gave her pause, and then she remembered all the times she'd thrown herself at the guy.

Yeah. No. Skin color hadn't been a factor in what had kept them apart.

"Given that you've now fainted twice, I'm thinking it's time to try hypnosis. We need to get down to the root of the problem and figure out how to stop these episodes from recurring before it happens while you're driving a car."

"I'm afraid I can't submit to hypnotherapy right now. I'm working on a criminal case and can't divulge details. As my issues are related to my work, hypnotherapy would necessarily have to probe that area, but I could jeopardize the investigation."

"I appreciate your concerns, but doctor-patient privilege protects you in this instance. No one can call this session into question. And you do know of my work with the CIA and FBI. I maintain the highest security clearance so I can continue to work with patients I helped when I worked for the government."

Hazel shifted in her seat. "I understand, but I still can't go into a hypnotic trance right now. It would be unethical for me to do so."

"Fine. We'll do this the hard way, then."

There was a biting edge to the doctor's voice, and Hazel was glad Sean was listening in. It could be simple annoyance because she'd rearranged her schedule to accommodate Hazel and now Hazel was rejecting the quickest path to the heart of her issues, or she could be irritated because she'd hoped to get Hazel into a suggestive state.

"We'll have to discuss your work, of course, because that's why you're here, but I'll avoid questions about your analysis. Fair enough?"

"That's fine."

"Okay, then. When last we spoke, you'd recovered bones from a lake, and you were conducting analysis in a lab at your cousin's estate, with Mr. Logan present to help you if you suffered an episode at work. Has that worked out for you?"

Hazel frowned, remembering her last session. In all the chaos that had gone on in the preceding days, she'd forgotten that Dr. Parks knew where the lab was. In fact, aside from the Virginia ME and a few engineers at Talon & Drake, had anyone else known?

Of course, someone from the ME's office or Talon & Drake could have divulged the location if the person asking appeared to have good reason to ask the question—as the sheriff who might make arrests based on Hazel's findings could easily claim.

But Dr. Parks's question today could also be a clever way of asking if the bones had been destroyed in the blast.

Surely there were news reports on the explosion? But then, the FBI had probably released a report stating a gas water heater in an old outbuilding blew. Hazel had been too focused on her analysis to remember to ask the cover story.

She looked at the doctor and gave her a tight smile. Should she be honest with her psychotherapist, or lie to a suspect? Finally, she said, "Yes. The lab is very comfortable and close to home. The work itself has been easier than I expected." That was all true.

Dr. Parks smiled. "I'm glad to hear it! I read something about an explosion on the Ravissant estate and feared for you, but the news report said everyone who lived on the property was out of town for a wedding."

"Yes."

"And then there was that footage of you with Senator Ravissant at the rally. Which was also published on Voigt Forum. Didn't look like much of a wedding to me."

"That was before the wedding." Hazel's unease grew. What was Dr. Parks probing for? And now she wondered if the woman usually visited Voigt Forum, or if she'd only gone to the site today to prep for their session. "You know, I called you today because…well, I'd just passed out. But after that, Sean and I talked it through, and I'm really feeling better about the whole thing. I'm mean, who cares if sex pictures were posted on Voigt Forum? Only racists go to that site, and only morons believe the crap posted there."

"Studies have shown there is always a kernel of truth to tabloid stories, something verifiable, which is what leads readers to believe even the most outrageous statements. For instance, when I read about your former SEAL stealing and selling arms in Afghanistan, I wondered if that was the kernel of truth."

Hazel bolted to her feet. "I think we're done here."

All at once, she felt a tingling sensation that started in her ears and traveled outward. Her fingers and arms felt like they were floating, yet she was pretty sure she was on the floor, looking up at the ceiling, not the other way around.

She'd read up on infrasound the last few days, and Isabel had shared some of her experience with it, to help Hazel understand what Chase had gone through. Isabel had described deep, excruciating pain. But this…this was light. Airy. Surreal.

Like vertigo, but without the unpleasant aspects. The whirling and giddiness, without nausea.

A few articles she'd read said some infrasound frequencies were pleasant. They could even cause arousal. Was this infrasound on that end of the spectrum?

As soon as the thought flitted through her mind, it escaped, lost in a swirl. Her head spun as if she was on a merry-go-round. Dr. Parks's face became a blur as Hazel laughed with the freedom of the ride.

Chapter Thirty-Eight

Sean watched the door, expecting Hazel to emerge. But she didn't. Over the radio, she made a giggling sound. The doctor said something he didn't understand, and Hazel responded, "I love him."

Okay. Had the doctor said something to make Hazel reconsider staying? What could she possibly say that would change Hazel's mind?

The doctor's voice was softer now. "Of course, I don't believe it. But I needed to elicit a reaction from you. We need to probe the dark places if we're going to get to the bottom of your issues."

Sean wasn't buying it, and he doubted Hazel was, but maybe she'd decided to stay to give the doctor more rope. The conversation was being recorded, after all. He'd keep listening. In the meantime, he texted Rav.

SEAN

Dr. Parks knew the bones were in the annex. Hazel told her last week.

RAV

Don't like the sound of that. She's Isabel's and Chase's doctor too.

SEAN

Exactly. Hazel is recording the session with a Raptor headset. I'm listening in. I want to know why Parks missed the signs Chase is still messed up.

I think the FBI is looking into her. She was assigned Chase and Isabel because she'd done analysis for CIA of infrasound testing by foreign intelligence agencies. I don't know details.

Any chance she knew Beck?

If she did, she managed to hide it from the CIA. They'd never have let her near Isabel or Chase.

Maybe she knew Westover. If she was studying infrasound, she could have met him when he was working for DIA doing the same thing. When is the FBI going to get the search warrant for Small's lake house?

Supposed to execute it today. No word yet.

What if Parks is the doctor who developed the implants? Did Parks know Isabel was set to survey the reservoir?

No. Iz hasn't seen her since last spring. But Small would know. All property owners were notified of the drawdown and survey.

SEAN

> Hazel's first appointment was before she was called to the field. Right? Hazel would have told her about her job, and that she was living with you. Was that before or after the note included the word redhead?

The circle spun as Rav typed a reply. It felt like an eternity as Sean waited.

RAV

> Before. The appointment was before the first redhead note.

> Parks would guess if Isabel found the bones, Hazel would be called in.

> Yes.

> Parks could want her here to pump her for information. To find out what the FBI knows.

> Get Hazel out of there.

> On it. Turning on cell broadcast for my headsets.

With the cellular link turned on, everyone with a Raptor headset—even operatives thousands of miles away—could join the conversation and hear Hazel's session with Dr. Parks, as if it were a conference call.

Parks spoke in low murmurs, words that couldn't really be made out, but Hazel's voice remained clear. She was answering questions. Her answers were innocuous at first. *Yes, no. I don't know.* Nothing that gave a hint at the questions.

Sean was carrying concealed and had a special permit, but if he charged into the doctor's office brandishing a weapon, not only was Hazel likely to get hurt, but the doctor would have plenty of reason to claim self-defense if she shot Sean.

And with the article on Voigt Forum accusing him of selling weapons, people would be more than primed to believe it. He left his gun in its holster.

He'd glimpsed a short hallway with two doors on the left, one on the right, before the door had swung closed behind Hazel.

He paused by the door, listening to Hazel's soft voice. "Twenty-six men. One woman."

Sean knew what that answer meant. The number of skulls Hazel had examined. She was talking, which meant somehow Dr. Parks had put her in a trance.

He shoved the door open, glad it swung on silent hinges. He entered the hallway and studied the closed doors. Which one was Hazel behind?

Before he could try one, the first door opened, and a white guy charged him. Sean thought he might look familiar, but it was all a blur as they rolled in the hallway, the guy trying to punch him in the ribs and neck. Sean popped him in the jaw, and the man went slack.

As Sean dragged him into the room he'd jumped from, he got a good look at the man's face. He'd been at the rally. One of the faces in the crowd that had stared at Sean with hate. He'd been in the news footage, which Sean had seen earlier in the week.

He relayed this information into the radio. Rav chimed in with message received.

Keith was listening too, as were Josh and another operative in the DC office only two miles away. The three former SEALs were mobilizing to provide backup.

A sound came from the hallway that turned Sean's blood cold. Pump-action shotgun.

The door was pushed open with the barrel of the gun, and there was none other than Sheriff Taylor and one of his toadies.

"Well, boy. Looks like you're in the wrong office."

Sean put his hands on his head. "Guys, Sheriff Taylor is here. And he brought a friend."

"You expect me to believe anyone can hear you on that stupid radio? I got men stationed all around the building. You's here alone."

"Tell him I just got a call from the FBI," Rav said on the radio, "and they're serving a warrant on his office right now. Another team is raiding Small's vacation home."

"My boss wants me to tell you that your office is being searched by the FBI right now," Sean said.

The sheriff's cell phone rang.

"That's probably one of your deputies calling to share the good news. Go ahead. Take the call. I'll wait."

Taylor glared at him until the phone stopped ringing.

Then another phone rang. The deputy glanced at the phone on his belt. "Should I take it?"

"You really should," Sean said. "It's going to be the FBI. Calling about the bodies in the lake. The illegal immigrants your boss rounded up so Dr. Parks could use them as test subjects in her infrasound experiments."

Taylor cursed and shoved the shotgun into the deputy's hands, then yanked the phone from the guy's belt. "Taylor," he grunted into the phone. Then he glared at Sean and said, "Did you read the warrant?" He cursed some more and said, "Put the asshole on the phone!"

But it appeared the FBI didn't care to talk to Sheriff Taylor at the time, because no one came on the line. He threw the phone to the floor in disgust and yanked the shotgun back from the deputy.

Sean knew the man's look. He'd seen it on enemy combatants when defeat was near. If he got his hands on the trigger, he'd blow Sean's head off.

Sean lunged before the gun fully changed hands. He shoved the barrel up, ramming the deputy in the chin with it as he kneed the sheriff in the balls. The man released the gun, which Sean had by the barrel. He slammed the butt into Taylor's head, dropping him to the ground. He kicked at the deputy's chest. He flew backward, into the wall.

Taylor was unconscious, so Sean pinned the deputy first and handcuffed him with his own cuffs. Then he did the same for the sheriff, telling the others listening in what was happening as he did so.

"I'm going after Hazel now."

They'd made so much noise, Dr. Parks had to be on the alert, and she had Hazel as a hostage.

The weird floaty sensation ended as abruptly as it started. In the hallway, Hazel could hear shouts and banging. It took her a moment to realize her hands were tied in front of her. Dr. Parks pressed the barrel of a gun into the soft flesh between mandible and hyoid bone.

Hazel's brain filled with images of what a bullet fired through the skull from just that spot would do. It was a popular placement for suicides. The bullet would travel upward, shattering the sphenoid and parietal bones. Depending on the angle, it could go out the back or straight up, taking out the frontal bones. Destroying the forehead.

"I said get up!"

Apparently, the good doctor had been shouting orders while Hazel took a grim mental stroll through craniums past.

"You're a crappy psychotherapist if you failed to realize the gun won't induce calm, compliant behavior in a patient who suffers panic attacks thanks to documenting the damage bullets do to skulls."

"Shut up and get up."

"You know, I don't think this relationship is working out. I'm going to find a new doctor, and I will insist you release your notes on our sessions."

The doctor pulled the gun back and slammed it into Hazel's cheek. Not enough to break the zygomatic arch, but damn, it hurt.

"Well, now you're breaking your Hippocratic oath." She raised her bound hands to cup her cheek as she got to her feet. Sean was listening. He'd get to her when he was done with whatever was happening in the hall. And no matter what happened, there would be a recording. "But then you aren't big on the Hippocratic oath, are you, Doc? How many men did you implant with the chip? How many are like Chase and still have the chip in their head?"

Parks said nothing as she shoved Hazel toward a door on the side of the room opposite the hall.

Dammit. The woman had an escape route, and she intended to use Hazel as a hostage. "You realize it's all over, don't you? The FBI knows everything."

The door led to a short hall, at the end of which was a staircase. It was an old building in DC, a house converted into elegant office space. Of course it had a back staircase. Servants needed stairs too.

Hazel had no idea if there were any other tenants in the building, but it had looked and felt empty when they arrived. A cry for help would do nothing except entice Parks to pull the trigger.

"So are you racist like the others, or were you in it for the science? I mean, you'd have to be racist to do what you did to the victims, but was that your primary motive, like Small?"

She pushed Hazel down the narrow staircase and surprised her by answering. "The science is really quite fascinating. Westover worked the pain end. I worked with pain too —you have to for it to be fully effective, plus the memory element works better with the pain—the human brain is so eager to erase trauma. But I learned to incorporate the pleasure receptors first. To get the subject into a trancelike state quickly. You know I never used anesthesia for any of the surgeries? I just told them it didn't hurt, and they believed me."

They reached the bottom of the stairs. She pushed open the exterior door, then surprised Hazel by shoving her through an archway, into a narrow corridor and then to another set of stairs. "You're taking me to the basement?" Sean would hear that and know the open back door was a decoy. "I hate basements. I think it might send me into a panic attack."

"Then I'll just have to shoot you."

"What does the implant do? Isabel thinks it's an infrasound translator of sorts. So you don't need a mask like Westover did."

"Isabel is very smart. It's a shame Westover didn't have more time with her, or I'd have put the same device in her head too."

The basement was dank, and Parks didn't turn on any light to guide Hazel down the dark steps.

"Did you know that Robert Beck is turning on you and Small?" Hazel asked. She had no idea if her words were true, but it might trigger a response. "He said you rounded up all your test subjects when he was arrested, and you gassed them, then pulled the chips from their heads and stripped them. You burned them, but because you couldn't use the incinerator in the compound, the fire wasn't hot enough to turn them to ash. So you dumped all the bones in the lake."

"That was Taylor's bright idea. Small and I had nothing to do with that, and Beck didn't know about it because he was in custody at the time, so anything he said is pure speculation without proof."

It wasn't good that the woman said that so freely. She clearly didn't intend for Hazel to leave this basement alive.

"Why did you send the threatening letters?"

"That was Small. He was panicking about Isabel finding the bones. He was trying to get the project delayed so it would be impossible. I wasn't nearly so worried until you stepped into my office and I realized you'd be right there, ready to examine any bones Isabel found. Taylor figured he could hire someone to play county coroner who'd insist the bones were part of a burial ground. He planned to salt the area with artifacts once the bones were located. But then you walked into my office, and I knew that if Isabel found the bones, she wouldn't waste time with the coroner, and Taylor wouldn't have a chance to salt the site. She'd call you, the state-certified forensic anthropologist living in her goddamn mansion. We were fucked."

In a burst of anger, Parks kicked Hazel in the back, and she fell down the steps into a void. For the half second she was airborne, she wondered if she'd fall forever or if death would be swift. But then she hit earthen floor covered with torn plastic sheeting and guessed she'd only fallen about four feet.

"Ironic that it might not have been an issue if Small hadn't worked so damn hard to delay the survey. If Isabel had begun fieldwork when she was supposed to, she might have finished before you returned from Croatia. Or even better, she might've surveyed that part of the lake bed when the water was a foot higher. I just want you to know, Hazel, that everything that happens to you is Small's fault."

"I feel so much better knowing you're on my side. Now why the fuck are we in this disgusting, dark basement?"

Parks pulled out her cell phone and directed the light at the back wall, and Hazel saw the small, three-foot high door. All at once, she realized what this was. "The building next door to this house was a speakeasy, wasn't it? There's a connecting tunnel, and we'll come out next door?"

"Shut up and crawl."

Hazel crawled on bound hands, which wasn't easy. She hoped to hell the radios could transmit through several feet of earth and wood and whatever else separated them from the world above.

"The photos on Voigt Forum, those were a lure to get me here today, weren't they? So you could put me in a trance and find out what I learned from the bones. What I've told the FBI."

When Parks didn't answer, Hazel continued, "What would you have done if I hadn't seen them? What if I didn't call for an appointment?"

"I'd have called you, expressing concern over the post, and invited you to come in for a session."

"I'd have asked what the hell you were doing on Voigt Forum."

"And I'd have said I have a Google alert set up on Alec Ravissant and Isabel Dawson so I can anticipate Isabel's needs. I'm such a conscientious psychotherapist."

Jesus. This woman had been inside Isabel's head for the better part of three years. Hazel's heart ached for her friend. For Chase.

"What about Chase? Are there others like him?"

They crawled in silence for a moment when the doctor finally said, "Sadly, no. But he is my crowning glory. If I can repeat my success with Chase, I will sell the process to Russia."

At last, Hazel came to another door and was forced to walk through another dark basement and up another flight of stairs. She continued to pepper Parks with questions, but the woman was done answering. She was probably too busy freaking out over the fact that her only option at this point was a life on the run. No big Russian payoff. And there was no way she could claim innocence and return to her private practice.

They reached the top of the stairs. Before Parks had a chance to stop her, Hazel shoved the door open and lurched through it.

She caught a glimpse of a person to the left, but she dove forward, determined not to give anything away. Behind her, Parks caught her ankle and pulled her back. "Not so fast, bitch."

All at once, there was the sound of a fist on skin, and her foot was released. She rolled to get out of the way as she heard Sean say, "You're screwed, Doctor. We recorded it all."

He dragged Parks out of the enclosed staircase and slammed her to the floor next to Hazel just as sirens sounded, roaring down the street and halting in front of the building.

Sean had Parks pinned and cuffed by the time the police entered.

He raised his hands as the cops circled all three of them, shouting orders. Hazel raised her bound hands too.

"I'm the one who called it in," Sean said. "This is Dr. Elizabeth Parks. The FBI is working on getting a warrant for her arrest. They'll be here any moment."

The standoff lasted ten minutes, with Sean and Hazel answering shouted questions. Not surprisingly, Parks said nothing.

At last the FBI arrived, including the Deputy Special

Agent who'd spent hours with Hazel on Monday. Dr. Parks was taken into FBI custody.

Hazel's hands were untied, and Sean pulled her into his arms. As she snuggled against his side, her whole body shaking with adrenaline and relief, she had a thought that made her laugh.

"What?"

"I was just thinking that after all this, maybe our first date isn't the time to play with bondage. I might need another week."

He chuckled. "You can have as long as you need. But sweetheart, I thought I was going to be the one tied up?"

Epilogue

Virginia
December

Their first party in their new house had Hazel nervously excited. The housewarming would be the first time Sean's family and hers would all be together. With Christmas less than two weeks away, this would also be a holiday gathering.

There was a lot to celebrate. Katrina was done with chemo and getting stronger with each passing day. Ivy and Matt's adoption of Julian had been finalized, and Ivy was twelve weeks pregnant.

Selena Ramirez and others had been identified. Others remained nameless, but they'd been counted. All would be buried, honored, and mourned. And their killers would face justice.

The search of Senator Small's property had provided enough evidence of the human testing conducted by Parks that there was no need to cut a deal with Robert Beck to convict Senator Christopher Small, Dr. Elizabeth Parks,

Sheriff Carl Taylor, and his deputies, who'd been the ones in the Audi in the high-speed chase, burned the cabin, and blown up the annex.

Dr. Parks had kept meticulous notes about the experimentation. With that data to reverse engineer the process came the best news of all, Chase Johnston was finally and truly on the mend. The implant had been removed and slowly, the memory blocks were being peeled away.

Boyish Chase was disappearing, and a new man was emerging in his place. His voice was deeper, and the occasional stutter was gone. He stood taller and projected a confidence that Westover and then Parks had stripped from him.

Now, at last, Hazel could see the man who'd been hired for Raptor's elite team at a young age. He still had a long road to travel, but he had a chance now.

As far as he could piece together, he'd blown up his own Prius in a desperate act that mimicked his orders from Parks. He'd been instructed to put the explosive under Isabel's car and set it so it would blow up during Alec and Isabel's drive home.

Alec's death would have solved many of Small's problems and distracted everyone. Plus the blame would have fallen on Chase, his own employee known to have been obsessed with Isabel in the past.

Chase had driven one of Taylor's deputies onto the estate in Isabel's Prius in the middle of the night. After his failure with the Prius, no one trusted him to see the job through. The man had rigged the gas furnace to explode. Afterward, Chase had driven to the compound and hidden in Sean's quarters as his mind fractured. He didn't remember the visit to the estate at all, but security had captured him on camera along with the use of his personal entry code.

Chase hadn't sent Sean and Hazel to his cabin out of malice. He honestly hadn't known that his cabin was the place where Dr. Parks ran her tests on him and repro-grammed him on a monthly basis.

Once Parks learned where Sean and Hazel were, she'd sent Taylor's other deputy to burn the cabin down and destroy the evidence of her experimentation on Chase as well as her DNA. Parks had victimized Chase in every way possible.

Chase had also explained his decision to hide in Sean's quarters. Every time in the past he'd tried to go to Keith or Alec to tell them he was missing time again or memories weren't quite syncing, he'd shut down. Like he'd been programmed with an automatic off switch. With his success in evading the order to kill Alec and Isabel, he hoped that in making a plea to Sean, he'd be able to get the words out before his body shut down. The gap in his memory for that very night terrified him. He feared he'd hurt Isabel or Alec. He knew Sean might recognize the cause, having been one of the few who were in Alaska at the end.

Now, finally, Chase could talk about his ordeal.

But not tonight. Tonight would be fun only. A celebra-tion. Food. Music. Family and friends. The buffet was set up, and the first guests were set to arrive in an hour.

Hazel did a walk-through of the kitchen. Food was warming in the oven, and the house smelled heavenly of sweets and spices.

She headed up the stairs to change for the party. She'd purchased a new backless dress that she knew would drive Sean wild. In the early hours of the morning, after the last guest had left, she fully expected he'd hike up the dress and take her against whatever surface was nearby to support her. She couldn't wait for the after-party party. But then she was a party girl at heart.

In their bedroom, she found Sean at the bathroom mirror, shaving. She walked up behind him and ran her hands over the muscles of his bare back. "We're just about ready. All I need to do is change and fix my makeup."

He finished with a last swipe of his razor against his jaw, then wiped down his face. "I'm glad we're doing this, but I'm already exhausted."

She laughed. "Me too." They'd only been in the house for two weeks. It had been a marathon to get everything ready for tonight. "But I'm looking forward to introducing my parents to your mom and Julian to the girls."

"Me too." He turned and kissed her, then stepped into the bedroom and grabbed his shirt from the bed. "When you're done getting dressed, join me on the balcony? I'd like to have a glass of wine, just you and me, before the crazy starts."

"Sure. It'll take me about ten minutes."

She slipped on her dress and fixed her makeup, then grabbed a thick shawl from the closet. There was a heat lamp on their upper balcony just for nights like this, so they could sit outside and take in their view of lake and mountains. They weren't on the lake, but they had a perfect view of it, and watching the sun set over the hills was a new ritual they both enjoyed.

She stepped out to see the sky lit with orange. Perfect timing.

Sean stood at the railing, looking out over the lake and trees. She stepped up beside him, and he draped an arm around her shoulders. A cloud of white formed when she expelled a deep breath.

He dropped a kiss on her forehead, then released her to pour the wine. "We do a lot of things out of order. Our first date happened months after I fell in love with you and a week after we became lovers."

She laughed. "Well, we tried to go on a date sooner, but the worst psychotherapist ever screwed up our day."

He smiled. "True, but it was still late for a first date. I was thinking for once I'd like to do something early. Can I give you your Christmas present now?"

"Now? Before the party? Sure, but it can wait until later. I don't want to rush it."

"Believe me, nothing about this present is rushed."

"You better not have done anything big. We just bought each other a house. You promised to keep it simple." Did this mean she should give him his present early too? She'd been looking forward to seeing his face when he opened the bag of sex toys on Christmas morning. She had other presents for him, of course, but that was the one that would make him laugh the hardest. And she loved making him laugh.

"Don't worry. It's simple." He pulled a box wrapped in gold cloth with a black ribbon from his pocket and handed it to her.

"It's beautiful."

He laughed. "You haven't even opened it yet."

"The wrapping is gorgeous." She ran the ribbon between her fingers. Slick, smooth silk. The texture grounded her. But everything about this house and this man grounded her. She pulled at the end of the ribbon.

"Wait! Before you open it, I need to ask you a question."

"What?"

He went down on one knee, and her stomach dropped. She might even be floating. He reached for her hand. "Hazel MacLeod, will you marry me?"

Tears sprang to her eyes before she could shout, "Yes!"

Sean stood and scooped her up and spun her around, then he set her down and kissed her. Hard and deep. He raised his head and whispered in her ear, "You can open your present now."

She yanked off the bow and tossed it on the table next to the wine. The fabric fell open to reveal a jewelry box. Sean took it from her hand and opened it. A beautiful, elegant solitaire diamond sat in an antique filigree setting.

She'd never been a ring person, had never even thought about rings, but this, clearly, was the best, most beautiful ring she'd ever seen.

"You never wear rings, so I didn't really know what you like, so if this isn't what you want to wear every day for the rest of your life, we can take it back and you can pick out one you like."

"No. I love it. It's stunning."

He took it from the box and slid it on her finger. "There. *Now* it's stunning."

She kissed him, then swiped at her eye. "There's just one problem."

"What's that?"

"You've upped the ante. Now I need to go shopping. I really need to get you a better present."

He laughed and pulled her into his arms. "Oh, sweetheart, you're the only present I've ever wanted."

Acknowledgments

Thank you to forensic anthropologist Pete Morris for answering my questions about forensic examinations as a private sector practice and all my technical, procedural questions. Inaccuracies due to error or fictional license are all on me.

Thank you to Toni Anderson for fielding random plotting questions and helping to shape the story. Thank you to Jenn Stark, Annika Martin, and Toni (again!) for our fabulous retreat where major elements of the book finally came together.

Huge, gigantic thanks to Gwen Hayes, who was vital to making this book happen. Not only did we meet early on in the writing and she helped me figure out the characters and their dynamics, but also in the end, when I hit a wall and couldn't see my way out, she listened and talked through the ending with me.

Gwen Hernandez and Annika Martin both provided excellent beta reads, for which I am forever grateful!

Thank you to my children for being the magnificent people you are. I am so incredibly proud to be your mom.

Lastly, as always, thank you to my husband, who helps me plot and reads every word I write and helps me make it better. Thank you for showing me what happily ever after looks like every single day.

About the Author

USA Today bestselling author Rachel Grant also writes thrillers as R.S. Grant. She worked for over a decade as a professional archaeologist and mines her experiences for storylines and settings, which are as diverse as excavating a cemetery underneath an historic art museum in San Francisco, survey and excavation of many prehistoric Native American sites in the Pacific Northwest, researching an historic concrete house in Virginia (inspiration for her debut novel, CONCRETE EVIDENCE), and mapping a seventeenth century Spanish and Dutch fort on the island of Sint Maarten in the Caribbean (which provided inspiration for the island and fort described in CRASH SITE).

She lives in the Pacific Northwest with her husband and children.

For more information:
www.Rachel-Grant.net
contact@rachel-grant.net